FATE &
FREEDOM

FATE &
FREEDOM

BOOK I: THE MIDDLE PASSAGE

K. I. Knight

First Freedom Publishing

First Freedom Publishing, LLC

Fate & Freedom
Book I: The Middle Passage

ISBN 9780990836520

Library of Congress Control number 2014952109

www.firstfreedompublishing.com

Book Design by Pro Production Graphic Services
Jacket Design by SJulien.com

Printed in the United States of America

First Edition

IN MEMORY OF GRANNIE.

CONTENTS

Contents

Contents

Contents

HOW THIS STORY
CAME TO BE WRITTEN ...

As a genealogist, I believe that "if you can prove it, it's genealogy, if you can't, it's mythology." The phrase circulates frequently among those who search historical records looking for that all important clue that may give a glimpse into the past. So when a story appeared through the ashes of time that kept insisting it needed to be told, I made the choice to write a novel in order to tell the greater truth only mythology can convey.

Fate & Freedom is a historical novel loosely based on the documented evidence I found over the course of seven years of intense research tracing the journey of the first Africans to arrive at America's first English settlement of Virginia. The storyline is the product of my imagination.

Many of the characters in this novel were historical figures, both in England and in Virginia. Some, like Robert Rich and King James I, played large roles on the stage of history. Others—John Jope, Edwin Sandys, Lady Isabel Wray—are less well known, yet their actions, struggles, and personalities are just as fascinating. I have tried to be as true to what we know about them as possible, reserving a novelist's prerogative not to let the truth stand in the way of a good story.

Other characters are invented, of course, but the two main characters—Margaret and John—are also historical figures. How I found them is a pretty amazing story of its own.

How This Story Came To Be Written . . .

Growing up in the small Florida town of Winter Garden, I was fortunate to have three of my four grandparents and my great-grandmother whom I saw most every day. They all told wonderful stories, but it was the early adventures told by my great-grandmother who peopled my mind and thrilled my imagination from generations past. I trace my interest and passion for genealogy to her. It would be much later when I learned to flesh out her tales with information I could find in archives, court records, and other documents. For me, these materials added legitimacy, allowing my forebears to come even more alive.

Questioning my husband as to his own ancestry, I realized he knew very little of his family's heritage. He had very few stories about who they were or where they came from, so on a lark, I decided to see what I could find. It quickly becomes like a hidden treasure map, soon finding one, then the next, with many of the men in his direct paternal line being men of elevated standing during their time. His grandfather—a state attorney, his great-grandfather—a senator, the next a war hero-if I may, who his opponent could never hold, but one in the same as the lieutenant who lost several cousins riding under his command in Florida's First Calvary.

Proudly reporting back to my husband, with one find then the next, I easily go back several generations, finding more and more. The hunt became an addiction. Who or what would I find next? For Christmas of 2007, as we give Bo, my father-in-law, a family tree of his direct lineage back to the 1600s, I received the best gift I could've asked for. Not a gift as a package would be, but a request to find a new story. Bo wanted to know about the Minorcan heritage he always heard about through his grandmother's line, the senator's wife.

What I didn't expect—none of us did—was that tracing his ancestry to prerevolutionary times, to the very founding of our country, would allow me to discover John and Margaret. They did not have historians to write their stories. Their names appeared in a court record here, a census taken there: hints of where they lived, loved, struggled, and thrived with their families.

Both came to Virginia from Africa on the "black *Mayflower*," which arrived on these shores three years before the pilgrims set foot in Massachusetts, and before slavery was institutionalized in the American colonies.

Their story fascinated me to the point where in my dreams and waking thoughts, I would hear a little voice pleading for me to listen and to keep exploring, to imagine who this girl and boy were, how they found themselves in their situations, and finally to tell their story.

Because the archival evidence was limited, I decided that there was not enough material to merit a historical account. At some point I realized that in a novel, a fictional narrative, I could tell more of their story.

And that is how this book came about, a combination of genealogy and mythology, a story of survival and discovery at the dawn of our American history, resurrected from the ashes of time. I hope that Margaret and John's story will shine a light on their existence and significance, and that others will enjoy taking part in their journey the way I enjoyed listening to my great-grandmother tell me her stories.

If there are any errors in the telling, they are of my own making. For those interested in the historical background and documentation, I have gathered much of the information on my website, *www.kinfolkdetective.com.*

—K. I. Knight
2014

FOR BO

ACKNOWLEDGMENTS

I could not have created a book of such vast historical scope without the generous help, input, and expertise of others.

On my production team, I want to thank:

Chris Angermann (*www.bardolfandcompany.com*) for his tireless guidance, advice, and contributions too numerous to count. *Fate & Freedom* would not be what it is without him.

Sharon Julien of Sharon Julien Web Design (*www.sjulien.com*) for working with me through several incarnations of the cover until we got what we liked.

Bob Land (*www.boblandedits.blogspot.com*), editor extraordinaire, for putting finishing touches on the manuscript.

Richard C. Moore (*www.ship-paintings.com*), whose beautiful works of maritime art and other paintings grace the collections of many museums, for the lovely cover images for both volumes of the book.

Rosanne Schloss, creative director of Pro Production Graphic Services (*www.proproductiongs.com*), for the interior layout.

I also want to express my appreciation to Victoria Lee and Daniel Y. Cooper for lending their likenesses to Margaret's and John's images on the cover, photographed by Michelle Brown Photography (*www.michellebrownphotography.com*).

Acknowledgments

I want to give a heartfelt thanks to my husband, Tom, and my children, James, Jesse, and Jessica, for putting up with me for the many years during which I was preoccupied with this project when I would bury my head in history books, archival material, and Internet research for days on end.

And finally, I want to thank my parents, Willis G. Hall and June G. Hall, for their ongoing support and for reminding me, whenever they can, that there is nothing unachievable if you just believe.

FATE & FREEDOM

BOOK I: THE MIDDLE PASSAGE

PROLOGUE
Africa—Summer 1618

In later years Margarita does not remember the long climb up the back of the large black rock. On a dare she has joined a group of friends to scale one of the *pedras negras*, the black mountains that surround the town of Pongo in the kingdom of Ndongo in Angola like a herd of sleeping elephants. Tall for her age, Margarita looks almost as old as Francisco, the fourteen-year-old leader of the pack. They've taken her along because she is the daughter of the *soba* of the district, and her participation gives the outing a kind of legitimacy. They are all skipping school and know the nuns will be angry. Perhaps with Margarita in their midst, they will get into less trouble.

They sneak through a gap in the palisades and make their way past gently rising meadows where goats and cattle are grazing lazily. The morning air on the high plateau is cool and dry, and the scorching heat of the day is still hours away. The youngsters chatter excitedly, but when they reach the steeper slopes where dark gray boulders poke out among the tufts of grass, withered by the remorseless summer sun, they lumber on in silence. By the time they reach the sharply rising cliff walls and begin their ascent, Margarita wishes she had not come, but she doesn't show any sign of fear or weakness.

She is the headman's daughter and has a reputation to uphold.

Fortunately, her toes and fingers manage to find purchase in the cracks and crevices carved by the downpours of many rainy seasons

Prologue

as she slowly climbs up the rock face. There is a moment when she gets stuck and can't move forward or back, and begins to panic, but Gustavo extends a helping hand from above and pulls her up to a ledge.

From there Margarita looks back down at her town below. Its thatched huts and buildings extend far into the interior of the high plateau. She can make out the roof of her house, larger than the rest. As *soba*, subject only to the new iron king, Ngola Mbandi, in Ndongo's capital city, Kabasa, her father has to have a domicile that reflects his importance and status.

She notices the nearby compound where the Portuguese Sisters teach her and the others about Jesus, who loves all people, but especially children. The younger nun, Sister Inez Theresa, has told her that the son of God is unlike her ancestor spirit, who pays attention to the living only after they have undergone the rites of passage and become adults. Although Jesus was busy performing miracles and telling parables to his followers, he took time to talk to little children, even when his disciples objected!

Margarita likes Sister Inez Theresa. A little younger than her mother, the nun always has a ready smile for Margarita, especially when she remembers her lessons well. She feels a pang of guilt for disappointing the Sister today and skipping school.

Margarita looks toward the large common area in the middle of the town, a brown rectangle surrounded by houses. Today it is empty except for a few makeshift wooden tables. But twice a week it turns into a teeming place, crowded with tradesmen, cattle and goat herders, and farmers from the surrounding villages hawking their wares—axes, iron hoes and other metal tools, copper hair pins and bracelets, lion skins, grains, vegetables, meat, salt, and medicinal herbs.

Her mother doesn't bother with the market, sending servants to buy food supplies as needed. Many of the locals bring provisions from their farms directly to the home of the *soba*, offering the best yams, peppers, millet, and Margarita's favorite treat—coconuts.

She and her mother go only once a month, when foreign merchants, men with bushy, dark hair on their chins, come from far away with wagons and pack animals laden with silken fabrics, ivory, and trinkets. Margarita loves the noisy bustle—the bleating goats, clucking chickens, guinea fowl, and other pent-up animals lowing nervously, mingling with the sounds of traders bartering in Portuguese, Spanish, and occasionally Dutch, French, and English. The speakers of the latter have blond and red beards and are the palest men she has ever seen.

Her mother always brushes past the colored glass beads and baubles laid out on the tables. They delight Margarita, but the time she asked her mother if she would buy some for her, she received a disdainful reply, "You mustn't be charmed by glitter. They are worthless things."

So Margarita was surprised when, after the ceremony for her Christian naming—the Sisters called it "baptism"—her mother gave her a sparkling pearl on a string to hang around her neck.

"To remind you what 'Margarita' means," she said, smiling proudly, caressing her cheek. "You are my dearest pearl."

Margarita treasures the pea-sized gem and often fingers the smooth, hard surface. It feels so different from the silk fabrics hanging on wooden racks on the side of the merchant carts. She still remembers the time she ran her fingers over a glistening, bright blue cloth and how soft it felt compared to her rough cotton dress. When the black-bearded trader with olive skin started shouting at her in Portuguese, Margarita looked at him uncomprehendingly, and her mother yelled right back with such ferocity that the man bowed apologetically. No one treats the daughter of the *soba* with disrespect!

At other times, she watches her mother bartering with cleverness and subtlety. She wrinkles her nose disparagingly, sighs in exasperation and makes as if to leave when the trader won't go any lower in price, and finally acquiesces with studied reluctance, allowing the merchant to feel like he's put something over on her.

Prologue

Later she explains to Margarita, "Always look as if nothing strikes your fancy. If the trader sees your eyes light up at what you really want, he'll drive a harder bargain."

People the size of ants are coming out of the houses to start their day, and Margarita, rested, resumes her climb. By the time she finally makes it to the crown of the rock, the sun is already high in the sky. Breathing heavily, she wipes the beads of sweat from her brow.

Francisco and some of the others are already standing at the far edge of the flat top. When Margarita joins them and carefully looks over the rim, she is amazed. The rock face plunges so much farther down than in back toward the interior. From the bottom of the precipice, yellow green foothills with gray rock outcroppings extend to small villages and cattle farms. Beyond them is a vast expanse of undulating grassland and ocher plain, dotted with palms and baobab trees. In the distance, the sky meets the earth in a flickering dance along an indistinct line that stretches as far as her eyes can see.

She turns to Francisco standing next to her and, pointing, asks, "Is that the edge of the world?"

Wrinkles appear on his ebony forehead. "No. Beyond that is a big lake, so big you can't see to the other side, with waves bigger than the ripples on a pond during a thunderstorm!"

"Is there anything on the other side?"

"We're not supposed to speak of it," Francisco says quietly. "It's bad luck to just look at it. Even Ngola Mbandi, now that he is king, will never lay eyes on it again!"

Margarita frowns. "How do you know all this?"

"I overheard the elders talk about it one evening."

Margarita breaks into a smile. "You listened in on them in secret!" she crows triumphantly.

Francisco grips her by the arm, hard. "Don't you dare tell anyone!"

Margarita pulls away. "Don't worry. I won't."

She glowers at him. Francisco pulls a millet cake wrapped in a large leaf from the pouch by his side and extends it to her as a peace offering.

For the rest of the day they sit around talking, eating, and sharing water from gourds they brought along. Margarita feels pleased to be included in their conversations.

At some point Gonzalo indicates the sun, which is way past its high point and heading toward the far edge of the plain. "Time to go back," he says.

Margarita takes a final look at the gold-drenched, shimmering expanse. That distant view—the endless thread of the iridescent horizon—is what she will remember for the rest of her life.

*　*　*

It is almost dark when they return to the town. The first person Margarita encounters in the enclosure of her home is Joana, the young housemaid. Relief is so evident in her face that Margarita is surprised. They were worried about her! She feels a twinge of guilt. It hadn't occurred to her that anyone would be concerned about her absence. After all, she is eight years old and can take care of herself!

But then her mother rushes from inside the house and embraces her, squeezing her so hard it hurts. Then she pushes Margarita away by the shoulders, her eyes flashing with anger, and says, "Don't you ever frighten us like that again!"

Margarita doesn't know which is worse—her mother's wrath or the curious, accusing faces of her younger brother and sister peeking around the doorway. Even her father, who normally dotes on her, looks stern and forbidding at supper that evening and refuses to speak to her, driving home the lesson that she has disappointed him. Although the goat stew smells delicious and she's hungry from the exertion of the climb, she has lost her appetite and just stabs at the food.

So it isn't until a week later when everyone seems to have forgotten her adventure that she gets up the courage to ask her father about the big lake far to the west. To her surprise, he doesn't get angry, just nods thoughtfully.

Prologue

"Kalungu—the foreign men with facial hair call it the 'Atlantic Ocean.' It is the gateway to the Other World."

"Have you seen it, Father?" Margarita asks, wide-eyed.

"Yes. As a younger man I once took a boat trip down the Kwanza to the mouth of the river." He smiles mischievously. "It was an adventure even worse than yours—I was gone for more than a week!—and my family was terribly upset with me."

Margarita blushes. To hide her embarrassment, she quickly asks, "What's it like?"

"There are waves as far as the eyes can see with whitecaps like the hood of a bird. And there is a constant roar, like the echo in a cave. It is the voices of the ghosts calling from the other side where Kalunga Ngome rules the underworld." He hesitates before going on. "Everything there is upside down. When the sun is at its highest point in Pongo, it is the dead of night over there."

"I don't think I'd want to go there," says Margarita.

Her father smiles kindly. "That's good. No one who ventures there ever comes back."

Margarita ponders the conversation for the next few days. She contemplates what the ghosts look like, if they are like ancestral spirits. She wonders if some of the traders from other lands have been across the Atlantic Ocean and what they found there.

But soon other events overtake such musings and crowd them far into the back of her mind.

PART ONE

&

KALUNGU

1

PONGO

Late Summer 1618

The talking drums have been beating for weeks now, carrying reports of Portuguese warships, loaded with conquistadors in shiny armor, musketeers, and cannons, traveling up the Kwanza River from Fort Massangano. Ndongo scouts are monitoring their progress in the hope that the armada will turn toward the south at some point, but as the days go by it becomes clear that they are headed straight for the capital at the heart of the kingdom.

Margarita doesn't understand what the rumors are all about. She has never seen a conquistador and can't imagine canoes or boats so big that they can ferry whole wagonloads of people and weapons. When she asks her parents or the holy Sisters, their replies are evasive or confusing. So she continues her religious lessons and household chores as if nothing was happening, but from the worried expression on her father's face in private and his frequent meetings with the elders, she knows that trouble is brewing.

There are still a few gray-haired men alive who fought in the great battle at the Lukala River thirty years earlier, when a great Ndongo army faced the Portuguese soldiers and their muskets and routed them in a decisive victory. Since then, peace has existed on the borders of the Angolan mountain kingdom.

But the new governor, Luis Mendes de Vasconcelos, who arrived in Luanda just over a year ago with dreams of conquest and enriching himself, has decided to take advantage of the recent civil war that has divided Ndongo. When the great Ngola Kiluanji attempted to strip the power of the *sobas*, he angered many of them and they rebelled. Some, including Margarita's father, conspired to lure him into an ambush during a hunting trip. They captured him, cut off his head, and installed his son Mbandi in his place.

But the young king has only been on the throne for a few months after fighting off other pretenders, and he doesn't have the experience and statesmanship to make peace with the dissenting *sobas*.

Margarita's father has traveled several times to the royal compound in the capital city of Kabasa to participate in discussions with the ruling council. He always returns shaking his head, frustrated that the Mbandi doesn't express enough interest in unifying the kingdom and pursuing alliances to combat the Portuguese threat.

"He is like a young gazelle who sees the lion downwind and doesn't believe it will hurt him because he can't smell it," he tells the elders.

Fortunately, the talking drums' accounts of early clashes are favorable. The *soba* Kaita ka Balanga is an experienced fighter, and he and his warriors inflict a stinging defeat on the elite Portuguese troops. Just as in the battle thirty years earlier, heavily armored musketeers in tight formation are no match for the curved battle-axes, iron swords, spears, and arrows wielded by the Ndongo tribesmen, who move lightly and quickly. Years of training and hunting lions and other wild animals have made them formidable.

But then the rhythmic messages beat out a word that strikes terror into the hearts of the most courageous Ndongo warrior: "Imbangala!"

The news that the brutal mercenaries are massing at the side of the Portuguese invaders spreads like wildfire through Pongo. It disrupts Sister Inez Theresa's morning lessons. Her older companion,

Sister Maria Gracia, arrives and beckons her to another room for a private conversation, leaving the children to their own devices.

In the past Margarita has heard adults invoke the savage raiders only as bogeymen to scare younger children when they misbehave. Although her mother has never threatened her or her siblings with, "Act right, or the Imbangala will come and eat you!" everyone is familiar with the phrase.

Now the older boys share what they know, as the rest of the children listen with eyes big as wood owls.

"They rub ashes on their faces and bodies until they look whiter than the Dutch traders," says Julio, the son of a coppersmith.

"They pull out half their teeth on purpose, so they have gaps between them and look like wild beasts," says Lorenzo.

To Margarita it sounds like the ghosts and monsters that live on the other side of Kalungu, the great ocean lake.

"They're like a plague of locusts," says Francisco. "When they swarm over a place, there is nothing left." He continues, "They chop down all the palm trees and steal all the corn and grain."

"Why do they cut down the palms?" Margarita asks.

"For the sap. To make wine and get drunk."

An edge of hysteria creeps into Julio's voice when he says, "They're cannibals. They slaughter all the cattle and goats, and kill everyone and eat them!"

Gonzalo adds, "Yes, and they bury babies and small children alive."

Juan, the five-year-old son of a cattle herder, starts to cry. He doesn't attend the school regularly because he helps out on the farm and doesn't always remember his lessons.

As Margarita goes to comfort him, she shoots Julio and Gonzalo an angry look. "My father says that we are safe here," she assures the boy, although she's not so certain herself.

That evening, she tells her father what she heard and asks, "Is it true?"

He looks at her thoughtfully. "Yes, they are evil men—outlaws who have no lands of their own, no kingdom, no desire to settle down and build something lasting. They worship violent spirits and live only for momentary pleasure, bloodshed, and destruction. But don't worry. The walls of Pongo have never been breached."

Margarita believes him, trusting in his strength and assurance.

So it comes as a shock to her when a few days later during morning lessons the clanging of the iron *ngongo* bells erupts in a cacophony of noise, calling on all warriors to defend the kingdom. Outside the Sisters' compound, there are shouts of "Ita! Ita!" (War! War!) as the thunder of battle drums shakes the town.

Everyone rushes to the market square, where young and adult men are assembling. Some are dressed in lion and leopard pelts—totems of their power and prowess. They carry iron weapons and ox hide shields. Margarita sees Francisco next to his father holding a curved axe, looking determined and self-contained. When he notices her staring at him, he looks away but straightens and stands more erect.

Margarita finds her mother and younger siblings among the older men, women, and children in the large circle around the warriors. Then she sees her father in battle dress emerging from a meeting in the elders' hut, followed by the members of his council. Everyone quiets.

He looks over the assembled warriors and addresses the crowd in a loud, confident voice. "Today we march to Kabasa and join our Ngola's great army. We will defend our country and beat back the invaders! They'll be sorry they ever set a foot on our land. I promise it."

The warriors shout in affirmation and tap their shields with their weapons. The sounds are deafening and fill Margarita's heart with pride. She has never felt happier as her father's daughter.

As he leads the regiment out of the town gates, none of the men look back. They have said their good-byes in the quiet of their homes. But the women follow them to the gap between the two humpbacked mountains and watch as they march down the path sloping toward the foothills leading to the vast plain. They call encouragements after them until they are visible only through a cloud of dust.

Heading back to town, Margarita's mother whispers to her, "I need you to be strong now. People will look to us."

Margarita nods, cognizant of the heavy burden of being wife and daughter of the *soba*.

＊　＊　＊

For the next week, the citizens of Pongo wait anxiously for news of their husbands, fathers, and sons. The talking drums tell of further massing of warriors in anticipation of a big battle, but nothing about the fate of individuals. Only half of the *sobas* have sent troops to face the brutal onslaught of the Imbangala.

The big clash occurs at the Lukala River. The battle rages for hours, and the Ndongo militias fight with indomitable spirit. But in the end, they have to yield to the superior numbers and Portuguese artillery and retreat. The Imbangala stream through the gaps like lava from a volcano and scorch the nearby villages and countryside.

There are stories of terrible atrocities as the Imbangala march to the capital city of Kabasa, where the royal forces led by *Soba* Balanga fight them in desperate hand-to-hand combat from one street to the next and barely manage to hold them at bay.

What ultimately halts the Imbangala and their Portuguese over-lords is not the heroic courage of the Ndongo forces but the arrival of the rainy season. The daily torrents of water pouring from the sky drench the parched earth and turn it into mud and muck, making roads impassable and disrupting the invaders' vital supply lines. The rains also soak the fuses of the Portuguese muskets, rendering them useless and depriving the Imbangala of their decisive edge in battle.

Pongo

So they retreated across the Lukala River to wait out the season.

In Pongo, Margarita is with the other children in the nuns' compound when the clanging of bells and talking drums announce the return of the warriors.

She and the others join a flood of women and children rushing to the edge of the *pedra negras* where they said good-bye just a fortnight ago. Through the sheets of rain, they make out a line of straggling, mud-covered men trudging up the long slope to the mountain gap. Their clothes are torn and covered with blood. The few without visible battle scars help the others stagger along or carry on makeshift stretchers wounded men who can't walk.

As they come closer, their wives and children surge toward them to help.

When Margarita sees her father at the head of the troops, tired and unbowed, her heart leaps in her chest. He is unhurt! She is about to run toward him, but her mother holds her back, insisting on preserving a dignified appearance. Margarita, feeling her mother's fingers dig into her shoulder like the talons of an eagle, can tell how upset she really is.

Then she sees Francisco shuffling next to his father. His left arm hangs limp by his side, and his eyes have a haunted look. Otherwise he seems all right, and Margarita offers a silent prayer for his return.

As the end of the line comes in sight, a sudden outburst of anguished wailing rises from the crowd—all the women and children who do not see their loved ones and realize that they have perished. Some collapse on the muddy ground, keening and sobbing, sputtering in agony over their loss. Others stand like forlorn statues.

Margarita wants to run, to escape from the heartrending sounds, but her mother holds her by her side with an iron grip, her face a stoic mask of defiance. Margarita does her best to imitate her, but her lips quiver and she is barely able to hold back her tears.

Later, in the quiet of their home, after her father has visited all of the families who have lost fathers, sons, uncles, and cousins, offering what comfort he can, he sits in the living area with them. The fact that he allows Margarita and her siblings to stay as he talks with his wife tells Margarita how serious things are.

"We fought valiantly, but we didn't have a chance," he says wearily. "There were too few of us and too many of them. If it hadn't been for the rains, the Imbangala would have slaughtered everyone."

It pains Margarita to hear the exhaustion and resignation in his voice.

She asks, "What about the king and his family?"

"They are safe for now. Their compound was never penetrated."

"So are we safe?"

"For now, yes. But I doubt that their blood lust has been sated. We'll have to get ready for them when they come back in the spring." A bit of his steely resolve returns as he insists, "And we will be."

It takes a long time for Margarita to get to sleep that night.

*　*　*

Over the next weeks, her father and the elders do their best to help the citizens of the town restore a sense of normalcy. The downpours help, keeping people inside in an ordinary, waterlogged existence.

For the youngsters, daily lessons and prayers with the Portuguese nuns continue, but they're cut short now because the Sisters go out to nurse and give solace to the wounded warriors and bereaved families. Margarita sometimes accompanies Sister Inez Theresa. The visits aren't easy. Some of the gashes made by the axes of the Imbangala are horrific. But the nuns and the family members work well together. The Pongo women have medicinal herbs that prevent the wounds from festering and promote healing. The nuns are good at making poultices and offering support with prayers.

Margarita is glad that Francisco is recovering from his wound, a sword thrust into his left shoulder. The first time Margarita and Sister Inez come to his house, he refuses to even look at Margarita, as if he is still far away in a nightmare country of his own. Margarita acts as if everything is fine, and by the third visit he ventures a small smile when she teases him about his fingers moving like a bird scratching the ground.

The most difficult times for Margarita are when they are helpless to prevent the inevitable. Sister Inez often sends her away to spare her the moment when the angel of death descends, but the sudden wailing from inside a hut pierces Margarita like a thorn, landing in the pit of her stomach, and no amount of prayer or thinking about good things can dislodge it for some time.

Still, after a month or so, life settles back into a familiar routine. Taking her cue from her mother, who has a ready smile for everyone she meets, she makes an effort to spread good cheer. Francisco has returned to the school, too, and recovered some of his natural swagger. Margarita even enjoys playing games with Juan and laughing at the antics of Julio, who entertains them with his imitation of different animals. In some stretches of time, Margarita forgets the dangers looming ahead.

2
CAPTAIN JOPE
October 1618

More than 5,000 miles to the north in the harbor of Plymouth, England, the Reverend John Colyn Jope stands on the quarterdeck of his ship, the *White Lion*. He has no idea that his fate will soon intersect with the young girl in Angola. He is watching a crew of sailors haul a heavy yardarm up the ship's main mast. The crew chief calls out, "Heave," and the men answer, "Ho," in rhythmic response as they pull on the thick ropes, their muscles rippling from the strain. Slowly the spar rises perpendicular toward the topmast platform, where other workers are perched on the ratlines that cross the two shrouds on either side of the mast like the rungs of a ladder, waiting to lash the heavy beam into place.

Jope is not wearing the habit of a Calvinist minister, but breeches, a plain linen shirt, and an open jerkin against the cool of the fall afternoon. As he surveys the ship, his eyes flash with pride. Even though the ship still looks like the skeleton—it has no sails, rigging, cannons, supplies, and provisions to make it seaworthy—he can now see it finished in his mind's eye. Just standing on the deck and feeling it gently swaying on the harbor waves after years in drydock give him a thrill.

When he bought the thirty-year-old galleon nearly a decade ago from an old sea captain who belonged to his congregation, it was in bad shape, a wounded veteran of many sea battles. The hull and deck had rotted in numerous places, and salt water seeped in the gaps between the timbers where tar and caulk had become brittle. The sails were beyond repair in many places, and the cannons were worn out and rusted.

But the first time Jope set foot on the creaking vessel, he felt at home in a way he had never experienced during his trips across the channel to Holland to study at the seminary in Vlissingen. When he reached the spot on the deck where he is standing now, a surge of energy flooded through him, leaving him trembling with excitement, and he knew without doubt that this ship was his destiny. He and the *White Lion* were bound up together in a larger purpose as certain as it was unfathomable at the time.

Getting the ailing galley into shape has been no easy task, however. There were large timbers to replace, rope and caulking to press between the cracks of the hull planks, new masts and spars to mount, not to mention cleaning out the lower decks and holds. While Jope had some training as a cabinetmaker and wasn't above getting his hands dirty, most of the jobs required many craftsmen and shipbuilding experts.

His older brother Joseph, who had inherited the family estate upon their father's death, helped by becoming an investor in the ship. And Jope scrimped what he could from his measly salary as a minister, sinking every penny into the project. But with limited funds, the refurbishing work proceeded at a snail's pace.

Not until four years earlier, when he entered into marriage with Mary Glanville, a pretty young woman from Tavistock, did his fortunes change for the better. Jope is glad that his family name is still respected and worth something in Cornwall, because Mary was quite a prize. Her father, John Glanville, is well connected in London and Parliament through her uncle of the same name, and he provided his only daughter with a generous dowry. As a result, Jope has been able to proceed apace and is now just months away of finishing and outfitting the *White Lion* for her second maiden voyage.

At thirty-nine, he knows this is the one big opportunity left to him in life to make something of himself—by taking to the sea and becoming a buccaneer like his father before him—and he is confident that he will succeed. As a good Calvinist, Jope believes with every fiber of his being that he is one of God's elect and has been chosen for a special purpose. Looking out of Plymouth Harbor toward the open sea, past rows of merchant ships moored at the docks, he wonders what destiny the Lord has in store for him.

Everything is coming together in a timely fashion. He has recently obtained letters of marque from William of Orange that will allow him to raid Spanish vessels with impunity. His friendship with the Dutch king's brother, whom he met at the seminary along with a number of English Puritans, has proved a godsend. At a time when privateering is considered a crime in England, an act of piracy punishable by death, the only way to be safe as a marauder is to have a document from another sovereign country that is at war with Spain. Having such letters of marque in one's travel trunk makes it possible to attack Spanish vessels legitimately and avoid the hangman's noose or executioner's axe.

Jope blames this state of affairs on the cowardice of King James. He enacted the law against privateering at the behest of the Spanish ambassador to England, Don Diego Sarmiento de Acuña, Count of Gondomar. Having converted to Catholicism shortly after ascending to the throne, James doesn't want to incur the displeasure of the urbane diplomat who keeps dangling before him the offer of marriage of Prince Charles to the Spanish infanta.

Gondomar has been clamoring for the head of Sir Walter Raleigh, imprisoned in the Tower of London after he returned from his ill-starred expedition to Guiana to search for the mythical city of El Dorado. Not only did he not find an ounce of gold, but the voyage ended in disaster when one of Raleigh's captains attacked a Spanish village. Along with his own son, several of the inhabitants were killed, which meant the old privateer ran afoul of the law. He had risked everything on a foolish rumor, promising James riches he desperately wants—Parliament keeps refusing to fund his extravagant lifestyle with new taxes—and it has all come to naught. Raleigh not only lost his reputation and his only son; now his life hangs in the balance.

Jope still remembers the time he met a younger Raleigh when the dashing courtier visited his father. They were good friends from their marauding days. Raleigh wore a pearl in his left ear and told marvelous stories about his exploits in the Americas. As he talked of raiding Spanish galleons, he had a gleam in his eyes. It kindled a burning desire for adventure in the twelve-year-old Jope, and that flame never diminished—not during his brief apprenticeship as a cabinetmaker, nor during his days at the Calvinist seminary in Holland, nor during his ministry in a small town outside of Plymouth in rural Cornwall.

But rather than chase after rumors of a fabled golden city in the jungle, he plans to raid Spanish ships on their way home from the New World. So much easier to let Spain and its slaves do the backbreaking work of digging gold and silver from the mines in Mexico and Brazil and relieve their masters of their riches at sea. The cargo in the hold of just one gold galleon will make his fortune for life, and is well worth the risk. Jope doesn't consider such pilfering a crime. His letters of marque will prove otherwise, and he will be doing God's work, striking at the heart of the Catholic Spain, embodiment of the devil!

A shout from the docks below interrupts his reverie. "Ahoy the *White Lion!*"

Jope walks to the starboard railing. A familiar figure looks up at him from beneath a wide-brimmed plumed hat. The man cups his hands to the sides of his mouth and shouts, "Permission to come aboard, Captain!"

A broad grin spreads over Jope's face. "Diego Grillo! You old sea dog. Come on up!"

Jope clambers down the steps with surprising agility to meet a dark-skinned man on the poop deck. They clasp each other in a hearty embrace.

El Mulato, also known as Grillo—the cricket—is a good twenty years older than Jope, and a foot shorter, but just as muscular and robust. His broad, brown face betrays his illegitimate origins. Born on an island near Cuba, his father was a Spanish conquistador and his mother an African slave.

He got his insect surname from Sir Francis Drake, the greatest of the English privateers, because of his permanent squint from beneath bushy black eyebrows. He is a legend on the Spanish Main himself, known by his enemies as "Lucifer de los Mares"—Lucifer of the Seas. He has devastated the Catholic fleet ever since Drake captured him as a youngster on the Isles of the Pines, adopted him as his own son, raised him as a Puritan, and further fanned his already considerable hatred of everything Spanish.

"Diego, how good to see you." Jope eagerly searches his older mentor's face. "What news from London?"

Grillo's face clouds instantly. "You haven't heard? They cut off Raleigh's head two days ago. There have been riots and demonstration against the King and Condomar all over London."

The news strikes Jope like a dagger. "The bastards!"

"He died nobly, they say," Grillo says. "When they showed him the axe, he said, 'This is a sharp medicine, but it is a physician for all diseases and miseries.' Always the wordsmith and poet, even at the bitter end."

"The bastards!" Jope repeats between clenched teeth. "How did it happen?"

"I think he was tired of the world, John. They gave him several opportunities to make his escape, but he ignored them all. His son getting killed must have devastated him. He had nothing to live for anymore."

Jope has a hard time reconciling his memory of the high-spirited courtier with Grillo's image of a worn-out old man ready to accept his fate on the scaffold. He feels a burning rage for the cowardly James, for the oily Gondomar, for all the arrogant Spaniards and their devilish Catholic religion.

"The bastards," he spits the word out for the third time. "We'll make them pay."

Grillo clamps his arm with an iron grip, draws close, and whispers. "That we will, John. But we must take care. The Spanish weasel is out for more blood. London's afloat with rumors that the son of the Earl of Warwick is using Jamestown as a pirates' base, and Gondomar would like nothing better than to prove it and separate him from his head, too."

"So we're going to lie low for now, like cowards?" Jope's nostrils flare in anger.

"Nothing of the sort." Grillo closes with him again and murmurs in his ear, "I'm about to ship out on a fishing expedition."

When he pulls back and raises his bushy brows significantly, Jope can see hatred burn in his dark eyes.

Grillo turns toward the main deck and watches the work crew preparing to hoist another yardarm up the mast. "I see you're coming along well. When will you be ready?"

"I plan to ship out in the spring."

"You'll need a good navigator. I know someone who knows the West Indies like his backyard," he says, smiling humorlessly. "*And* he's got angling experience." He lowers his voice again so only Jope can hear him. "If you make it to Cuba by June, we can meet up. Show you the ropes and catch some Spanish gold fish."

"That's more like it," says Jope, matching Grillo's grim smile.

"You'll have an easier time shipping out from Plymouth. In London, the King's police keep sniffing around the docks looking for evidence of our trade. The last time, I had to hide my powder, shot, and muskets beneath fishing tackles and nets, and pay a hefty bribe to boot, to convince them I was on legitimate business."

"I'll keep that in mind."

Grillo pulls back and announces in a loud voice, "I'm heading back to London tomorrow. Why don't we hoist a pint in the Crown & Anchor later tonight? I'll introduce you to our fellow fisherman. His name is Marmaduke. You'll like him. That is, if it's all right with your fair mistress."

Jope flushes crimson from the neck up. "I'm not a henpecked husband, you old dog."

"No, but I've seen your eyes go soft whenever someone mentions Mary's name." He squints. "Sure you're ready to leave her for a year or two?"

"Mary knew about this when we got engaged and had the bans read," Jope answers huffily. "She'll be just fine."

"If you say so," Grillo teases. He mock salutes and turns to leave. "See you tonight then."

"Yes," Jope calls after him with more conviction than he feels.

Alone, he wonders about his young wife. Their four years together have been a surprise to him. Mary loves him with a child-like affection he did not anticipate when they were betrothed. They met only twice before they got married, surrounded by stern-faced chaperones, and exchanged meaningless pleasantries. He did most of the talking as Mary seemed too shy to venture any thoughts of her own. That didn't last long after they exchanged vows, however. She is not only a chatterbox, but her disposition is sunny and full of ardor. She has taken to him so completely that she has won his heart.

Jope doesn't want to admit to himself how much he will miss her, so he keeps telling himself that he's doing all this for her, too, not just because it is his destiny.

3
LORD RICH
November 1618

Meanwhile, in London, another man who will figure prominently in Margarita and Juan's story is having one of the worst days of his life. Sir Robert Rich, the oldest son of the Earl of Warwick, is attending an emergency board meeting of the Virginia Company. As one of the largest investors, he wields considerable influence, though not as much as Sir Thomas Smythe, who has been treasurer and board president since 1609 when he obtained the royal charter for the company.

Rich has a good idea what it is all about. He imagines it is to determine the successor to Lord De La Warr, the titular head of the Virginia Company, who died under mysterious circumstances on his way to Jamestown to investigate irregularities there. Ever since his ship, the *Neptune*, returned from Jamestown with the news, London has been awash with malicious gossip. Rich's name has come up because his own ship, the *Treasurer*, and its captain, Daniel Elfrith, met up with the ship at sea. After a joint dinner, half the crew of the *Neptune* became sick, and several men, including Lord De La Warr, died soon after. The rumor of foul play, ordered by Rich to cover up his own wrongdoings, is utter nonsense, of course; but idle speculation spread by the crew of the *Neptune* and its captain, Edward Brewster, has tongues wagging.

Lord Rich

Thomas Smythe, who called the meeting, has troubles of his own. He and his fellow merchants hold a monopoly to bring essential food and supplies to the Jamestown colony at inflated rates. Their magazine ship is a sore subject with many shareholders, who have seen Smythe and his cohorts grow wealthy while they haven't received a penny from their investment and the company slips ever further into debt.

Rich doesn't like the magazine ship either but has ignored the issue so far. With his ailing father close to death, he is about to become one of the richest men in England. Looking around the room, he imagines that either he or Henry Wriothesley, the flamboyant Earl of Southampton, will be nominated to head the company. Southampton, being older and having more eminence, is the more likely candidate.

So Rich is taken by surprise when Smythe calls the meeting to order and immediately confronts him. "We have received word that the *Treasurer*—your ship, Sir Robert—did not go to Virginia on a fishing and trade expedition, as you claimed, but was outfitted for privateering. Worse, there are charges that Samuel Argall, the governor you had us vote into office, has been using Jamestown as a pirate base for your vessels to attack the Spanish gold fleet. These are serious accusations and, if true, threaten the very existence of our enterprise."

There is a collective gasp from the merchant board members.

Smythe raps his gavels once and asks, "What say you?"

Rich rises. His handsome face is a mask of calm, but beneath it he is seething. "Who is making these outrageous claims?"

"Captain Brewster of the *Neptune* says the *Treasurer* was outfitted with cannons and muskets and had no fishing gear at all. When he got to Jamestown, Governor Argall apparently confiscated his cargo, and when he complained, had him arrested, tried for treason, and sentenced to death. He escaped with his life only because members of the court and the clergy, shocked by the severity of the punishment, interceded to have him pardoned."

Barely able to contain his fury, Rich raises his voice. "These are blatant lies! Daniel Elfrith and Samuel Argall are above reproach."

Southampton comes to his aid. "Since when do we accede to idle hearsay? Captain Brewster has not presented one shred of evidence in support of his contemptible accusation. Are we to believe his word over those of his betters?"

A merchant dressed in a fancy doublet answers him. "A number of the sailors with him have corroborated his version of the tale."

"No doubt well prepared and suitably paid," Southampton scoffs.

Sir Edwin Sandys rises. Like Smythe, he is nearly twice as old as Rich, but while his pointed beard is gray, his eyes are sharp, and his voice is resonant from many years of speaking in Parliament. "I am inclined to take Sir Robert at his word," he intones. "We have more important matters to discuss. The survival of the colony is at stake. We must send more settlers there and give them the wherewithal to become independent, to stand on their own feet."

Rich is surprised. He did not expect support from that quarter. As a fellow Puritan with a firm belief in separation of church and state, he shares Sandys's antiroyalist sentiments. But Sandys represents the small investors, while Rich sides with his fellow aristocrats, and the two have never warmed up to one another.

Smythe takes note as well. He knows that Sandys's barb was aimed at him, but he must tread carefully. Much as he loathes his opponent for his democratic ideas—in Parliament Sandys is the leader against King James's efforts to raise taxes to pay for his lavish lifestyle—the man is a powerful adversary.

"Your concerns are apt, Sir Edwin," he says smoothly. "Let us discuss them in detail at our upcoming quarter court meeting. Today we must deal with the matter at hand. These allegations are serious enough to merit investigation."

The merchants on the board murmur their assent. No doubt Smythe has organized their response in advance. Rich bides his time to see what else he has planned.

Banging his gavel again, the treasurer says, "Therefore, I intend to nominate Sir George Yeardley to replace Samuel Argall as governor when his term is up this month. He knows Jamestown and the Indian affairs from personal experience. He is above reproach and will conduct a thorough investigation."

Rich did not see this coming. He leaps to his feet. "This is an affront to Samuel Argall, who has given his all for Virginia for many years!"

Smythe continues, unruffled, "As all you know, Yeardley and Argall fought together as lieutenants under Captain John Smith in the early days of the colony. Yeardley will treat him fairly and with respect." He continues, affably, "If, as we all expect, he discovers nothing amiss, he will say so. Surely, Sir Robert, you don't think Captain Argall has anything to hide?"

Rich knows the old bastard has outfoxed him. "Of course not!" he says huffily and sits down.

After Smythe garners the necessary votes for the nomination to be brought to the quarter court, which is attended by all the shareholders, he quickly brings the meeting to a close. Rich takes only the time to thank Southampton and Sandys for their support before leaving. He needs to gather his thoughts.

In his carriage on the way home, he muses about the irony that his accusers are right. He is a privateer. Ever since he attended Emmanuel College in Cambridge, Rich has held the belief that the future of England lies in developing colonies overseas. Spain got into the game early on and grew rich beyond measure from its gold and silver mines in South America. If it hadn't been for buccaneers like Sir Francis Drake, Walter Raleigh, and Rich's father, who built the largest private fleet in England and amassed immense wealth of his own, England would be a minor nation instead of a major force in international trade.

People thought Rich was nothing but a wastrel at Cambridge University, the spoiled child of a wealthy patron, who preferred dueling, hunting, wenching, and drinking to getting an education. But his instructors, extremist Puritans all, had a more lasting impact on the young man than anyone could have imagined. In line with his father's views, they inculcated in young Rich a hatred of Catholicism and its most fervent agent, Spain, as well as love and patriotism for all things English.

Although there is no love lost for his father, Rich considers him a daring visionary and happily followed in his footsteps. It's been six years since he sent the *Treasurer*, under the command of Captain Argall, to Jamestown with sixty-eight men and supplies and provisions. He has invested heavily in the stock companies of Virginia and the Somers Islands—Bermuda—and financed most of Raleigh's doomed expedition to Guinea. Yet none of these ventures in the New World have borne fruit, except for one. If it wasn't for his marauders relieving the Spanish of their treasure, the whole enterprise would have been a catastrophe.

He needs Jamestown as a base from which to launch his ships. It may not rival Cuba and Tortuga in the Caribbean as a pirates' haven, but it has served his purposes very well for the past two years. Rich managed to make it so when Samuel Argall, then captain of the *Treasurer*, brought John Rolfe and his wife, Pocahontas, on a visit to England to promote the Virginia colony. The Indian princess caused a sensation. People flocked to see her; King James was smitten and had her participate in his Twelfth Night revels. The members of London's elite fawned over her, although privately they were aghast—a princess of royal blood marrying a commoner!

Rich had no such qualms. He met in secret with Rolfe and Argall and forged plans. He installed Argall and Rolfe as governor and secretary-treasurer of the colony, respectively, and they have outfitted his ships as needed for their raids into the Spanish Main. Daniel Elfrith took over as captain of the *Treasurer* and, along with other of Rich's ships, has been fleecing the Spanish galleons successfully, which paid off handsomely.

But now there's trouble. Rich knows that the squall raised by Brewster's report is not likely to blow over on its own. He must warn Argall and Elfrith. Fortunately, he has time until February. No one in his right mind ships out in winter and braves the Atlantic's violent storms.

Still, he must be watchful. Smythe is an experienced political hand, and his connections reach all the way to James's closest advisers. It is a good thing that Rich's mother, Penelope Devereaux, may her soul rest in peace, introduced him to the King as a youngster. James has a predilection for good-looking young men, and Rich took after his mother, who was considered the most beautiful woman in England at the time. If anything, at thirty-two he is even more handsome, with piercing black eyes, dark brown curls, and a dashing goatee and mustache, Although the King has never made a pass at him, he enjoys Rich's company. Being in the inner circle of the self-indulgent Catholic monarch isn't always easy. Championing the Puritan cause while profiting from illegal acts of piracy requires Rich to walk a fine line. One misstep and he could end up on the chopping block like Sir Walter Raleigh. Keeping James well-disposed toward him is important.

He leans back in the cushioned seat and dares to relax for a moment. But if he thinks his problems are over for the day, he is mistaken.

When he arrives at his residence, a large town palace with a courtyard and stables, he tells his groom to have his butler bring him a decanter of wine. "The good claret! I'm in desperate need of libation!"

Then he heads to his study where Alfred greets him, carrying a flagon and goblet on a silver tray. Rich has inherited the butler from his ailing father. He is loyal, incorruptible, and utterly humorless, but has the uncanny ability to anticipate his desires. Alfred is stoop-shouldered and has a bulbous nose, Rich has often wondered how much of the wine the butler reserves for himself.

As Rich sinks into his favorite chair, Alfred sets the tray on a side table next to him and, cognizant of his master's tastes, fills the glass nearly to the brim. Rich drinks deeply.

Alfred clears his throat. "Your cousin would like a moment of your time, m'Lord."

Rich sighs. More bad news, no doubt. But he nods. "Send him in."

By the time there is a knock on the large oak double doors, Rich is on his second glass of wine. "Come," he calls.

Nathaniel Rich enters, carrying a number of scrolls and documents. A portly man, he is just two years older than his cousin, but with neither his good looks nor his youthful energy. Still, his eyes are as lively and his mind is perhaps even sharper. A lawyer by training, he has an amazing head for all the details of the many business interests Rich pursues. Most important, he understands how to skirt, bend, and if necessary, break rules and laws that get in the way.

Rich likes and appreciates his cousin. "So, Nathaniel, what crisis du jour don't I know about yet?" he says languidly.

Ignoring the attempt at levity, Nathaniel hands Rich a letter. "The kingdom of Savoy has made peace with Spain."

In response, Rich hurls his goblet at the fireplace. The glass shatters against the wall, adding to a large, dark stain on the wood. The rest of the wine splatters onto the glowing logs, raising small, sizzling tongues of smoke. Sighing heavily, Rich walks to the window. He breaks the seal and peruses the missive only to get his emotions under control. His quicksilver mind has already grasped the implications.

As long as the kingdom on the southern coast of France was at war with Spain, the letters that he obtained through bribery provided official cover for his privateering exploits. Now the *Treasurer* lacks legal protection for its raids on Spanish galleons. The documents in Elfrith's trunk aren't worth the parchment they were written on. His frigate and men are in direct violation of James's edicts against piracy and, if caught, will have an appointment with the hangman's noose.

Nathaniel doesn't move a muscle during Rich's outburst. He simply waits for his temper to run its course.

When Rich finally turns in his direction, he seems almost surprised that Nathaniel is still in the room. "Anything else?"

Nathaniel crosses to a handsome wooden desk and puts down the scrolls. "A few documents that need your signature. Captain Brewster and Lady De La Warr are threatening to bring a lawsuit against you for wrongful death, but I don't think we need to worry about that."

Rich comes over, scrutinizes them briefly, takes the quill Nathaniel has dipped into the ink glass for him, and scratches his name at the bottom of the parchment sheets. Nathaniel sprinkles talcum powder on them to aid in drying the ink.

"Anything else, m'Lord?"

As Rich finishes the last signature with a flourish, he says, "Actually there is."

He is about to yell, "More wine, Alfred," when the butler materializes with another decanter and two glasses. Rich invites Nathaniel to take one and fills it. "I need your help with the Virginia Company. I'm losing ground to Smythe and his greedy merchants."

Nathaniel waits for Rich to pour himself a glass and says, "I will buy some shares. That way I can officially attend meetings and vote and—"

"—work your magic behind the scenes," Rich finishes for him.

They clink glasses and drink, cementing their arrangement. For the next hour, Rich fills his cousin in on the different factions, major shareholders, and issues. Nathaniel pays close attention and makes a few suggestions. By the time he leaves, the decanter is empty and Rich's temper much improved.

If he has to give up Argall's governorship to satisfy the small-minded gaggle of shareholders, so be it. He still has John Rolfe in Jamestown. He remains loyal and will mind his affairs. And when George Yeardley ships out to Virginia, he will take with him as secretary John Pory, who has been in Rich's camp for some time.

November 1618

A line from Shakespeare's *Hamlet* comes unbidden to his mind: "How all occasions do inform against me, and spur my dull revenge!"

Rich's smile is vulpine. With Nathaniel by his side, his revenge on Sir Thomas Smythe will be anything but dull.

4

IMBANGALA!

Spring 1619

I t is the depth of the wet season on the high plateau. Everything looks gray in Pongo and waterlogged, even when there is a break in the relentless torrents of rain. Margarita can make out the hump-backs of the surrounding mountains only in outline. When the water comes streaming down from the dreary skies, raising small splashes on the muddy roads, the mountaintops disappear from view completely.

Unlike previous years, when everyone hunkered down until the sun comes out in the spring, Margarita's father and a small delegation have braved the miserable weather and traveled to the capital. He has waded across washed-out roads, forded streams that have swollen to the size of rivers, and endured downpours that have soaked him to the bone in order to confer with the King's council.

When he returns after several weeks, he looks grim but refuses to say anything until he meets with the elders.

Late in the afternoon, Margarita watches Joana bury yams in the cooking pit in the kitchen and cover them with a layer of clay. Then she brings embers from the fireplace in the main living area, places them on top, and fans them with a large palm frond until they glow white hot. Margarita feels the heat from several feet away and relishes the smell of cooking yams that starts to waft from the pit.

Imbangala!

Suddenly she hears the raised voices of her parents from deeper in the house. She sneaks to the curtain at the door to hear better.

"Mbandi doesn't understand the danger. Now that he sits on the throne, he thinks he's invincible," her father says. "We kept telling him to make peace with all of the *sobas* and forge alliances with the other kingdoms while there is still time, but he wouldn't listen!"

Margarita has never heard her father sound so agitated before.

"Are you sure it's as bad as all that?" her mother attempts to soothe him.

"The Imbangala have only withdrawn to Ambaca, but they'll be back as soon as the wet season ends. If it was just the Portuguese, we'd be fine, but we're facing a horde of powerful, vicious fighters. We can't defeat them unless we're united."

"What are we going to do?"

Margarita hears the fear in her mother's voice and it worries her. The young servant girl is upset, too. She stabs repeatedly at the yams in the pit. Her fingers tremble from gripping the iron poker so hard.

"We have to make preparations on our own. Our elders think Pongo is impregnable, but the *pedras negras* won't protect us against the onslaught of the Imbangala."

"Shhh," says her mother. She has realized that they were speaking loud enough for everyone in the household to hear.

Margarita strains her ears, but with her parents' voices reduced to whispers, she can no longer make out what they're saying. At dinner, her parents act unconcerned, as if their conversation never took place.

The next day at the Portuguese Sisters' compound, no one seems aware of the danger either. Margarita's age mates and the younger children show no signs of worry. Juan prattles on about his father's new calves, born at the beginning of the rainy season. They're filling out and following him around. One in particular has captured his affection.

"She comes up behind me and nuzzles me when she wants to be petted," he says happily.

Spring 1619

Margarita hardly pays attention. She looks out the window at the drip lines of water coming off the palm-thatched roof and the dark gray rain curtains hiding everything beyond from view. Much as she hates the wet season, she prays that it will not end this year.

* * *

A month later, in late January, the sun returns to the high plateau land along with hazy morning mists. Soon the talking drums resume their distant thumping, bringing dire news. As her father predicted, the ground has barely dried out and the Imbangala are on the march again. Once more the war bells clang, calling for Pongo's warriors to protect the kingdom.

Margarita's father says his good-byes at their house. He kisses her and her siblings and hugs them. Margarita doesn't want to let go of him, so he gently pulls her hands away.

He looks her in the eyes and says gravely, "Whatever happens, never forget that you are the daughter of a warrior."

He embraces her mother for a long time. Then he asks them to go to the market area ahead of him while he stays behind to pray.

On the way Margarita feels a painful knot in her chest, but she doesn't let on how desperate she feels. Once again, Pongo's fighters have assembled. They still look formidable, but their numbers are not as large as before, and they don't swagger as before. Margarita notices fearful glances among them as they mill about.

Francisco stands off to the side looking glum. His left arm hangs uselessly by his side. Margarita knows that he doesn't want to stay behind.

She comes up to him and says, "We need you here to protect us."

He looks at her, surprised, and his pained expression lifts for a moment.

Then her father appears, and the warriors slowly come to attention. His eyes flash, and he addresses them with a force and vitality

Imbangala!

Margarita has never seen in him. He appeals to their sense of honor and nobility and rouses their courage with words of inspiration. They start banging their axes and swords against their shields until the cacophony becomes a frightful din.

Margarita wants to remember him this way. She looks to her mother, who is watching her husband with stone-faced dignity and eyes sparkling with pride.

The women, children, and men too old to go to war follow the warriors to the edge of the mountains as before and watch them march down the foothills toward the vast expanse of plain. They keep vigil long after their loved ones have disappeared from sight.

* * *

For the next week Margarita and her mother go about their daily duties and rituals, doing their best to act like everything is normal, but there is an edge, a tension in the air everywhere they go. And when the talking drums begin to pound, everyone stops to listen.

The day of the big battle they rattle on nonstop, their throbbing beat echoing relentlessly across the plain. During the first clashes Ndongo's forces manage to hold the line, but soon the superior numbers of the Imbangala overwhelm the king's army and rush through the gaps. The defenders fall back to protect the capital.

The drumming intensifies, telling of heroic stands, last-ditch efforts to repel the attacks of the white-faced marauders, but to no avail. Kabasa is overrun. King Mbandi flees, leaving his mother, his wives, and his children behind at the mercy of the barbarians. He's heading south for safety, pursued by bands of Imbangala whose blood lust hasn't been sated.

The drums strike fear into the hearts of Pongo's citizens, but then they suddenly stop altogether, and the silence is even more frightening, leaving people to contemplate the worst their imaginations can conjure up.

Spring 1619

The next two days are quiet, except for the arrival of farmers and livestock herders from villages on the plain who have escaped the marauders and seek shelter in the mountains. Like Pongo's residents, they hope that the Imbangala will pass by the rocks, content with raping and plundering the easier targets—stores of grain, herds of cattle and goat, and the groves of palm trees on the open plain. Everyone knows that the makeshift palisades at the entrance of Pongo, guarded by youngsters and old men with bows and arrows, won't offer much resistance.

During the daylight hours, Margarita and the other children of the town take refuge with the Catholic nuns. Her mother reassures her, "You'll be safe there. Even the Imbangala won't violate the sanctuary of the Portuguese Sisters."

Margarita isn't so sure. She would prefer to stay with her mother, but Margarita obeys her wishes. In the evening she returns to her home for supper and the comfort of her own bed. But the nights are anything but restful. She wonders what happened to her father and listens for unusual sounds, staring fearfully into the darkness when she hears an owl hooting or the scratching of a wild animal, before falling into a fitful sleep.

The next morning Margarita is on her way to the Sisters' compound when the iron alarm bells sound throughout the town. The frantic clanging can mean only one thing: the Imbangala are attacking!

She races to the compound where the two nuns are surrounded by frightened children. As Margarita joins them, she hears Sister Maria say with a firm voice, "Gather close. If we pray together, we will be safe."

They all huddle, kneel, and clasp their hands in prayer, reciting the Pater Noster ever more fervently as the cries, screams, and sounds of clashing weapons come closer.

Suddenly, there is a brutal shout, and a large figure leaps into their midst. His face is covered with white ash, his eyes are wild, and he brandishes a bloody axe. The children scatter, screaming, but Margarita trips and falls. The ghostly warrior bends over her, his leering face close to hers. She can smell the rancid breath issuing from his mawlike mouth.

When Sister Inez Theresa surges forward to protect her, the brute swings his axe. Blood spurts from her throat as she falls to the ground. Her body twitches uncontrollably, then lies still.

The monster turns back to Margarita when Francisco appears behind him. He swings an axe in a great arc and buries it in the monster's neck with all his might. There is a loud thud. The Imbangala grunts and crashes to the ground like a gored water buffalo. Margarita scrambles backward, away from his thrashing body.

But the victory is short-lived. Other white-faced attackers pour into the compound. One of them slashes with his sword and nearly severs Francisco's head from his shoulders. Margarita sees the light extinguish in his eyes as his body crumbles and she cries out.

Suddenly, she's lifted up and slung over the muscular shoulder of one of the intruders. When she kicks with her legs, a fist cuffs her head and she goes limp, half-dazed.

She comes to as she's being lowered to the ground next to the sundial in the courtyard of the compound. The iron stick tilting toward the sky throws a shadow on the numeral IX. Incongruous as it seems among the surrounding mayhem, it is another image Margarita will carry with her for the rest of her life.

There is blood spattered over her dress. At first she thinks that she's been hurt, but when she feels no pain, she realizes that it must be from Sister Inez Theresa when she gave her life trying to save her.

She notices other children next to her, crying softly. Juan sits nearby, lost and shivering. His face looks gray, and his lower lip quivers. Margarita crawls over to him and squeezes him by the hand until he looks at her.

"We will be all right, you and I," she says with a sense of conviction she doesn't feel.

Juan searches her face. His lips tighten, and he nods several times.

The Imbangala call out for them to get up and move. They kick those who comply too slowly and herd them away. Everywhere, there are bodies lying on the ground grotesquely twisted, blood seeping from gaping wounds in their heads, limbs, and trunks—all the men and women the brutes have slaughtered.

Margarita puts her arm around Juan. "Don't look," she says. In response, he clamps his small hands around her waist, letting her guide him.

When they get to the marketplace, there are other captives, a few young men and mostly women. She sees people from elder families crouched next to herders and servants. The Imbangala make no social distinction.

Margarita searches frantically for her mother but doesn't see any sign of her. Just as a wave of desperation threatens to overwhelm her, she notices Joana, their young servant girl. Her rust-colored dress is torn at her shoulders, and she holds it up against her chest. She looks wild-eyed with fear. When she sees Margarita staring at her, she bursts into tears and looks away. That's when Margarita knows her mother is dead. She closes her eyes and a moan escapes her.

She doesn't know how long she has stood there immobile as a stone when she receives a rough shove from behind and stumbles. Recovering, she turns to face an Imbangala brute. He rips off her dress. When he sees the pearl around her neck, his eyes light up. Her hand covers it involuntarily, then drops to her side in resignation. He yanks it from her neck, and it disappears in his leather pouch. Then he takes her hands, ties them together in front of her, and attaches the hemp rope to Juan, similarly bound.

When all the prisoners are naked, the Imbangala lash forked tree branches to the necks of the older men and women. They yoke them together and attach their hands to the boughs with ropes and chains.

Margarita feels her arms jerked forward, and she joins the line of captives. They stagger past more bloodied bodies lying in the streets, some of them hacked to pieces, and avert their eyes as best they can. An eerie quietness has descended, interrupted by the crackling bursts of exploding wood from the burning houses. It has taken only an hour or so to destroy the beautiful town completely.

Margaret looks up and sees buzzards and vultures circling high in the smoke-filled sky above.

The caravan makes its way through the gap in the dark mountains, down the green foothills onto the plain. Everywhere are signs of devastation and savagery—the ruins of farm homes, dark smoke rising into the hot afternoon air, the carcasses of slaughtered cattle making small mounds in the landscape, palm trees felled and hacked apart for their sap.

The captives stagger on as if in a daze. The Imbangala drive them without mercy, prodding them with their swords and axes. When someone stumbles and falls, they're whipped until they regain their feet. They do not stop to rest until the sun is setting, a bloody ball far ahead above the horizon.

The captors remove the yokes from their captives' necks to allow them to sit, but keep them in chains. The captors give them a bit of water and mashed grain for supper.

While they build a large fire, Joana manages to get close to Margarita. "Your mother stuck a knife in the eye of the brute who attacked her," she whispers. "He bellowed like a wounded panther. I thought you'd want to know."

Before Margarita can answer, there is a horrific scream. Four Imbangala have pulled up a naked man from the resting captives. As they yank him toward the fire, he shrieks in fear until another warrior buries an axe in his neck and he crumbles to the ground. More Imbangala swarm over him and hack his body to pieces. They tear into the flesh like hyenas feasting on the carcass of a gazelle. Some bring parts of arms and legs to those guarding the prisoners, so that they can partake in the ghastly meal. The white faces, smiling bloody lips, and teeth of the cannibals, illuminated by the dancing flames, make for a gruesome spectacle.

Spring 1619

Margarita hugs Juan to her, trying to shield him from the horror. She prays for her parents, her friends, and all the people of Pongo who have died. She prays for the poor man who was just killed. And she prays for all the survivors of the massacre until exhaustion overwhelms her and she falls into a restless sleep.

5

ENGLAND

Spring 1619

Robert Rich lunges furiously at his fencing instructor, who nimbly turns his rapier aside and touches his padded chest protector with the blunted tip of his own sword. Rich curses and walks away, jerking a towel from a servant standing by to wipe his perspiring face.

"You're too aggressive, too wild today, m'Lord," the Italian master says. "To parry and riposte in one tempo as taught by Grandmaster Fabris requires a measured approach."

"Again," Rich counters.

He faces the older man and feints a stab to his inside. But instead of parrying, Lorenzo counterfeints to Rich's head. Raising his rapier to ward off the attack, Rich leaves his low line exposed, and the master in one smooth motion thrusts his sword into the soft wadding protecting his belly.

Disgusted, Rich throws down his Italian blade and stalks from the room.

"Till next week," the fencing master calls after him as he bends down and picks up the rapier with a loving gesture.

Bursting into his drawing room, Rich kicks off his shoes. He can barely stand still enough for Alfred to undo the knots of the protective gear and peel it off before he starts pacing. The butler picks up the shoes and disappears.

Smoldering, Rich continues to pace. Of course Lorenzo is right. He is too preoccupied; he should not have insisted on the lesson. Newly invested as the second Earl of Warwick, he hasn't had much time to enjoy the trappings and privileges of his new title. After burying his father at Leez Priory, the family estate in Essex, he returned to London only to be beset by difficulties all around. Captain Brewster and Lady De La Warr have made good on their threat and filed a suit against him and Elfrith for wrongful death. Rich would like nothing better than to skewer them with his sword.

More annoying and troublesome are matters at the Virginia Company, where the investors continue to act like nervous ninnies. "The smaller their stake, the more their worries and the louder their protests," Rich mutters.

As predicted, in the quarter court meeting in November, at Smythe's bidding, they voted to remove Samuel Argall as governor of Jamestown and install George Yeardley in his place. They even gave him 300 acres in addition to the 1,000 he already owns in Virginia, "to defray his expenses." Now, with the coming of spring he is about to cast off with a mandate to bring parliamentary government to the colony and to investigate Brewster's claims and discover the whereabouts of the *Treasurer.*

"That nosy popinjay," Rich sputters. "He'll stick his nose where it doesn't belong, and there is nothing we can do about it."

With slippers in hand Alfred returns, kneels, and slides them onto Rich's feet. He rises with a regretful expression and says, "Lady Rich is here to see you."

That's all Rich needs—the scheming widow of his father! As if dealing with the Virginia Company isn't infuriating enough, he has had to sort through the contract he made with his second wife. After less than three years of marriage, she and her relatives are getting a small fortune and more property than any of them deserve.

Before he can say anything, Lady Frances sweeps into the study, preceded by a cloud of lavender perfume. Although it has been less than a week since his father was laid to rest, she wears a fancy dark green dress with embroidery and jewelry. Only the black veil of her hat indicates that she is in mourning.

As she curtsies, Rich eyes his stepmother suspiciously. He can see why his father married her. With her face made up, he can't tell whether she is in her forties or fifties. She is attractive and vibrant, although she couldn't hold a candle to his own departed mother.

"Lady Frances, how nice to see you," he says with more gallantry than he feels. "Won't you have a seat? May I get you a glass of wine?"

She declines, coming straight to the point. "This won't take long. I need more money than the niggling amount specified in the will. My townhouse will need to be remodeled and—"

Rich can't resist a dig. "You have your estate in Snarford."

Lady Frances laughs, but her eyes are blazing. "I don't intend to withdraw to the backcountry like my sister Isabel. London is expensive. As Lady Rich I am required to entertain in a certain style."

"Talk to Nathaniel," Rich offers languidly. "He is handling all matters regarding the settling of my father's estate."

"I have, and he's making things difficult. That is why I am here." She shakes her finger at him. "I know you, Robert. It is at your behest, and I won't stand for it."

Rich sighs inwardly. "I will talk to him."

"Do, or London society will know you're a skinflint who keeps his relatives in poverty. I don't think that is the reputation you'll want to cultivate as the newly installed Earl of Warwick!"

Rich glowers at her with hatred. "I don't respond well to threats, m'Lady."

She looks at him fearlessly. "News has a way of traveling, Robert, quite beyond my control."

Rich knows he cannot win against her. She and her sisters hid Calvinist ministers from persecution and stared down soldiers sent for them by the King. If he wants to remain a leader of the Puritan cause, he must keep to her good side.

"I will do what I can."

"That is all I ask," Lady Frances purrs. "I'll see you this evening at the King's reception."

Rich nods curtly, and she flounces from the room, leaving behind a lingering scent. As the earl wrinkles his nose in disgust, Alfred materializes. He takes a clay pipe from a sideboard, fills the bowl with shredded dark brown leaves, and hands it to his master. With an iron tong he picks up a glowing ember from the fireplace and holds it over the bowl. Rich sucks on the stem several times until the tobacco leaves glow bright red. Then he takes a leisurely draft and expels a cloud of smoke that curls in the air. The sweet, pungent aroma fills the room, extinguishing all remnants of Lady Frances's visit.

"A glass of wine, m'Lord?"

"Yes, thank you, Alfred."

The Earl of Warwick tries to banish his stepmother from his mind, but her reference to the King's banquet this evening reminds him of an unpleasant duty. He will have to bring his strongest pomander, spiked with cloves and freshly dusted with cinnamon. Sitting at the side of the King may be an honor, but it comes with a high price and requires considerable fortitude. James may be of royal blood, but he is also a slob who never bathes and wears the same shirt until it all but falls off his rancid body. Joining him in his favorite activity—hunting—is one thing. Being in the open air dissipates the miasma that surrounds him like a noxious cloud wherever he goes. But in closed quarters, it takes every ounce of Rich's self-control not to screw up his nose in disgust in the imperial presence. It would help if James didn't consider smoking tobacco a disgusting habit and join in the mania that has overtaken his subjects.

Alfred returns with wine. "M'Lord, your cousin is here to see you."

Rich snorts, "Let's hope he brings some good news."

Nathaniel Rich, dressed in a simple doublet, jerkin, and pantaloons, enters and bows.

Waving impatiently, Warwick asks, "What news from the docks?"

"Sir Yeardley's vessel has been unexpectedly delayed by a week." Nathaniel shrugs. "Accidents happen."

For the first time this day, Warwick feels a ray of sunshine. "Well done! We must send a messenger to Plymouth that there is not a moment to lose!"

"I've taken the liberty of dispatching a horseman already. The *Eleanor* is outfitted to go to Bermuda. It is but a small matter to add more provisions for her to voyage beyond and to Jamestown."

"Will she suffice? Argall must be gone before Yeardley sets foot on shore."

"She's a smaller and quicker ship and would beat him in an even race by three days. I'll make sure she'll be ready and out to sea before Yeardley weighs anchor."

Rich is pleased. He can always count on his cousin to anticipate his needs. He lays his tobacco pipe aside and is about to get to his feet.

Nathaniel directs his gaze to the fresco-covered ceiling and says casually, "I had a visit from Lady Frances this morning."

Warwick sighs. "I know. Give her what she wants."

Looking at his cousin askance, Nathaniel asks, "Are you sure?"

"Yes!"

"Very well."

Rising with determination, the earl is suddenly all business. "Now, what shall we do about the next quarter court of the Virginia Company? Thomas Smythe is stepping down as treasurer, but he'll surely have handpicked his successor."

Nathaniel considers for a moment. "Sir Edwin Sandys is standing for election. Whoever we throw our support behind will win."

They discuss their options. Neither faction's candidate is ideal. Getting Sandys elected will certainly extract revenge and be the first step toward braking the merchants' magazine ship monopoly. But he also wants to limit the cultivation of tobacco in favor of food crops and other plants like flax and indigo—this at a time when the mania for tobacco from the Americas and Bermuda provides hope for finally turning a tidy profit. Smythe's faction is with Rich and other large landowners, supporting growing as much tobacco as possible. Still, it may be time for a radical change. Encouraging self-determination on the part of Jamestown's colonists would drive a wedge between the settlers and the covetous merchants and irritate the power-mongering King.

"We have some time to decide," counsels Nathaniel.

Warwick nods, thoughtfully. "Whatever we do, it must be in the service of establishing a Puritan colony in the New World."

* * *

It has been a frustrating three weeks for Captain Jope. With the reconstruction work on the *White Lion* finished, he hoped to set sail with the first spring breezes, but a series of setbacks have delayed his departure several times. Some of the cannons did not arrive in time, and the ropes securing the main spar to the main mast slipped; it turned out they were defective and needed to be replaced, which required a thorough checking of the rest. And just when loading furnishings and weaponry was proceeding apace, the Earl of Warwick's men descended on the harbor and snatched all the flour, salt, grains, and dried fish he had counted on to outfit his ship. The captain of the *Eleanor* came and apologized in person for the inconvenience, claiming he had to ship out at short notice—an unfortunate emergency in the colonies.

Jope watches the *Eleanor*, a sleek vessel, clear the buoys at the harbor's entrance and sail into the open channel. How he wishes it was him. He swallows his annoyance: Patience. Patience. His time will come. His purser has talked to the suppliers, and they promise to have his provisions within the week. Perhaps it is God's will.

A deckhand approaches. He pulls off his cap self-consciously. "Excuse me, Cap'n, your wife has arrived."

Jope looks at him, puzzled. Then it dawns on him. Of course! In all his irritation he has forgotten that today is the day when Mary comes aboard for a tour of the ship. While the *White Lion* was being renovated, he insisted that she stay at home. A construction site is no place for a woman, but now he's run out of reasons to keep her away. She has traveled to Plymouth from their home in Tavistock, as promised.

Grinning, Jope moves to the starboard railing, just in time to see Mary maneuver the gangplank, with raised skirt and petticoats. Her blond curls peek out from under her hat, and the men eye her appreciatively. Then she is on the main deck, looking around curiously, taking in the tall masts with the sails rolled up and tightly lashed to their yardarms.

Bounding down the steps from the quarterdeck, Jope greets her with an exaggerated bow. "Welcome aboard, my lady!"

She bestows an amused glance on him as he takes her by the arm and promenades with her toward the bow for a tour of the ship. Along the way, sailors, stevedores, and deckhands make way for them, casting sidelong glances in their direction.

Jope points out various parts—crow's nest, fo'c'sle, capstan, chocks and scuppers and ratlines. Mary listens politely, but Jope can tell that the words mean little to her. She is trying to figure out how such a vessel can be home to her husband and crew for months on end at sea.

It isn't until they return and he brings her to his cabin at the rear of the ship below the quarterdeck that Mary becomes genuinely interested. She looks at the small bed in one corner, the desk already strewn with maps, and the oak dining table with a candelabra and four chairs. She notes the small altar and Bible with approval.

They step out together onto the galley in back of the cabin's windows, overlooking the docks and other moored ships gently bobbing in breeze.

"I will sit here in the evenings and look back toward home, thinking of you," Jope says.

Mary blushes, and a small, contented smile starts to play at the corner of her lips. "It is a snug corner," she says approvingly. "I almost wish I could come."

Jope laughs. Part of him wishes it, too, but women onboard a ship, other than as hostages or prisoners, are considered bad luck. He would lose the respect of his crew long before they hoisted the anchor.

"I can't imagine you on deck giving orders and shouting at the sailors, but I can think of you here at night praying and resting and thinking of me," she says.

Jope hears the unspoken question in her voice and embraces her. He kisses her fiercely, wanting to impress the memory of his love on her lips, and she kisses him back with a fervor he has come to cherish.

It almost feels as if they are saying their good-byes that afternoon.

During another week of waiting for provisions, a restlessness invades their presence. There is little for them to do in Jope's small room at the harborside inn. They have already withdrawn from one another into the privacy of their own lives, looking inward in preparation for having to survive alone without one another for a long time.

When the day of departure finally arrives, it is a relief for both of them. Mary, at the dock with her maid, stands apart from the cheering crowd. She does not expect her husband to look in her direction, but her eyes are fixed on him high up on the quarterdeck.

Jope; his navigator, Marmaduke; and his first and second mates by his side look over the crew assembled on the deck below—sailors, deckhands, cabin boys, cannoneers, and musketeers—many of them veterans of the Spanish Main. They eagerly await his orders to hoist the anchor, but he surprises them by first calling out, "Let us pray."

They look at one another, then doff their hats and caps. To their amazement, Jope sinks to his knees, closes his eyes, and begins to speak, his sonorous voice carrying forcefully to all corners of the ship and the dockside below:

Spring 1619

My Lord and Savior Jesus Christ, please grant me the strength to command this vessel. Guide our path and fill our sails with the winds from your heavens above. Light our way with your guiding star. Watch over this crew of worthy men and give them the strength to be the great heart of this *White Lion*, to overcome all obstacles and challenges and fulfill their destiny. Bless us with your treasures and guide us to a safe and happy return home. In your honor and name, Jesus Christ, my blessed Lord and Savior, Amen.

His words reach deep into the souls of the gathered men. Many have been battle tested and wear a thick scab covering their emotions, but something about Jope's earnest, heartfelt prayer touches them. As their captain rises, they greet him with respectful silence.

Jope looks to the skies, as bright blue as his shining eyes, and calls out, "Raise the flags and hoist the anchor!"

A cheer erupts from the men below, and they scatter to their work stations. The sailors climb the rigging lines and untie the ropes that hold the sails to the spars. They unfurl and flap impatiently in the wind until others secure them at the bottom and they fill out. Soon the masts creak, eager as racehorses straining their reins at the starting line.

Another cheer goes up on the ship, echoed on the dockside as the English flag, Saint George vanquishing the dragon, climbs the mast.

The mooring ropes untied, the *White Lion* drifts away from the dock and slowly moves into the shipping channel toward the harbor entrance.

Jope does look back at the diminishing figure of Mary waving after him and wonders if he will ever see her again.

6

KALUNGU
April–May 1619

The slave caravan has been traveling for nearly two weeks. Every morning the Imbangala rouse their captives, check their chains and bonds, tether their necks to the yoking branches, and continue their march west. There are few rests along the way. When people sink to the ground from exhaustion, the brutish slavers whip them until they struggle to their feet and stumble onward. If they can't make it, a vicious blow with the axe finishes them off and their bodies are left for the vultures and hyenas. The other prisoners avert their eyes, knowing they could be next.

Margarita and Juan stumble along over the brown earth. To break the monotony, Margarita makes a game of it by imagining how far it is to the next plane tree, the next bush, the next rock formation, and then tallying their steps in bunches of ten, but she often loses count. She marvels how Juan bravely tramps along, putting one foot in front of the other with determination.

But at night when they lie next to one another, exhausted, he snuggles up to her, seeking refuge in her arms. He hugs her especially tight under the assault of the horrific screams when the Imbangala pick out another hapless man or woman to satisfy their cannibalistic blood lust, hacking and disemboweling the victim and tearing at the organs and raw human flesh like wild beasts. Margarita has decided that she and Juan are safe, too small to feed the entire band of their tormentors. Not that the Imbangala rely on humans for their main meal. They conduct their ghastly ritual as much to intimidate their captives and keep them submissive. They eat plenty of grains, tubers, and antelope meat cooked at the fire along with their revolting fare, leaving only thin gruel and a few handfuls of millet for their prisoners.

The days blend into one another with dull monotony. The only good thing is that their path mostly slopes downhill as they leave the high plateau. Gradually the plain changes from the familiar clay grassland with a smattering of palms and baobab trees to softer, darker earth and green wooded regions.

At some point, they reach a river, wider than any of the swollen streams Margaret has seen in Pongo during the rainy season. Its light brown water drifts lazily past sandy banks. The caravan wends its way along the shore until it reaches a fording point. As the Imbangala herd their captives toward the water, Margarita starts to panic. She does not know how to swim! Trembling with fear, she awaits her turn, watching the first adults who have reached the middle. They're up to their waists in water.

There is a jerk on her tether, and Margarita stumbles forward. She catches herself and wades into the river. She can feel rounded rocks underfoot. She takes a few steps, more confident. The mud-colored stream rises to her chest, and then she loses her balance and falls. Water washes over her head. Flailing, she sees images—her mother, father, the yellowish teeth of an Imbangala warrior, carrion vultures. She feels the tether tighten around her neck as she is pulled to the surface. Choking, she gasps for air, and before she knows it, she is on the other side standing on firm ground.

The Imbangala who has pulled her up and carried her ashore laughs uproariously and puts Juan down, having scooped him up because he is tied to her.

Juan looks at her, concerned. "Are you all right?" he asks in a small voice.

Margarita nods, but there is no time to rest. The Imbangala shoves them forward and joins his compatriot in driving the caravan on mercilessly. They head downstream, keeping to the river's edge for some time. It's easier going than trying to slog through the dense shrubs farther inland.

At some point they meet up with another slave coffle. It is from the capital city of Kabasa and larger than theirs, but the captives look just as bedraggled and exhausted as Margarita's group. As the two caravans merge, she loses sight of familiar faces from Pongo. She catches the eye of Joana, who looks back in her direction before she disappears among the rest of the new prisoners.

That evening, the stories of atrocities, shared in anguished whispers by the newcomers, open wounds in Margarita's heart. She sobs quietly, praying for all her friends and family who are gone, while the shrieks of the Imbangala's most recent victim pierce the night.

Over the next few days they continue to descend from the high plateau, plodding through densely forested land where the air feels heavy and musty. But as they emerge onto the coastal plain, Margarita feels a cool breeze that brings a salty smell with it.

Excited whispers of "Kalungu, Kalungu" issue from the front of the caravan. Then, reaching the top of a small rise, she sees for herself what has everyone else so agitated: a dark blue expanse as endless as the sky above—the great Atlantic Ocean, She remembers her father's words about the ghosts on the other side and shudders.

They soon reach the outskirts of a large city—Luanda—and they hobble through streets past houses and gawking strangers. Their bearded, sallow faces remind Margarita of the Portuguese and Spanish traders who came to the market in Pongo, but these people's eyes, although not as calculating, are hard and unpitying.

Suddenly the roadway opens up to the bay, and the sight takes Margarita's breath away. The curving seaboard and a long sandbar farther off shore create a kind of lake. Beyond the bar are the darker waters of Kalungu and several large ships bobbing on the waves.

Kalungu

They are bigger than any canoe Margarita has ever seen, and they have tree trunks mounted atop. The few branches on them stick out straight as lances, and there are ropes like spiderwebs hanging down from their sides. The wooden hulls rise high out of the water, and the side wall of one of the boats has small windows all in a row. She can't imagine what these ships are for. Then it occurs to her that they must be the transport vessels the talking drums mentioned.

Juan stares at them just as amazed.

Soon they're all herded into large enclosures surrounded by bamboo palisades. Their wooden yokes removed, the captives sink to the ground, exhausted under the shade of small open huts covered with large palm leaves. Rice and beans and water are brought in large buckets, and those who can eat and drink greedily. Then some of them take food to their fellow prisoners who are too weak to move.

Margaret sees one of the tan-skinned bearded men drop several handful of cowrie shells into the pouch of one of the Imbangala leaders. The brute grins, gesturing to his men, and they all leave. Margarita is glad to see them go and prays she'll never set eyes on them again.

Cries of pain suddenly issue from one corner of the enclosure. Some of the prisoners surge in the opposite direction toward the entrance gate, but they are met by soldiers and vicious barking dogs. One by one, the captives are brought to a spot where a large brazier is filled with glowing coals. While two soldiers hold them by the arms, a third takes a branding iron and burns a mark in their side.

When it is their turn, Margarita takes Juan by the hand. She goes first, determined to show him how to be courageous. The hot iron sizzles as it scorches her skin and hurts like nothing she's ever experienced. She cries out in pain. Juan closes his eyes and squeezes her hand so hard it quivers. He grimaces and emits a high-pitched cry through his clenched teeth. They are now officially the property of the Portuguese trader.

Once branded, the men are fitted with an iron collar that has a small ring welded to it. Then a chain is threaded through, linking six at a time. If they want to move about or relieve themselves, they all have to get up and do it together. The women and children are segregated from them in another area, but not put in chains, allowing Margarita and Juan to move about and play with the other children.

Her prayers about the Imbangala are not answered. Over the next few days more Ndongo prisoners arrive from all over the kingdom, herded by the white-faced brutes. The enclosure fills up, and Margarita wonders what will happen to them. The stench of so many people crowded into close quarters becomes nauseating. Days pass in the merciless heat, and Margarita loses track of time. Although the images of her town being destroyed are still vivid in her mind, it all seems to have happened ages ago.

Then one morning a soldier arrives, decked out in a shiny golden helmet and armor, a sword by his side. He gives orders in what Margarita recognizes as Spanish, and from the diffident way the others treat him, she knows that he is an important man. He moves around the enclosure with the trader in tow and points at different men and women. His eyes fall on Margarita, who has Juan by the hand. They glisten like black sapphires, hard and shiny and without pity. He points a slender finger at them and several other children before moving on.

Guards roughly herd them toward the rear of a large crowd of captives by the entrance. Surrounded by guards and soldiers, they march down toward the water. There is a long dock. Up ahead, Margarita sees the first chained men and women being forced to climb into small boats. Bearded men row them across the lagoon and drop them off on the shoal. Then the boats return for the next load.

The transport goes on all day long, and the remaining captives sit and lie on the dock in the sweltering heat, waiting their turn. Wispy clouds drifting overhead provide occasional relief from the blistering sun.

When Margarita and Juan finally get to the head of the line, they face a Portuguese man in a dark robe covered with a white lace bib. From her time with the Sisters she knows that he is a Catholic priest. He waves a censor in her direction. The pungent smoke tickles her nostrils; she almost sneezes. Then he sprinkles water in her face, makes the sign of the cross over her, and mutters a phrase in Latin. Margarita makes out "Maria." The priest does the same with Juan, calling him "Jiro." Remembering the naming ceremony with the Sisters, Margarita understands that he has baptized them, but wonders why he has given them strange names.

A soldier lifts her into the boat. It rocks unsteadily as others climb aboard, frightening her. The other captives crowded next to her look just as afraid. Then the boat casts off and heads for the sandbar. The oars of the rowers slap the water, and the wake in back has little bubbles in it. As the dock and the people on it get smaller and smaller, Margarita shivers, and the knot in her chest aches when she swallows. It is the last image of her homeland, and she wonders if she will ever see it again.

At the sandbar they climb out and have to wade the last few feet in the water. It feels cool and soothing on her blistered feet. Margarita scoops up a handful and drinks. Grimacing, she spits it out and stops Juan from taking a drink.

"It tastes of salt," she warns him.

On the other side of the shoal, a ship towers overhead. Up close it is even bigger than when she first laid eyes on it. The wooden hull looms higher than the tallest baobab tree she's ever seen, and it is longer than several houses put together. The little windows have black iron tubes sticking out of them.

A long, wide plank extends from the sandbar up to the ship. It bends under the weight of the captives making their way aboard. Margarita's eyes follow them as they scramble through a gap in the railing. She looks farther up to an even higher level, where the haughty Spaniard from earlier in the day stands, arms akimbo, watching.

Juan asks, "Is he the *soba* of the ship?"

Margarita nods. "I think so."

Before she has time to consider it further, she's pushed toward the wooden plank. As she sets foot on it, she feels movement and drops on all fours. She clambers up to the railing and steps onto the ship. As she gets to her feet, she looks up at the tall tree trunks in wonder. A soldier shoves her to an opening in the wooden deck and down the steps into the dark belly of the vessel.

It is dank and humid, and flickering torches provide the only light. Margarita can smell the sweat of the men and women crowded there already. Soldiers are chaining them to large iron rings in the floor and on the side beams. Since no room is left in the main hold, they squeeze the remaining prisoners into side bays. Margarita and Juan end up in the crawl space under the stairs, with barely room to sit up.

When the last captives are secured, the soldiers leave. Through the gaps in the treads, Margarita sees a large hatch cover fall on the opening. It hits with a thud, sending tremors down the stairs. The torchlight grows dim through the timber lattice work, and darkness descends.

In the impenetrable blackness, the men and women begin to talk quietly. Their voices are strained with fear. Like Margarita, they wonder what is going to happen to them. A rumor quickly makes it through the entire hold that they will be taken to the land of the white ghosts who will eat them, just like the Imbangala. Juan holds on more tightly to Margarita.

"We will be all right," she says.

Time passes while the ship rocks gently on the waves. Suddenly there are shouts from above and the sounds of eager footsteps going every which way, echoing into the hold. The whole ship is abuzz with activity. Margarita hears distant flapping noises and chains clanking. The ship's timbers creak as if straining to awaken, and then there is movement, at first a gradual drifting, then stronger swaying and seesawing.

She grasps Juan's hand and whispers, "The ship is walking on Kalungu!"

7

ELECTIONS

London—Late April 1619

H aving been held up in traffic, the Earl of Warwick arrives in an agitated state at the house of Sir Thomas Smythe in Pilpot Lane. Although the meeting of the Virginia Company of London will not start without one of its most important shareholders, he hates being late, especially for the most important quarter court of the year. With Smythe stepping down as treasurer, this gathering will determine the direction of the company for the immediate future. Considering its financial difficulties, who will be elected is of utmost significance.

As Warwick emerges from his carriage, he straightens his velvet doublet. He looks up in irritation at the impressive façade of the palatial townhouse. It is newer and larger than his own residence, reflecting the financial success of its owner. As a founding member of the East India Company, importing spices, fancy cloth, and other exotic goods from the Orient, Smythe is one of the wealthiest merchants in London. He and his investment partners have thrived even when other participants in their commercial ventures have not fared so well. Unlike Warwick, whose reasons for becoming involved in Virginia and Bermuda are in part religious—which has not always blessed his enterprises—Smythe and his associates, with only money on their minds, have made fortunes.

Elections

It continues to rankle Warwick as he hurries from the impressive vestibule down the hallway, past a large painting depicting Smythe and his favorite dog, a marble bust on a pedestal, and dark wooden sideboards covered with rugs, statues of elephants, and other exotic trinkets. The roar of lively conversations spills from the large doorway farther down the gallery.

As Warwick enters the great hall, many eyes turn toward him. There is an eager crowd, nearly 100 shareholders, representing some of England's most successful and powerful nobles, merchants, craftsmen, and artisans. Thomas Smythe, the host, resplendent in his treasurer's robes, stands in front of the board table at the other end of the room, talking with several of his merchant friends; among them is his choice to replace him, Alderman Robert Johnson. From time to time Smythe's eyes rove over the expectant crowd with a smug, self-satisfied expression. Warwick wishes he could erase it from his face.

Off to one side, he notes Edwin Sandys in animated discussion with Nicholas Ferrar—businessman, fellow member of Parliament, and close friend. Listening attentively is Lord Cavendish, the notorious gambler and rake. It surprises Warwick to see the self-indulgent nobleman so openly aligned with the leader of the smaller shareholders. He will have to ask Nathaniel Rich about that.

Before he can locate his cousin, however, Warwick is waylaid by Thomas Weston, a London ironmonger and importer of talc and other goods from the Netherlands. The man has tried to cozy up to him at a number of company meetings. The earl tolerates him because he is closely connected with the Leiden Separatists, a radical group of Puritans who fled to Holland from James's persecution and are looking for a permanent home in the New World. Weston has smuggled seditious religious pamphlets to them and is passionate about their cause.

He bows deeply and speaks with fawning intensity, "I wonder if you have had time to consider my proposal, m'Lord?"

His servile familiarity annoys Rich. "Not yet."

"When do you think you might be able to?"

Continuing to sweep the room with his gaze, Warwick waves him off impatiently. "Now is not the time, Thomas."

Weston seems oblivious to his displeasure. "The Separatists are getting quite desperate," he says with urgency.

"Later."

The earl finally locates Nathaniel Rich and catches his eye. The lawyer disengages from his group and comes to his rescue. Taking Warwick by the arm, he says, "Excuse me, but I must discuss election matters with my cousin," and smoothly ushers him away.

"Of course, m'Lord. Later then," Weston calls after them and bows to their backsides.

Warwick bestows a grateful smile on Nathaniel and heads to the council table, where he offers his hands in greeting to the Earl of Southampton and some of the other board members. He and Thomas Smythe exchange polite nods. Then he and the earl take their seats on either side of the treasurer. Smythe bangs his gavel three times on the table to call the meeting to order. It takes several additional raps to quiet the excited crowd.

When he has everyone's attention, Smythe rises and surveys the crowded room. Relishing the expectant hush that has descended, he begins to speak in measured tones, "This quarter court of the Virginia Company of London is now in session."

He pauses, holding his audience's attention like an actor the stage, before continuing. "For the past twelve years, I have willingly spent my labors in support of this great enterprise, to establish and grow our great plantation of Virginia. But now that the King has seen fit to honor me and appoint me commissioner of His Majesty's navy, I can no longer give a good attendance, as required to continue to lead this fine undertaking. Therefore, I have resolved to relinquish my office as treasurer in order for you to elect someone worthy to take my place."

It is a pretty speech that, although it does not come as news to anyone, receives generous murmurs of approbation.

Smythe bows in acknowledgment and says, "We have three candidates who wish to stand for the office: Sir John Wolstenholme, Alderman Robert Johnson, and Sir Edwin Sandys—commendable gentlemen all. Do I hear nominations for them?"

There are shouts of support from different sections of the crowd as each contender receives an official nomination by someone representing the faction they represent—a knight, a merchant, and in the case of Sandys, his friend Nicholas Ferrar. No discussion or campaign speech is needed. Everyone knows who the three men stand for.

Smythe raps his gavel once and says, "We will now proceed to the vote—tan for Alderman Johnson, brown for Sir John Wolstenholme, and red for Sir Edwin Sandys."

He gestures to a large side table where there are three bowls filled with colored balls the size of small marbles. The company deputy, a merchant board member, positions himself at the end of the table with a large velvet bag.

One by one, the shareholders file past the table, pick up a ball, and drop it in the bag. The line is so dense with people crowding from behind that it is impossible to tell which ball individual voters pick. The board members go last. By the time they approach the table, the bag is so heavy and bulging that the deputy has set it on the table.

Smythe, going last, can't see which marbles those before him have chosen. When he finally steps up to the table, he selects a tan-colored marble for Alderman Johnson, deliberately holds it up for everyone to see, and drops it into the bag with a confident smile.

Then he returns to his place at the center of the table, bangs the gavel, and intones, "The voting is closed. We will now proceed to the count."

One by one, the deputy extracts balls from the bag and places them into one of three empty bowls. Warwick watches Smythe and is delighted to see his self-satisfied expression yield to shock and dismay as a small mountain grows in Sir Edwin Sandys's bowl. At some point, he catches Smythe's eyes and offers a half bow with a smirk, letting him know who is responsible for his defeat.

When the deputy announces the final tally, Smythe's candidate, Alderman Johnson, has received the least votes—eighteen balls. Wolstenholme, the representative of a group of independent knights, has garnered twenty-three balls. But the overwhelming victor, with fifty-nine balls, is Sir Edwin Sandys.

For Smythe and his faction, the day goes from bad to worse. Not only does his candidate for deputy lose handily to Nicholas Ferrar, but every committee and auditor election makes more clear that a sea change is taking place. The tide has turned in favor of Sandys's faction at every turn. The mercantile faction has been roundly defeated.

When the final election is complete, the room buzzes with exhilaration and excitement, punctuated by celebratory shouts of congratulations. The merchants' corner is quiet, however, an assembly of glum faces with downcast eyes and tight lips.

Sir Thomas's face is a stoic mask of acceptance as he removes the great seals of office from around his neck and hands them to his successor without a word. Sandys puts them on and moves to the seat at the center of the table. He takes the gavel and silences the crowd with a single rap.

His voice is higher pitched than the sonorous tones of Smythe, but it vibrates with energy and elation. "I thank you all for your vote of confidence. We have much work ahead of us, and I will do my utmost to deserve your faith in me."

He turns toward Smythe and continues, "But before we begin, I want to recognize my predecessor for his years of service. In consideration of the great trouble mixed with much sorrow which Sir Thomas has endured during the term of twelve years past from the infancy of the plantation to this present, it would be fitting to express our thankfulness for his good endeavors by conferring twenty great shares of the company stock upon him."

Elections

The suggestion receives scant discussion before Sandys puts it to a vote, and it passes by a unanimous show of hands. Warwick smiles to himself. It is a double-edged act of recognition that must gall the greedy merchant. Considering that Smythe leaves office with the company mired in debt by his practices—close to £8,000—he is not likely to reap any rewards from the shares.

Sandys announces that, with the change in leadership, weekly council meetings will take place at the home of Nicholas Ferrar's father and brings the great quarter court to a close.

Altogether, Rich is pleased. Not only has he taken fitting revenge on Smythe, but Sandys owes him a great deal for his election. Without the earl's noble friends and their supporters, he would not have succeeded. Warwick will remind him of it the next time uncomfortable questions about arise the *Treasurer* and Lord De La Warr. In the meantime, he will have to keep Sandys's more radical ideas for the Virginia Colony in check and make sure the company pursues a course more congenial to his own interests.

8

THE PASSAGE

Atlantic Ocean—June 1619

Don Manuel Mendes de Acuña is pacing on the quarterdeck of the *San Juan Bautista*. He wipes the perspiration from his dark brows with a silk handkerchief and scowls. His navigator and the ship's doctor are standing at attention, watching their captain with serious expressions on their faces.

Acuña is worried. They are only four weeks out of Luanda with their cargo of 350 slaves, and already close to 100 "pieces," as he and his men refer to the prisoners, have succumbed to the bloody flux. The stink of vomit and diarrhea wafts from the hold to his men's cabins on the lower deck. It upsets their stomachs and makes it hard for them to sleep. Fortunately, it does not reach his cabin at the rear. How the pieces shackled deep in the belly of the ship can tolerate the revolting stench is beyond him. He can only attribute it to their being subhuman and therefore being able to get used to anything. Except they are dying.

On the upper deck below, several sailors, with scarves covering their mouths and noses, emerge from a hatch. They haul two naked, emaciated black bodies to the railing—a man and a woman—and, lifting them by their hands and feet, toss them overboard. Acuña hears the splashes as they hit the water.

He fingers the gold chain around his neck nervously. Another two pieces gone. With each death, his profit erodes. He rues the day he decided to gamble his fortune on this cursed ship. The *San Juan Bautista*, a war galleon, was never meant to be used as a slave ship. Built in Japan, she carried the last Portuguese missionaries home when that country expelled all Westerners and closed itself off to the outside world. When Spain conquered Portugal, the ship fell into his hands. It seemed like a gift from heaven at the time, but has been nothing but trouble.

Carrying forty cannons on the main deck, it is not really outfitted as a cargo ship. While the guns provide safety from pirates for the journey through Caribbean waters, the hold for the slaves is two decks below with no ventilation at all. Bringing the prisoners to the upper deck daily for food and exercise makes extra work for his soldiers and sailors. Now that dysentery is ravaging the ranks of the slaves, making things even more difficult, they have begun to grumble that the ship is cursed.

Acuña turns to the doctor, a short, pudgy man wearing a dark robe. "Can't you do something? I don't want to arrive in Veracruz with a shipload of ghosts."

The medic ponders the options. None of them will please the aggravated captain. He clears his throat and says, "We could bring them up for air twice a day. That will help. Better yet, we can stop in Jamaica and get medicine."

Acuña flushes red but restrains his anger. He knows the medic is not a miracle worker. He gestures to his navigator to follow him to his cabin. "Let's look at what a change of course would mean."

* * *

In the hold below, Margarita and Juan lie prone in the fetid darkness. Filthy and hungry, they no longer notice the horrible stench. The heavy heat that presses down on them is almost unbearable. Sometimes Margarita wonders if this is the hell the Sisters talked about, where sinners are condemned for eternity, but she can't bring herself to believe it. Nothing she or Juan have done in their lives deserves such punishment.

Soon after they were under way, the gentle swaying of the ship gave way to turbulent lurching and seesawing, which made her nauseated for a while. Now she gets queasy only when they're herded up on deck to be fed and allowed to walk about. She has learned not to look at the horizon rocking up and down as the ship plows through the mountains of waves.

It frightens her that there is only the vast ocean as far as her eyes can see in every direction. At least she and Juan are not sick like so many of the other prisoners languishing beside them in the hold. When they first began to vomit and void watery stool, she thought it must be because of the dreadful swill the soldiers feed them. But not everyone got the flux even when some of the sailors fell sick, too.

Then the first captives died. The soldiers came and dragged them away up the stairs, no one knew where. That's when the rumors of being eaten by cannibals on the other side of Kalungu gave way to even more frightening notions—the Spaniards were pressing the dead bodies into oil or grinding them up for dye to make blood-red garments. She tries to convince Juan that the rumors are foolish nonsense and to cover his ears when he hears the whispers.

Some of the men who had been warriors in Ndongo talk about staging a mutiny and killing as many of their tormentors as they could, but hunger robs them of their strength and all plans of rebellion vanish when sickness invades the hold. Those too ill to climb the two flights of stairs to the upper deck are soon among the dead being dragged and carried from the hold.

At one point when they are let out on deck, two of the young men shackled together break free from the other captives, dash to the railing, and before anyone can stop them, leap overboard to their deaths. Margarita, who recognized them from Pongo, knows that they preferred the churning waves to their wretched existence in the hold because they thought dying would return them home. As a

Christian, she doesn't believe that. Besides, after that incident, the soldiers put short ankle chains on the prisoners and linked more of them together, making it impossible to do anything but hobble along, and they watch like hawks until everyone is locked up again safely below.

Much as Margarita longs for the brief periods when she can feel the sun on her skin and breathe the clear, salty sea air, it makes the return to the belly of the ship so much worse. The short-lived respite forces her to realize how squalid her prison is. The horrendous stink assaults her nostrils again until she can't smell it anymore. She understands why the sailors and soldiers feed them up on deck. They avoid entering the ship's hold prison as much as they can, disgusted by the miasma of vomit, human waste, and death.

She prays that she and Juan will be spared from the bloody flux. And she thanks the Lord for the one friend he has sent them. If it wasn't for the cabin boy, they might very well be among the dead already.

When they were first shackled in the hold and fell asleep, the sound of the hatch woke her up. Rays of torchlight seeped through the rickety wooden steps above her. The treads shook as men came down carrying pails and small bowls. One of them was a boy not much older than she. They went around to give the prisoners water.

At some point the boy came over and peered down at her and Juan. He dipped the bowl in the pail and held it out to her filled with water. Margarita slurped it down gratefully even though it tasted stale, and she handed the bowl back with a shy smile. The boy repeated the process with Juan and left without a word.

But the next time, after he ladled out water, he put a finger to his lips and handed her a small hunk of bread. Margarita took it, nodding that she understood and hid it in the dark of their cupboard. Then she touched the youngster on his extended palm and brought her hand to her heart. He looked surprised, and a small smile flitted across his lips.

Since then, he always brings something for her and Juan to supplement their meager diet—a chunk of bread, a piece of meat, an extra yam. He must spend most of his time in the ship's kitchen because she has seen him only once when she's been outside. That time, he was swabbing the deck and ignored her. As Margarita walked past, she kept looking at him. She wanted to remember their savior—his tanned skin; wavy, dark hair; thin lips; and calloused hands.

With the hatch to the hold closed and darkness once again surrounding her, Margarita feels for the piece of bread she has stashed in the corner. She and Juan pray the "Our Father" the way the Sisters taught them. When she gets to "Give us this day our daily bread," she stops for a moment. It means more to her now than when she simply repeated the words by rote.

After Juan echoes her "Amen" in a small voice, they share the cabin boy's gift to the last crumb. Then Juan curls up beside her. Margarita tries to comfort him, holding him like a mother holds a child. She sings him songs she remembers from Pongo about giraffes and elephants and playful monkeys. When he has fallen asleep, she sends a silent prayer to Jesus, who loves all children, imploring him fervently not to let them perish.

9
EDWIN SANDYS
London—July 1619

Sir Edwin Sandys, recently elected treasurer of the Virginia Company, strokes his gray beard as he reads over the letter he has written to the new governor of Jamestown. He knows he's pursuing a dangerous course of action. It's one thing to inform Sir Yeardley that the *Treasurer*'s letters of marque from the Duke of Savoy are no longer in force. It's another to order him to seize the vessel and her crew when she puts into harbor in Virginia to sell the spoils from its raids on Spanish ships.

When he is finished, he hesitates. The Earl of Warwick will be furious when he finds out, and Sandys does not want to make an enemy of him, but he must protect himself and his fellow shareholders in the Virginia Company. He scratches his signature at the bottom and folds the parchment several times. He takes a stick of sealing wax and melts one end with a candle until it drips onto the overlapping edges. Then he embeds his signet ring in the soft, reddish-brown clump.

The arrival of George Yeardley's first official letter from Virginia caused an uproar. When he reached Jamestown he found Samuel Argall, the man he'd been sent to investigate for illegally seizing assets of the company, "gone with his riches." The former deputy governor had sailed a week earlier on the *Eleanor* sent by Lord Rich.

The *Treasurer* was gone as well, but Yeardley confirmed that Argall had outfitted her with "ordnance and provender for war," readying her for a profiteering voyage.

Argall landed in England a few days after the incriminating letter reached London, having stopped in Bermuda along the way. He visited the residence of the Earl of Warwick, no doubt to report on the success of his venture. But then he demanded to meet with the council of the Virginia Company and made his appearance, sword at his side and swaggering like a rake, to contest "any and all false allegations" against him.

Sandys knew he had to tread lightly. After all, Warwick is an esteemed member of the company with influential connections to the Privy Council and King James. Even if he was using Jamestown as a base from which to launch his privateering ships—and Sandys was as certain of it as the nose on his face—there had to be definitive proof before any measures could be taken against him.

At the council meeting, Argall's performance more than matched his brash entrance. He rejected all charges of feathering his own nest at the expense of the company and of being secretly allied with the Earl of Warwick in pirating ventures. When confronted with Captain Brewster's sworn testimony that, upon the *Neptune*'s arrival in Jamestown on its ill-fated voyage with Lord De La Warr, Argall had confiscated all of the supplies aboard ship and used them for his own purposes, he called his accuser a self-serving liar who was trying to cover up his own incompetence. He scoffed at the report that he had Brewster arrested, court-martialed for sedition and mutiny, and condemned to death; he laughed at the claim that he had agreed to let Brewster sail for England only after making him swear an oath that he would never set foot on Virginia soil again.

When it came to the most damning allegations—that the *Treasurer*, Warwick's "fishing" vessel, was outfitted for war and profiteering, with Argall providing additional men and supplies—he was at his most defiant. He not only rejected the contention but reminded the council of his many years of service to the colony, both as soldier and deputy governor. Then, in good military fashion, he went on the offensive and bitterly complained about the magazine ship and certain members of the company enriching themselves by robbing the settlers blind at a time when they were barely holding on. It was a masterful stroke, blaming the former treasurer and his cohorts when they no longer wielded power and appealing to the interests of Sandys and his faction.

If the situation wasn't so grave, Sir Edwin couldn't have been more pleased. Argall's attack on the merchants is just what he needs to help rid the company of its stranglehold in order to improve its financial health.

But then one of Smythe's minions left on the Council asked pointedly, "And where is the *Treasurer* right now?" bringing everyone back to the original purpose of the gathering.

Warwick, as the owner, replied, "I have had no news of my ship since it made Jamestown," and tried to deflect the renewed attention on his affairs with a little joke. "I'm as much at sea as everyone else."

When all eyes turned to Argall, he shrugged and said, "The Atlantic Ocean is large. How should I know?"

His smug tone didn't help, and the council meeting quickly descended into accusations and counteraccusations with words such as "infamy," "treason," "outrage," "slander," and "calumny" swirling about like flotsam in a tempest. It took all of Sandys's efforts and parliamentary skill to cool the heated tempers and bring the meeting back to order to deal with other, more pressing matters.

When it came time to vote, Warwick, his cousin Nathaniel Rich, and the Earl of Southampton strongly supported Argall, and the council cleared him of all charges and officially thanked him for his service. Sandys joined in to absolve him, even though he was certain of Argall's guilt. He is well aware of how much he owes his success to Warwick. Later in private, he has to assure Lord Rich that he was on his side against the firebrands out to get him. It galls Sandys that he has to provide cover for him. The arrogance of someone thirty years younger protesting that others are fanning the flames against him when it is Warwick himself who is playing with fire! If he gets burned, it is his own fault.

Even if the truth lies somewhere between Brewster's claims and Argall's protestations that they are false, it would be serious enough, threatening the very existence of the Virginia Company as a privately owned enterprise. If any of the accusations prove true, it would bring the wrath of the Privy Council and King James himself upon their heads. And now there is Yeardley's letter supporting Captain Brewster's version of the story.

There is a knock on the door. Nicholas Ferrar pokes his head inside and announces, "The Leiden Separatists are here."

Sandys sighs. Just what he needs—another pet project of the Earl of Warwick at his doorstep. As champion of the Puritan cause, Lord Rich has for some time favored the religious exiles in Holland and their desire for a home of their own. Since he helped them obtain a patent from the company, they have been petitioning to be allowed to settle in Virginia.

It would actually be a good thing. The colony is in need of hard-working men and women, but this is not the time to have an autonomous group beholden to Warwick establish itself in Jamestown—not when Sandys is doing his best to scour Virginia of smuggling and privateering. To think that he actually entertained having the earl fill the vacancy left by Lord De La Warr's demise and offer to make him titular head of the company. Yeardley's letter arrived just in time to scotch that foolishness.

Ferrar ushers in two men dressed in black coats, black breeches, and large white collars. Robert Cushman, a deacon with a fierce gaze from beneath bushy black eyebrows, is a firebrand. His fellow Puritan, John Carver, has softer brown hair and a gentler disposition.

They have barely bowed before Cushman bursts out, "We are concerned about the rumors from last night's meeting, Sir Edwin!"

Sandys tries to diffuse the tension. He points to the sofa and armchair. "Won't you sit down, gentlemen?"

But Cushman won't have it. "I prefer to stand. We all need to know where we stand with our petition!"

Sandys smiles amiably. "You know I support your cause. The separation of church and state is important to me, especially since our Catholic monarch heads both and thinks he should have power absolute, unrestrained by law."

In a softer voice Carver offers, "You need not sweeten the news for us, Sir Edwin."

Cushman is pacing like a tethered bull. "Yes, come to the point. The situation in Holland grows desperate. We have heard that James is about to send men to kidnap our leaders and bring them back to England to be tortured and executed."

"The company has issued you a patent to establish your people in the New World and we will—"

"We have met all of your conditions to settle in Jamestown," Cushman interrupts impatiently. "We are tired of waiting and want to ship out as soon as possible."

Undeterred, Sandys continues, "The situation is more complicated now. Due to some unforeseen issues, this is not a good time, and your petition to go to Jamestown has been tabled indefinitely."

There is a moment of silence. Then Cushman erupts. "I knew it!"

"I understand your disappointment, and I assure you—"

"Disappointment? Have you any idea—"

"But you will honor the patent," Carter intercedes. "We can apply to go elsewhere in the Virginia Company's vast territory?"

Sandys shoots a glance at Nicholas Ferrar, who hovers in the back, ready to join in if necessary. This may be the opportunity for him to smooth the waters with the Earl of Warwick.

He clears his throat to gain time and says, smiling, "I think that may be a suitable alternative. Let me confer with the Earl of Warwick on it. I am certain we can come to a mutually agreeable solution."

Edwin Sandys

He stresses the name of the great Puritan benefactor, hoping that inserting him into the conversation will smooth ruffled feathers. It does. Cushman takes a deep breath. Sandys pretends not to notice the look that passes between him and Carver.

"I'm sure the Earl of Warwick will look out for our interests. We will wait to hear from him and you, Sir Edwin," Carver says with a curt bow.

Cushman barely nods and stalks from the room. Ferrar sees them out. When he returns, shaking his head, a bemused smile plays on his lips. "Shakespeare's Hotspur has nothing on that hothead," he volunteers.

"I understand their concerns and admire their passion," says Sandys.

He goes to his desk, picks up the letter, and contemplates it for a moment. Then he hands it to Ferrar. "See that this gets into the secret pouch for Governor Yeardley on the next ship to Jamestown."

Ferrar looks at his friend and benefactor for a moment, then nods and withdraws.

Sandys sighs again. He can only hope that Yeardley is discreet and takes action quickly to find incontrovertible proof of Warwick's involvement in the privateering trade. Surely that will give Rich bigger worries with King James and encourage him to leave Jamestown alone.

In the meantime, the two will work together to further neutralize Smythe and his faction and make sure Yeardley's mission to put the colony on sound parliamentary footing succeeds against any backstabbing efforts in the London office of the Virginia Company or at the royal court. And offering a solution to the situation of the Leiden Separatists will help keep Sandys in Rich's good graces.

10
DANIEL ELFRITH
Cuba—Late June 1619

It is late afternoon when the *White Lion* sails into Havana Harbor with the red, white, and blue stripes of the Dutch flag flying high. Captain Jope has heeded his navigator Marmaduke's advice and struck the English banner. Although Spain and his country are not at war, ever since Francis Drake and his fellow buccaneers devastated the Spanish treasure fleets, the inhabitants of the busiest port in the New World do not look kindly on the Union Jack.

Jope has been well pleased with the man Grillo urged him to hire. The Cricket didn't exaggerate Marmaduke's abilities. He may be a man of few words, but when he speaks they count, and he knows the best routes and shipping channels. Under his expert guidance they have crossed the Atlantic in record time and negotiated the chain of Caribbean islands guarding Cuba without mishap.

As they drift past the heavy fortifications of Castillo del Morro, Jope is amazed at the size of the harbor and its facilities. The shipyard where boats are being repaired rivals Plymouth in capacity, the row of storage sheds lining the wharf seems to go on forever, and the sheer number of ships berthed and anchored is an impressive sight. He notes the slavers and merchant vessels, easily identifiable because their upper decks are closer to the water line than on the Spanish war galleons. Without the need for cannons, the main deck can hold crew cabin and storage areas.

There is no sign of Grillo's ship yet, but Jope spots another familiar English warship, the *Treasurer*. Last he heard, it was captained by his childhood friend from Cornwall, Daniel Elfrith. As they come closer within hailing distance, he is surprised to see no one on deck.

Jope nods to his ensign, who yells across the gap, "Ahoy, the *Treasurer*!"

A suntanned sailor with a head scarf like a pirate emerges at the railing. He squints at the Dutch flag of the *White Lion*, then hollers, "Who would be doing the asking? What do you want?"

Striding to the quarterdeck railing, Jope cups his hands and shouts, "Is Captain Elfrith aboard? We're old friends from Plymouth."

The tar looking up at the Dutch flag again has Jope glancing at the *Treasurer*'s pennants. He does not recognize the colors.

Marmaduke comes up behind him and says, "It's the Duke of Savoy's banner. He must be carrying letters of marque from the French kingdom."

By now the sailor has made up his mind that they are a friendly crew and calls back, "Our captain's gone into town with some of the gang. You'll find him in one of the taverns."

"Much obliged," Jope yells back.

It takes several hours before the *White Lion* is safely anchored, her sails struck, and all rigging made fast. By the time the dinghy is lowered to take Jope, Marmaduke, and some of his men to the town, it is long past sundown. The ride to the main pier across smooth waters is brief. They disembark, light their lanterns, and climb up the stone steps to the street. While the mates and sailors look for quick entertainment in the first dockside tavern they come to, Jope and Marmaduke continue on in search of Elfrith.

They find him in the third tavern. The air is thick with tobacco smoke and the laughter of drunken men. Sailors of different nationalities are gambling—playing taroc, knucklebones, and El Mundo—and enjoying the company of eager wenches.

A well-endowed trollop, her breasts bulging from the top of her blouse, sidles up to Jope. He ignores her and takes another few steps into the room, peering into the hazy interior, dimly lit by smoking wall sconces.

Suddenly a loud voice hails him from an alcove. "By James's thorny cock, if it isn't John Jope of Cornwall!"

When Jope wheels around, he makes out a thickset man with a dark beard and bulbous nose sitting between two men. His open doublet reveals a shirt stained with the remnants of their meal. Pewter cups surround the carcass of a roast pig in the middle of the wooden table.

"Daniel Elfrith, you old rapscallion. I've been looking for you," Jope calls out in delight.

The captain of the *Treasurer* staggers to his feet, totters toward Jope, and embraces him with a mighty hug. "Odds bodkins, I never thought I'd see you in these waters."

Jope untangles himself from his old friend's drunken stranglehold. "You knew I had the *White Lion* almost ready when you shipped from Plymouth a year ago."

"Took you so long, I figured you never finished the job on purpose, you being spliced to your fine mistress and all," says Elfrith, grinning. "Come and have a drink with us. The rum here is excellent."

He introduces Rollins, his first mate, a well-muscled, younger version of himself; and Kipling, his navigator, a sinewy beanpole by comparison. When Jope nods to them and presents his own navigator, "Marmaduke Raynor," Elfrith looks at him shrewdly. "Bugger all, John, how'd you manage to get one of the best pilots in the Caribbean to steer your ship?"

"Grillo recommended him," says Jope.

The others nod, impressed.

Jope pulls up a stool and calls to a passing barmaid, "Cerveza. And another round for my friends!"

The serving wench collects the empty cups and squints suggestively at Marmaduke. "And what's your pleasure?"

"What they're having," he replies tersely.

Rollins grins approvingly. "That's more like it." Handing his cup to the waitress, he addresses Jope: "Much obliged, Cap'n. But why do you want to drink that swill instead of fine island rum?"

Elfrith intercedes, knowing that Jope's Calvinist beliefs forbid him to drink liquor of any kind. He figures his friend is making an exception with beer to fit in among his fellow seamen. "John here hasn't been far away from England long enough yet to develop the taste for the finer things Havana has to offer."

Kipling chuckles knowingly. "You'll be sorry!"

When the waitress brings a tankard overflowing with suds and four cups of rum, Jope ventures a sip and spits it out immediately.

"Zounds! That is the vilest brew I've ever tasted."

The others laugh uproariously. Elfrith claps him on the shoulder. "Told you."

Marmaduke changes the subject. "We were looking to meet up with Captain Grillo. Sail in consort with him. Have you seen him?"

"You're a fortnight too late," says Kipling. "The Cricket raided a ripe Spanish treasure galleon. He set sails for England not two days ago, his hold bulging with enough riches for ten merchants to retire on."

Jope's face clouds. That is bad news indeed. The delays in England have cost him dearly.

Elfrith notices his chagrin and reassures him, "The season is young!"

Jope scratches his beard and asks, "Will you be sailing to Virginia?"

"Eventually. But not with an empty hold."

He bends toward Jope and whispers so that only he and his tablemates can hear. "Why don't you sail in consort with me? We'll head for Virginia and fill our coffers with Spanish gold and other valuables along the way. The settlers at Jamestown are in such need, they'll barter for anything we plunder."

It doesn't take Jope more than a second to agree. "I'll be proud to sail in consort with you."

Elfrith claps him on the shoulder again. "S'blood, we'll make a splendid team." He downs the last of his rum. "Let's have another round. Tomorrow we get ready to sail, but tonight we celebrate!" He winks mischievously. "Sure you won't join with us in a cup of rum, John?"

Jope hesitates. Is this the way destiny is meant to unfold? Could this chance meeting be a sign of what God has in store for him?

He decides to take the plunge. "All right. Just this once."

The others cheer, their merriment adding to the bawdy din in the tavern.

11
RESCUED
The Gulf of Mexico—July 1619

It takes Jope and Elfrith less than three days to take on provisions and make repairs on their ships before they leave Havana Harbor, but they trawl the shipping lanes from Mexico to Cuba for the next two weeks without sighting any suitable prey. Instead they encounter a small summer storm.

It is Jope's first experience with rough seas. He is familiar with the winter storms that rage through the English Channel, but nothing has prepared him for riding waves the size of mountains, which toss the *White Lion* about like a cork in the surf. He prays that God did not include shipwrecking so early in his marauding career as part of his destiny.

Marmaduke, noticing his captain's discomfort, laughs as they're standing on the quarterdeck, running ahead of the heart of the storm, dark billowing clouds to the stern. With each wave that clashes against the hull of the ship, warm, salty water from the Gulf sprays over them.

"This is but a squall," the navigator shouts over the howling wind. "Wait till we encounter a hurricane."

"Can't wait to experience that," Jope mutters.

After two days, the rugged seas return to normal, becoming gentle rolling hills again. Jope is pleased when Marmaduke tells him how well the crew has performed.

Rescued

When they reunite with the *Treasurer* and catch their bearings, they discover that they've been thrown far off course. They're much closer to the Mexican coast than they had planned. As far as Marmaduke can tell, they're somewhere in the Bay of Campeche, just a few hundred miles east of Veracruz.

The next morning, a thick fog hangs over the calm waters. In the pale sunlight, as the mists begin to clear, a voice rings out from the crow's nest on the forward mast: "A ship! A ship to the south!"

By the time Jope hurries on deck, Marmaduke and the crew are already on the lookout, crowding the railings on the starboard side of the ship. Across the waves, Elfrith is pacing excitedly on the deck of the *Treasurer*. When he sees Jope, he bellows across, "A warship flying red and white flags! A Spanish galleon!"

Jope looks at the tiny vessel in the distance. Marmaduke comes up next to him. "Only one reason for a Spanish warship to be in these waters."

"Treasure out of Mexico," Jope shouts happily.

He gives the order to make the *White Lion* battle ready, and the crew springs into action, buzzing with excitement.

* * *

In the hold of the *San Juan Bautista*, Margarita wakens to the urgent sound of bells. Disoriented, she thinks she is under attack in her hometown of Pongo. "Imbangala!" she whispers, terrified.

Then she becomes aware of the impenetrable darkness and remembers where she is. Her throat is parched, and she feels weak. Something is happening aboard the ship. There are scurrying footsteps in the cabins above. Shouts in Spanish waft below. The ship is on alert.

Juan stirs next to her and cries out in fright at the chaotic noises above them. Margarita tries to comfort him but can't explain what's going on. All she knows is that something has upset the normal routine. At least the ship is riding calmly after the interminable pitching and rolling and the dreadful howling of the wind. For the first time in days, Margarita doesn't feel nauseated.

In the sweltering darkness, she can't tell whether it is morning or nighttime. Even the hunger pangs in her belly don't provide a clue to what time of day it is. They have gone without food and water since the beginning of the terrible storm—the small stash of bread from the cabin boy has run out. She hears the breathing, moans, and cries of the other prisoners in the hold and wonders if her jailers have forgotten all about them.

There are slapping noises as the hull plows through the waves, and the ship sways more—they are picking up speed. Margarita hears distant thunder rumbling. It is coming closer. Has the storm returned?

Suddenly there are booming sounds above, sending tremors through the ship. They come one after another in short succession, roaring thunderclaps intermingled with more shouting. Margarita has never heard blasts so loud and close before, not even during the height of the storm that just passed. She begins to pray.

During a short respite, hoarse whispers from the young men who fought for Ndongo make their way through the hold: "Cannon fire, big white guns, spewing rocks of iron."

Margarita can't imagine what they're talking about, but she hears the fear in their voices. Everyone in the hold is terrified.

There is another round of bellowing thunder blasts above, followed by cheers and excited Spanish shouts. Margarita reaches out to Juan. He has pressed his palms against his ears to shut out the noise. She throws her arms around him.

Suddenly there are blistering blows against one side of the ship, sounds of splintering wood, ear-splitting explosions, and men crying out in terror. There is a mighty crack up above, followed by a deafening crash, like a giant tree smashing to the ground, shaking the whole ship. The *San Juan Bautista* starts listing to port.

Rescued

Margarita tightens her arms around Juan and prays more fervently.

* * *

The *Treasurer* has borne the brunt of the Spaniard's counterattack. Several cannon shots have penetrated the hull above the waterline. But she has given as good in return, blowing holes into the sidewalls of the Spanish galleon.

Marmaduke has kept the *White Lion* just out of reach of the adversary's fire, and her superior guns shower the *San Juan Bautista* with cannonballs. They slash through sails and rigging and blow apart railings and storage casks on deck. When one of them topples the main mast, the ship starts to lean in the water. Soon the white flag of surrender climbs the mizzen mast. Cheers rise from the decks of both English ships.

Jope and Elfrith arrive at the ailing Spanish vessel in their tenders at the same time. They and their men climb up rope ladders. Although the main deck is a shambles of singed sails, torn ropes, and splintered wood from the toppled mast, there is a large area clear of debris where the vanquished crew—soldiers and seamen—has assembled. Their blackened, smoke-stained faces emanate fear and defeat. Some have blood dripping from wounds or seeping through hastily wrapped bandages.

Ascending the curved stairs to the quarterdeck, Jope notes the exquisite workmanship of the warship's carpentry. The Spanish soldier in bronze armor awaiting them, with his navigator and second in command by his side, has a furious expression on his face.

His raven black eyes blazing, he announces in broken English, "I am Captain Manuel Mendes de Acuña, cousin of Diego Sarmiento de Acuña, Count of Gondomar and Spanish ambassador to England. You are in violation of your King's treaty with Spain!"

Elfrith looks at him with contempt. "We will have your sword of surrender first, Captain."

The Spaniard obeys and hands his sword over. "I can recognize an English corsair. This is piracy!"

Jope regards him blandly and gestures toward the *White Lion*. "If you will direct your gaze to my ship, you will see the Dutch flag. I hail from Flushing, Holland, with Dutch letters of marque."

Before the Spaniard can reply, Elfrith presses on, "What treasures do you have aboard?"

The question surprises Acuña. "I have no treasure. We are headed for Veracruz with a cargo of slaves."

Elfrith's face darkens. "This ship was built for treasure. Why would a warship be carrying slaves?"

"I purchased them from the Portuguese in the port of Luanda in Africa. I have the papers."

Acuña gestures to his second, who comes forward with a parchment scroll. Elfrith snatches it from him, unfurls it, grimaces, and hands it to Jope.

Looking it over, Jope scratches his head. "This is in Spanish."

Impatiently, Elfrith gestures to his first mate. Rollins steps up, takes the document, and translates slowly, "Three hundred fifty slaves sold to Captain Manuel Mendes de Acuña for transport to the port of Veracruz."

"You see, no treasure aboard," the Spaniard asserts haughtily.

"By God's teeth, we'll see about that," says Elfrith. "In the meantime, *mi capitán*, it is time for you and your crew to abandon ship."

Acuña's face darkens. The veins in his forehead throb with fury. "This is an outrage!"

Elfrith bows and twirls his hand in a mock flourish, ending by pointing in the direction of the main deck.

"Mark my words, this is not the end of it," Acuña blusters.

He stalks down the stairs to the main deck and says a few words to his surviving men. They stand at attention as best they can, then follow him and his officers down the rope ladders on the side of the ship and climb into three large rowboats. When they cast off, Acuña sits in the bow of the lead boat still as a statue. He does not look back.

Elfrith and Jope descend to the main deck and down a hatch into the bowels of the ship. They pass dead soldiers, overturned cannons, fallen timbers, and wide, gaping holes in the hull. As they descend to the level where the crew's cabins and provisions storage areas are, the smell of burned wood and gunpowder mingles with a pungent outhouse stench. When they get to a dark, wooden hatch with iron cross pieces, the fetid smell is so revolting that Jope takes the scarf from his neck and places it over his face.

"Bring torches," Elfrith calls to one of his crew. "By God's wounds, we're not going down there without light."

As seamen lift the trapdoor, Jope peers into the darkness below. The ambient light from above reveals wooden stairs heading down and dark shapes below. Sounds of moaning and soft crying float up along with a more intense, putrid odor.

Jope takes the first lit torch in hand and holds the scarf tightly against his nose and mouth. As he descends, one of the steps breaks. His boot slips through a crack, and he reels backward. There is a cry from beneath the stairs as helping hands catch him from behind and push him upright. Jope pulls his foot free and carefully continues down the stairs.

At the bottom his feet sink into a soft layer of caked brown excrement covering the wooden planks. He almost vomits. Then the flickering light from his torch reveals rows of naked men and women covered in filth and offal, chained to the floor. Most are lying down; a few sit up, their white eyes fearfully darting back and forth.

Jope is at a loss for words. He has heard about the wretched conditions on Spanish slave ships, but never in his life has he seen such an appalling sight. Behind him he hears Elfrith swearing and a seaman throwing up.

He aims his torch farther into the hold, but the light does not reach to the end. The rows of misery extend far beyond its reach.

He turns to find out who cried when he broke through the stairs and shines his torch into the nook underneath. In the quivering light, he sees a thin, naked girl and a small boy kneeling next to her, chains around their ankles. She stares at him with large fearful eyes. Jope feels an instant stab of anguish, and then he has the shock of his life. The girl moves her hand to her bare chest and makes the sign of the cross.

In her weakened state, Margarita sees a lion face surrounded by reddish-blond hair. She expects him to roar and tear into her, but instead he says something in a language she doesn't understand. A large paw reaches for her leg. She flinches as it grabs her, but it has no claws. Instead fingers search along the chain to unshackle her from the floor.

As the leonine face comes closer, Margarita realizes that it is a bearded man. He reaches for her and pulls her from her prison cupboard. Lifting her up, he cradles her in his arms and carries her up the stairs. Along the way he barks orders to a sailor. Then up another flight, and another, until they're up on deck, where he puts her down. The afternoon sunlight blinds her, and when she squints and opens her eyes, she sees a man looking down on her, his face glistening, his hair golden flames of fire. His sparkling eyes are blue as the sky. She has never seen such eyes before.

Kneeling beside her, he reaches his arm back and someone puts a metal cup in his hand. He raises her head and trickles drops of water past her cracked lips. The liquid soothes her swollen tongue and raspy throat. She eagerly extends her lips, and he pours a bit more water into her mouth. When she sucks greedily for more, he pulls the cup back.

He smiles and takes her hand in his tough paws and utters words she can't understand, but from the gentle tone she realizes that she's safe now.

When he picks her up and carries her to the edge of the deck, she settles into his arms. She feels herself being handed down the side of the ship into a waiting boat. For a moment, she is terrified she has lost him, but then he appears next to her and cradles her in his arms again. As the boat moves away from the large galleon that has been

Rescued

her prison for longer than she can remember, she feels tension leave her body, succumbs to the gentle swaying, and passes out.

* * *

When Margarita comes to, she is lying on a bed, a wet cloth draped across her forehead. A piece of cloth like a small blanket covers her from the waist down. She struggles to sit up and looks around the room. It is a wooden cabin with a table and chairs in the middle. Near the door there is a small desk. Books and papers are neatly stacked with a weighted cross of gold placed on top. On the other side of the bed, she recognizes a makeshift altar with candles and a small cross. If this cabin belongs to the lion man, he is a Christian.

Suddenly the door swings open and he enters, carrying Juan. He gently places him on the bed next to her, takes a wet cloth from a wash basin, and wipes his face. Margarita watches attentively. His large hands caress Juan with surprising tenderness. He leaves the cloth on Juan's forehead and looks at his small chest rise and fall. Satisfied, he notices her staring at him.

He walks around to her side of the bed. Hunkering down before her, he points to his chest and says, "Jope. Captain Jope."

When she doesn't respond, he takes her hand and taps his chest repeatedly, saying "Captain Jope" each time.

Margarita looks at him attentively. She mouths the words, "Captain Jope."

He smiles and nods, "Captain Jope."

Then he takes her hand and touches her chest with it. When wrinkles of puzzlement furrow her forehead, he drops her hand. He points his finger at his chest and says, "Captain Jope," then touches his finger lightly to her chest. He repeats the words and gestures several times with a questioning look on his face.

Margarita tries to say her name, but her throat is so dry that she can make only a rasping sound.

Jope goes to the table and brings back a small cup of water. He holds her head and helps her take several small sips.

When she is finished swallowing, she clears her throat and says in a small voice, "Margarita."

Jope leans his head back and smiles. "Margarita!"

She points to herself and says her name again. Then she touches the chest of the boy lying next to her and says, "Juan."

Jope laughs happily and points at her and the boy. "Margarita and Juan."

She rewards him with a smile.

There is a knock on the door, and another bearded man enters carrying a metal trencher. On it is a hunk of bread and two oranges. When Jope puts his finger to his lips and indicates the sleeping boy, the man nods in understanding, carefully places the plate on the table, and leaves quietly.

Jope breaks off a piece of bread and hands it to Margarita. While she gnaws at it, he takes a knife and cuts an orange into slices. He hands one to her and takes another for himself. Putting it to his lips, he bites into it and sucks the juicy marrow into his mouth. Margarita follows his example gingerly. Her eyes grow big. The juice tastes sweet and wonderful and reminds her of home.

Suddenly tears stream down her face and she sobs uncontrollably. Jope sits on the bed, pulls her on his lap, and rocks her gently until her crying subsides. Then he lays her back down next to Juan, and she falls asleep immediately.

Jope looks at the two slumbering children for a long time before he leaves the cabin.

* * *

The sun is setting behind the *San Juan Bautista*, smoke still rising from its crippled hull. Nearby, the *White Lion* and *Treasurer* are floating side by side in the water, lashed together with ropes. Jope walks across the planks that have been placed as a bridge between them to confer with Elfrith. He notes the damage to the ship—several holes in the hull above the waterline, exposing the interior of the ship, torn sails, blasted railings, and the main deck littered with debris. He feels fortunate that his ship made it through the battle without sustaining any damage.

When he climbs up to the quarterdeck, Elfrith greets him with an assessment of the situation. "The Spanish bugger told the truth, blast him," he growls. "Except for a few trinkets in his cabin, there's not an ounce of treasure."

Jope takes a deep breath. "What do we do now?"

"We'll have to make the best of it. We have enough provisions to each take twenty to thirty extra men and women aboard and make it to Jamestown. We can trade them there. The plantations there are always in need of workers and field hands."

Considering their options, Jope nods. It makes sense, especially with the *Treasurer* seriously damaged. "What about the rest of the unfortunates in the hold?"

"Acuña will come for them once we're gone. I'm certain of it. He'll want to salvage what he can."

Jope glances at the listing hull of the *Bautista*. He knows Elfrith is right. The galleon is badly battered, but the lower hull is solid and will keep her afloat.

"Tomorrow then. We'll make our selections and be on our way." He hesitates before asking, "You're sure your ship will make it?"

Elfrith laughs, but there is no humor in his outburst. "Don't worry about me. We'll be fine. Not my time yet to kiss the bottom of the sea."

That is exactly what Jope expects him to say. "All right, then."

But as he heads back to his own ship and notes again some of the injuries to the *Treasurer*, he's not so sure. If they have to travel through another storm, there could be trouble. He stares at the *Bautista* for a moment. The glowing beams of dying sunlight shining through a bank of clouds enfold the ship like giant fingers.

The Gulf of Mexico—July 1619

Back in his cabin he contemplates the two sleeping children, their innocent faces relaxed now. He wonders again what strange currents have brought him to this situation. Their fate and his are now intertwined—he can feel it in the core of his being that they are a part of his destiny. He kneels at his altar and prays to God, thanking him for the opportunity to save these two chosen souls and asks for help in what he must do now to guide their lives.

12

SAMUEL ARGALL

London—July 1619

The long driveway leading to Southampton House is crowded with the horse-drawn carriages of members of the Virginia Company. The shiny private coaches of the wealthy merchants, knights, and nobles are parked close to the entrance, while the shabbier carriages-for-hire of the less prosperous shareholders have to pull up closer to the street, requiring their passengers a longer journey on foot. The company still can't afford its own headquarters, and while Nicholas Ferrar's house can accommodate the council meetings, it is too small for the larger quarterly assemblies. Fortunately, the Earl of Southampton has graciously offered his London residence to host the quarter court meetings.

Inside, a large crowd of investors mingles under the lofty hammer beam ceiling of the great hall, eager to share the latest news and rumors floating about town. Sir Thomas Smythe's faction congregates in front of a large tapestry depicting a hunting scene, which covers most of the wood-paneled wall above the carved wainscoting. Sandys's supporters occupy the area by a large stone fireplace, while the Earl of Warwick's followers are gathered by the large windows overlooking the extensive gardens.

The leading board members of the company—Edwin Sandys and Nicholas Ferrar—are busy looking over documents at the large oak table at the head of the room. Southampton and Warwick are engaged in conversation. Lord Rich seems at ease despite the tension in the air, but inside he is churning. The De La Warr business is turning into a protracted legal battle, and he still has heard nothing of the *Treasurer*. His private meetings with Sandys about the situation of the Leiden Separatists have been productive, raising the hope of establishing a Puritan community in the New World. But he is beginning to believe that the new treasurer is playing a double game. While personally assuring Rich of his good wishes, he is having his minions sue Samuel Argall over misappropriating company supplies as governor. It is an indirect attack on Warwick designed to keep the issue of Jamestown as his pirate's lair alive.

He looks over at Argall engaged in earnest conversation with Nathaniel Rich. Warwick knows that Argall's loyalty to him is unquestioned, but he will need to reassure him that his participation in the Jamestown ventures won't reflect badly on him. That is one of the reasons Warwick has been working to persuade King James to reward Argall with a knighthood for his many services to the realm.

There is a small commotion by the entrance at the far end of the hall. The crowd parts to make way for Captain Brewster. Stocky and self-important, he struts into the room and scans the assembly as if looking for someone in particular.

A brief look passes between Warwick and Nathaniel Rich. Brewster's arrival means trouble.

Brewster stares briefly in Argall's direction, then heads toward the fireplace, bowing curtly to various members of Sandys's faction. As he finds Lord Cavendish and starts talking to him, the rest of the shareholders in the room relax and go back to their conversations.

Warwick sees Thomas Weston heading in his direction and renews his conversation with Southampton. The last thing he needs is to listen to the man bend his ear. He is like a burr. Once he sticks to your coat, you can't get rid of him.

He is saved by the sound of distant church bells tolling the hour. The council members take their places behind the table, and

Edwin Sandys in his role as treasurer brings down his gavel three times to quiet the crowd.

He announces, "The quarter court of the Virginia Company is now in session. I trust that we will conduct ourselves with dignity and decorum. We have a full agenda."

There is a prayer followed by acceptance of the minutes of the April quarter court, as well as the interim council meetings. Significantly, there is no mention of the discussion about Brewster's allegations regarding the *Treasurer*, Warwick's privateering, or Argall's spirited defense. Sandys, at the suggestion of Southampton, has decided not to air the company's dirty linen in public.

Instead, he provides an update on the latest news from Virginia. According to the most recent letter from Sir George Yeardley, the new governor has wasted no time in instituting reforms in Jamestown.

"As we meet, he is holding elections for the House of Burgesses in the General Assembly of Virginia to select the two members representing each of the eleven settlements established on the James River," says Sandys. "The first meeting will be held at the end of the month to administer the Oath of Supremacy to each representative and to review the Great Charter that Sir Yeardley took with him to Virginia."

One of the merchants of Smythe's faction steps forward and challenges, "I'm still not persuaded that it is a good idea to leave governance in the hands of people thousands of miles away who may not have our best interests at heart."

There are low murmurs of assent, and Sandys quickly scotches them. "This matter has been settled. The Council of Estate here in London will advise the governor in Virginia, who acts on our behalf and has veto power."

Warming to his task, he continues, "The health of the colony must be our main concern. Its future, and our financial success, lies in creating its own manufacturing capabilities—ironworks, glassworks, tanneries, and shipbuilding. But above all, we need more investors and able-bodied men to go there. We have been working on a proposal that we believe will encourage more immigration."

He nods to Nicholas Ferrar. The deputy rises, brandishing a document. "We want to reward new investors with 100 acres of company land and fifty acres for each additional person they bring to Virginia. Immigrants who pay their own fare will receive fifty acres as well. Those who cannot pay their way will receive their allotted land after they complete a contract of indentured servitude."

"As an incentive, we also propose to supply them with food, clothing, and livestock so they can make their own start in the colony," Sandys adds.

As he pauses, there are rumblings from the crowd, many of them unfavorable.

"You want to give away our precious company assets!" challenges one of the merchants.

Sandys responds with confidence. "Our charter gives us territorial rights over thousands of miles along the coast of North America. What we propose will take but a tiny fraction of our vast lands. To encourage more immigration, I propose that we—"

"And what about the magazine ship?" calls out another shareholder near the tapestry.

"Whatever recommendation comes from Virginia will require the approval of all shareholders here," Sandys explains, unruffled. He doesn't really want to deal with this issue, although he feels secure in the knowledge that he has the votes to have his way when the time comes to allow the settlers to trade with whomever they want.

Suddenly, the air is pierced by a gruff voice coming from near the fireplace. "What about the *Treasurer*? How can we keep the colony safe when Jamestown is a pirates' haven?"

There is instant silence as all eyes turn to Argall and the Earl of Warwick. Surprised by being ambushed, they are momentarily at a loss for words.

Immediately, other shouts fill the air: "Where is the ship?" "We have a right to know." "There is no room for privateers in our ranks." "Treason!"

Sandys bangs the gavel to restore order. When he has everyone's attention, he turns slowly to Warwick with a questioning look.

The earl clears his throat and says blandly, "I have no more intelligence of the *Treasurer*'s whereabouts than the last time this matter was raised."

"Which is nothing!" accuses a red-faced shareholder from Sandys's faction.

Before the chorus of critics can start up again, Argall steps forward and glares at the incensed shareholders. "Your accusations are baseless. As deputy governor I have worked tirelessly to advance our cause in Virginia, and I have seen firsthand what goes on over there. The Indian situation is under control, but the settlers don't have enough workers to bring in their crops. They grow so much tobacco that they don't have food enough to live on. And there are people here who would choke the lifeblood from Jamestown just to protect their profits."

The shouts of indignation that echo through the hall rise to the roof. Sandys has to wield his gavel repeatedly before the din of outrage starts to subside.

But just as the meeting is about to return to normal, Captain Brewster parts the crowd. He points his finger at Argall and shouts, "You're a blustery bastard and a thief. You appropriated goods from the *Neptune* in Virginia for the very people you claim to champion. You took them as your own bounty."

Argall leaps forward incensed. "You're a contemptible liar!"

In response, Brewster draws his sword. "And you're a vulgar prygman. I challenge you to a duel."

Argall's hands itch to reach for his own sword, but he thinks better of it. "You have already brought a legal suit against me. Now you want a pound of flesh, too? Why don't we let the courts decide the truth?"

Sandys calls out in his high-pitched voice, "Gentlemen, gentlemen! This will not do. This wrangling is unbecoming, and it hurts our cause!"

But Brewster charges, only to be intercepted and restrained by others. They hold his raised arm, sword pointing to the ceiling, until he calms down.

Warwick notices Lord Cavendish smirking, enjoying the chaos. No doubt he had something to do with it.

At last Brewster sheathes his sword. But as he withdraws to the group by the tapestry, he calls out to Argall, "Just let me catch you away from here, and we'll see how pretty you talk then."

Argall smiles coldly, "It will be my pleasure."

He rejoins the ranks of Warwick's supporters at the windows while Brewster enjoys the approbations of Sandys's faction. Lord Cavendish claps him on the shoulders.

Although order has been restored, Sandys realizes that no more substantial business is likely to be concluded this day. He says with passion, "We cannot continue in this fashion. Our strife will be the talk of the taverns and drawing rooms at court. If we can't act in a civil manner and show a united front, we'll have others interfere in our business."

Everyone knows he is talking about King James and his Privy Council, who would like nothing better than to take over the Virginia Company if given the right excuse.

"All pending matters are tabled till next time," Sandys says. "The meeting is hereby adjourned." He bangs the gavel once and leaves the table to confer with Southampton.

Warwick gestures Nathaniel Rich over and whispers in his ear, "Have Argall come see me later."

When Nathaniel nods, Warwick joins Sandys and Southampton to confer about what happened and strategize on how to proceed.

* * *

In the late afternoon, Captain Argall arrives at Lord Rich's lodgings. He takes the secret entrance in a side alley, where Alfred is waiting to convey him to the drawing room of the mansion. As he climbs the marble stairs, he muses again why Warwick wants to see him. As co-owners of the *Treasurer*, now that Lord De La Warr is dead, they do have matters to discuss. Or is it about Brewster and what might have happened if he had taken him up on his challenge? At thirty-nine, Argall is a seasoned veteran of many a battle on land and sea, and he has no doubt that he would have skewered his nemesis. But the King hates dueling, and it would get him in trouble with the law.

He removes his sword and hat outside in the parlor and strides briskly into the study when Alfred announces him. Warwick, lounging in an armchair, gestures him over and holds out a glass of red wine.

"Come and join me, Captain. This is a most excellent claret."

Argall bows. "Thank you, m'Lord. You always teach me to appreciate the finer things."

He sits down on a sofa across from Warwick, takes a sip, and nods in acknowledgment.

Rich, noting the tension in his shoulders, smiles and says, "I was impressed earlier at your self-control in the face of that boisterous lout. I could tell you were itching for a fight."

"I'd like nothing better than to run that loudmouth through and through!"

"Wouldn't we all, and good riddance. But self-restraint is better. You don't want to do anything to jeopardize your impending knighthood."

"No. But all these accusations are more than troublesome. And now there is a lawsuit against me. What if—"

Rich puts up his hand. "Rest assured. Nathaniel will take care of it. You have my word."

"I'm very glad to hear it, m'Lord," Argall says, relaxing visibly. He takes another, longer sip.

Filling his glass from a crystal decanter, Rich continues, "I could use your help with another matter. As you know, the Leiden Separatists' petition to go to Jamestown has been tabled for now. I'd love for them to go there—the place is run by Anglicans who are really Catholics in disguise. But they need another place to settle.

Samuel Argall

In your explorations to discover a shorter route from Virginia to England, did you come upon any other place that might be suitable?"

Argall purses his lips. He immediately understands that Rich plans to send the Puritans to the New World without a specific patent from the Virginia Company. He thinks back on his voyages, including the time he looted and destroyed Port Royal in Arcadia, far to the north. "It would need to be far enough away from Jamestown not to interfere with its interests," he says.

Rich is pleased. He can always count on Argall to understand the bigger picture without having to spell things out for him. "Yes, the Virginia Company claims territory along the coast of the Americas for more than 1,000 miles, all the way north to New France."

"Let me think on it and consult some maps, m'Lord. I'm sure I can find several spots that will fit the bill."

"Excellent. We will need to work closely on this and other matters."

Rich downs the last of his wine and places his empty glass on the silver platter by his side. Argall takes the hint and rises from the armchair.

"Will there be anything else, M'Lord?"

"No, thank you, Captain. Just keep a cool head," Rich says, smiling.

Argall bows and withdraws.

But he does not heed Warwick's advice. The next morning, he visits the Sheriff's Court in the Guildhall in Cheapside to pay a bond on a warrant sworn against him by William Oxbrigg, one of Sandys's allies, as far as he can tell, regarding the claim that he appropriated company goods for his own purposes.

When he is finished, he exits the large gate, and Captain Brewster is waiting for him with his blade drawn.

"There's no one to run interference here, you runt-faced coxcomb," he says. "Will you take my challenge now?"

Argall doesn't hesitate and draws his sword. "It will be my pleasure to turn you into a pin cushion!"

"I will make mincemeat of you!" Brewster blusters.

"Come to me then, sweetheart," Argall goads him.

When the irascible captain lunges at him, Argall steps aside and thrusts his sword below Brewster's ribs, but the blow glances off. Argall pulls back, surprised, and Brewster uses the opportunity to recover. As they continue to fence, a crowd gathers around them. Some of the onlookers make bets regarding the outcome.

Argall, a superior swordsman, manages two more thrusts into Brewster's body, but neither pierces him.

"You're wearing body armor, you piss-pot pillock!" he shouts.

Brewster smirks. "I've got you now, you miserable cacafuego."

The crowd, wanting to see blood, urges them on. Argall considers his options. The game has just gotten more dangerous. Since his opponent feels invulnerable, he can fight recklessly and just might land a lucky blow. Perhaps this is a time when discretion is the better part of valor. What settles the matter is when he sees a constable striding toward them. When Brewster lunges again, Argall parries across his body and steps into him. Trapping his adversary's sword arm with his own, he wrests his weapon from him. Then he elbows him in the face, sending him staggering backward.

By the time the constable arrives, Argall has sheathed his sword and calmly hands Brewster's sword to the officer of the peace and says, "The codger attacked me."

When they look around, Brewster has taken the opportunity to disappear in the crowd.

* * *

Later that day, Rich and Sandys receive separate reports about the altercation. They both heave a sigh of relief that nothing serious happened and say so in public, but secretly they regret that their man didn't run the other through with his sword.

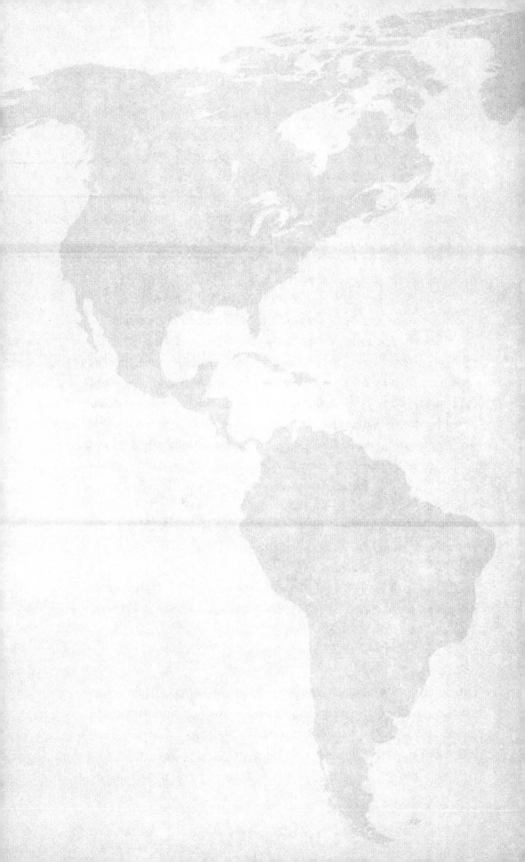

13

TO POINT COMFORT

Virginia—August 1619

Margarita wakes. It is nighttime. In the dim light of a lantern hanging near the table, she sees Juan next to her, asleep. She remembers she is onboard the ship of the lion-faced man—Jope . . . John Jope . . . Captain John Jope!—and exhales, reassured. Barefoot, she goes to the row of windows at the rear of the cabin. The shutters are up, and the moon glows ghostly in the distance over the lapping waves. She sits on the bench hugging her knees and thinks of her mother, father, brother, and sister. She would like to think that they are still alive but knows it isn't likely. A dull ache grips her heart, and she says a prayer for them.

Then she hears heavy footsteps, and the cabin door opens abruptly. In the lantern's glow she sees her rescuer, his blue eyes glistening, surrounded by reddish-blond hair. He notices that she is at the window and goes to the sleeping boy on the bed. Bending down, he touches his shoulder. Juan wakens immediately and sits bolt upright, his eyes wide with fear. When he sees Jope, he lets out a sigh of relief.

The captain gestures them over to the table and places two bowls filled with a steaming liquid before them. When Juan sits down on the chair, he barely can see over the edge. The captain finds a box and slides it under him.

"There, that's better," he says, grinning.

Margarita lifts her bowl to her dry, cracked lips. The hot liquid smells and tastes unfamiliar, and she grimaces. She looks to the captain, who motions her to eat.

"It's soup," he says.

She takes another sip and finds it not too unpleasant. She nods gratefully and starts to slurp the soup. Juan watches her and follows her example. Only when the warm liquid settles in her stomach does she realize how hungry she is.

After Jope leaves, she repeats the strange word out loud. "Soup."

For several days, she and Juan don't leave the cabin. Time passes like a dream between sleeping long hours and eating hungrily whatever the captain has to offer. From time to time the dull ache in her heart returns, and Margarita distracts herself by repeating the words she hears the captain say.

Sometimes Juan has a faraway look, too, reliving unpleasant memories of their ordeal. When Margarita notices it, she gently takes his hand or puts an arm on his shoulder to bring him back to the present. In turn, he hugs her when a sudden noise startles her— bells being rung or someone shouting on deck—and a muscle starts to twitch in her cheek.

Soon, with the resilience of the young, they recover and greet their rescuer with smiles when he looks in on them or brings more food. For Jope it is heartening to see them starting to relax and take an interest in their surroundings.

When he thinks they're ready, he takes them outside. Margarita holds onto Juan by one hand and grabs Jope's big paw with the other as they walk onto the main deck. The breeze feels fresh and cool against their faces. The sun is bright and blinding, and they squint until their eyes adjust. Jope has told his crew to act normally, so the sailors go about their work as if seeing two African children promenade on the ship is an everyday occurrence.

Looking about, the first thing Juan notices—and points out to Margarita—is another ship nearby, cutting through the waves.

It is close enough so that they can see the deckhands working the sails. Margarita wonders about the gaping holes in the hull and the quarterdeck's beams partially destroyed. Are they from the thunder balls and the battle with the slave ship?

Then she sees the other captives rescued from the *San Juan Bautista*. They are lying asleep on the foredeck or leaning against the railing, dozing. There are more women than men, and they are no longer in chains. Jope feels Margarita tightening her grip and notes the surprise of the few Africans who are awake when they see the children by his side.

Margarita and Juan are just as surprised. Although none of the men and women are from Pongo, she remembers some of them from the times they got fed on the deck of the slave ship. Tentatively, almost shyly, they exchange greetings in Kimbundu, their native language, and remind each other of their names and where they come from. Margarita realizes that some of them are farmers and cattle herders from the Pongo region—Juan's people. Others grew up in Kabasa, the Ndongo capital, but none of their parents were nobility like hers.

As the days pass and the adult Angolans gradually regain their strength, the amount of time Margarita and Juan spend with them becomes more extended, and conversations flow more freely. A sign that the adults are recovering, too, is that they salt their musings about what's going to happen to them in the future with humor.

"I don't think they're going to eat us after all," says one of the women.

"They're just fattening us up so we'll taste better," jokes another.

At some point when they are sailing within sight of the shore, a yellow line of sand with trees and greenery above it, one of the men comments, "We are *malungu*, the ghosts who have walked across Kalunga."

Margarita remembers the conversation with her father and shivers. Her cheek twitches involuntarily.

To Point Comfort

When some of the women ask her about Captain Jope, she tells them he is a good man, a kind man, to reassure them. Margarita is more talkative than Juan, who responds only when asked a direct question. But he is fascinated by the workings of the ship and never tires of watching the sailors climb the ratlines to the spars and crow's nest high above the deck, tying up and unfurling sails to adjust to changes in the wind.

Jope cannot follow the conversations his charges have with the others, but he is glad that Margarita and Juan feel comfortable and are establishing relationships with them. It will make it easier to let them go when they reach Jamestown. Caring for them, he has grown more attached than he expected, and he wants the best for them.

Since the shock of the first encounter in the hold of the slave ship, each day with the children brings a new surprise. When he overhears Margarita sounding out English words with Juan, he becomes more deliberate in his conversations, pointing to different objects in the cabin and on deck and saying their names. The children repeat words—table, chair, bed, plate, cup, mast, sail, salt, water, waves—after him. Then they say something to each other in their own language. It sounds like noise to Jope, and Margarita's attempts to teach him the rudiments of Kimbundu fall on deaf ears. What amazes him is that he rarely needs to reinforce a lesson. Even days later, the children remember words he said only once and can repeat them accurately.

One afternoon, Jope decides to teach them how to count. He spreads out kernels of rice on the table in the cabin.

"Rice," says Margarita, echoed by Juan.

"Rice, yes," says Jope.

But when he puts the kernels in a row, points to them one at a time, and counts, "One, two, three," to his amazement Margarita grins knowingly, points to more grains, and continues, "Four, five, six." Then she repeats all of the numbers in Spanish, and again in Dutch! Juan matches her confidently, word for word.

Another surprise comes when Margarita first sees him pray at his altar at night. She and Juan kneel next to him, fold their hands, and start to say the "Pater Noster." Jope recognizes the Latin prayer. How is it possible that they know that? Reluctantly, he teaches them the English version.

In time, as her English improves, Margarita conveys to him that she and Juan were schooled by Catholic nuns. Jope has heard about Spanish and Portuguese missionaries in Africa, but it still astonishes him that these two children are so clever and—yes, he has to admit it—civilized. How did they find themselves in such dire circumstances, imprisoned on a slave ship, bound for certain death? Is it his fate to redirect their paths? And if so, what responsibility does he bear for their future?

On some days, he doesn't have time to pursue such musings. A storm requires all hands on deck. While he and the crew cover the hatches and battle heavy gales and towering seas, Margarita and Juan cower in the cabin frightened by the howling wind and holding on to whatever they can grab as the waves toss the *White Lion* back and forth. When the tempest finally settles, everyone onboard sends a prayer to heaven for their safe delivery.

In the morning sun and calm seas, the sailors inspect the damage to the ship and discover that they've survived relatively unscathed. There are some broken spars and ripped sails, and a good deal of water has invaded the hull and needs to be pumped out, but that is all. The other Africans have survived as well. When Marmaduke establishes the *White Lion's* current bearings, he figures that it will take them only a day or two to get back on course.

But there is no sign of the *Treasurer*. She must have been blown even farther off course, or worse, crippled as she was, taken on too much water and sank beneath the waves. Jope worries about Elfrith and his crew and hopes that the old seadog's prediction that he wasn't ready to kiss the bottom of the ocean held true. He prays that he will see them again at Jamestown.

To Point Comfort

As they sail farther north, the sweltering humidity yields to dryer, cooler air. The forest vegetation on the shore becomes a lusher, darker green, and on the few occasions when they travel close enough for Margarita to make out details on the trees, she realizes that they are unlike any other she has seen. They have long, thin needles instead of leaves. Jope calls them "pine trees."

The weather stays sunny and clear. Occasional squalls bring a few hours of relief from the heat, and the rain caught on deck in large, open barrels replenishes their supply of drinking water. But feeding twenty-two extra mouths is straining the provisions onboard. The soups and stews that Jope brings to the children from the ship's kitchen get thinner, and Margarita notices that he is eating smaller portions than before, although theirs remain the same. Everyone on ship is getting short-tempered, with small quarrels among crew members growing into near bare-knuckle disagreements.

So everyone is glad when, during a meeting of Jope and his officers, Marmaduke, poring over a map, announces, "Tomorrow we will reach the Chesapeake Bay."

Margarita and Juan have looked at some of these charts from Jope's travel trunk before and didn't understand what they were for. All they saw were large blue and yellowish-brown areas separated by a dark, jagged line. Small offshoots from the blue parts burrowed into the yellow regions like wiggling snakes. Jope called them rivers, but for once he was at a loss trying to satisfy their curiosity, and his explanations only increased their befuddled looks and furrowed brows.

Now the relief on the faces of the men in Jope's cabin, followed by spontaneous laughter and backslapping, tells Margarita that the maps help Marmaduke determine where they're going and that the troubles onboard are about to be over. At the same time, she understands that they are about to reach their destination, and it worries her, not knowing what to expect on arrival. While she does not have the heart to upset Juan with her concerns, she spends a sleepless

116

night sitting by the rear windows looking up at the star-filled sky and fretting about their future.

When they reach the mouth of the Chesapeake Bay, it is so wide that Margarita and Juan can only see shore on the port side of the ship. But as the *White Lion* heads toward the James River, they suddenly make out a coastline to starboard as well. Excited, Juan races back and forth from one railing of the quarterdeck to the other.

Before long, a small fort with a few houses and storage sheds appears on a promontory reaching into the bay. As they get closer, Margarita is surprised at their rundown condition. There are gaps in the uneven palisades, and the thatched roofs are in need of repair. From her time with Jope she expected a grander settlement, but this smattering of buildings doesn't come close to the size of Pongo, much less Luanda—the only other towns she's seen—and she is disappointed.

Marmaduke, who has been here before, echoes her feelings. "Not much to look at, is it?" he says to Jope. "Jamestown upriver is not much better. A few more buildings, a church, and a tavern, but altogether a sorry sight. Most of the people live on the surrounding farms and plantations and try to take better care of them."

Jope orders the crew to drop anchor and secure the sails. Deckhands spring into action, manning the capstan, while sailors scramble up the shrouds and ratlines, energized by catching a glimpse of civilization.

Suddenly a lookout in the crow's nest of the foremast hollers down, "A skiff with oarsmen and three military officers approaching from the wharf!"

Jope takes the children to the cabin and prepares himself. He removes a roll of parchment from his trunk and puts it on the table. Then he straps on his sword.

"Stay here and don't show your faces outside," he orders.

Margarita and Juan obey reluctantly, apprehension on their faces. Jope understands that they want to know what is going to happen to them, but he has to make a good first impression with the

Jamestown reception committee, and it won't do to have two African children by his side.

By the time the three men in uniforms climb onboard, Jope awaits them on the main deck. He has drawn himself to his full height, his arm resting casually on the hilt of his sword, with Marmaduke and the first and second mate standing behind him.

The tallest visitor strides forward with military bearing, bows, and says, "I am Captain William Tucker, commander of the fort, and these are my lieutenants. What is your business here?"

Jope takes the measure of the man. He seems straightforward, like a good soldier. There is neither fear nor guile in his eyes, only curiosity.

Smiling, he says, "I am Captain Jope, sailing from Flushing, Holland, carrying letters of marque from Prince Maurice of Nassau. This is my navigator, Marmaduke Raynor."

Sweeping his hand in the direction of the Africans sitting on the foredeck, he continues, "We came upon a foundering Spanish galleon carrying slaves to Veracruz. They were starving and lying in decay. We managed to rescue about fifty. We understand that you are in need of able-bodied men and women."

Tucker looks over the dark-skinned men and women crouched on deck, eyeing him with suspicion. "That's scarcely half of them. Are the rest below?"

"No, they are on another ship, the *Treasurer*, captained by Daniel Elfrith. We sailed in consort but lost sight of each other in a potent storm. He assured me we would be welcome here in Jamestown."

At the mentioning of Elfrith's name the three men grow visibly tense and exchange uneasy glances.

"Well, Captain, you have arrived at Point Comfort. Jamestown is some forty miles upriver," says Tucker. "We will send word to Governor Yeardley apprising him of your arrival. He will decide if you can conduct your business there. May I have a look at your letters of marque?"

Marmaduke steps forward. "Why are you questioning the word of our captain?"

Jope does some quick thinking. Argall is no longer governor, and Elfrith's name provokes discomfort. Things have changed since the *Treasurer* shipped out from here nine months earlier. Not sure which way the wind is blowing now, caution is in order.

Placing a placating hand on his navigator's arm, he says, "Certainly, Captain Tucker. They're in my cabin."

While Marmaduke goes to retrieve them, Jope apprises the three men of their plight. "Our hold is bare, and we are in need of food and water." He indicates the Africans again. "These poor souls are starving. They cannot wait for the governor's decision." He adds indifferently, "It would not be Christian to throw them overboard."

When Tucker stares at him hard, he quickly continues, "I assure you, Captain, my only desire is to find victuals and shelter for these poor souls, which I humbly bring to your port, and ask only for provisions for myself and my crew in return."

Tucker gives him a calculating look. "You don't want to sell your cargo?"

"I have no inclination to profit from their suffering, which has been more than sufficient already."

When Marmaduke returns with the scroll and hands it over, Tucker unfurls it and studies it carefully. Finally, he says, "Your letters of marque seem to be in good order."

"Told you so," Marmaduke mutters, and Jope shoots him a warning glance.

As Tucker gives the documents back, he asks offhandedly, "Would you know Captain Elfrith's whereabouts?"

"Not since the storm," Jope replies. "Last we had sight of him, he was sailing here with thirty more Angolans aboard."

"Coming here to Point Comfort?"

"Aye."

The three men shift uneasily, and another uncomfortable look passes among them.

"And under what letters of marque would he be sailing?"

"The Duke of Savoy's."

Anxiety displaces discomfort on the faces of the men. Tucker looks pained when he offers, "Those letters are no longer valid. The Duke of Savoy declared peace with Spain some months ago. If Captain Elfrith claims he acquired his cargo under that commission, he is guilty of piracy."

Now Jope understands what's at stake here. "I believe he has no knowledge of such a declaration," he says.

Tucker responds severely, "Be that as it may, we will have to detain him and impound the *Treasurer* if he reaches our shores."

"Under whose orders?"

"We have our instructions from England."

Now it is Jope's turn to exchange an apprehensive glance with his navigator and first mate.

Tucker makes up his mind. He looks at Jope intently and says, "We want no trouble here. I will get word from Governor Yeardley as quickly as possible regarding your Africans. In the meantime, I will see what I can do about provisions for you and your men."

"We are much obliged to you," says Jope and bows.

After he accompanies them to the railing and watches them climb down the rope ladder to their skiff, he turns to Marmaduke. "This is hardly the open-armed reception we were promised."

"No," his navigator replies with a perplexed expression. "It looks like we're in something of a pickle."

Jope taps the parchment roll in his hands thoughtfully. "It almost seems like they want us to warn Captain Elfrith. We better be on the lookout for his arrival."

14

CONSPIRACY

Virginia—Late August 1619

Tucker is as good as his word. The next morning a small skiff arrives carrying a cask of corn and several freshly caught fish, and at lunch for the first time in weeks, everyone enjoys corn porridge and leaves the meal with a full belly. Marmaduke and the crew assess the wear and tear of the voyage on the *White Lion* and the damages from the recent storm to start repairs—sewing torn sails, reinforcing spars, replacing the frayed ropes that secure barrels and other supply containers stored on deck, and tarring seams between planks in the hull and on the decks, as needed.

That afternoon Tucker returns with his retinue seeming less guarded. He bears good news. Word has come from Jamestown that Dutch letters of marque are in order and that there is considerable interest in the *White Lion's* cargo.

He launches into an explanation of how things have changed in the past four months since the new governor, George Yeardley, arrived with orders from the new company treasurer in London, Edwin Sandys, to create a democratic parliament in Jamestown. Highly respected as a military man from his previous postings in Virginia, Yeardley instituted a legislative assembly, the House of Burgesses, which was sworn in just a few weeks earlier. It has completed its initial work: refining a new charter; passing and revising laws regarding conduct, religious observances, and trade; and regulating the price of tobacco.

"We are poised on the threshold of a new era in Virginia," says Tucker proudly. Looking in the directions of the Africans on deck, he adds, "We are limited in obtaining most of our goods from the magazine ship of our company, but for certain cargo we can trade with any *legitimate* supplier."

Jope nods significantly and says, "I understand, Captain."

Tucker quickly goes on, "Abraham Piercey, our cape merchant and keeper of the company store, will be here tomorrow to look at the African men and women in your charge and negotiate on Governor Yeardley's behalf."

"For the governor himself?" says Jope, surprised.

"Yes, his plantation, Flowerdew, is in need of laborers to harvest this year's tobacco crop."

"I'll be honored to make Mr. Piercey's acquaintance,"

For the first time, a smile plays on his rugged face. "You better be prepared, Captain. The man isn't the wealthiest merchant in James-town by accident. He's shrewd and drives a hard bargain."

That evening Jope has supper in the cabin with Margarita and Juan. By now the children have learned enough English to engage in lengthier conversations. Jope is in good spirits—for the first time in weeks, things are going his way—and he entertains the children with stories of England.

But then Margarita asks, "What will happen to us?"

A hush descends on the cabin, interrupted by the creaking tim-bers of the ship swaying at anchor.

Jope has dreaded that question for some days, but he decides to answer honestly. "You will go ashore with the others. I will make sure that you are well taken care of."

Juan pipes up, "Will you go with us?"

"No, I have to take my ship back to England."

"We want to come with you!"

Sighing, Jope says, "That won't be possible."

But when Margarita asks, "Why not?" he has no satisfactory answer, at least not one that she and Juan find acceptable.

"I thought you cared about us," she says accusingly, and her cheek twitches.

Her plaintive tone shook Jope to the core, but he insists, "It's the best way."

With that, conversation ceases. The children poke listlessly at their food, all appetite vanished. They say their prayers and go to bed heavyhearted. Juan hugs Margarita the way he used to in the hold of the *San Juan Bautista*. Neither falls asleep for a long time.

Out on deck Jope paces and looks at the hazy moon, praying that he is making the right decision.

* * *

In the middle of the next day, a pinnace comes downriver and anchors next to the *White Lion*. Jope and Marmaduke watch as a dinghy carrying several passengers crosses the short distance between them.

Two young men help a portly older man climb up the side of the ship. When he reaches the opening in the railing, he pulls himself laboriously onboard. He is Jope's age, and his waistcoat looks fancier than Tucker's, befitting his status and wealth. His dark hair spills out from beneath a wide-brimmed hat.

He takes a moment to catch his breath, then walks toward Jope and extends his hand. "I'm Abraham Piercey."

Jope shakes it and says, "Captain John Jope. Welcome to the *White Lion*."

Piercey indicates the young men in back of him. "My assistants."

Nodding to them, Jope introduces Marmaduke. He notes the merchant's quick, appraising eyes that seem to absorb everything at once. Taking Piercey by the arm to assert his being in command, he says, "Let me show you the cargo."

As they advance toward the group of Africans who have assembled on deck, Margarita and Juan sneak out from the entrance to the cabin and watch warily. The dark-skinned men and women stand there awkwardly, as if on display, their eyes fearful and attentive. Piercey walks among them, evaluating and calculating. From time to time he whispers to one of his assistants. He gestures to one of the older women to come forward. She complies slowly, and the merchant looks her up and down and walks around her before moving on.

It reminds Margarita of the Spanish conquistador in the compound in Luanda striding among the Ndongo prisoners and making his selection. Her cheek twitches, and her lips compress into a thin, angry line.

When Piercey has assessed every single one of the twenty rescued Africans, he turns to Jope and announces. "They're all in good shape and will do very well on Yeardley's plantation and mine. We will give them the same contracts as the indentured servants from England—seven years' service and then they're free, with food, clothing, cattle, and fifty acres to call their own."

Jope nods. "That is fair." He hesitates before asking, "What about the children?"

Piercey notices Margarita and Juan, who have come up behind the captain. Surprised, he narrows his eyes and purses his lips. He looks from the children to Jope with undisguised interest, expecting some sort of explanation, but receives none.

"The boy's too young. Just an extra mouth to feed," he volunteers. "The girl will make a good servant. Strong legs, good carriage. Yeardley will want her for his household."

Margarita bristles. "We're together."

Juan nods defiantly.

Piercey is taken aback. He does not expect any of the Africans to understand English, much less speak up for themselves. He screws up his face and says to Jope, "I gather they don't belong with any of the others."

Jope shakes his head. "They're orphans."

Looking toward the adult Africans, Piercey says, "If any of them will take the children on as their own, we might be able to work something out. I'll talk to the governor, and we'll see what we can do. They won't add much in value, though."

Margarita's face burns with anger and shame at being discussed like one of the animals for sale in the marketplace of Pongo. Her cheek spasms.

Oblivious, Piercey goes on. "I understand you want to trade for provisions, Captain. I can offer you a casket of maize, another of barley, and two barrels of salted pork."

Jope looks to Marmaduke who nods imperceptibly—it's enough to get them back to England. "Make it three barrels of pork and you have a deal," he says.

Piercey smiles. "Agreed. You make things easy, Captain. We will bring the provisions from our storehouse tomorrow morning and take the Africans off your hands. I'll bring the indenture contracts with me ready for signing. It is good doing business with you. Next time, come up to Jamestown to my home."

They shake hands again, and the merchant returns to his skiff with the help of his assistants.

Marmaduke rubs his hands in satisfaction, but Jope feels uneasy and conflicted. Margarita refuses to look at him. Juan's glances are accusatory and forlorn.

* * *

The next morning, Piercey arrives in a bigger skiff. While his assistants and the *White Lion*'s crew haul caskets and barrels aboard, the merchant and Jope repair to the cabin to sign the contracts on behalf of the Africans. Piercey is surprised to see Margarita and Juan by themselves on the gallery in the back of the ship.

At some point there is a knock at the door. The first mate pokes his head in and beckons to Jope. In the hallway, he whispers, "The *Treasurer* has been sighted at the mouth of the river."

By the time Jope finishes his business with Piercey and they return to the deck, the second half of the Africans are aboard the skiff and on the way to the pinnace. An eerie silence has descended on the deck of the *White Lion*.

Looking downriver, Jope can make out the sails of the *Treasurer* in the distance. Piercey notices them, too. His expression clouds. They watch for a while, the congenial atmosphere broken.

When the skiff returns, Piercey hands the stack of documents to one of his assistants and asks, "What about the boy and the girl?"

Distracted by the approaching frigate in the distance, Jope doesn't hear him.

The merchant repeats, "The boy and girl. What about them?"

Jope hesitates and takes a deep breath. "Leave them with me for the night," he pleads. "I will leave them for you with Captain Tucker."

Piercey looks at him inquisitively for some time before venturing, "You are an intriguing man, Captain." He rubs his cheek. "Very well. I'll expect them in Jamestown the day after tomorrow."

Then he grabs hold of the rope ladder and lets his assistants help him down to his transport below.

Jope calls after him, "Thank you."

As he looks up, he can make out the Union Jack with the cross of St. George flying high on the *Treasurer's* mast. The ship seems to list somewhat toward starboard, bouncing on the waves like a limping charger.

He calls to Marmaduke, "Get a boat ready. We have to warn Elfrith before he drops anchor."

But by the time he and Marmaduke reach the *Treasurer*, Captain Tucker and his lieutenants have beaten them to it. As they climb aboard, past the remnants of the shattered wooden railing, they see him and Elfrith in heated conversation. His corpulent friend paces up and down the deck, and Tucker has a hard time keeping up with him.

When he sees Jope, Elfrith bellows, "Bugger all, John, this knave keeps telling me that my letters of marque are no longer good and they won't be able to trade with me!"

Tucker, his face contorted in an exasperated expression, pleads, "Now listen, Daniel, you know my hands are tied—"

Elfrith turns on him. "If you can't do anything for me, get off my ship!"

Tucker throws up his hands and beckons to his lieutenants. As he leaves he shrugs apologetically to Jope.

When they have disappeared over the side, Elfrith explodes, "By God's bones, blast the Duke of Savoy for making peace with the Spanish swine!" Suddenly, he breaks out into a radiant smile. "But it's good to see you, John! And you, Marmaduke."

He throws his arms around his friend in a crushing bear hug, lifting him off the ground.

"You, too, Daniel," says Jope, disentangling himself.

"Glad you made it here in one piece. We got blown hither and yon—way off course. Plus, we're taking on water like a sponge. I've had our bilge pumps going round the clock. My crew is exhausted, and we need food."

"Captain Tucker told me they have orders to arrest you," Jope says, straightening his doublet. "What are you going to do?"

"It'll be taken care of, don't you worry. Tucker's all right. His brother-in-law is Maurice Thompson, Lord Rich's business manager here in Virginia. He's not going to do anything rash. But I may have to make a hasty exit."

Jope looks around the battered ship: tattered sails, torn ropes, and splintered yardarms. It appears unsalvageable, not likely to survive a chase. In a tight voice, he asks, "What can we do to help?"

Elfrith shrugs. "Let's wait until we get word from Jamestown."

On the way back to the *White Lion*, Jope listens to the oars slapping the water. He looks at the moon rising above the houses and prays for guidance.

* * *

The following afternoon, a small skiff arrives from upriver. When it makes land by the fort at Point Comfort, three men get off and enter the palisades. They are dressed formally in waistcoats, breeches, and boots. After half an hour, they return with Captain Tucker, get into their boat, and head for the *Treasurer*.

Jope watches them climb aboard. After a few minutes, they return with Elfrith in tow and climb into the waiting skiff. He fears the worst for his friend, but instead of heading back to the shore, they make a beeline for the *White Lion*.

Elfrith's head is the first to emerge above the railing. He clambers aboard and roars with laughter when he sees Jope's bewildered expression. "We come to meet with you, John," he shouts. "Your cabin is more congenial since the Spaniards blew holes in mine."

Soon, the three men from Jamestown and Captain Tucker arrive on deck. The leader pulls off his cap, revealing a full head of brown hair. His chiseled, furrowed features suggest a man older than his years.

When he sees Jope's navigator, his face brightens. "Marmaduke, it's good to see you again in these waters." He turns to the captain. "And you must be the Dutchman." He extends his hand. "I am John Rolfe, treasurer and recorder for the Virginia Company in Jamestown." He smiles wistfully and adds, "At least for another fortnight, until my replacement takes over."

Jope is surprised as he shakes his hand. He did not expect Jamestown "royalty." He well remembers when Rolfe visited England three years earlier with his wife, Pocahontas, and her name was on everyone's lips even as far from London as Cornwall.

When Jope reminds him of that time and expresses his condolences for her untimely death, Rolfe's face clouds. "Yes, she rests in English soil," he says solemnly. Then he smiles. "I recently remarried." He introduces one of the other men, who is not much older than he. "In fact, this is my father-in-law, William Pierce, a lieutenant in the militia."

Jope notes the military bearing, nods to him, and receives a nod in return.

"This is William Ewen, a merchant who has a plantation next to mine, and you already know Captain Tucker."

Jope nods again, unsure what this is all about.

There is an awkward pause until Elfrith blusters, "Well, aren't you going to invite us in?"

In response, Jope laughs and says, "I'm forgetting my manners. This way, gentlemen."

When the visitors enter the cabin, they are surprised to see Margarita and Juan. The children greet them with looks of curiosity and apprehension. Jope asks them to go aft, out to the gallery, and starts to clear nautical charts from the table to the bench by the windows. Rolfe watches attentively as Margarita and Juan head outside. He observes them through the open door and glances speculatively at Jope.

Offering seats to his guests, the *White Lion's* captain says, "I hope you'll forgive me that I have nothing stronger to offer you than water, gentlemen, but we have been through trying times getting here."

"Think nothing of it, Captain," says Rolfe. "Do you mind if we drink some tobacco?"

When Jope shakes his head, the three Jamestown men and Tucker pull out pipes and pouches. They go through an elaborate ritual of packing the pipes with dark brown fibers, tamping them down, and lighting up using the candles on the table. Tucker shares his pipe with Elfrith. Soon the cabin is hazy with pungent smoke.

Rolfe offers his pipe to Jope and Marmaduke. "The Indians pass it around at gatherings and call it smoking the peace pipe," he explains.

Marmaduke accepts and takes a puff, but Jope declines. "Perhaps another time."

"Then let me come straight to the point, Captain," says Rolfe. "Your raid on a Spanish ship could not have come at a worse time."

He goes on to detail the changes that Yeardley has instituted since taking over as governor of Virginia. Then he proceeds to the most serious development—Edwin Sandys's letter with orders to arrest Elfrith and impound the *Treasurer* upon arrival, and to detain and try for treason anyone purchasing from the Earl of Warwick's ship or giving aid to its captain and crew.

Pierce interjects, "As you can see, Daniel, Jamestown is no longer a safe haven for privateers."

Elfrith scratches his head. Jope, well aware of the gravity of the situation, asks, "What can we do to help?"

"We know you're not a Dutchman, Captain," says Ewen. "Your Cornwall brogue betrays you. Besides, Captain Elfrith speaks too fondly of you."

"I guess the cat's out of the bag," says Jope, grinning.

Rolfe exhales an aromatic cloud of smoke. "Actually, we want to put it back in the bag," he says. "Your letters of marque are legitimate. If you claim that you attacked the Spanish galleon and took the slaves on your own, and that Captain Elfrith purchased them from you, everyone will be well covered."

"So you want me to continue to be the Dutchman from Flushing, Holland."

Rolfe says, "Yes." The others nod eagerly.

Jope thinks about it for a moment and remembers a phrase from his student days in Vlissingen. "*Ik ben blij om het te doen*—I'm happy to do it. You have my word."

The conspirators burst out laughing. Elfrith, leading the chorus, slaps Jope on the back. "I knew I could count on you."

When the merriment dies down, Tucker speaks up. "Now that that's settled, Daniel, I would like to purchase two of your Africans. I can make good use of them on my farm."

"The same goes for me," Ewen chimes in. "We'll provide you with plenty of provisions in return."

"At least to get you to Bermuda," says Rolfe. "The governor there is Warwick's man, and you can hide out for as long as needed. We will tell Yeardley that you disappeared before we got here. The others will back me on that."

He turns to Jope. "It would be good if you can get to England ahead of the *Treasurer*."

"Our repairs are almost done. We will set sail within the week," Jope assures him.

By the time the meeting breaks up, it is getting dark outside. Marmaduke takes a lantern and hangs it on the mast. Light and shadows play over the deck.

Elfrith slaps Jope on the shoulder again. "By Jove, I won't forget this, John."

"May the wind be at your back," says the Dutchman, embracing his friend and kissing him on the cheek.

Rolfe is the last one to leave. "Thank you again, Captain. It is good to make your acquaintance."

"Until next time," says Jope.

At the railing, about to descend to the skiff, Rolfe stops. He says quietly, "How much do you think the children overheard of our conversation?"

Jope is instantly vigilant. "I don't know. But I doubt they would have understood anything of what we talked about."

Reassured, Rolfe nods, but hesitates. The flickering light from the lantern plays over his face. He makes up his mind and whispers so that only Jope can hear him, "That little girl is a beauty, Captain. I hope for her sake and yours that you aren't going to trade her away, too."

Jope fixes him with an indecipherable stare.

The hint of a smile twitches on Rolfe's lips as he disappears over the side of the ship. Jope looks after him, deep in thought.

As the skiff pushes off, the oars hardly make a sound over the waves lapping against the hull of the ship.

After Marmaduke withdraws, Jope remains alone on deck for some time, looking into the darkness on the starboard side of his ship. He prays for God to reveal his destiny to him and hopes he has made the right decision.

Taking the lantern off the hook on the mast, he returns to his cabin. Entering quietly, he smells the remnants of the tobacco smoke. It itches his nose. He holds the lantern high and looks down on the bed where Margarita and Juan are sleeping entwined in each other's arms.

PART TWO

&

ENGLAND

15

TO ENGLAND

The Atlantic—October–November 1619

As the *White Lion* leaves the calm waters of the Chesapeake Bay and heads for the open seas, it dawns on Margarita that her captain is not leaving her in Jamestown after all. Watching the last of the land become a thin line on the horizon, she feels such joy and gratitude that the next time she meets him on deck, she impulsively throws her arms around him.

"Thank you for taking us with you," she says in a husky voice.

Jope is surprised and just a bit embarrassed at such an open display of affection, and in front of the crew, too. He knows that most of them don't understand why he did not trade the children away; he doesn't fully understand it himself, only that he is somehow fulfilling a divine purpose. Fortunately, his men respect their captain too much to question him, even if they look at him a bit askance and talk about him behind his back.

So Jope returns Margarita's hug and smiles kindly down at her. Juan stands off to one side watching. He is happy to stay aboard, too, but he is not one to wear his feelings on his sleeve.

For the next few weeks, the children roam freely above and below deck, from the *White Lion*'s beakhead to the stern gallery. At times they play hide-and-seek among the cannons and barrels stored in the hold, but more often they watch the crew go about their work. They sit with the sailors fixing pulleys and replacing rotted rope, visit the cook in the galley as he boils chunks of rock-hard salt pork and skims off the fat to be used later for making candles, and accompany the cooper on his rounds to make sure none of the water barrels has sprung a leak.

At first, some of the old tars growl at the children interrupting and asking endless questions. Others let them participate in their tasks, handle some of the tools, help with simple tasks, and teach them new words—bowsprit, capstan, topgallant and mizzen sail, orlop deck. The second mate, a young Welshman named Gareth, is especially friendly and introduces them to areas of the ship below deck they wouldn't be allowed to explore on their own. In time Margarita and Juan's innocent curiosity and excitement melt even the most hardened old salts, and everyone is happy to see them when they make their rounds.

Juan is fascinated by the sailors working high above deck. He wishes he could join them scurrying up the ratlines and shrouds and straddling the yardarms as they lash the sails to the wooden beams. Instead, he spends hours watching them adjust the rigging, shortening sails with martnets and clewlines to prevent them from getting damaged when the wind gusts, and then using the sheets to pull them taut again at the lower corners on calmer days to capture every bit of breeze and propel the ship forward.

Marmaduke, noticing his interest, takes Juan under his wing. He shows him how to use the compass and quadrant to determine the ship's position and course. He introduces him to the whipstaff below the quarterdeck, a long vertical lever that connects to the tiller another deck down, and explains how the helmsman steers the ship. The wooden rod is nearly twice as tall as Juan, but Marmaduke lets him hold it, steadying it from above. Juan feels the vibrations and force of the ocean waves and currents and holds on proudly with determination and the serious expression of a boy doing a man's job.

During supper, the children tell Jope all about their adventures and discoveries, and he marvels how much they absorb and how quickly they learn. He realizes that they are brighter than many of the members of his crew, who understand only the task at hand, and he wonders once again how they came to be so special.

With warm weather, clear skies, and fair winds for much of the voyage, it is a carefree time for Margarita and Juan, a respite from the suffering and hardship they have endured, an interlude before new difficulties rear their head. Margarita's nervous tic all but disappears. No longer bothered by seasickness, she loves watching the rising and falling waves and gets excited when large fish—the sailors call them "leviathans" or "whales"—rear up from the ocean and blow water-spouts into the air. In the evenings, she likes to sit in the stern gallery outside Jope's cabin and watch the blood-red sun sink into the sea.

From time to time she peppers Jope with questions about where they are going, and when he says, "Home," she feels a momentary twinge, knowing that it is his home, not hers. Beyond that she cannot imagine what he means when he talks fondly of "country estates," "moors," and "heath" and tries to explain what they are. How could she and Juan ever become part of that?

For Jope these questions are troubling for different reasons. He knows he is returning like Raleigh from his last expedition—from a failed voyage with nothing to show for it in the hold by way of booty and riches. His older brother will have to be patient and wait another year before seeing any return on his investment. Jope is confident that he will understand. What really gnaws at him is what to do about the children. How will Mary react? Where in the countryside can he hide them? And beyond that, how can he ensure their safety when he goes off on his next expedition?

Until he met with Rolfe and Tucker, he did not realize just how dangerous rescuing the destitute men and women from the *San Juan Bautista* would turn out to be. Looting a Spanish treasure ship of gold and jewels is a less risky endeavor—the spoils tell no tales after-ward. But these Africans are not only living reminders of the raid; at some point they could bear witness to what happened.

To England

He knows that Elfrith is in even greater trouble because he plundered the Spanish galleon with expired letters of marque under the English flag, and he still carries twenty Africans onboard as evidence. Jope's documents from Holland don't offer much protection either. King James, under the influence of the Spanish ambassador, does not recognize such legal subtleties as they pertain to Englishmen. If Jope was discovered with African children from the Spanish slaver, it would mean his head. He is grateful to Rolfe and Tucker for coming up with their plan for him to play the Dutchman for the authorities.

When he broaches the subject with Marmaduke, whom he has come to trust implicitly, the navigator is quiet for some time. He has wondered why his captain is taking such risks with the children. It is an unusual thing to do, even if it is because of divine inspiration, as Jope claims. As an ordained minister, he may know things others don't, but he is still taking a great risk that puts them all in danger. True, there is something special about the children, especially the boy, who is sharp and seems to have an affinity for the sea. He is certain that none of the crew members will talk. To do so would open them to charges of piracy, and no one is that foolish. "What happens aboard, stays aboard," as the saying goes.

"We can't sail into Plymouth," he volunteers. "Everyone there knows you for who you are, and there's bound to be talk about the children."

"What other choices do we have?"

Marmaduke searches for a map of England among the naval charts in Jope's cabin. He unfurls one on the cabin table, putting the pewter candle holders at either end to keep it from curling up. Pointing to specific spots, he says, "We can go to Bristol, or even Newport or Cardiff in Wales, and smuggle them ashore. From there you can take them overland to Cornwall, while I bring the *White Lion* to Plymouth."

Jope strokes his beard. "It's cumbersome, but makes sense. I say Bristol. It's the closest port."

The navigator eyes Jope thoughtfully before venturing, "It would be best if they can pass as being English, even with the dark color of their skin."

Jope nods. He has been thinking along the same lines. It occurs to him that Margarita and Juan also need protection from someone powerful enough to deflect idle questions and, if necessary, claim them as members of his household. The seeds of a plan are sprouting in his mind.

That evening at prayer before supper, when Margarita and Juan cross themselves, Jope stops in midsentence. Startled, the children look up and take note of the serious expression on his face.

"Have we done something bad?" Margarita asks.

"No. Not at all." He smiles reassuringly. "I know your faith in God and Jesus is strong, and the Portuguese nuns who taught you had your best interest at heart. But in England, our ways are different ways, and I must teach them to you. From this day forward, you cannot speak of your Catholic upbringing."

The children look at him bewildered.

"There is danger for you in England—evil people who do not understand who you are and might do you harm. You would not want to be returned to the ship where I found you, would you?"

The thought sends shivers down Margarita's spine, and her face twitches for the first time in weeks. She and Juan shake their heads vigorously.

"From now on, no more making the sign of the cross before prayer. Fold your hands by linking your fingers as you have seen me do."

He interlaces his fingers, and Margarita and Juan imitate him awkwardly.

"And you will go by your English names—Margaret and John. Marmaduke and I have told the crew to call you that from now on."

In response to the questioning looks on their faces, he points at them one at a time and says, "From now on you are Margaret. And you are John. "

Slowly, they repeat pointing to themselves. "Mar-ga-ret. John."

"We will practice," says Margaret earnestly. She turns to her companion and says, "You are John, like John Jope."

"John," he says and grins merrily. "Big John, little John! And you are Mar-ga-ret."

"We will practice," Margaret repeats.

The next day on deck, everyone calls the children John and Margaret as if they have had those names all their lives.

16

BRISTOL

England—Late October 1619

The weather gets decidedly cooler in the weeks before they glimpse the English shoreline. The children appreciate the woolen blankets Jope gives them to keep them warm at night. As they approach the coast and start to travel up the Bristol Channel, Margaret and John only catch glimpses of the seaside towns from the windows above the stern gallery because Jope insists that they stay inside the cabin. Large sailing ships attract the attention of the populace on shore—farmers and fishermen wave as they pass by—and he wants to make sure that they remain out of sight. The children endure as best they can the tedium of being cooped up again.

One morning, they hear orders being shouted, followed by the boatswain's high-pitched whistle and the sounds of feet running back and forth on deck. Before long, the *White Lion* glides to a halt and drops anchor; they have arrived in Bristol Harbor. The children can make out the masts and hulls of other ships, but they can't see what's on land because the stern of the ship faces away from the shore toward the channel.

Jope leaves soon after, wearing a wide-brimmed hat and his sword strapped to his side. He is gone for most of the day. When he returns late in the afternoon, he comes into the cabin and hands them each a small woolen overcoat with a hood. The one for Margaret fits her pretty well, but John's is much too big—he all but disappears inside it.

"I'll have it hemmed up," says Jope, pulling out a travel trunk from the corner. "We leave early tomorrow morning. I've hired a coach to take us south to Plymouth." Seeing the uncomprehending looks of the children, he adds, "We are going to travel over land."

He packs a change of clothes, some documents, and coins. Then he brings out two pistols and cleans them thoroughly, making sure they're in good order. "Just in case we meet up with some highwaymen," he explains, smiling grimly.

None of it makes any sense to Margaret and John. They've never seen firearms before. All they understand is that there is danger ahead and that their captain will take care of it.

Excited and apprehensive, they stay awake most of the night. At some point they doze off for what feels like minutes before Jope rouses them. Outside the sky is pitch-black. Even wearing her new coat with the hood drawn over her head, Margaret shivers in the chilly morning breeze.

Deckhands carrying lanterns escort them to the railing where Marmaduke is waiting. As he helps them over the railing, he says to Jope, "Safe travels. See you in Plymouth."

They climb down the side of the ship into a small dinghy bobbing in the water. Two sailors steady it against the hull of the ship while two others bring Jope's trunk. Gareth lifts the children one at a time from the rope ladder into the boat. Margaret is glad the second mate is going with them; she doesn't know Trevor and Corbin, their other two traveling companions, as well. She and John huddle together on Jope's trunk. The captain comes down last. When he is settled, the sailors push off from the *White Lion* and start to row to shore.

By the time they reach the dock, the sky in the east lights up with a sliver of blue. There are a few men ashore, setting up tables to get ready for when the fishermen come in with the fish they caught during the night. They look briefly in the direction of the boat and get on with their work. The four travelers step ashore with Jope's trunk, and the two sailors who brought them cast off quickly to return to the *White Lion.*

When the children climb up the stone steps to the wharf, they are in for a surprise. Standing in front of one of the buildings is a big wooden box the size of a small hut with wheels attached at both ends and an open door in the middle. A man bundled in a dark overcoat, his face hidden by a large cap, sits up high to one side. Four strange brown animals that look like zebras, only bigger, are hitched to the box in front of him, and leather straps lead down from his hands to their mouths.

Gareth notices their amazement and explains. "It's a called a coach or carriage. That's our driver up there and his horses. They'll pull us so we don't have to walk."

Before they can ask any questions, Trevor and Corbin have secured the trunk on a shelf in back of the carriage, and Jope hurries them inside. There are wooden seats on either side of the door. Margaret and John settle into one corner, and Gareth joins them, while the others take the opposite side. Jope steps inside last. He closes the door and calls out the window. There is a cracking sound. The coach jolts forward and starts to bump and clack over the cobblestones.

By the time they reach the outskirts of Bristol, the sky is bright with rose-colored light illuminating wisps of clouds. The cobblestones yield to dirt and clay, and they are riding at a more leisurely pace, but it is still rough going. Margaret and John can feel every rut, pothole, stone, tree root, and branch the coach bounces over. The other sailors, John, Corbin, and Gareth, seem uncomfortable, too. After being on the open decks of the *White Lion,* they don't like their cramped traveling accommodations any more than the children do.

As the sun comes up, they see lush green meadows and pastures out of the window in the door. They recognize the brown farm fields with yellowish stubble as having been harvested, but the forests they pass and travel through are overgrown with unfamiliar shrubs and trees. Gareth points out elms, poplars, and maple trees, covered with brightly colored leaves.

At times the coach stops to let small herds of animals cross the road. The children are excited when they see cattle, although they look different than the ones they know from Africa. But they're bewildered by the smaller, bleating creatures covered with curly white and yellow fur.

When they ask Jope, he says, "Those are sheep. And the 'fur' is actually wool. It's what your blankets and coats are made of."

The explanation leaves them even more confused. The dark woven cloth keeping them warm looks nothing like the fluffy yellow fleece of the animals.

That evening, they stop at an inn. It is the biggest house the children have ever seen, with dark upright timbers and crossbeams visible on the outside. They spend the night on the second floor, in a comfortable, toasty room much larger than the cabin on the *White Lion*. It has wood-paneled walls and a fire going in a stone enclosure. The beds are soft with straw mattresses, clean linens, and blankets.

The food is a new experience, too. Margaret likes the stew they get for supper, thick with vegetables—carrots, peas, and parsnips—and pieces of meat.

"It's called rabbit," Jope tells them.

To drink, the adults share with the children a sour-tasting liquid called beer, served in pewter tankards. When they pucker their faces in disgust, Jope laughs.

"You'll get used to it," he says. "It's good for you. The water will make you sick."

"Next time, we'll get you some cider," says Gareth, grinning.

Their favorite part of the meal by far are the sweet, stewed pears for dessert, and the men share amused glances as the children lick the wooden bowls clean to the last drop.

Early on, Jope has Margaret and John duck low in the coach as they meet the ostlers at the entrance to the courtyards of the inns where they stop for the night. Then he sneaks them upstairs into the private rooms. But after a day or two, he gets more lax. The children have to go to the privy at night and in the morning, and it becomes impossible to hide them from sight at all times.

At one of the stops along the post road, a constable from the nearby town, alerted to their presence, pays them a visit in the morning while they're eating their porridge. When he asks about their business, Jope puts on a Dutch-sounding accent and says, "We're castaways from a Flemish ship on our way to Portsmouth to find a ship to take us to Holland."

The official laughs and says, "Then you're headed the wrong way. This is the road to Exeter." He points out the direction they should be going.

"Much obliged," says Jope.

After that, they take to back roads to avoid the bigger towns. The inns and ale houses are less luxurious and comfortable. Some nights, they find a private home or farm willing to take in lodgers. Margaret and John are delighted to see chickens and goats in the farmyards—familiar creatures—and the rooster crowing in the morning brings back a flood of memories, not all of them unpleasant.

During the day, they eat cheese and bread they buy from their hosts.

Taking back roads means slower going and more travel through forests, where the musty smell of fallen leaves invades the coach. They encounter new animals—deer and foxes. At one point, they startle a brown rabbit. He raises his head in fright and then darts into the bushes. When Margaret asks Gareth what it is called and he tells her, she makes the connection between the living creature she's just seen hop away and the tasty meat in her stew.

Although the weather is mostly sunny and only the nights are cold, it rains on several occasions, and then the road becomes muddy and impassable for hours afterward.

"When are we going to see highwaymen?" asks John at some point.

Bristol

Jope laughs and replies, "With luck, we won't."

More often than not, he has to answer the age-old questions of every child getting tired of traveling: "How much longer?" and "Are we there yet?"

"Soon," Jope answers patiently. "Very soon."

But the closer they get to their destination, the more he worries and wonders how his wife, Mary, will respond when she sees the children.

17

THE BERMUDA COMPANY

London—November 1619

The November quarter court of the Virginia Company of London commences once again at the home of the Earl of Southampton. The great hall is filled to capacity with nattering shareholders awaiting the start of the meeting. But if they expected another explosive session, they are disappointed. To the relief of the main stockholders, matters proceed in a civilized manner without the squabbles and fireworks of previous gatherings. Although their legal battle continues in court, Captains Brewster and Argall have declared a truce of sorts, allowing them to encounter each other in public without coming to blows. While Edwin Sandys waits for a reply to his secret letter to Governor Yeardley, he has scaled back his attack on the Earl of Warwick for using Jamestown as a privateering base. News of the *Treasurer*'s arrival in Bermuda has deflected further accusations from other aggrieved parties, and Lord Rich has enjoyed the respite to the fullest, spending the fall hunting on his estate in Essex.

Yet, while Warwick and Sandys may have made peace for the time being, there is no love lost between them. Required by custom to sit next to each other at the council table, they act as if they occupied separate rooms. Warwick has his body turned away from his adversary and responds only to questions concerning company business. Sandys pretends to keep busy, conferring with Nicholas Ferrar and Southampton. Still, the lull in unwanted excitement bodes well for settling a number of important issues.

After calling the quarter court into session, Sandys begins with the announcement that Governor Yeardley has successfully instituted a democratic parliament in Virginia. As one of its first acts, the company deals with the petition of the House of Burgesses to make a few changes in the charter. The main modification concerns the proposed allocation of private land to newcomers who have paid for their passage from England to Jamestown. The Burgesses don't wish that share to come from the property of established planters "after so much labor and cost, and so many years habitation." Other requests include granting the male offspring of planters a share in the company, appointing a local treasurer to oversee finances in the colony, and sending more laborers for the plantations.

Sandys characterizes the petition as "humble, mild, and reasonable," and calls for a vote. There are only a few dissenting murmurs and many more hands raised in favor than against.

The report on some of the laws the Burgesses have passed on their own meets with a mixed response. When Sandys mentions the ban against attacks on Indians, some of the military veterans who spent time in Virginia scoff. The most vocal critic is John Smith, an early colonist who published two books about his adventures in Jamestown, including the time he was captured by the Powhatan Indians and only the intercession of Pocahontas saved his life.

With his full dark beard and flashing eyes beneath furrowed brows, he looks like an angry biblical prophet, and his voice carries the force of someone used to commanding soldiers. "These Indians cannot be trusted. They are a devious lot and they hate us, no matter how gentle and fawning their appearance." He declares, "We can rely only on the superiority of our English muskets to keep the colony safe."

Lord Cavendish jumps in, "They are wicked heathens who deserve any punishment they receive."

But the general assembly is not as bloodthirsty and agrees with Southampton when he suggests, "Why don't we let the settlers in Virginia be the judge of that?"

When Sandys reads the rest of the list of prohibitions—against idleness, gaming, drunkenness, and excess in apparel—there is general merriment. One wag calls out, "These laws would serve us well here in London," and he is rewarded with much laughter from the other attendees.

The setting of the price of tobacco, the crop that everyone hopes will make them rich, passes without comment. The announcement that the settlers may purchase provisions not readily available from the magazine ship from other suppliers provokes grumblings from the Smythe faction, but Sandys disposes of them quickly, pointing out that the matter has been settled since the last quarter court.

Then he turns to the most important business of the day. "As you all know, the population of Virginia is in great need of further settlement and greater stability," he announces. "Therefore, after considerable discussion, the council has decided that the next shipment to Jamestown will, along with the regular supplies, include 100 women."

Before the assembled shareholders have time to react, Southampton springs to his feet and says, "We understand that it is a radical proposal, a change in the practice of shipping able-bodied men, regardless of their background, to replenish the labor supply needed for the cultivation of tobacco."

He turns to the most prominent Puritan among the shareholders and yields the floor to the Earl of Warwick, who rises with a suitable air of self-importance and says, "I have no objections. On the contrary, I believe that there is nothing more important than to encourage the formation of families in the colony." He pauses for effect and continues, "Ensuring a stable, self-sustaining community is the only way I see to put the company on sound financial footing and stem the tide of mounting debt."

The well-coordinated presentation on the part of the council members precludes objections on financial and religious grounds, and discussion proceeds without the usual melodramatic outbursts of those voicing their objections. Soon, Sandys is able to call for a vote, and the measure passes by an overwhelming margin.

When the Virginia Company's quarter court adjourns, there is a break before the meeting of the Somers Island Company. Since many of the larger shareholders—Warwick, Smythe, Sandys, Southampton, Cavendish, and Ferrar—hold stock in both ventures, they have conveniently arranged to convene the gatherings back-to-back. The smaller shareholders who have invested only in the Virginia enterprise vacate the premises while others arrive for the business of the Bermuda Colony.

Much to Warwick's pleasure, Thomas Weston is away on a trip to Holland and does not stalk him today to inquire after the status of the Leiden Separatists' petition. The earl has been working on finding them a suitable place to establish a colony in America, but progress is slow.

Just as he is about to leave the council table to seek out his cousin Nathaniel, Southampton approaches him. "A word with you, Robert?"

Warwick would prefer to avoid the conversation, but he follows his handsome host to one of the windows. People give them a wide berth as they stand next to each other like the best of friends, surveying the assembled group and bowing ceremoniously to the notable arrivals.

Southampton smiles and says, "That went surprisingly well."

Warwick nods, wondering what Southampton has up his sleeve.

The earl continues, "What do you make of the rumors that two Africans and four Flemish sailors having been sighted in Somerset a week ago?"

It is news to Rich, and he is instantly on guard, although nothing betrays his heightened sense of alertness. He flicks a speck of dust from his brocade doublet and says languidly, "I haven't the slightest idea, Henry. Any word on whether they've been seen since?"

Southampton shakes his head. "No. No one seems to know where they went."

Warwick has a pretty good idea where they have come from and gone to, having received secret letters from Rolfe and Pory informing him of what transpired at Jamestown in August. He pretends to give it some thought. Finally he volunteers, "Bermuda is too far for them to be part of the *Treasurer's* cargo. Too bad, really, since Captain Elfrith swears his Africans were properly obtained."

"Yes, that is not at issue," says Southampton. He adjusts the collar of his doublet. "The question is *who* they belong to."

Warwick hears the warning tone, but responds teasingly, "Aye, there's the rub. And here I thought we were having a pleasant conversation, Henry."

Southampton bows in acknowledgment. "Just wanted to give you fair warning which way the wind is blowing."

"I am in your debt."

Pleasantries concluded, Southampton returns to his seat.

Warwick looks after him thoughtfully. The earl didn't have to alert him about an ambush from Sandys—he is expecting as much—but what Southampton didn't say is as significant as his warning.

When Elfrith's badly damaged ship lumbered into Bermuda's harbor in September, then acting governor Kendall, a Sandys man, impounded the *Treasurer* and confiscated its human cargo, claiming fourteen of the thirty Africans for himself. Four weeks later when Nathaniel Butler arrived to take over the governorship, he forced Kendall to give them up and settled them on Warwick's tobacco plantation. The rest were dispersed among other landowners. Sandys didn't take kindly to the news.

Warwick gestures to Captain Argall and Nathaniel Rich. When they come over, he points to a squirrel on the lawn outside the window and whispers, "Be prepared for a blistering attack from

Sandys about the ownership of the Africans on the *Treasurer*, and keep your heads. They don't know what happened at Jamestown—yet."

Sure enough, when Southampton calls the meeting of the Somers Island Company to order, the thirty Africans Elfrith brought to Bermuda are the main bone of contention.

Sandys, speaking softly, engages in a legal argument, "Since the *Treasurer* was carrying supplies on behalf of the Virginia and Somers Companies and is technically leased to them, all cargo—human and otherwise—belongs to the company shareholders."

Lord Cavendish adds, "It is only fair that Lord Rich return his fourteen Africans or pay a fair price for them."

Warwick, a thin smile on his lips, replies from his place at the council table. "In the interest of fairness, may I inquire at whose behest Governor Kendall impounded my ship?"

Argall joins the fray from the floor. "And for what reason? That's what I'd like to know."

That brings Sandys to his feet. "The Earl of Warwick and Captain Argall are trying to muddy the waters. The only thing at issue here is who the Africans belong to."

Rising swiftly, Warwick declares with calculated fury in his voice, "No, gentlemen, I refuse to answer to the issue of ownership until this disgrace is addressed. This is about the rights of an Englishman for due process. I have been denied my property from the beginning on dubious grounds. Will no one here admit to having given that illegal order?"

Assenting calls of "Yes, tell us!" "We have a right to know who," and "This is unpatriotic!" erupt from members of his faction.

Sandys's supporters retaliate with mocking shouts and catcalls worthy of the unruly crowds at the theaters in Southwark.

Warwick looks pointedly at Sandys. He has a good idea that he gave the order but is loath to admit it, having argued against that kind of tyrannical overreach himself in Parliament when King James claimed that he was above the law.

It's a standoff. Sandys knows that he has lost this round. It galls him that Warwick wraps himself in the mantle of patriotism and stands upon the laws he flaunts whenever it is convenient for him! But for now he has to admit defeat. He signals his supporters to calm down and suggests that the discussion be tabled for later and go on to other business.

Warwick smiles to himself. He knows that he has done little more than postpone the inevitable. At some point he will have to deal with the ownership of the Africans—in a court of law, no doubt. In the meantime, it gives him a great feeling of satisfaction to have spit in Edwin Sandys's eye. What will happen when it comes out that the *Treasurer* first banked at Jamestown is another, more dangerous matter altogether.

18
MARY
Tavistock—November 1619

Aweek later, the travelers reach the Dartmoor, a bleak, hilly expanse of low shrubbery and grasslands with nary a tree in sight. The rugged outcrops of rocks Jope calls "tors" remind Margaret of Pongo. Unlike her homeland, however, this is a forbidding and unwelcoming landscape. She can't understand why Jope raved about it when they were still at sea. Looking at the gray mist outside the carriage, she shudders and draws her blanket closer around her.

An air of restlessness has overtaken Jope. He knows they are nearing the end of their journey and is already anticipating their arrival. But near Lydford a violent thunderstorm overtakes them. Bolts of lightning strike the ground nearby, and the wind whips curtains of rain across the open land. They make it to the small, nearby village and seek shelter in a tavern and spend the night.

The next morning a rooster crowing at the break of dawn signals clear weather ahead. Soon the sun comes out and burns off the blankets of fog covering the brown heath and peat bogs. Jope impatiently hurries the children to get dressed and eat their breakfast. When they're ready to head out, he climbs onto the box seat up front next to the coachman to give him directions as they get close to their destination.

With the moors behind them, some of the land turns green again. Margaret marvels at the verdant meadows and hillsides beyond stubbled fields. Mid-morning they arrive at the River Tavy. The water flows high on the banks from the November rains, and as they enter the ford, it soon reaches up to the hubs of the wheels. Midway in the river when one of the horses loses its footing and stumbles, they come to a sudden halt and remain stuck, despite the coachman yelling and cracking his whip. Margaret is terrified that they'll have to wade the rest of the way, remembering the time she nearly drowned. It isn't until Corbin, Trevor, and Gareth get out and push the carriage from behind that they get moving again and make it safely across.

The land rises gradually on the other side, and the horses have no difficulty climbing the winding road up the hillside. As they come over the rise, Jope suddenly whoops in joy and shouts, "Tavistock!"

Sticking their heads out the carriage window, the children see a town ahead with tall houses built of gray stones. The gabled roofs are covered with dark, blue-gray slate tiles and topped with black and gold weather vanes.

Jope shows the coachman a path that keeps them on the outskirts, and before long they come to a large wrought-iron gate. The driveway leads to a pleasant-looking two-story house. To Margaret it looks like one of the small inns where they stayed on their journey.

When the carriage pulls up to the front door, Jope leaps to the ground. Margaret and John, unsure of what to do, remain inside the safety of the carriage while Gareth, Trevor, and Corbin unload his travel trunk.

Jope takes several silver coins from his purse and hands them to the coachman. "Thank you, Hugh," he says, and points south. "That'll take you to the road to Plymouth. When you get there, take my men wherever they want to go in town." Then he holds up another coin. "I'd appreciate if you would keep quiet about this trip."

Hugh's look mingles covetousness with cunning. "Understood, Captain," he says, grinning. "I'll be as quiet as a grave."

The front door of the house opens, and a servant woman, wearing a cap and white apron over her brown dress, comes out.

"Sarah," Jope calls to her. "Where is your mistress?"

A smile of recognition crosses her face. "It's the captain!" she exclaims. "We didn't know to expect you. The mistress is out back in the garden."

"Well, what are you waiting for?" Jope says, laughing. "Go fetch her!"

Sarah hikes up her skirts and hurries back inside.

As Gareth helps the children down from the coach, Jope turns to Trevor and Corbin. He shakes their hands and presses a coin into each of their palms. "Marmaduke will have your wages. This is something extra. Godspeed and safe journey."

The two tars salute and climb into the carriage.

Gareth bends down to John and says, "Next time, we'll have you in the crow's nest in no time." He tousles his hair and gives Margaret a peck on the cheek. Then he straightens and salutes Jope. "See you in Plymouth, Captain."

He leaps up onto the carriage box next to Hugh. A flick of the whip and they're off. Jope and the children wave after them.

A voice calls out from behind them. "John!"

They turn to see a pretty young woman come running toward them. She is wearing a faded blue bodice and skirt, and her blond tresses bounce at the side of her beaming face. "You are home and safe!" she cries out and throws her arms around Jope. Then she covers his face with kisses.

Jope responds in kind. At some point, he holds her at arm's length to get a good look at her. His eyes sparkle with delight as he strokes her cheek and hair. "It's a fine thing to see you, Mary Jope, and good to be home."

Suddenly she notices the children, and her expression changes from pleasure to puzzlement. "John, what is the meaning of this?"

Jope smiles and gestures to the children to come forward. "Mary, this is Margaret and John."

Margaret curtsies and little John bows, as they have been taught. There is an awkward pause. No one knows what to say.

Mary

Finally Jope says, "These children are a gift from the Lord, Mary." When she continues to look dubious, he adds, "Why don't we go inside and I'll tell you all about it?"

He picks up the travel trunk as if it weighed no more than a serving tray and heads toward the house. Mary and the children follow, eyeing each other uncertainly.

* * *

Inside, the practical Sarah takes over, bustling Margaret and John into the kitchen. From the entrance hall they pass through a cheerful drawing room with comfortable furnishings and a stone fireplace. Sunlight pours through large windows overlooking a garden and meadows and trees beyond.

In the kitchen, Sarah shuts the door and ushers the children to a table where bread, milk, and cheese are waiting. At first, they take only small, tentative bites, but at Sarah's prodding they soon dig in heartily. At some point, they hear raised voices coming from the drawing room and look up anxiously. While they can't make out the words, they know that they are the cause of the argument, and the haunted expressions that appear on their faces touch Sarah's kind heart.

"It is so pleasant outside. Let us go outside and explore the garden," she says, and Margaret and John follow her eagerly.

In the drawing room, Mary paces agitatedly by the fireplace, her face flushed. "You pirated them from a Spanish warship?"

"I could not leave them to die a miserable death as slaves."

"They are stolen Spanish cargo. Here! On Glanville grounds!" Her voice rises higher with each exclamation. "This cannot be! How will we explain their presence here in the house my uncle gave us?"

Jope stands awkwardly, not sure how to reach her. "I tell you, these children are a gift from our Lord. They are so far beyond their years. I just know they have a special purpose. They are my destiny!"

Mary looks at her husband as if he was mad. When Jope tries to take her hand, she shies away and goes to the window. He follows, pleading, "Mary, they know of our Lord and Savior. He placed them in my path. I cannot turn away from my holy duty."

His solemn tone touches her. When she turns to him, there are tears in her eyes. "Oh, John, I understand you and your circumstances. You are a good man. But my uncle is a member of Parliament. His name will be tarnished if they are discovered here."

"It was never my purpose for them to stay with us," he says. "I just want them to be safe while I figure out how to take care of them. But I need your uncle's help."

She looks up at him with questioning eyes and lets him lead her to an oak bench near the windows. They sit, and he tells her his plan.

* * *

While they await Sir John Glanville's return from London, the uneasy truce in the house soon turns to acceptance. Mary's kind nature, sweet disposition, and sense of humor make it impossible for her to stay angry. She marvels at the children's resilience after she hears about their horrific experiences. For their part, Margaret and John try to fit as best they can into a way of living they know nothing about, which leads to amusing misunderstandings.

The first evening in their bedroom, John finds a clay chamber pot. When he asks Jope why there is a drinking jug under the bed, the captain is for once at a loss for words. Seeing him all flustered, Mary laughs with mirth. Good-humoredly, Jope shrugs helplessly and joins in. Margaret and John trade glances, unsure of what the adults find so funny, but happy to see them in good spirits.

The next day, Mary tends her garden. The flowers are no longer in bloom, but some of the herbs are ready for harvest. When she notices Margaret watching her from the doorway, uncertain but curious, she beckons her over. She crushes a thyme sprig and some rosemary between her fingers, holds them under Margaret's nose, and is pleased to see her eyes widen in wonder and delight. Later, she shows her the dried versions in the kitchen cupboard and adds new words to Margaret's vocabulary—sage, rosemary, fennel, savory, tarragon, mace, nutmeg, cloves, and mustard.

By the time they get news of Sir Glanville's arrival, Mary has to admit to herself that she has grown quite attached to the girl and boy.

* * *

Leaving the children in Sarah's care, Mary and Jope attend a family gathering at her uncle's mansion. The clan includes his family, Mary's parents, two sisters and three older brothers, and some of their children.

Sir John Glanville welcomes them into his home. Like Jope, he has a full beard, but his is brown—as are his eyes, which don't miss much. He is a few years younger and not as muscular as Jope, and an appreciation for good food and drink has left him more rotund at the waist. He has the weighty bearing of a man who believes in the importance of his work as a lawyer and a member of Parliament.

Mary asks his blessing like a good niece and his eyes light on her—he has always had a special feeling for her. When he kisses her, she leans close to him and whispers in his ear, "John needs to see you alone sometime today."

Glanville glances at Jope, who nods imperceptibly.

Dinner is a lavish three-course affair with meat pies, roasted capons, boiled lamb, cucumbers, carrots, parsnips, cakes, and gingerbread. It is a trying occasion for Jope because everyone wants to hear about his exploits and adventures. He deflects their questions as best he can—without treasure, he cannot talk about his raid on the Spanish galleon—and entertains them with tales of Havana and storms at sea. He is glad when the meal is finished and Mary and her mother and sisters repair to the drawing room for games with the children while her father, cousins, and brothers go off to smoke tobacco and indulge in after-dinner conversation.

Glanville invites Jope to his study, a dark room with wood-paneled walls and oak furniture. One shelf is filled with heavy books, legal tomes mostly. He offers Jope a pipe of tobacco. "From Virginia. It's smoother than the stuff from the Caribbean or Bermuda."

When Jope declines, Glanville says, "Surely I can tempt you with a glass of Madeira? The Spaniards may be godless heathens, but they do know how to make a good wine."

Once again Jope shakes his head.

Glanville pours himself a glass from a crystal decanter and settles into a large wooden armchair, rearranging the pillows beneath him until he feels comfortable. He gestures for Jope to sit in a chair opposite and asks, "Now, what is this all about?"

He listens in silence as Jope tells of rescuing Margaret and John and sailing to Virginia, keeping to the story he agreed to at Jamestown. Glanville affects a genial manner, occasionally taking a swallow of wine, but his watchful eyes never leave Jope's face. The only time he expresses surprise is when Jope mentions the *Treasurer* appearing at Jamestown. That revelation has not been part of the version that has been making the rounds in London.

Nor does Glanville interrupt when Jope outlines his plan of approaching the Earl of Warwick for help. Lord Rich's stepmother and step-aunt, Lady Frances and Lady Isabel Darcy, are both radical Protestants who helped Puritan ministers when they lost their livelihood on account of their beliefs, and he thinks one of them might willingly hide Margaret and John.

He concludes passionately, "They gave support to our new order without question because they believed it to be their destiny, just as these children are mine."

Glanville finishes his wine as he ponders Jope's situation. Then he puts the empty glass on the silver tray on the table next to him.

Mary

He clasps his hands before his chin and says, "I knew who you were and what you were planning to do when you asked for my niece's hand; so I will not withdraw my support now, however tempting it may be."

Having offered that slight reprimand on behalf of his family, he continues as a practical man of the world. "You were wise to come to me. I am on familiar terms with Lord Rich through our mutual interests in the Americas and can facilitate a meeting with him. You may not know that he played a blackamoor as a boy in a theater masquerade called *The Masque of Blackness.* Your African just might intrigue him." Leaning forward, he adds, conspiratorially, "His aunt might well serve your needs, but given his negative feelings about his stepmother, I don't think mentioning Lady Frances would be a good idea."

Jope is about to express his gratitude when Glanville holds up his hand. "I can open the door, but nothing more."

"That is all I wish for," says Jope.

A small smile plays at the corners of Glanville's lips. "Why don't you have Mary invite me over before I go back to London? I wish to observe what she has done with her garden and see your Africans with my own eyes."

19

THE BARGAIN

London—December 1619

Sir John Glanville is good to his word, and a week later Jope is granted an audience with the Earl of Warwick. He rides to London on horseback, changing mounts every ten miles at the postal stations, and makes the trip, which takes coach travelers more than a week, in just three days. He spends the night at his uncle-in-law's townhouse.

The next morning he rises early, puts on his best Venetian breeches and burgundy doublet, dons his broad-brimmed hat with feather, and arrives at Lord Rich's townhouse before the church bells strike ten o'clock.

When Alfred ushers him into the anteroom of Warwick's study, two men are waiting there already. By their simple dark breeches, coats, and white collars, Jope recognizes them as Puritan Separatists from Holland. Absorbed in conversation, they look up briefly and, when he introduces himself, tell him their names: John Carver and Robert Cushman. Then they return to murmuring quietly to each other.

Jope removes his sword and takes a seat on an upholstered chair. From time to time, Cushman looks up at him from beneath his bushy eyebrows. The first time Jope nods courteously, and thereafter ignores him.

The Bargain

When Alfred calls him, Jope rises and marches into the study like a man about to be knighted. The heels of his shoes click smartly on the stone floor, but then he halts in midstride, surprised. There are two men standing by a dark oak table covered with maritime charts. He had expected to meet only with Lord Rich.

The younger man is handsome with black curly hair, a fashionable short beard and mustache, and a face whitened by makeup. He is wearing a green silk doublet with matching breeches and satin slippers, and looks at him with calculating interest. Jope has never seen such a fancy garment before and realizes he is looking at the earl. Only a man as wealthy as Warwick could afford it.

The other man has a darker face with a full brown beard and the tanned, weathered skin of someone who has spent many years at sea. He is wearing a leather jerkin with stuffed sleeves. When he steps forward, he appraises Jope like a general evaluating a new recruit.

Jope removes his hat with a flourish and bows to the earl. "M'Lord. Captain John Colyn Jope at your service."

Warwick nods his head, an ironic smile playing about his lips. "So this is our Dutchman. I must say, he is everything John Rolfe promised."

At the mention of Rolfe's name, Jope perks up his ears. The conspirator he met at Point Comfort must have been in contact with the earl. He wonders how much Lord Rich knows already.

Warwick indicates the older man beside him. "I have asked Captain Argall to join our conversation. As part owner of the *Treasurer*, he is most interested in what you have to say."

Argall comes forward and shakes Jope's hand. "Glad to meet you, Captain. We are somewhat acquainted with what transpired at Jamestown, but we're eager to hear from someone who has firsthand knowledge."

Rich adds, confirming Jope's suspicion, "Yes, Rolfe sent a letter—understandably vague—and we want to know what really happened."

He gestures for Jope to be seated on a plush sofa by the fireplace while he occupies a large armchair across from him. Argall takes a smaller chair between them.

Sinking into the soft upholstery, so unlike the solid wooden furniture on his ship and in his home, Jope feels uncomfortable. Leaning forward, he asks, "Do you know if Daniel Elfrith is safe?"

Warwick snorts derisively. "Yes, he is sitting pretty in Bermuda. I'm afraid the *Treasurer* is a total loss, though. Apparently, it was a small miracle that he made it there at all."

Jope nods, pleased. At Warwick's prompting, he launches into an account of his adventures, starting with meeting Elfrith in Havana. Rich and Argall listen carefully, interrupting only occasionally to ask for further clarification. But when Jope gets to Point Comfort and Tucker telling him about his orders from Governor Yeardley to impound the *Treasurer* upon arrival, they both shift in their chairs.

"Do you know from whence these orders came?" Argall asks pointedly.

Jope realizes this is something they did not know beforehand. "Tucker told me they came from London," he says. "Later on, John Rolfe mentioned a letter from Sir Edwin Sandys to the governor that came in July, which said as much."

At that, Warwick erupts from his chair, shouting, "I knew it! That windbag bastard has had it in for me all along. I could wring his scrawny Puritan neck!"

Amazed at the earl's outburst, Jope looks for help to Argall and receives a reassuring shrug. They watch Warwick pace to and fro, muttering, until he has himself under control and returns to his chair. He sits, brushing his satin breeches as if nothing has happened, and looks up expectantly.

Continuing with his account, Jope describes the arrival of the *Treasurer* and the meeting with Elfrith, Rolfe, Pierce, Ewen, and Tucker, in which they hatched the plan to use the *White Lion* and his legitimate letters of marque from the Prince of Nassau to conceal what really happened.

Rich, fully recovered, smiles at Jope and opines, "I must say, it is a most excellent solution to a most difficult problem." Then his eyes narrow. "But why would you agree to it? It can't be just to save your childhood friend?"

Jope considers how best to proceed. "This is what I came to talk to your Lordship about, but I would appreciate it if we could discuss it in private."

A cunning expression appears on Warwick's face. A glance and slight nod to Argall, and the captain rises and says, "I'll make my excuse then for the moment."

"Take the map with you and show the Separatists from Leiden the Hudson River," Warwick calls to him. "I will speak with them anon."

Argall rolls up one of the charts on the table. As he leaves, he says to Jope, "Captain, it is a pleasure to meet you."

Jope nods. "Likewise."

Before Argall has shut the door behind him, Warwick turns to Jope, all business. "Now, what is on your mind?"

Jope decides it is time for a bit of fawning. "I appreciate you making time for me in your busy schedule, m'Lord," he says humbly. "I have a favor to ask."

Warwick waves his hand impatiently. "Enough with the flattery, Captain. I understand you're a forthright man. Out with it!"

So Jope tells him about rescuing Margaret and John from the *San Juan Bautista* and how he got the idea to have the earl's aunt hide them at her home in Yorkshire, because she is known for supporting Puritan causes.

To his consternation, Warwick burst out laughing. "Two African children from a Spanish slaver here in England? You must be mad. I have listened to a lot of harebrained schemes, but this one's deranged enough to land you in Bedlam."

"I can scarcely believe it myself, m'Lord. If I didn't know with all my heart that they are a gift from God, I'd be the first one to have myself committed to the lunacy asylum."

Warwick looks at him with renewed interest. "You believe this is your God-given mission?"

"It is my destiny."

"I knew you were a man of the cloth, Captain—a most unusual background for a privateer—but I had no idea your beliefs are so strong."

"It is my destiny!" Jope repeats with conviction.

Pulling at his beard, Warwick rises and walks to the window. "I am well-disposed toward you, Captain," he says, with his back to Jope. "I am potentially in your debt, and I reward those who are loyal to me and my cause."

Jope approaches him eagerly. "I will gladly take the blame. If necessary, I'll swear under oath that I raided the *San Juan Bautista* alone and that Elfrith purchased his Africans from me."

Warwick observes him carefully. "Oh, it would be necessary. You'd have to swear out an affidavit, and you'd have to stay hidden. No one who sees you in person will believe that you're a Dutchman."

"I am yours. You can count on me, m'Lord."

"What about the others on your ship?"

"My crew will back me, including my navigator, Marmaduke. It's their necks, too."

Warwick is pleased that there is no hesitation in Jope's replies. He thinks for a moment and says, "My dear Aunt Isabel is actually a good candidate. She's kind and just mad enough to go along with this scheme of yours. And she likes me, so she'll listen to me, unlike her sister, that greedy, good-for-nothing harridan."

Afraid that he's about to erupt again, Jope quickly interjects, "M'Lord?"

But Warwick is already considering the implications. "It is a worthy proposition. Let me ponder on it this day. You are lodging in town?"

"Yes, at my wife's uncle's."

"Sir Glanville is a good man. Alfred!"

Jope is startled at the quicksilver change in Warwick's demeanor and even more surprised when the butler materializes as if he has been in the room all along, waiting in the shadows to carry out the earl's wishes.

"See Captain Jope out."

Much as he would prefer a certain answer, Jope knows this is all he will get this day, and it is more than he hoped for. He bows. "M'Lord, I will await your word."

He dons his hat and leaves. In the anteroom, Argall is in animated conversation with the two Separatists. He gets up and gestures for them to go into Rich's study.

Before he joins them, he stops and turns to Jope. "I hope you got what you came for, Captain."

"Time will tell," says the Dutchman.

* * *

He doesn't have to wait long. Early the next morning, a messenger calls at his lodgings, inviting him to another audience with the earl.

This time Warwick is dressed in a lilac velvet doublet and matching gathered trunk-hoses whose folds extend to just above his knees. He greets Jope warmly and comes to the point without delay. "I have considered the matter and decided to grant your request, Captain."

Jope bows, barely able to contain his joy. "I can't thank you enough, m'Lord!"

"Just make sure you stick to your story."

Alfred materializes and takes Jope to another room, where Argall, a scribe, and someone he doesn't recognize are waiting for him. The unfamiliar man's clothes are stylish, though not as fancy as Sir Robert's outfits, and he has shrew eyes that take in Jope from head to toe.

Argall introduces him. "This is Sir Nathaniel Rich, the Earl of Warwick's cousin, a member of Parliament."

"I know your wife's uncle, Sir John Glanville, well, Captain Jope," he says. "We both have legal backgrounds and share certain interests regarding the Americas."

Jope bows to him, realizing that he is here in his role as Warwick's attorney and confidant to make sure his testimony is suitable.

"Time to tell your story again, Captain," says Argall, grinning.

For the next hour, Jope gives the Dutchman's version of what happened at Point Comfort. He goes slowly so that the scribe can follow and write it down. When he is finished and has signed the document, Nathaniel Rich witnesses it.

Suddenly, Warwick sweeps into the room. He looks to his cousin and receives a slight nod. He picks up a sealed letter from a side table and hands it to Jope.

"This is a note introducing you to my aunt Isabel Wray Darcy," he explains. "You will find her a sharp-witted woman, and you'll do well to convince her that it is God's will that brought the children to her, not just mine. I will send word to her. By the time you arrive, she will be well acquainted with what we are asking her to do."

Sputtering with gratitude, Jope says, "I don't know what to say, m'Lord."

Warwick waves him off. "This is in the way of a straightforward business deal, Captain." Then he smiles, but his eyes are hard as flint. "We must be sure to keep both sides of the bargain."

Jope appreciates the velvet threat of a powerful man who won't take kindly to being crossed. He smiles in turn and says, "You have my word, m'Lord."

"In that case, it would be good if you set out to sea again—soon. You will need to be far from the clutches of the law when this matter becomes public, as it no doubt will."

"I will make preparations to leave as soon as I have delivered the children, m'Lord."

The Bargain

With matters settled, Warwick makes as if to leave, but stops at the door and says, as an afterthought. "You'll have to do without your navigator, though. I have a personal mission for him, befitting his talents and knowledge of the Virginia coast. When you get back to Plymouth, send Marmaduke to me. Tell him it will be worth his while."

Although taken aback, Jope understands immediately that Warwick wants to exercise more personal control over Marmaduke. It is a small price to pay, and he bows politely in acknowledgment. Then he slides the letter into his doublet and takes his leave.

When he emerges from the dark entrance hall into the street, the sun is shining and he has to squint until his eyes adjust to the bright day. For the first time in months he feels like a burden has lifted from him. He feels light on his feet and muses that if he weren't a serious minister and pirate, he just might dance a jig for joy.

20
LADY ISABEL
Aldwarke—December 1619

To deliver the children to Aldwarke in Yorkshire, Jope hires a frigate. The ship is smaller and sleeker than the *White Lion* and cuts through the winter waves with greater speed. Little John enjoys the choppy voyage, which sends salty spray over the bow on their way through the English Channel and the North Sea, but Margaret is seasick again and spends most of the voyage in the cabin. She is much relieved when they finally make land at the town of Hull on the Humber River and transfer to a coach for the trip to Aldwarke Manor, even if it is a jarring, bumpy ride.

It is an overcast day and noticeably colder in Yorkshire than in Devon, and she and John bundle up in blankets. As they travel past York, she hears the bells from the cathedral and notices the three belfries towering over the town. She thinks back on their time in Tavistock. In the few weeks they spent there, she became quite attached to Sarah and Mary, and neither she nor John wanted to leave.

But when they ask Jope why they have to go, he explains, regretfully, "It's the only way for you to be safe."

When they say their good-byes, they all have tears in their eyes. Margaret wonders if she will ever see Mary or Sarah again.

By midday they reach the Ouse, a wide, slow river, and watch a tree branch drift by lazily. Traveling along the eastern bank, they enter a forest. Most of the trees have lost their leaves, and the gnarled, bare branches of oak and chestnut trees reaching into the gray sky look unwelcoming and foreboding. When they get to the other side, however, the sweeping meadows and farmlands bordered by low fieldstone walls are more appealing.

Soon they approach the outskirts of a small town—Aldwarke. A shepherd directs them, and they travel on a rutted country lane until they come to a large gate with high stone walls on either side. The long driveway lined by tall poplars leads to a large manor house. It is by far the most elaborate edifice Margaret and John have ever seen.

The façade of the main building is made of dark red bricks and gray stones and has large windows on the ground floor. The steep roof, lined with dormers and chimneys, looks like someone planted a small row of houses there. A large side wing extends toward them on one side with the skeletons of bare trees partially obscuring the view. On the other side, several large, connected utility buildings—Jope points out that they contain a dairy, bakery, smithy, and stables— complete the horseshoe shape of the estate.

As Margaret and John step down from the coach and Jope escorts them to the entrance, the cold, wet December wind chills them to the bones. One of the great oak doors swings open, and a butler dressed in black livery welcomes them inside. He ushers them through a large entrance hall and a spacious drawing room into a parlor.

"Lady Darcy is expecting you. She will be along shortly," he declares and withdraws, closing the door after him.

The children go to the stone fireplace and huddle before the crackling, glowing logs to warm themselves. Jope looks around at the upholstered furniture, elaborate wall tapestries, and high, timber-beamed ceiling.

Moments later, an elderly woman dressed in a black bodice and gown, her silver-gray hair pinned up under an embroidered coif, enters the room. Lady Isabel Wray Darcy may be small of stature, but she has a naturally regal bearing. While she doesn't wear any jewelry, her outfit made of glistening, coal-black silk conveys wealth and stature. She has an aquiline face with thin, tight lips.

Jope removes his hat and bows gracefully. "Thank you for seeing us, m'Lady."

He introduces Margaret and John, who curtsy and bow awkwardly.

Lady Isabel surveys her visitors with lively gray eyes that seem to take in everything important—the children's makeshift clothes, their anxious expressions, and their guardian's muscular, bearlike presence.

Taking a letter from his doublet and handing it over, Jope says, "I have a dispatch from the Earl of Warwick to explain our appearance in your home."

As Lady Darcy breaks the seal, she replies, "My nephew has acquainted me with this matter in some detail." She peruses the letter and continues, "I would like to hear more from your own lips, however."

She turns to Margaret and John. "Do they speak any English?"

"Poorly, your Ladyship. Only the small amount I have taught them," Jope offers. "I have found that they speak a bit of Dutch, too." He purposely doesn't mention their greater proficiency in Spanish.

Lady Darcy walks over to the children. As she extends her palm to John, he impulsively hides his hands behind his back, scowling up at her. Jope is mortified.

But her stern expression yields to a smile. "I am Aunt Isabel, John. You will be safe here."

She takes one of Margaret's hands in both of hers. "You must be hungry from your journey. Would you like something to eat?"

When Margaret nods, shyly, Aunt Isabel calls out in a surprisingly loud voice, "Agnes!"

Lady Isabel

A side door opens, and a pale-faced, matronly woman wearing a simple brown dress enters the parlor. Younger and plumper than her mistress, she curtseys. "Yes, m'Lady."

"Come and meet the children. This is Margaret and John. They will be staying with us for some time. Take them to their part of the house for some food, and find them some proper attire while I speak with Captain Jope."

"Yes, m'Lady."

If Agnes is surprised at the appearance of the African children, she hides it well. She bustles over to them like a mother hen and fusses, "You two must be hungry and tired from your journey! Well, come with me, and we'll soon take care of that."

Margaret and John relax, but when Agnes takes them by the hand and starts to usher them from the room, Margaret's eyes grow wide with fear and her cheek twitches. She looks pleadingly to Jope, who nods reassuringly and gestures for her to go along.

When the door closes after them, he exhales slowly. Things are going better than expected. He won't have to persuade their host to take the children into her care. But he soon discovers that it doesn't mean he gets off scot free.

Lady Darcy fixes on him with her clear gray eyes and inquires, "My nephew tells me that you are a Calvinist minister and this situation is something of a mission for you."

"Yes, m'Lady. Margaret and John are a gift to me from God. They are chosen souls and my destiny."

Hearing cast-iron conviction in his voice, she nods. "You are an unusual man, Captain Jope, not at all the rough privateer I expected. Come walk with me. At my age I like to keep moving whenever I can."

As they amble through a large meeting hall toward the west wing of the mansion, Jope tells her how and where he found the children, why he brought them to England, and why he needs a safe haven for them. From time to time, Lady Isabel asks him clarifying questions. Her manner brooks no dissemblance, and he tells her more than

174

he meant to, explaining that they are Christians but were raised by Catholic nuns.

"They are in need of a good Puritan education, as well as a good upbringing," he concludes.

If Lady Darcy is shocked by any of his revelations—the appalling conditions in which he found the children on the Spanish slaver, or Margaret and John's religious background—she does not let on.

She halts by the sculpture of a small angel and chooses her words carefully. "I have given this matter some thought already and prayed on it. Now that I hear you, I am convinced that the children must be properly educated, but not just in the way of my station in society. They must be prepared for whatever the Lord has in store for them."

Jope nods gratefully. "I leave it in your expert hands, m'Lady."

"You can rely on me. Rest assured that the children will be safe with me. My husband, Lord Darcy, prefers to spend his time in London or on his own estate, and my staff are loyal and will not betray their presence here. I will keep you informed of their progress."

"Thank you, m'Lady."

Resuming their walk, she looks at him shrewdly. "I imagine you must be of considerable service to my nephew. He is not the kind of man to take risks without benefit to himself."

When Jope is about to launch into an explanation, she holds up her hand. "I do not wish to be acquainted with the details, Captain. Just wanted you to know that we understand each other."

He bows slightly in acknowledgment.

"You are welcome to visit whenever you can. For now, let us go and see that the children are settled before your departure. Normally, I'd invite you to stay the night, but I think it is better if you take your leave now. I have given orders for your horses to be fed and readied."

"Whatever you think best, m'Lady."

He follows her down a corridor to another parlor, where Margaret and John are sitting on upholstered stools by the hearth, dressed in warm gowns and eating buttered scones. They look up, tense and expectant, and for a moment Jope shares their apprehension, but his encounter with Lady Darcy has given him faith that he is making the right decision.

He hunkers down before them. "Margaret, John, this is your new home from now on. Lady Darcy will take good care of you. I will come to see you whenever the *White Lion* sails on England. But for now, I must say good-bye."

Margaret fidgets nervously and tears well up in her eyes. John's lips quiver. Jope clasps them in his arms and kisses them. He rises and gives them his blessing. Then he bows to Lady Darcy and follows the butler, who is waiting at the door, down a corridor to a side entrance and from there to his carriage.

The children only hesitate for a moment before running after him. They stop in the shelter of the entranceway just as Jope climbs into the carriage and departs. Shivering, they wave after him until they can't see him anymore.

Agnes, who has watched them quietly, scolds them tenderly. "What's the matter with you two? You'll catch your death," and she bundles them inside.

She takes them to a kitchen and feeds them a proper supper. The smells of pottage and roasted chicken make their mouths water, and the cider is rich and sweet. For dessert, they have gingerbread and marzipan, and Margaret's and John's eyes grow with wonder and delight at their first bites.

At some point, a young man enters. His brown beard and mustache haven't filled out yet. He is dressed in a simple overcoat and breeches and wears a cap. Agnes makes the introductions, "Margaret, John, this is Samuel. He will be your companion and tutor."

Samuel looks at them with undisguised fascination. "Welcome to your new home," he says and joins them at their meal.

By the time they're all finished eating, it is getting dark outside. Agnes lights a small candelabra and leads the way upstairs. Samuel brings up the rear carrying another candle.

Wall sconces illuminate the long, wood-paneled hallway. Agnes halts at an open door and says, "This is your room, Margaret. John's is next door."

Both children go inside and stop in amazement. The bed in the middle of the room has draped curtains on three sides, tied back with tasseled cords. A clean nightshirt and cap lie waiting on the covers. There is a chamber pot by the side of the bed, and Margaret and John exchange knowing looks.

They watch in fascination as Samuel takes hot stones from the fireplace, places them into a dented brass pan with handles, closes the cover, and places it between the sheets in Margaret's bed. "To warm things up," he says, grinning.

When they go next door, John's room looks similar to Margaret's, but with darker-colored fabrics for the bedcover and curtains. Agnes helps them remove their clothes and put on the nightshirts.

Samuel is readying another bed warming pan when Lady Isabel enters the room. The servants bow, and Agnes gestures for Margaret and John to kneel. The cold from the floor seeps through their gowns. They ask Lady Isabel for her blessing the way Mary has taught them.

She puts her hands on their heads and says, "I pray to God that he bring happiness and comfort to your lives here."

Then she says, "Good night," and withdraws.

Back in Margaret's room, Agnes takes the warming pan back to the fireplace and covers the embers for the night. When Margaret climbs into the bed, the sheets feel warm and comforting. The feather bed feels soft like no bed she's ever slept in before. Agnes kisses her on the forehead and closes the curtains. She blows out the candles on the nightstand and leaves, closing the door behind her.

Although the room is pitch black, Margaret is too preoccupied to go to sleep. Her mind is awhirl with everything that has happened. She listens to the wind blowing and rattling the windowpanes. At some point, she hears the door creak open and holds her breath.

Then she hears John whisper, "Margaret, are you awake? I can't sleep."

Relieved, she calls to him, "I can't sleep either."

He climbs up into bed with her, and Margaret is glad. They fall asleep with their arms around each other.

The next morning when she wakes, John is next to her, still sound asleep. She parts the bed curtains on her side. The room is bone-chilling cold. Gray light comes through the window. Margaret is amazed to see crystal flowers covering the panes in intricate patterns, like delicate lace fabric—ice and hoar frost, Agnes tells her when she asks about it. By the time she climbs out of bed, puts on slippers, and takes a closer look, the sun has come up and illuminates the floral display with a bright glow. When she peers through a clear part of a pane not completely covered by ice, she is even more amazed. As far as her eyes can see, the ground, trees, roof, and balconies are covered in a white blanket, whiter than the whitest linen.

"Snow," Samuel explains at breakfast.

Margaret gobbles down her bread and porridge as fast as she can. She can't wait to go outside and find out what the mysterious substance is. John is just as eager.

When Samuel takes them to the grounds behind the manor house, the snow crunches softly under their feet. Margaret picks up a handful of the soft, powdery substance, which melts quickly, leaving her hand wet and prickly cold.

Samuel mashes a handful into a small ball and tosses it at John. It shatters against his coat, and before long he and the children are having a snowball fight and rolling in the snow.

Aunt Isabel, watching from her parlor window, smiles to herself.

21
COUNCIL BUSINESS
London—February 1620

In late January, William Ewen returns to England from Jamestown with a letter from John Rolfe for Sir Edwin Sandys, reporting what happened at Point Comfort in August when the *White Lion* and the *Treasurer* arrived with their cargos of Africans. It is the version the conspirators agreed on that satisfies the concerns of the company treasurer. Everything appears to be legitimate, from the letters of marque that the Dutch captain carried to the colony's refusal to trade with the *Treasurer* before it made its escape.

Sitting at his desk in the study of his townhouse, Sandys muses that the ship and its captain, Daniel Elfrith, are now safely beached in Bermuda, and he heaves a sigh of relief. While Rolfe's account raises some questions, nothing untoward seems to have occurred that would reflect badly on the Virginia Company.

But then a week later, a letter from Sir George Yeardley arrives that puts the matter into an entirely different light.

"A pox on that flap-mouthed bastard," Sandys yells so loudly that it brings Nicholas Ferrar running into the room.

"What's the matter?"

Sandys thrusts the epistle at him. "Warwick!"

He paces about the room in agitation, pulling distractedly at his wide white collar, while Ferrar peruses the document. In it, Yeardley

179

tells of capturing a seaman from the *Treasurer* who jumped ship at Point Comfort. Under interrogation, he admitted that Elfrith sailed in consort with the Dutchman and attacked the Spanish galleon, committing an act of piracy at the instigation of the Earl of Warwick and the ship's co-owner, Samuel Argall.

Returning the letter, Ferrar says, "Yes, that is a decidedly different account from what John Rolfe says."

Sandys snatches it from him. Ferrar's tranquil response irks him. He doesn't seem to get the seriousness of the situation, while the revelation strikes fear into Sandys's heart. If the King's Privy Council gets wind of this, the scandal could be the end of the Virginia Company, just when some of the measures he has instituted to make the colony self-sufficient have the potential of paying off—the new parliament, the influx of hundreds of new immigrants, and the use of common lands to grow crops other than tobacco.

He curses Warwick's recklessness and feverishly thinks about what he can do to distance himself and the company from this disaster. "We must take preemptive measures right away!" he sputters.

Ferrar is familiar with Sandys's tendency to panic in a crisis—overreacting and jumping to conclusions. He prefers a less dramatic, more deliberate approach. "The difference in accounts may be to our advantage," he offers. "It will buy us time while we determine which is the more reliable."

"Of course, Yeardley's account is the truth," Sandys fumes. "We installed him and can trust him. I'm not sure about the others. Call an emergency session of the company council!"

"Don't you think that's a bit hasty? We will alert others that there is a problem."

"This is a catastrophe! Call the meeting!"

Ferrar sighs inwardly. "Very well," he acquiesces and keeps his own counsel: Fireworks serve no good purpose.

But Sandys, better than his younger colleague and friend, knows how dangerous the situation is. He was twenty-nine when the

Spanish Armada sailed into the English Channel with more than 100 ships, determined to attack and drive Queen Elizabeth from her throne. Only the heroic efforts of—he hates to admit it—English privateers and a mighty storm, which scattered the Catholic fleet, thwarted the invaders.

In the past decade, Spain has used diplomacy where warfare failed. Count Gondomar, who has recently returned to England, considers Jamestown and Bermuda rival outposts limiting Spain's sphere of influence in the New World. He has lobbied with King James against their existence in the past, and would like nothing better than to quash the English colonies. Sandys does not think it too far-fetched that, under the right pretext, Spain would even send warships to attack the poorly defended settlements and destroy everything he and his fellow investors have sought to create.

So he decides to engage in some secret diplomacy of his own and, unbeknownst to anyone else, uses his backdoor channels to make overtures to the Spanish Embassy and Count Gondomar in order to distance the Virginia Company from the whole affair.

* * *

The council meeting takes place at the house of the Earl of Southampton in a small parlor off to the side of the great hall. The attendees include Warwick, Nathaniel Rich, Sandys and Nicholas Ferrar, and Thomas Wale, the leader of the merchants on the board representing Thomas Smythe's faction.

As Ferrar anticipated, the fireworks are not slow in coming.

Sandys lays out his case by reading out loud the letter from Yeardley. There are gasps from the merchants and fearful glances in the direction of Warwick, whose scowling face is turning a deep shade of red.

Fixing his eyes on his adversary, Sandys concludes, "There is no doubt that the *Treasurer* attacked a Spanish vessel and committed piracy at your behest. Do you deny it, my Lord?"

Warwick leaps to his feet, furious. "I most certainly do! This is an outrageous lie!"

Sandys thrusts the letter at him. "Do you call Sir Yeardley a liar?"

"I am disinclined to believe any account based on the interrogation conducted by someone who is acting under orders to find evidence against me."

"You are endangering the very lifeblood of the company!"

"No, Sir Edward, it is you who is endangering the company with your high-handed methods. You sent a letter to the governor in June ordering him to impound my ship upon return to Jamestown long *before* the reputed incident with the Spanish galleon took place. Do you deny that?"

The accusation takes Sandys by surprise. "How . . . how do you know that?"

"You have your letters, I have mine! How dare you take such liberties with my property!"

With Sandys at a loss for words, Warwick drives the rapier home. "I'm sure the Privy Council will be interested to hear that a leading member of Parliament who insists on the rule of law with King James flouts English law at will when it suits his purpose!"

"You, sir, are a villain!"

By then, the other council members are their feet, shouting to be heard. Southampton's voice thunders above the rest. "Gentlemen, enough! Contain yourselves."

The aggrieved parties pull back but refuse to take their seats, glaring angrily at one another.

"As a member of the Privy Council, I can tell you that this is serious business—on both accounts. We must certainly inform the Privy Council if a British ship raided a Spanish galleon. But we cannot compromise the reputations of our members or the decorum of our company."

When he looks pointedly at Sandys, Nicholas Ferrar asks, "What do you suggest?"

"That we dissolve this meeting and work out a solution amongst ourselves." He indicates Warwick, Nathaniel Rich, Sandys, and the deputy. "This is a delicate situation, and we must be sure that cooler tempers prevail!"

Thomas Wale speaks up for the Smythe faction. "We insist that we be informed of all decisions made on our behalf before any actions are taken!"

Nicholas Rich, his hand placed soothingly on his cousin's arm, answers, "That goes without saying. But Sir Henry is right. The initial discussions are best conducted among a smaller audience."

After making eye contact with his fellow merchants to gauge their views, Wale bows to Southampton. "We yield to your wisdom, m'Lord."

He and his colleagues withdraw.

Southampton waits until a servant closes the door behind them and says, "I think we should conduct this session in the chapel." Trying to lighten the tense atmosphere, he adds, smiling, "A little divine guidance might help."

He leads the adversaries and their seconds through the great meeting hall to the family chapel. There is a table in the rear of the high-ceilinged room. A small partition separates it from the pews and the altar, where a simple crucifix hangs in front of a large painting of angels.

Southampton waits until everyone is seated at the table. He offers a brief prayer before plunging ahead and addressing the crux of the matter. "You both have legitimate grievances, gentlemen, but neither of you is without blame. So let's dispense with excuses and be honest about where we stand. You, Lord Rich, have been using Jamestown as a haven for your privateering exploits on the Spanish Main for some time; and you, Sir Edwin, have made a mockery of the law."

He looks at them both sternly, daring them to disagree. When they remain silent, he continues, "This is a dangerous state of affairs for everyone. The only way out is a suitable compromise that will satisfy all parties, keep the Virginia Company intact and in the shareholders' hands, and ensure the safety of everyone involved."

For the next hour, Southampton expertly mediates, giving the two antagonists plenty of opportunity to save face and voice their concerns—not always in the most measured tones. He encourages them to confer with their seconds and propose solutions. Like a good navigator, he always steers the discussion back to the issues at hand when it threatens to veer off course because of the pride and bluster of the adversaries.

When Warwick digs in his heels, Southampton invokes Sir Walter Raleigh's fate, suggesting that the earl is in danger of being sent to the Tower and having his head on the chopping block. When Sandys starts to rant against the arrogance of noble privilege, Southampton reminds him that the King is looking for a pretext to revoke the company's charter.

In the end, he gets them to agree to a simple compromise: Warwick will forswear using Jamestown as a pirate base. Sandys will make a presentation to the Privy Council, guided by Southampton, deflecting all blame from the Virginia Company, and Warwick's name will be kept out of it.

Just as everyone is about to agree, Sandys raises a final objection. "How can we be sure the Earl of Warwick will keep his word? We cannot prevent his ships from docking at Point Comfort."

It is a contemptible accusation to levy at a peer of the realm, and even the placid Southampton is about to lose his patience when Nathaniel Rich, after whispering to his cousin, offers an acceptable solution. "My Lord Rich will swear to it here and now before God."

Without further ado, Warwick and Southampton make their way to the altar. As the others watch from behind the partition, Robert Rich kneels and says in a firm voice, "I do so swear before Almighty God."

Then he gets up, stalks past the others, and leaves the chapel without as much as a glance in Sandys's direction.

22
ALDWARKE
February 1620

Living at Aldwarke opens up a whole new world for Margaret and John. Lady Isabel insists that they enter the main part of the mansion only with her permission or accompanied by Agnes or Samuel. But they have the entire west wing of the mansion to themselves and use their free time to explore the warren of parlors, drawing rooms, bedrooms, kitchen, larder, and hallways like pirates looking for treasure. They plunder dusty cupboards and musty storage closets for booty, uncovering things both ordinary and unusual that enflame their imaginations. When Lady Isabel hears from Agnes about their excursions, she gives them her blessing and uses what the children find to enhance their daily lessons and knowledge of English words, idioms, and customs.

One day Margaret and John come upon a chest filled with toys that belonged to Lady Isabel's son, Godfrey, from her first marriage.

"Look, a frigate," John shouts excitedly and pulls out a small boat with masts and sails. "Just like Captain Jope's!"

He is just as delighted with the hobby horse and wooden toy soldiers.

Margaret finds a doll with a pretty red dress, painted face, and blond curls. It reminds her of Mary, Jope's wife. She holds it up next to her own face in front of a looking glass and notes how much lighter the doll's skin color is to her own. After a week at Aldwarke, when John overcomes his fear of the dark and sleeps in his own bed, the doll becomes her nighttime companion.

Under Agnes and Samuel's supervision, Margaret and John investigate the estate from the gardens to the stables, barns, and animal pens. Just as with the sailors aboard the *White Lion*, the children's good spirits and innocent curiosity soon endear them to servants, grooms, and craftsmen and artisans alike.

For Margaret there are moments when the past and present converge unexpectedly. The first time the children venture with Agnes into the extensive gardens surrounded by tall evergreen hedges, there is not much to see. The flower beds are mostly bare. But in the middle of the rose garden among the unadorned rootstocks, there is a large stone circle with signs and lines carved into the granite slabs. An angled iron pole at the center throws a thin shadow across one of the meridians.

To Agnes's astonishment, Margaret says, "This tells the time of day, doesn't it?" She has a sudden vision of the bloody ground where she lay next to the sundial in the courtyard in Pongo during the Imbangala massacre. Her cheek starts to twitch uncontrollably, alarming Agnes even further.

Lady Isabel recognizes Margaret's occasional facial tic as a sign of the terrible ordeal she has endured and tries to instill a calm resolution in her. "You must overcome your fear. It is God's will!" she says sternly whenever it happens.

In many ways, she reminds Margaret of Sister Maria Gracia in Pongo—strict, but not unkind—and her exhortation becomes a refrain Margaret chants to herself whenever she feel anxious.

But such moments are increasingly rare. Soon she and John settle into a daily routine. When the cock crows at dawn, they linger in their cozy beds before jumping out and putting on their clothes as fast as they can because the rooms are freezing cold. They splash their faces with the ice-cold water from their washing bowls before hurrying downstairs to the kitchen to warm up by the fire. Lady Isabel insists on proper behavior, so while the cook prepares breakfast, they go to her parlor, kneel before her, say their prayers, and ask for her blessing.

After a breakfast of porridge and milk, or sometimes bread and butter, they spend the morning in a parlor at lessons with Lady Isabel and Samuel. Sitting at a low wooden table, they work to improve their English, learn ciphering—numbers and algebra—and receive religious instructions. They become adept at using wax tablets—wooden boards covered with a thin layer of soft beeswax—into which they carve letters and numbers with a stylus, and rub them out to create a clean writing surface.

During the initial ciphering lesson, Margaret and John amaze their teachers as much as they did their rescuer when they demonstrate that they can count from one to ten in several languages. That and their ability to absorb things quickly convince Lady Isabel that Captain Jope was right when he insisted the children were a gift from God with a special purpose.

Margaret, older and more mature and articulate than John, often speaks for him; but when it comes to sounding out words and reading, they are equally adept. Learning to write with a goose quill is more of a chore for them because of their small fingers. The day John scratches his name in ink on paper for the first time without a mistake is a cause for celebration. It takes Margaret much longer to match his dexterity with stylus and quill.

Dinner, the main meal of the day, takes place around noon in Lady Isabel's dining room, whose paneled walls are brightly painted. The children wash their hands before and after the meal. Servants bring food on trenchers with meat already cut into small pieces. There is a cornucopia of new smells and tastes—savory meat pies and pottage; all kinds of fowl, including capons, quail, Cornish hens, pigeons, ducks, and geese; game like deer, rabbit, and wild boar; roasted lamb and chicken; pig's feet and tripe; and freshwater trout and eels. But what Margaret and John like best are the sweet custards, trifles, tarts, and candies served throughout the meal.

The afternoon is taken up with lessons from Agnes and Samuel, who teach the children skills considered appropriate for young girls and boys. Margaret learns to knit, darn, and spin flax into linen threads. She helps the cook make butter and cheese in the kitchen and assists the baker with bread, biscuits, and scones.

John spends time in the barn helping the stable hands and grooms brush and feed the horses. He loves being with the large animals, rubbing their warm, muscular bodies and inhaling the pungent smell of hay and sweet feed. In the smithy, he enjoys watching the sparks fly on the anvil as the farrier, clad in a dark leather apron, hammers red-hot iron rods into horseshoes. To the amusement of the adults, he holds his nose during the hot shoeing when the horse's hooves sizzle and emit a caustic stench that lingers on unpleasantly long after they're finished.

The rest of the afternoon and on weekends, Margaret and John are free to roam the estate to their hearts' content. When the sun goes down and the distant church bells from Aldwarke village ring, it is time for supper. In the early months of their stay, that happens around five o'clock, but as the days grow longer, it happens at later hours, giving Margaret and John plenty of time on their own. In preparation for supper, Margaret and John help Agnes light the candles in the dining room. Once again, the children wash their hands before and after the meal, and enjoy bread pudding, stew, and cider.

The day closes with prayers and blessings from Lady Isabel, and then it is time for bed. John lies awake for a long time, a welter of images from the day tumbling through his mind. Margaret tells her doll, Mary, everything that happened to her. With so many novel impressions and activities to share, it is difficult for her to fall asleep, too. Clasping Mary tightly she whispers her innermost secrets to her as she drifts off to sleep.

When tradesmen and local farmers come to the estate, the household staff make sure they remain out of sight in their quarters.

One day, Agnes and Samuel keep them in their wing of the mansion from morning until night and serve them their meals in the kitchen there.

When Margaret asks why they can't go outside and into the rest of the house, Agnes tells her, "Lady Isabel's son, Godfrey, is here for a visit."

"I'd like to ask him about the frigate and his toy soldiers," John pipes up. "Perhaps he wants to play with them."

Samuel smiles kindly. "I'm afraid that won't be possible."

But that evening while going to their bedrooms, there are sounds coming from the main part of mansion unlike any they have ever heard before. After Agnes and Samuel have bid them goodnight, Margaret and John sneak out of their rooms and along the corridor until they reach the second-floor gallery overlooking the great hall. Peeking between the wooden newels of the railing, they see strangers with odd-looking instruments. The sounds issuing from them remind the children of the songs the seamen sang when they hauled in ropes, but these melodies don't have words and are much more beautiful.

Lady Isabel is sitting next to a middle-aged man with a brown beard and curled locks. He is younger than her, but older than Captain Jope. It must be Godfrey, Lady Isabel's son. Margaret can see the resemblance between him and his mother and notes the way she keeps glancing at him with unmistakable affection. But what captivates her and John more are the beautiful sounds. When a worried Agnes finds them there, she is amazed at their rapt, glowing faces and bodies responding to the music. She gently pulls them away from the railing to make sure they're out of sight, but she lets them stay until the musicians finish before shunting them off to bed.

When Lady Isabel hears about it, she isn't surprised. She may be a Puritan who eschews jewelry and fancy gowns, but she believes that music comes from God. The fact that the children responded so powerfully convinces her further that Captain Jope was right when he insisted they were a divine gift.

Aldwarke

When Godfrey leaves the next day, she returns to teaching Margaret and John with renewed resolve, determined to instill her Puritan beliefs in them. She explains that God has chosen an elect group of people to be saved at the end of time. This selection is not based on merit, goodness, virtue, or faith, but because of his unfathomable, infinite mercy. At the same time, she insists that God continues to create and work in the world and, echoing Jope, puts the idea into Margaret's and John's heads that they have a divine destiny.

"You are here for a reason," she insists.

Margaret would like to understand. She asks with uncertainty in her voice, "What do you mean?"

Lady Isabel looks at her intently with her deep gray eyes and answers, "Your destiny will reveal itself in time. The ways of God are mysterious to us; but make no mistake, he has a special purpose for you."

John accepts Aunt Isabel's teaching as grown-up stories he doesn't fully understand, but Margaret wonders what it all means. It makes sense to her that God would reveal himself to humans only through Jesus Christ, the savior, who loves children, because it makes her feel good and reminds her of the teachings of the Portuguese Sisters.

She relates the Calvinist notion of "total depravity" Lady Isabel mentions—the inability to save herself from sin without God's grace—with what the Sisters said about original sin, but it doesn't make any more sense to her now than it did in Pongo. Nothing can convince her that she was born evil and deserves the terrible things that have happened to her and John. Lady Isabel's insistence that they have a special purpose is a more attractive explanation for all the difficulties and suffering they have endured.

She wishes she could talk to someone about them, but she keeps her promise to Jope not to say anything about her experiences and what she saw and overheard aboard his ship. Only her doll at night hears murmurs of what goes through her mind.

23

COMPANY BATTLES
Leez Priory–London—
Late March–May 1620

The Earl of Warwick is riding his favorite stallion at a gallop across the fallow fields at his country estate of Leez Priory. There are patches of snow here and there, and yellow and blue crocus and white lilies of the valley are pushing through the dark earth, harbingers of an early spring, but he pays them no heed. He normally loves to ride, but he takes no pleasure in this outing. He has decided to be conspicuously absent from London while Edwin Sandys meets with the Privy Council, as if it is of no concern to him. But he has been thinking of little else. Ever since the disastrous Virginia Company council meeting at Southampton's, he has been like a prowling animal, licking his wounds and dreaming of revenge. He would gladly wring Sandys's neck.

When the lake by the manor house comes into view, he pulls up to rest his horse. The large hall made of red brick looks like an old castle with towers, turrets, and parapets. It always strikes Warwick a bit old-fashioned—the conceit of his father, who had a sentimental streak for things medieval. He built it on land that belonged to an Augustinian monastery for 300 years. It fell into his family's hands when Pope Clement refused to grant Henry VIII a divorce from

Catherine of Aragon, and the angry monarch separated the Church of England from Roman Catholicism, abolished all monasteries, and distributed their riches to his loyal followers.

His father may not have had the best taste in architecture, but at least he had the foresight to buy his title from King James before he died. That Catholic wastrel, always in need of money, was only too happy to oblige, and £10,000 barely made a scratch on the newly installed Earl of Warwick's immense wealth.

When Sir Robert inherited the title, he decided to keep Leez Priory as his country home. He had the interior renovated to hold court there in a style to rival the monarchs of Europe. Far richer than James, he can indulge his own expensive tastes—food, wine, hunting, music, and theatrical events—as he pleases. Everyone who seeks his patronage makes the forty-mile journey from London to Leez Prior when Warwick is in residence, no matter how rough the roads. Early springtime is especially difficult because frequent rains make the muddy terrain all but impassable.

Warwick spurs his horse into action. As his mount ambles toward the manor, his thoughts return to the Privy Council, where his fate lies in the balance. Although he trusts Southampton to look out for his welfare, one never knows. The Privy Council can be fickle, and Warwick can only hope that no further measures are required to assure his safety. He does not want to flee the country and live in exile, even if he has joked in the past that he would like nothing better than to lead a Puritan colony in the Americas.

After the meeting at Southampton's, he had briefly considered remaining a member of the Virginia Company, but he withdrew in a huff when the council voted to confiscate the *Treasurer* and its cargo in Bermuda. Invoking the technicality that the ship was leased to the company, Sandys persuaded enough board members that the Africans belonged to them. Well, let him try to take them from him! In the meantime, Nathaniel Rich can represent his interest on the council.

Not that Warwick has been idle since the Virginia Company closed its ranks against him. He has been in negotiations with King James's advisers to obtain approval for the Council of New England to further his colonial ambitions in the New World. Since Warwick's wealth and generosity give him ready access to the court, it required only the promise of a handsome financial settlement to dispose the King favorably toward the venture, along with assurances that the colony would be established far to the north of Jamestown so as not to interfere with Virginia's territory. Now that the groundwork for a royal charter has been finished, Warwick has sent word to his contacts—Thomas Weston, Robert Cushman, and John Carver—that they can get their ships ready to transport the English Puritans and Leiden Separatists to America.

They first will have to make the journey to Leez Priory, however, even if they don't approve of his trappings of wealth. Warwick knows they don't understand how a devout Puritan can enjoy such pomp and circumstance. They are not men of the world like him, but they will work hard to find a safe haven for their beliefs. Perhaps they will succeed where Guinea and Jamestown have not and manage to be at least as profitable as Bermuda in their pursuit of religious and spiritual freedom.

As he reaches the stables, Warwick sees a mud-spattered carriage standing by the front entrance of the hall, and his pulse quickens—news from London! He dismounts, hands the reins to his groom, and hurries to the mansion. He enters the main building through a side door, where Alfred meets him carrying a fresh set of clothes. No one else is in sight. When Warwick has visitors, his wife, Frances, not to be confused with his harridan stepmother of the same name, knows to keep their five children out of the way in the family quarters of the mansion.

As Warwick hurries toward his study, one of his foxhounds bounds toward him and rubs against his riding breeches. Rich rewards him by pulling and rubbing his ears. The dog rolls on his side, exposing his belly, and yips with pleasure when the earl scratches his fur.

Warwick turns to Alfred and says, "If only people were that loving and loyal."

"Yes, m'Lord."

As he approaches his study, he slows down and makes a dignified entrance, nodding to Nathaniel Rich and Samuel Argall. They are waiting for him in their travel clothes. Warwick barely acknowledges their bows and flops into his armchair to let Alfred pull off his riding boots.

That chore accomplished, he looks up and notes the serious expressions on his visitors' faces. Steeling himself for the worst, he snarls, "For God's sake, Nate, out with it. Am I to be condemned to the Tower?"

His cousin holds up his hands in an appeasing gesture. "Southampton has been true to his word and made sure that you were not involved. All the letters Sandys presented to the Privy Council had your name blotted out."

"And I got all the blame," Argall interjects, a dark scowl on his face. "I've been cast as the villain in this piece!"

"I told you it will be taken care of," Nathaniel hisses in his direction.

Argall takes a step back and worries his mustache.

Nathaniel laughs mirthlessly. "The Privy Council actually rebuked Sandys and the Virginia Company for condoning privateering practices!"

Warwick looks from one to the other. "So what is the problem? I can see from your faces there is more."

His cousin decides to try a roundabout approach. "As expected, Sandys presented letters from Yeardley, settlers at Jamestown, and council members disavowing the actions of the *Treasurer*."

"'S blood, Nate, don't keep me on the rack!"

Nathaniel exchanges a look with Argall, who blurts out, "He also brandished a letter from Gondomar. It said that he had received satisfaction from the Virginia Company for the offense to his cousin's ship."

"Gondomar? He went to Gondomar on his own?"

"Yes, which means the Spanish bugger knows all about your involvement now."

The bearers of ill news hold their breath, waiting for the eruption they've been dreading. Warwick's face turns red and he clenches his fists, but the explosion never comes. Instead, a look of such savage, pent-up fury and hatred comes over him, his eyes glistening and hard as black onyx, that it frightens his visitors more than if he had burst out yelling and demolished the room.

When Warwick finally speaks, his voice is an eerie growl. "We must conduct this campaign like a battle fought on several fronts."

Argall, who normally has no difficulties with military metaphors, asks, "What do you mean, m'Lord?"

"Have it put out that Sandys has been passing company secrets to Gondomar, and blame the debacle with the *Treasurer* on his incompetent handling of the situation."

A wicked smile breaks out on Nathaniel's face. "It will be my pleasure."

"Set up a meeting with Sir Thomas Smythe. He has been carrying a grudge against Sandys for ousting him as treasurer and closing down the income from the magazine ship. He has access all the way to the King's bedchamber. Let's see what we can do if we put our heads together."

"We'll turn the tables on Sandys," Argall says happily.

Warwick is less sanguine. "Perhaps, but he'll keep pursuing this situation with the *Treasurer*. He's like a mongrel who won't let go of a bone. He and that cur, Gondomar, are the same breed."

Nathaniel nods, "Birds of a feather!"

"Yes. Fortunately, we have Captain Jope's testimony if they bring any legal actions."

"There is more good news on that front, m'Lord," says Argall. "Governor Yeardley heeded your request and petitioned the King for

Marmaduke Raynor to receive a commission to survey the southern coast of Virginia."

Nathaniel Rich adds, "I just received word from the Privy Council that the petition has been granted. It will keep him away from England for several years."

For the first time, a smile begins to play on Warwick's face. "Yes, if he wants to tell his version of what happened with the Spanish slave galleon, he'll have to content himself with the Indians for his audience."

They continue to strategize for another hour. Afterward Warwick has Alfred pour him a glass of Madeira. As he takes a sip and savors the aroma, along with the irony of enjoying a Spanish wine, he stares into the curling flames from the embers in the fireplace. He is done licking his wounds and will prowl like a wolf to have his revenge on Sandys. The man has no idea what beast he roused when he made the issue personal.

* * *

At the beginning of May, an anonymous broadside appears all over London, claiming that of the wave of new settlers who immigrated to Virginia in the past year, hundreds died shortly after their arrival in Jamestown. It lays the blame at the door of Edwin Sandys, who has been a tireless promoter of the colony. Needless to say, the company treasurer is furious. He knows the allegations are true, but only members of the council were aware of the actual figures, so someone must have leaked the information. Of course, he suspects Warwick and his oily cousin. They would like nothing better than to tarnish his reputation. But there is no way to prove it.

A week later, Captain Argall encounters Count Gondomar at a social function. Remarkably, the Spanish ambassador, normally subtle and devious, commits a diplomatic blunder. He accosts Argall and loudly berates him for stealing Angolan slaves belonging to his family and His Majesty, King Phillip. The rant includes damning details of the *Treasurer's* participation in the raid on the *San Juan Bautista* and causes an immediate scandal. Fanned by anonymous instigators, rumors spread like wildfire throughout London, from fashionable boudoirs and parlors to seaside taverns, that Edwin Sandys has betrayed Virginia Company secrets to Count Gondomar.

The flames reach all the way to the next quarter court of the company, where they ignite a passionate debate and threaten to obliterate the routine business of reelecting the officers for another year. Immediately after Sandys gavels the meeting to order, Nathaniel Rich rises and accuses him of the very offense that has been making the rounds of the city—divulging secrets to the Spanish ambassador.

He finishes his oration with a mighty rhetorical flourish. "I ask before the assembly what other matters of import the treasurer has poured into the receptive ears of the Spanish agent?"

Shouts of outrage flare up instantly. The loudest outbursts— "Traitor!" "Treason!" "Treachery!"—erupt from Smythe's and War- wick's factions and force Sandys to his feet. As he rises, the unruly crowd quiets.

He surveys the room and says with admirable composure, "These vile accusations are baseless. I vow here before the assembly that I never saw the Spanish ambassador but in the streets, and I have never sent any messages to him, neither by letter nor any other writings."

He fixes his eyes on Nathaniel Rich, as if to dare him to say otherwise. When he receives no reply, he continues, "Shall we resume our company business and move on to the annual report of the state of the colony?"

There is some grumbling, but most of the rejoinders affirm that the meeting should resume its regular course. But if Sandys thinks he has weathered the worst of the firestorm, he is in for an unpleasant surprise. As he starts to read from his prepared documents, there is a commotion in the back of the room. The great oak doors open, and an emissary from King James, wearing scarlet livery, enters.

He announces loud enough for everyone to hear, "I bear a message from the King for the stockholders and officers of the Virginia Company." Then he advances to the table at the front, unfurls a small scroll, and reads, "His Royal Highness, King James, out of especial care and respect for the Virginia Plantation, has decided that the slate of nominees for treasurer should include Sir Thomas Roe, Alderman Robert Johnson, Maurice Abbott, Thomas Smythe, and no other."

There is stunned silence. Nathaniel Rich shares a satisfied smile with Captain Argall.

Sandys stands rooted to his spot, like a groom jilted at the altar. Everyone expects him to explode, but nothing in his face betrays the slightest emotion.

"We thank His Royal Highness for his care," he says.

The messenger bows and departs.

When the door has closed behind him, Sandys resumes reading his report as if nothing has happened, "We now have 1,261 settlers in Virginia, and we raised £9,830, the lion's share through the lotteries, and spent £10,432. Most expenditures went to transporting settlers by ship, sending provisions to Jamestown, and paying interest on the company debt. I am pleased to announce that our business this year has not added one penny to that debt, although we still owe close to £9,000, outstanding from the period when Sir Thomas Smythe was treasurer."

He adds his concern that private plantations are growing at the expense of the company's lands and that the cultivation of tobacco to the exclusion of all other crops except sassafras does not bode well for the self-sufficiency of the colony.

Then he officially hands over to Nicholas Ferrar all accounts, invoices, and a list of names of everyone who traveled to Jamestown at company expense. "I thank my deputy for his dedicated service and thank the members of the company for their love in choosing me to be treasurer."

Then he slips the gold chains and seals of his office over his head and places them on the table next to the documents and steps away to join Lord Cavendish on the side.

For a while, the assembly seems at a loss on how to proceed. They are all aware that the gauntlet the king has thrown down regarding the leadership of the company puts them in a precarious position, and that they must proceed with caution if they wish to retain control. Slowly, the shareholders voice their concerns in line with their factions and self-interest.

To no one's surprise—after all, three of the candidates proposed by James are merchants loyal to the former treasurer—the followers of Thomas Smythe insist, "We are obliged to show our duty to the King by acceding to his demands."

Sandys's supporters, who share his democratic views in the House of Commons, counter, "But if we do so, we shall suffer a great breach into our privilege of free election!"

Nathaniel Rich, Captain Argall, and Warwick's faction keep above the fray.

Finally, the Earl of Southampton proposes a solution. "I recommend we table the decision until the next quarter court and appoint a committee to determine a humble answer unto His Majesty. Until then Sir Edwin Sandys shall continue in his office as treasurer."

It is an indication of how seriously the assembly takes the King's challenge to its authority that his suggestion prevails with unanimous support from all three factions.

* * *

When Nathaniel Rich and Argall relate what happened at the meeting to the Earl of Warwick at Leez Priory, he smiles like a naughty child.

"The bugger lied through his teeth about Gondomar. For certain he's a tattletale," he contends.

"Yes," Nathaniel Rich agrees. "Gondomar announced the next day that he knew all about the raid from a letter sent by his cousin, Count Acuña, who was the captain on the *San Juan Bautista*, but it came too late for Sir Edwin."

"Your most excellent broadside gave Smythe plenty of ammunition to persuade the King of his incompetence, Nate. I only wish I could have seen the look on Sandys's face when the messenger read the list and his name wasn't on it."

Argall wisely refrains from mentioning that Sandys actually comported himself with dignity. "Who do we want to install in Sandys's place?" he asks, steering the conversation to safer territory.

Nathaniel Rich purses his lips. "It can't be someone too closely aligned with our cause."

Warwick nods. "Whoever it is, he must be well disposed toward us."

24
LADY FRANCES
Aldwarke—May–June 1620

Over the next few months, Margaret and John become acquainted with English religious customs and holidays. They attend Sunday services in the manor chapel. The minister is a young Puritan staying at the manor. Lady Isabel has taken him into her confidence and provides a monetary incentive as well for him to officially ignore the children and keep quiet about their presence. They observe Easter and Pentecost with special services whose content and rituals are unfamiliar to Margaret and John, but nothing compares with their first May Day celebration.

Much as they would like to go with Lady Isabel to Aldwarke village to participate in the festivities there—as the shire's leading citizen she is obliged to officiate and add her blessing to the events—they are not allowed to leave the manor grounds. But Samuel and Agnes make sure that they follow the customs and conduct their own private ceremony commemorating the beginning of spring.

In the morning, Agnes gets Margaret up early, takes her outside into the misty meadows where cattle graze quietly, and has her wash her face with dew collected from the blades of grass.

"It will make you more beautiful in the coming year," Agnes explains. "Not that you really need it. You're such a pretty girl. Before you know it, you'll be a beauty."

Margaret stops splashing dew on her face. "Is it important to be beautiful?"

The question surprises Agnes. Mystified, she says, "It doesn't hurt, especially with the young gentlemen."

Although she doesn't understand what that means, Margaret takes it seriously. Later, alone in her room, she tries to reconcile the word "pretty" with her face in the looking glass. She knows flowers are pretty, and songbirds, but she has never thought of herself that way.

After breakfast, Agnes teaches the children to make garlands with leaves and flowers. They put them on and go outside where Samuel has put up a maypole in the courtyard behind the manor house. Colorful ribbons dangle from the crown up top, and Agnes encourages Margaret and John to grab them and dance in a circle around the maypole.

To the children it seems a peculiar thing to do, but then they remember celebrations in Ndongo and their bodies respond with energetic movements—foot stamping, stutter steps, leaps, and twirls. Pent up for so long, they burst out into a joyous, exuberant dance. Now it is Agnes and Samuel's turn to feel peculiar. Never have they seen such vigorous maypole cavorting and frolicking.

Lady Isabel, about to leave for the village, happens to see them from her parlor window and is shocked. She hurries outside and calls to them, "Enough! Not so wild! That is enough, quite enough!"

Margaret and John stop in confusion. They don't understand why Lady Isabel is so upset.

Agnes, who understands very well, curtsies and whispers, "Sorry, m'Lady. It won't happen again."

Noticing the children's bewildered faces, she takes them inside and makes up for the reprimand by sneaking them extra sweets after dinner. Lady Isabel doesn't mention the incident again.

* * *

With the coming of summer, Margaret spends more time in the vegetable garden, learning how to cultivate and pick artichokes, asparagus, cucumbers, spinach, cabbage, lettuce, leeks, parsnips, peas, and turnips. She enjoys learning how to prepare them in the kitchen. Experimenting with the spices from the garden, she surprises the cook with unusual, tasty concoctions for stews and side dishes.

John continues to work with horses and other farm animals. When Samuel teaches him to saddle, mount, and ride a pony, he beams with pride and trots around the paddock whenever he can. The tutor is amazed at how easily John takes to working with livestock on the farm. He is especially comfortable around cattle and pigs and participates in their breeding, birthing, castrating, and slaughter as if it were the most natural thing in the world.

When John, Margaret, and Samuel explore the woods behind the manor, they discover a small pond surrounded by oaks, poplars, and ash trees. Under Samuel's tutelage, John learns to fish there and in the nearby river for perch, pike, trout, carp, and minnows.

Margaret likes to go there alone when she feels anxious or melancholy. Sitting in the late afternoon sun and watching the breeze raise tiny ripples on the water's surface and rustle the leaves of the trees, she feels at one with nature—less isolated and, except for missing Jope, almost at peace.

* * *

One early June morning, Margaret stirs in her bed. As she yawns and rubs her eyes, she notices a bundle of rose-colored cloth lying on the chest by the window. Intrigued, she gets up and takes a closer look. It is a beautiful gown with red embroidery and ribbons. When she runs her hand over the smooth silk fabric, a fleeting image of the market in Ndongo and the bearded merchant yelling at her flashes through her mind. She feels a spasm of anguish as she remembers her mother standing up for her.

By the time Agnes arrives, she has recovered and holds it up to the light, examining the workmanship. "What is the occasion?" she asks. "Is there a special holiday?"

Agnes gives her a meaningful look and says, "Lady Darcy's sister is coming for a visit!"

She helps Margaret put the gown on, lacing it up in back, straightening the collar and the ruffles. It fits surprisingly well. Stepping back to take a look, she clucks admiringly, "My, don't you look like a proper lady?"

On her way to Lady Isabel's parlor for prayers before breakfast, Margaret meets up with John, dressed in an outfit just as fancy as hers—an indigo blue doublet and matching pleated breeches. From all corners of the manor, they hear the bustle of activity. They pass house maids and servants sweeping the floors, polishing windows, and dusting the furniture in the great hall, drawing rooms, and parlors.

Aunt Isabel, as always, is dressed in a black gown made of fine silk, and she bears herself more regally than usual. She evaluates Margaret's and John's appearance critically and seems satisfied.

"Today is a very special day," she tells them. "My sister, Lady Frances Rich, is coming to pay us a visit. She is a very fine and proper lady, and I want you to make a good impression when she meets you."

"Why is that?" John asks, unsuspecting.

"She is a very fashionable lady. Now that the weather is warm, she will come here often. She and I have no secrets from each other."

Margaret understands the significance. Until now, she and John have always been shunted away in their part of the house when guests spent time at the manor.

"We will not disappoint you, Lady Isabel."

"I'm sure you won't."

"She is the stepmother of the Earl of Warwick, isn't she?"

Lady Isabel is taken aback. "How do you know that, my child?"

"Captain Jope told us that's how we came to you," Margaret explains innocently.

"I see. Well, Agnes will take you to breakfast now. Then you will wait in your parlor until you are called."

As the children leave, she marvels once again at how much they know and understand. She smiles, pleased. Her younger sister is in for quite a surprise.

* * *

That afternoon, Margaret and John watch from a second-floor window in their wing as a large carriage with four horses pulls up at the front entrance. Servants and footmen hurry from the manor entrance in time to greet a woman dressed in a fancy gray traveling cape emerging from the coach. She has a feather decoration on her head and is carrying a matching feather fan.

Margaret and John cannot see her face from their vantage, but they marvel at her appearance as she makes her way inside like a barge that thinks it owns the river.

Downstairs, Lady Isabel waits in her parlor when the well-dressed woman floats into the room. Lady Frances Wray Rich is eight years younger than her sister, and while she may have spent two days traveling by coach, not a hair is out of place in her coiffure. She extends her arms from her sides to let a servant slip the cape from her shoulders, and she glides forward to kiss Lady Isabel on the mouth in greeting.

"I would have come sooner, but I was laid up with a dreadful cold that just wouldn't go away," she chirrups.

Feeling enveloped by a cloud of lavender, Lady Isabel resists crinkling her nostrils and says, "I'm glad you're here, Frances."

"Yes, your mysterious letter has me curious as a kitten. What possibly could be so exciting here, where you keep to yourself, cloistered like a nun?"

"Now, Frances, I am a married woman, as you well know."

"Yes, and your husband is suitably absent. It is the best way for a wife, I always say—provides her all the benefits of rank and wealth without having to put up with him!" She giggles like a young girl.

Happy to see each other, the sisters repair to the sofa where Frances takes off her gloves and launches into the latest gossip from London. Although Isabel is not interested, she knows Frances won't pay her any mind until she has unburdened herself of her treasure trove of rumors and news. So she pretends to listen with rapt attention to the affairs of various high-society ladies and gentlemen she knows distantly but cares not a whit about. More intriguing to her is the news of a treaty signed with Spain to arrange for the marriage between the Prince of Wales and the Infanta Maria Anna in return for relaxing laws concerning Roman Catholics in England. Isabel shares her sister's outrage and concern over what it will mean for the Puritan cause.

She is little affected by the troubles at the Virginia Company and the King's personal intervention to scuttle the reelection of Sir Edward Sandys as treasurer. Apparently, Sandys has petitioned one of the King's favorites, the Earl of Buckingham, to intercede on his behalf.

"That will surely come to naught," Frances concludes dismissively.

But Isabel perks up at intelligence of her nephew's newest colonial venture, the Council of New England. A ship called the *Mayflower* has recently docked in London in order to take Puritans from England to northern Virginia. Isabel is always pleased to hear when aid comes to those persecuted for their religious beliefs, and she approves of Warwick's intrigues in that regard.

Before she can get a word in edgewise, however, Frances launches into what has London all astir—a legal suit brought before the High Admiralty Court by Count Gondomar over the attack on a Spanish slave ship by one of Warwick's privateering vessels. Isabel's heart skips a beat, and she is glad that Frances is too self-absorbed to notice her agitation.

"With depositions from people as far away as Bermuda and Virginia, this will drag on for months, if not years," Frances clucks rapturously. "Not to worry, though. I will keep you abreast of every juicy tidbit!"

Having exhausted her storehouse of news, but by no means weary herself, Frances leans conspiratorially toward her sister. "Now, what is it that you have to tell me? You've had me on pins and needles for two days traveling."

Isabel can barely restrain herself from bursting out in laughter at her sister's disingenuous declaration. She feigns a cough and, when she has herself under control again, gets up and rings a bell.

"I think you better see for yourself."

There is a knock, and Margaret and John enter. They hover shyly by the door until Lady Isabel beckons them over. Then they walk up to the unfamiliar woman on the sofa and bow and curtsey to her.

"These are my wards, Margaret and John," says Lady Isabel.

For once, Lady Frances is dumbstruck. Her eyes dart back and forth from one child to the other.

Taking in the penetrating odor of lavender tinged with cloves and cinnamon, Margaret notes the resemblance between her and Lady Isabel even through the heavy makeup. She understands why they are wearing their finest clothes. She has never seen such a fancy outfit before. The vermillion gown has a low-cut body with ruffled sleeves, huge hanging wings, and a full gathered skirt. There are lace-embroidered borders and a ring secured by a narrow ribbon to her wrist.

Margaret marvels at the feathery contrivance perched atop Lady Frances's head like a bird guarding its nest. Then she notices the pearl necklace slung from her shoulder to the waist. Her eyes widen. She doesn't know the English word, but the Spanish *la perla* leaps unbidden to her tongue and her hand reaches out toward the glistening strand.

Lady Frances backs away and protests, "Why are you pointing your finger at me?

"My name . . . Margaret . . . la perla."

Lady Isabel is the first who understands. Her voice is filled with disbelief and admiration. "She means your pearls, Frances. Her name, Margaret, means 'pearl.'"

Recovering quickly, Lady Frances looks at the pearls on her dress. "Oh . . . of course. How do you do?"

"Well, m'Lady. I hope you had a pleasant journey," Margaret replies. "The coaches on our travels have not been very comfortable."

"Yes. Well, I have plenty of pillows to keep me company."

By now Lady Frances has recovered and, true to her breeding, resumes her role of graceful noblewoman. She turns to John and asks, "So your name is John?"

"Yes, m'Lady. I like ships better than carriages."

His earnest manner brings a smile to Lady Isabel's lips. "Why don't you two go back to your quarters for now?" she says. "We will meet again at supper. Lady Frances and I have much to talk about till then, I'm sure."

Relieved, Margaret and John curtsey and bow as before.

Lady Frances watches them leave. As soon as the door closes behind them, she rounds on her sister and exclaims, "Good Lord, Isabel, you must be out of your mind. These are the very Africans Count Gondomar accuses Warwick of taking from him."

"Yes, Robert has asked me to look after them."

Lady Isabel joins Frances on the sofa and tells her all about the children's arrival with the Calvinist captain who rescued them, their remarkable and surprising abilities, and their divine purpose. For once, her sister does not interrupt, except for occasional ejaculations of astonishment.

When Isabel is finished, Frances shakes her head. "This is a dangerous game you're playing. If word gets out that they're in England, you'll be in desperate straits."

Lady Isabel bristles. "Since when are you worried about such things? You didn't used to think this way when we were younger and harbored the nonconformists at our homes."

"Times have changed, my dear. Times have changed."

"Nonsense. The captain told me that these children are a gift from God, and everything I have seen of them since persuades me that he is right." She takes Frances by the hands and says urgently, "Promise me you'll keep an open mind. Get to know them and sleep on it. We will speak further anon."

The tension leaves Frances's shoulders. She sighs and says, "As you wish, my dear."

* * *

But neither supper, nor her encounters with Margaret and John over the following days, change her view. While she has to acknowledge that the children are remarkably poised, intelligent, well behaved, and devout, she cannot forget the danger they represent. Although she does not care much for her stepson, Warwick's wealth and power are what keep her in comfort, and she cannot see past the threat to his status and well-being.

When she gets ready to depart after her three-day visit, the sisters remain at an impasse, although Frances vows she will not interfere nor expose the children's presence at Aldwarke.

"I'll be back soon," she promises in the courtyards by the coach as she kisses her sister good-bye and nods to the children.

As they watch the carriage drive off, John whispers to Margaret, "I don't think she likes us."

25

JOPE

Jamestown—Summer 1620

As the *White Lion* nears the mouth of the James River and Point Comfort, Captain Jope stands on the quarterdeck, scanning the shorelines for familiar points of reference. Without Marmaduke as his navigator, he is not as confident in his approach as before. Not sure what to expect, he is once again flying the Dutch flag.

When Jope struck his agreement with the Earl of Warwick and promised to leave England, Nathaniel Rich suggested that Jope use the *White Lion* as a merchant vessel to transport tobacco from Virginia to Holland. It would serve the dual purpose of keeping him away from English shores and allow him to earn money easily, relieving him of his financial difficulties.

It so happened that there was need for his service. For seven years, the Virginia Company benefitted from a special royal dispensation, paying no import duties on the tobacco it shipped to England. But when the exemption expired the previous year, King James refused to renew it, and all efforts to change his mind have fallen on deaf ears. Although the tariff is half of what Spanish ships have to pay for their Caribbean and South American cargo, it cuts into the profits of shareholders of the Virginia Company. Looking for alternatives, the more enterprising members have decided to reroute a substantial portion of the tobacco crop directly to Holland, which charges no import duties.

Jope

Jope liked the idea. With his Dutch letters of marque, he could bring provisions to Jamestown, transport tobacco legitimately from there to Leiden or Antwerp or Amsterdam, and bring goods from the Netherlands to Plymouth—textiles, alum, refined sugar, cured tobacco, and tulip bulbs—profiting at every turn. He was not about to absent himself from England entirely. It would mean a steady income rather than pursuing a quick fortune. But if he happened to encounter a Spanish gold ship along the way, why not go on a little buccaneering excursion? Above all, it would allow him to return to Mary and visit Margaret and John more often.

So he outfitted the *White Lion* with English provisions and sailed to Leiden to make contact with the merchants there. He also visited the leaders of the Separatists. John Carver and Robert Cushman greeted him with suspicion until he presented them with a letter from the Earl of Warwick, informing them that the success of the Council of New England meant they should get their ship, the *Speedwell*, ready to meet up with the *Mayflower* for an imminent departure to the Americas. After that, they welcomed him as a fellow Puritan into their homes.

From Leiden, Jope made his own voyage across the Atlantic. Uneventful, it has allowed his new navigator to get to know his new crew. With Marmaduke soon to be in Warwick's employ, Captain Argall had recommended an old sea dog as a replacement. But Jope didn't want to have a spy aboard who would report his every move to the earl and his retainers. His contacts in Plymouth recommended Oswald Byers, and Jope has not been disappointed. The man may not be as experienced as Marmaduke, but he runs a tight ship and has made sure that the crew, a mix of old-timers from the last voyage and new hires, quickly learned how to work together.

When Point Comfort finally comes into sight, Jope is surprised how much the town around the fort has grown since his visit nine months earlier. There are more homes and warehouses facing the wharf. Two other merchant ships are anchored close to shore, while smaller boats ferry their cargo to waiting porters on the pier.

Before long, the welcoming skiff approaches, with Captain Tucker and his two lieutenants in tow. Stepping aboard the *White Lion*, he greets "the Dutchman" like an old acquaintance.

"Captain Jope! How good to see you."

"Captain Tucker."

"What cargo do you have for us today?"

"Nails, tools, plates and utensils, fabrics and clothes, and whatnot. I aim to trade them for tobacco."

Tucker seems disappointed. He leans in close and whispers, "I wish you had another load of you-know-who. The two from the *Treasurer* are good, hard workers—smart, too. Took over my tobacco fields in no time. I haven't had to worry about them since."

Jope grins. "I'm glad to hear it. Perhaps next time."

Straightening, Tucker resumes his normal tone of voice for the benefit of his seconds, "I'll let Jamestown know you're here. Come ashore tomorrow and you can meet with the agents for the plantations."

Jope spends the evening in his cabin, rereading the letter from Isabel Darcy that arrived in Tavistock shortly before his departure. Margaret and John are settling in nicely, receiving religious instruction and making good progress with their English. He is glad that they like their new home. After all they've been through, they deserve a spell of ordinary existence. He muses about how their destiny will unfold and what further role he will play in their lives.

The next morning, he goes ashore with Oswald to bargain with the plantation agents, who congregate at the pier among fishermen hawking what they caught during the night.

As he strides toward them, Tucker intercepts him. He is alone. "Morning, Captain. I just received word that you are cleared for travel to Jamestown. Abraham Piercey and Governor Yeardley are quite interested in what you're carrying in your ship's hold."

Jope wonders if Tucker is trying to tell him something between the lines, "This doesn't have anything to do with . . . ?"

"Not at all. I only sent word to John Rolfe that you are here. The others think you're a regular Dutch trader. Their plantations are in need of provisions. All above board."

Jope considers for a moment. He is curious to see Jamestown for himself, but he is also cautious. If this is a trap, he wants to be prepared. On the way back, he tells Oswald to get the *White Lion* battle ready.

The navigator is surprised. "Do you expect trouble, Captain?"

"Let's just say that my previous visit occurred under dubious circumstances."

Oswald isn't sure what to make of this but knows enough not to inquire further. During the forty-mile journey upriver, which takes most of the day, he has the crew ready the cannons, lay out muskets, and make sure that plenty of powder and shot is within easy reach of the cannoneers.

Staying on the quarterdeck for most of the journey, Jope keeps a watchful eye as they glide along forested banks overgrown with shrubs. The woods look denser here than in his native Cornwall. Occasionally, they pass wooden docks extending into the river, with storage sheds built atop and small boats anchored on their sides. None of them or the few people ashore present a threat. Jope imagines more activity when a ship arrives to be loaded.

By the time the *White Lion* reaches Jamestown's island, the late afternoon sun bathes in a rich glow the thatched roofs of the main settlement inside the fort. The tallest building inside the palisades, a simple church with a wooden cross embedded in the white wall under the gables, is the highest point on the island. Beyond the fortifications, a smattering of houses, some still under construction, occupy the ledge above the riverbank. Except for the stronghold, it looks like a small English seaside village and trading outpost, hardly a thriving community. After Havana and the bustling ports of Europe, Jope finds it a disappointing sight.

Still, he remains vigilant until the harbormaster arrives in a small pinnace. The portly man who steps aboard the *White Lion* wears a serious, self-important expression befitting his office. What surprises Jope is the quality of his outfit—his doublet has striped sleeves with gold trim, and his breeches are pleated—more fashionable than a mere uniform and more expensive than what his counterparts in London and Plymouth would wear. His two assistants are more suitably dressed in dark coats and pants and white Puritan collars.

The harbormaster introduces himself as William Rowley, offers his welcome, and delivers a message from Abraham Piercey. "Our cape merchant asks that you do him the honor and join him for dinner at his house tomorrow at noon."

Jope wonders what special reason Piercey has to want to see him, but he bows graciously. "It will be my pleasure."

"In the meantime, I suggest you may moor your ship at the dock," Rowley offers. "Michael here will aid your navigator."

By the time they've brought the *White Lion* alongside the pier, which thrusts from the shore into the river, and laid a walking plank down to it, the sun is setting. Reassured that there are no plans afoot to detain him and his ship, Jope gives the order to drop the anchor and strike the sails.

As the harbormaster and his assistants leave, there is a shout from the dock. "Permission to come aboard!"

When Jope strolls to the railing and recognizes John Rolfe below, he grins and relaxes further. He waves for him to come onto the ship. They greet each other with undisguised pleasure.

"It's good to see you, Captain," says Rolfe, shaking Jope's hand.

"And you."

As they head to Jope's cabin, Rolfe looks around for signs of Margaret and John. When he doesn't see them, he gives Jope a questioning look.

"The children are safe in England."

Rolfe smiles. "I am glad you decided to take them with you. I trust they are well."

When Jope doesn't reply, he changes the subject. "You missed Marmaduke by just a week."

Back on safe ground, Jope becomes more talkative. "Yes, I saw him off in Plymouth. He's in the Earl of Warwick's employ now and has his own ship, the *Marmaduke*. Named it after himself, but you know that."

Rolfe laughs. "Yes, he bought himself a new doublet and coat. He's quite the peacock."

"Well, he deserves it. He's a good man."

They catch up on other news. Rolfe reassures Jope that no one questions the legitimacy of his role in the raid on the *Bautista*.

When it is time to leave, he says, "By the way, I'll be at Abraham Piercey's dinner tomorrow noon. Why don't I pick you up beforehand and give you a tour of the town?"

"I'd like that," says Jope.

By the time Rolfe arrives the next day, the wharf is teeming with dockhands and purchasing agents. The new part of town is a beehive of activity. Carpenters and joiners are putting up frames of new homes. Their hammering echoes all the way to the ship. The front gate to the fort is open, and a steady stream of people pass through it coming and going. Jope is startled by two barefoot men in leather loincloths and loose garments draped across their shoulders. Muscular and lean, their skin is dark and reddish brown. Feathers stick out from their black, pleated hair falling to their shoulders. They are at ease, nodding to the people they meet and receiving their greetings in return.

"Are those Indians?" he asks, surprised that they are allowed inside the fort without escort.

Rolfe confirms his guess. "Yes, they are members of the Powhatan tribe. In the past, we've often been at war with them, but we are on good terms with them now. Some of them work on my plantation."

As they walk past the defensive trench into the fort, a drunken man staggers into their path. He squints and tips his hat in their direction and stumbles on. "Not so different from London or Plymouth, after all," Jope comments.

"Yes, many of the laborers spend their money on cheap wine that smugglers bring in on merchant ships—no offense to you, Captain. It's a popular drink and destroys their bodies."

Inside the fort, Jope notes the unusual layout—a triangle of palisades whose apex points north toward the interior countryside. The three corners are raised, circular bulwarks with cannons aimed downriver and into the hinterland. The arrangement of houses follows the lines of the palisades. In their midst is a large open area, the marketplace, with storehouses on both sides and the church between them. There are a number of booths and tables with all kinds of wares on display—pottery and glass beads, venison, fish, tobacco pipes, and wool and leather products.

"Whatever the Earl of Warwick may say about Edwin Sandys being the devil, he has done a lot to develop our colony," says Rolfe. "A year ago we didn't have glassmakers, coopers, millwrights, weavers, or tanners here. Now we're developing ironworks and vineyards and encouraging plantation owners to try growing other crops in addition to tobacco."

Jope is hardly listening. His attention is drawn to two women examining leather belts and pouches. Their gowns, made of fine, colorful silks, are bedecked with jewelry that sparkles in the sun. The beaver hat with a pearl band that one of them wears would be the envy of every society lady in London.

Rolfe notices his astonishment. "Those are the wives of the burgesses, in town because of the upcoming parliamentary assembly," he explains. "Tobacco has made their husbands rich, and they are eager to flaunt their wealth." He adds wryly, "We are no longer the beggars of the world."

By then they have reached Piercey's house. Although it is the largest on the block, it is modest in comparison with Jope's home in Tavistock. The interior is comfortable, though, with wooden floors, fine dark wood furniture imported from England, and tapestries on the walls.

Jope

Piercey greets Jope warmly. "Welcome to my house, Captain. I'm sorry my wife, Elizabeth, is not here to meet you, but she is on a visit to England with my two daughters."

Rolfe presents his pregnant young wife, Jane, who has arrived ahead of them, and introduces the other guests. Jope already knows William Pierce, Rolfe's father-in-law, from his previous visit. But the Reverend Buck is a new face, as are John Pory, secretary to Governor Yeardley and speaker of the assembly, and two plantation owners, burgesses whose well-dressed wives rival the two he saw earlier.

Pory intrigues him the most. A decade older than the others, his eyes shine with curiosity and mischief. Jope imagines that, as Yeardley's man, he will report every word to the governor.

Dinner is not as elaborate an affair as some of the banquets at John Granville's home, but liveried servants offer plenty of corn pudding, bread, and roasted duck. The oysters, Pory assures him, are a special treat from the northern islands in the Chesapeake Bay. Everyone is eager to hear the latest news from England, especially about the betrothal of the Crown prince to the Spanish infanta. Jope does his best to satisfy their curiosity.

Pory entertains everyone with tales of his travels across Europe—from the Low Countries to France to as far as Constantinople—and he and Jope trade reminiscences of Leiden and Amsterdam. When he hears that Pory has translated and published a book about African geography, he wonders if there is anything in it about Margaret and John's homeland.

"I would like to read it," he says.

"I'll be glad to get you a copy," replies Pory, pleased.

Dinner is followed by the men withdrawing to Piercey's study to smoke tobacco and talk well into the afternoon among dense clouds of smoke.

At some point the conversation turns toward the Africans Jope brought here on his last visit.

"They are an industrious lot and a boon to our plantations," Piercey says, echoing Butler's praise at Point Comfort. "We were surprised how much they already knew about cattle and tobacco. I imagine they were farmers in Africa."

"Better than some of the riffraff we've been getting from England. Sometimes I think they're just emptying Newgate prison onto our shores," says one of the burgesses with disdain as he takes a long puff on his pipe.

"The influx of newcomers does put undue stress on the resources of our colony. Many of them succumb to disease within a few months of their arrival," Reverend Buck observes.

"Yes, Jamestown has become an uncouth place, indeed," Pory agrees. "If it wasn't for present company, I'd despair of life."

"Now, now, the plantations are not so bad," says the other burgess. "People spend the week working hard and they observe the Sabbath."

"I yearn to escape and go back to Europe," Pory laments. "You wouldn't have an extra berth on your ship for me, Captain?"

Jope, realizing Pory is only half-serious, says kiddingly, "I'm sure we can accommodate you, should you so desire."

By the time the party breaks up, it is getting dark outside. Jope thanks his host "for a most entertaining day."

"I'll see you tomorrow on your ship," Piercey promises. "Then you can take the cargo upriver to unload at my plantation and Governor Yeardley's Flowerdew and pick up as much tobacco as you can carry!"

As Rolfe accompanies him back to the *White Lion,* Jope asks about John Pory's close connection to the governor. Rolfe reassures him, "You need not worry about him. He is an ally to our cause."

By the time they reach the dock, the land across the river is only dimly visible, a dark, high, uneven line above the water's edge.

Jope stops and looks at the hazy moon rising downstream reflected in the gentle ripples of the waves. "Is life really better on the plantations?" he wonders aloud.

Jope

Rolfe considers the question, realizing it may have another purpose besides making conversation. "Yes," he answers. "They are worlds apart from Jamestown. Why don't you see for yourself when you get to Flowerdew and Piercey's plantation?"

Jope nods. He has plans to do so already.

26
WARWICK'S GAMBITS
London—Late Summer 1620

The Earl of Warwick is sitting in his favorite armchair, dressed in a loose doublet and slippers, his bare legs covered with a blanket. He has been feverish and suffering from a headache and racking cough for two days. At the insistence of Nathaniel Rich, he has called for his personal doctor to attend him. Unlike many of his wealthy peers, Warwick is not a hypochondriac. He figures it is nothing more than a bout of influenza, which will pass with time, but his cousin has convinced him it is better to err on the safe side and endure the ministrations of his physician.

His illness could not come at a worse time. He is beset by too many difficulties and needs to remain sharp-witted. The investigation by the High Court of Admiralty into the *Treasurer's* privateering has reached a critical point. Various problems have delayed the departure of the *Mayflower* and *Speedwell* for New England. Meanwhile, Sir Edwin Sandys continues to agitate against him at meetings of the Virginia and Bermuda Companies.

The doctor arrives with the pompous air of a man who believes his arcane knowledge bestows a special superiority on him. He is a good ten years older than Warwick. Clad in a dark brown gown and wearing a skullcap, he carries a large book under his arm. His apprentice, a round-faced, pimply lad of fourteen, walks behind him, toting a medical bag.

They bow deeply before Warwick, who grunts in reply.

"M'Lord, you really should be in bed!" the doctor remonstrates.

"I am far too busy for that!"

Stroking his full gray beard, the doctor examines his patient critically from all sides. After listening to Warwick's complaints, he collects a urine sample from him in a glass vial. He swirls it, smells it, tastes it, and compares its color to a chart in the book the apprentice holds open for him. Then he mutters something about "bad blood," "yellow bile," and "imbalance of humors."

Warwick, anticipating a bloodletting, waves irritably in his direction. "Do your worst, leech!"

Ignoring the hostile epithet for members of his profession, the doctor nods to his apprentice, who rummages in the bag and brings out a jar of the very creatures Warwick has invoked. The doctor applies the black, sluglike worms to his bare legs. Then he goes to a side table and starts to crush with a mortar and pestle herbs he has brought to mix a potion.

Rich closes his eyes and leans back. The line from Shakespeare's *Hamlet* comes to his mind: "How all occasions inform against me."

At least he has had the satisfaction of hearing about Edwin Sandys squirm. Ever since King James vetoed his reelection as treasurer of the Virginia Company, Sandys has been hard at work behind the scenes to undo His Majesty's order. He even approached the young Duke of Buckingham, the King's current favorite, to plead his case. Warwick likes Buckingham. The man is amenable to bribery, as long as it is done judiciously; but Sandys, who believes too much in the sanctity of the law, didn't pursue so shady a course of action. Nor does he understand the monarch's profound personal antipathy toward him for frustrating his will in the House of Commons. James considers the Virginia Company under Sandys's leadership a hotbed of sedition and democratic rebellion.

So it was exceedingly gratifying to Warwick when Nathaniel Rich brought word of what happened in the King's bedchamber when Buckingham relayed the "official" plea for free elections from the company. James had a most royal fit and shouted at the top of his voice, "Choose the devil if you will, but not Sir Edwin Sandys."

But Warwick has to admit that Sandys is a tough old bird. Although he had to relinquish his post, he continued to battle in order to keep Thomas Smythe from taking over the reins of the company again. At the quarter court at the end of June, the secret deal he managed to wrangle came to light, surprising everyone.

The Earl of Southampton rose and said that the King had "graciously condescended" to withdraw his nominations in favor of free elections, as long as the shareholders chose "such a person as might at all times and occasions have free access unto his royal person."

Immediately Lord Cavendish jumped to his feet and called out, "I nominate Sir Henry Wriothesley, the Earl of Southampton, as treasurer."

Although Smythe's faction presented its own contenders, the vast majority of the assembly cast its balls for Sandys's compromise candidate.

It was a neat trick, Warwick has to concede. It keeps the wily parliamentarian as the man with the real power behind the treasurer's seat. Southampton is willing to play the figurehead as long as he doesn't have to slog through the morass of company business affairs. With Nicholas Ferrar reelected as deputy and most auditor positions in his camp as well, Sandys can pursue his vision for Virginia as a commonwealth and state unto itself without interruption.

And he will continue to be a headache worse than Warwick is feeling now. He will surely call for ongoing investigations of the *Treasurer* affair, even as the High Admiralty Court does its work.

Warwick's reverie is interrupted by the doctor plucking the leeches from his legs and depositing the swollen worms in a jar. He hands the earl a cup. "'Tis a potion for your headache, m'Lord."

The dark liquid smells of tar, rosemary, and something Warwick had rather not ask about. He takes a tentative sip and puckers his lips. The taste is bitter and loathsome. As he proceeds to take larger swallows, there is a knock at the door, sending Rich into a sputtering cough.

Alfred materializes and says, "Thomas Weston is here to see you, M'Lord. Shall I tell him you're indisposed?"

The doctor nods his head in warning, but Warwick ignores him. Between coughs he says, "No, send him in when the doctor is gone."

Knowing that it is futile to argue, the physician sighs and advises, "You should feel better in a day, m'Lord, although the cough will be with you for a seven-night."

Then he joins his apprentice who has packed up jars and bags of herbs. At the door he turns, bows, and says, "I will be back tomorrow, m'Lord."

Warwick waves him away like a bothersome fly. Feeling weaker than when the doctor first arrived, he finishes drinking the potion and takes a deep breath.

When Alfred ushers in Thomas Weston, wearing a cloak and garments that identify him as a merchant, Warwick gestures him to a nearby chair. Without preamble, he asks, "What news?"

Weston looks chagrined. "Not good, I'm afraid, m'Lord. The *Speedwell* sprung another leak in her hull near Penzance off the tip of Cornwall, and the two ships put into harbor at Newlyn."

Exasperated, Rich slams his hand on the armrest, all illness banished. "This is the second time after a month of unnecessary delays. What is it with this Dutch ship? Is this venture cursed?"

"Not at all!" Weston perks up. "The good news is that rather than do another round of repairs, John Carver and the others decided to transfer all of the pilgrims onto the *Mayflower*. She's headed for Northern Virginia on her own as we speak."

"Finally. Any later and the whole enterprise just might perish in one of the autumn storms!"

Weston nods eagerly. "You know how much the merchant investors appreciate your generous support. We would like to invite you to join the New England Council at our next quarter court in November."

"It will be my pleasure," Warwick says, gratified. At last, a company he can guide without the bothersome presence of Edwin Sandys.

"We will need to address the drawing of boundaries between Virginia and our colony after the *Mayflower* makes landfall," Weston continues. "We are counting on you bringing your influence to bear on our behalf."

Rich brightens. He and Argall found a protected area on the coast nearly a thousand miles to the north of Jamestown, but delineating the border between the two colonies presents him with an opportunity to spite Sandys in an entirely new way.

"Of course," he says.

Pleading illness, he cuts the interview short, but when Weston leaves, he feels better than he has in several days.

*　*　*

The following day at the strategy session on how to respond to Count Gondomar's revelations about the *Bautista* affair at the High Admiralty Court, Warwick is almost himself again. The headaches are gone. Even the occasional cough no longer hurts his lungs.

The meeting, conducted around a large oak table, includes Argall, Nathaniel Rich, and two attorneys conversant with maritime law. One is sallow skinned, the other has a ruddy complexion and jowls like a bulldog. Also present is Captain Daniel Elfrith, recently arrived from Bermuda to testify before the court. He does his best to appear comfortable, but it is clear that he would rather be on the quarterdeck of a ship. He is a lapsed Anglican, and the Puritans put up with his colorful language without letting him know how much it offends their sensibilities.

Warwick occupies the most prominent chair at the head of the table but lets the others take the lead.

The main issue is the letter from Gondomar's cousin, Count de Acuña. It describes the *San Juan Bautista* being attacked by two vessels, one flying the Dutch flag, the other the British Union Jack, and contradicts what Warwick has claimed all along—that the Dutchman and his *White Lion* raided the Spanish slave ship alone, and that Elfrith bought the Africans from him sometime later on.

"That scotches laying all of the blame at Captain Jope's feet," says Argall with regret.

It is Nathaniel Rich, with his crafty legal mind, who comes up with a solution. "We can still blame the Dutchman," he insists. "We'll just say that he coerced you and the *Treasurer* to sail in consort."

"By my gammer's withered leg, that is a fine cock-and-bull yarn," Elfrith bristles. "How could he do that when I had superior firepower?"

Nathaniel Rich retorts, "You just have to maintain that's what happened. As captain of the ship, your word carries a great deal of weight."

"Od-rat-it, it don't feel right."

"Best lay your scruples aside, Captain. You're in this up to your neck," Warwick warns him, ignoring his oath. "If you say it with conviction and stick to your story, they'll believe you."

He coughs and fixes Elfrith with a stern look until the captain nods in agreement. Then he adds, "My cousin will take you through your testimony word for word."

"It would be good if we had several crewmen back up the claim," says the bulldog-faced attorney.

"Yes, Nathaniel Butler in Bermuda can take care of that for us," says Nathaniel Rich. "He can identify who has the wit to testify in person and who best remain there to be deposed."

"I can help with that, too. I know my crew," Elfrith volunteers to make sure his powerful employer knows he is fully on board.

A look passes between Warwick and his cousin. They know whose judgment they trust more—their man in Bermuda.

As they go over the details of the testimony, Nathaniel Rich has another idea. "Why don't we call on one or two of the Africans to testify and support our cause? They will be considered unbiased and lend credence to our argument."

Argall joins in. "And it will irritate Count Gondomar to no end!"

Warwick recognizes the potential benefit and uses the opportunity to assure Elfrith of his favor. "Our captain here can tell us which ones will best serve our purpose. He'll go to Bermuda after his testimony to the court and bring them to Leez Priory in secret."

Elfrith straightens in his chair and slams his fist on the table. "Gadzooks! You can count on me, m'Lord."

Wincing at the sound, Warwick covers his bemusement at the oath invoking the nails of the cross with a fit of coughing.

There is more discussion, but Warwick is tiring. Nathaniel Rich notices him stifling a yawn and brings the meeting to a close.

"I will confer with Elfrith and Argall separately and return in the morning to go over what else needs to be done," he assures his cousin.

That night the Earl of Warwick sleeps soundly for the first time in weeks.

27
FRIENDLY VISITS
Aldwarke—Fall 1620

A lthough Lady Frances disapproves of her sister taking Margaret and John in as wards, she finds it difficult to stay away. Something about the children fascinates her, like a chipped tooth one can't help worrying with one's tongue, and she visits frequently during the summer and fall. She uses the High Admiralty Court's inquiry in London as a pretext, claiming that she wants to be sure that Isabel is thoroughly informed of the progress.

Before long, she has to admit to herself that she has grown somewhat fond of the children. Margaret in particular, looking at her with big eyes, touches something deep inside her. The young girl is serious, poised, articulate, and pious in a way that appeals to the jaded noblewoman, as if she recognizes a former part of herself, having been an outsider herself in the Catholic and Anglican communities of the English upper crust. She shows less interest in John, who spends more time in the stables and animal pens, although he is always courteous and shows no fear in her presence.

Margaret, in turn, is always somewhat uncomfortable around Lady Frances. Not only does her immoderate use of perfume threaten to overwhelm all else in her surroundings, Margaret often feels her eyes evaluating her. When they sit in the drawing room after dinner, Lady Frances likes to fill the air with idle chatter about the newest fashions in town. It is difficult to follow her comments about frounced farthingale skirts, lace standing-falling ruffs, and embroidered stomachers. Her extensive wardrobe seems excessive and affected—she often displays several dresses during a visit, each studded with jewels, fancy embroidery, and colorful ribbons—in stark contrast with Lady Isabel's simple, dark outfits and quiet elegance.

Nor does Margaret understand Lady Frances prattling on about the newest affair of this earl or that duchess, and she would rather be outside working in the garden with Agnes. But since Lady Isabel feigns interest, she pretends to listen attentively, too, while focusing on her knitting. But when Lady Frances mentions the newest developments in the trial in London, her ears perk up because Captain Jope's name comes up frequently and she is eager to learn anything of his whereabouts.

Apparently, sailors from the *Treasurer* have been giving testimony that the Dutchman, as Lady Frances calls him, coerced their Elfrith captain to sail in concert with the *White Lion* and attack the Spanish ship that held her and John prisoner.

The first time she hears of it, her brows knit—she remembers the easygoing, jovial exchanges between her captain and the portly skipper of the other ship, as well as the gathering that took place at night in Point Comfort. There was no tension between them, and they acted like the best of friends.

"What is it, Margaret?" asks Lady Isabel, observing her change of demeanor.

Margaret remembers Jope's instructions to remain quiet about what happened at sea and fumbles with her knitting. "I dropped a stitch," she says.

Lady Isabel looks at her long enough to make Margaret uncomfortable. Then she asks, "Do you need help?"

"No, it's fine now."

Lady Frances also gives a long, penetrating look before resuming her account.

After supper, while the children get ready for bed, she takes her sister aside. "What do you know about this, Isabel? The girl is hiding something, but won't say."

"Leave her be, Frances. When the captain brought the children here, he mentioned he had reached an accommodation with Robert, but I didn't press him. It is of no concern to me."

Frances knows her sister well enough not to pursue the matter any further, but many of her questions are answered sooner than she expected.

Two days later, while the women are in the drawing room, the butler enters and says, "A Captain Jope has arrived, m'Lady, and begs an audience with you."

As soon as Margaret hears that, she drops her knitting. Forgetting all proper decorum, she dashes from the room without asking for permission. Isabel and Frances are too shocked by her behavior to stop her or call after her.

Meanwhile, Margaret flies through the hallways to the entry, where Jope is waiting. "Captain! You're back!" she cries out and flings herself into his arms, burying her face in his leather jerkin.

In no time, his powerful arms lift her off the floor, and she sees the familiar bearded face smiling at her and the sky-blue eyes dancing with delight.

Jope draws her to him and hugs her for some time before putting her down. He takes a step back, looks at her in her purple gown, and says, "My, my, Margaret, you're turning into quite a young lady."

By then, Lady Frances and her sister appear with Agnes in tow. Lady Isabel's reprimand comes with a smile. "Margaret, remember your manners!"

Blushing, Margaret curtseys. "Yes, m'Lady."

But any resumption of proper decorum is shattered when little John barrels in from outside, crowing, "Captain Jope! Captain Jope!"

He nearly bowls the kneeling Jope over, throws his arms around his neck, and plants a kiss on his cheek. Margaret, forgetting her manners again, joins them.

When Jope smiles helplessly up at Lady Isabel, she yields to circumstances. Addressing her butler, she says, "Take them into the parlor, Jake, when they're ready." Then she whispers to Frances, "Come. We're unnecessary here. We will have plenty of time to see them later."

When Jope and the children are installed in the parlor, Margaret and John pepper him with questions. The captain, surprised at their command of English, does his best to answer and asks after them in turn.

When he conveys Mary's greetings, Margaret is chagrined for not having asked after her before. She does so now and is happy to see Jope's face soften. When he says, "She misses you, you know?" it brings tears to her eyes.

Then it is time for presents. John's eyes light up when Jope hands him a small dirk, and Margaret runs her fingers over the soft silk scarf from Holland.

Soon Agnes and Samuel poke their heads in the door to say hello. After meeting him, they marvel over the gifts, and Jope uses the opportunity to excuse himself and join the ladies in the drawing room.

Bowing smartly to Isabel, he says, "I apologize for upsetting your home, m'Lady."

"Think nothing of it, Captain Jope. We forget how impulsive we all were as youngsters," Lady Isabel replies graciously. "Let me introduce my younger sister, Lady Frances Wray Rich."

For a moment, they take each other's measure. Jope notes the ostentatious dress, slender fingers, thin lips, inquisitive brown eyes, and overbearing scent of lavender. Frances is surprised at his easy, courtly manners. She expected a rough seaman with calloused hands and awkward social graces.

She is further taken aback when he bows and says, "It is an honor to meet you, m'Lady. You are one of the beacons of the Puritan cause. We are all grateful for the aid you gave to my fellow ministers during the dark times and your ongoing support nowadays."

To regain her composure, Frances goes on the offensive. "So you are the infamous Dutchman. We hear a great deal about you at the High Admiralty Court in London these days."

Jope wonders just how much she knows of his arrangement with the Earl of Warwick. Her next comment confirms his suspicions.

"Doesn't it bother you to be the scapegoat for my stepson's privateering ventures?"

"My Lord Rich and I have an understanding that is mutually beneficial."

"No doubt, but why do your intrigues have to involve my sister?"

Jope draws back, and his face hardens. "It seems to me that Lady Isabel is perfectly capable of keeping her own counsel on this matter."

"Yes, Frances, that is quite enough," Lady Isabel interposes. "We have discussed this before. Captain Jope is my guest, as are Margaret and John."

Frances nods icily. "I just wanted to make sure we know where we stand."

Jope bows curtly in acknowledgment.

There is no thawing in their relationship at supper that evening, and everyone is secretly happy when Lady Frances announces that she will leave the next day to look in on her estate at Snarford before returning to London.

Her departure makes the time Jope spends with the children much more pleasant. They want to show him everything on the estate. John takes him to the stables, introduces him to his pony, which he has named Berwick, and shows off how well he can ride it around the paddock. Jope is impressed. He was much older before he ever sat on a horse on his own.

Friendly Visits

When he accompanies Margaret on a tour of the gardens, with Margaret naming all the herbs, vegetables, and flowers, he exclaims, "I wish Mary could see this!"

Together, they all visit the pond in the woods. The October sun sends shafts of light through the tree canopy, which glisten on the ripples in the water. Jope finds a small branch and shows John how to whittle with his dirk. For a while they sit quietly on the bed of fallen leaves by the shore, enjoying the musty fall odors and listening to the birds that haven't headed south yet. Margaret will remember this afternoon as one of the best times in her life.

* * *

But it is only an interlude, and all too soon, Jope has to leave again. Before he says his good-byes, he sits with Lady Isabel at a table by a window overlooking the gardens, where Samuel is playing hide-and-seek with the children.

"I can't thank you enough for all you're doing for Margaret and John, m'Lady," he says. "I appreciate your letters updating me about their progress."

"I am very glad you brought them into my life."

"I think both you and I know that it is God's will."

"Yes, I believe it is."

One of her hands lying idly on the table has started to tremble. Seeing Jope take notice, she draws it back into her lap.

Jope catches her eye for a moment and says, "Please continue to keep me informed of all matters as they develop."

Understanding his concern, Lady Isabel chooses to give him a partial answer, "You have nothing to fear, Captain. My sister would never do anything to harm me or her stepson. After all, Lord Rich pays her a handsome annuity. And I will make sure nothing ill befalls my charges."

Impulsively, Jope kisses her other hand in gratitude.

Later, riding in his hired coach on the way to Hull Harbor, where the *White Lion* is waiting for him, he looks out at the green countryside and thinks about his visit. Lady Frances's attitude is troublesome not only for the potential safety of Margaret and John but because it raises concerns about their future. While he trusts Lady Isabel, they cannot remain her wards forever—the tremor in her hand is worrisome—and they will never be accepted in England as more than household servants. He prays once again that he is following the Lord's purpose and will.

28

A SECRET MEETING

London—November 1620

"He's done it just to spite me!"

Sir Edwin Sandys paces in the smoke-filled study of the Earl of Southampton's London palace, fulminating. Henry Wriothesley and Nicholas Ferrar, sitting at a large table, look at each other in frustration. They've come together in secret to hammer out plans for the future of the Virginia Company, but their meeting has gone far astray from its purpose.

When the Earl of Warwick withdrew from the company, leaving his cousin Nathaniel Rich to look after his interests, they had hoped that the ongoing strife would yield to a more reasonable course of action and that their main difficulties would come from Thomas Smythe's faction. But Warwick continues to cast a malicious shadow over their affairs. Not content with sending the *Mayflower* to northern Virginia—as agreed to in the patent awarded by the company to the Leiden Separatists—he petitioned King James for a separate charter, asking that all lands north of the Virginia Company's domain be granted to the Council for New England.

Southampton pulls nervously on his tobacco pipe. As a member of the Privy Council, he was among the first to receive word of Warwick's success. Now he wishes he hadn't mentioned the terms, which sent Sandys into a paroxysm of fury. It turns out that the territory belonging to the New England Council extends south to the 40° latitude, overlapping Virginia's claim by hundreds of miles.

"How dare he encroach on our dominion!" Sandys sputters.

"I'm sure Lord Rich had to pay a pretty penny for the privilege," says Nicholas Ferrar.

"He throws his wealth around like every arrogant nobleman, thinking his money can buy whatever he pleases."

Ferrar glances anxiously at Southampton. How will the earl respond to a slur that includes him, if unwittingly? To his relief, Wriothesley expels a puff of smoke and allows it to pass in silence. He apparently understands that when Sandys is worked up, you have to let his choleric humor runs its course.

"I agree that it is most irritating," he ventures offhandedly, "but the line is so far to the north, it doesn't really signify."

Sandys stops in mid-stride. "What if it opens the floodgates to other royal charters at our expense? If James has his way, there'll be a throng of colonies throughout the new world."

Southampton chuckles. "That is not likely to happen."

"I pray to God you are right."

"In any case, the best way to thumb our noses at Warwick is to ensure the success of our Virginia venture," Southampton says languidly, trying to bring the conversation back to the more important subject at hand.

But Sandys is difficult to appease. "This couldn't have come at a worse time," he complains. "Our company is still mired in the debt incurred by Smythe and his predatory friends, and our new investments in iron and Italian glassworks at Jamestown have cost us nearly £5,000."

"But we have paid for that with subscriptions, and if the manufacture of metal goods, pottery, and beads to trade with the Indians succeeds, it will go a long way to making the colony more independent," says Ferrar.

Southampton adds further balm. "I need not remind you that they were your ideas, Sir Edwin, and when they take root and blossom, it will be to your credit."

Mollified, Sandys returns to his seat at the table, and Southampton heaves a quiet sigh of relief. As Warwick has known all along, he is primarily a figurehead for the company while Sandys guides the reins behind the scenes and Ferrar takes care of its day-to-day concerns. He looks longingly toward his desk, where various papers wait for him to resume his true passion—poetry. Acting as mediator is taking a great deal more time and effort than he anticipated.

"We must find new ways to raise money for the company," Southampton admonishes. "The Privy Council has learned of our diverting our tobacco crop to Holland to avoid import taxes and is not looking kindly upon it."

"It was a matter of time," Ferrar agrees.

"I'm not very happy with George Yeardley as governor," Sandys says, changing the subject. "He is too passive in demanding rents from tenants on our lands in Virginia. We must have that income! I want to replace him when his term is up next year."

"Who do you have in mind?" asks Southampton carefully, anticipating another long, drawn-out battle with the Smythe and Warwick factions.

"Sir Francis Wyatt."

"Isn't his wife, Margaret, your niece?"

"You are well-informed, m'Lord. But he is a good candidate in his own right!"

"No doubt," Southampton replies, offhandedly. "A wise choice."

Ferrar nods. "I will tell Lord Cavendish to rally our supporters and feel out the opposition."

Southampton takes another drag on his pipe, mulling over whether to comment on the agenda for the upcoming quarter court of the Somers Island Company. Any mention of Bermuda could set Sandys off again. While the Privy Council has insisted that its meetings be held at a separate time and place from the Virginia Company's, the Earl of Warwick continues to attend them, making it unavoidable that the two enemies encounter one another.

At the last session, when Sandys accused Warwick of having transferred his privateering base to Bermuda, they all but came to blows. Still, they might deal with matters affecting their financial interests if they weren't hewn from the same block, which is why it takes so little provocation for them to be at loggerheads.

But to his surprise, when he brings up Bermuda, Sandys is unexpectedly delighted. Southampton is immediately on guard, and sure enough, he soon has reason to despair.

"I have been following the inquest of the High Admiralty Court," Sandys says. "Count Gondomar has called witnesses from the crew of the *Treasurer* who are refuting Captain Elfrith's ludicrous claim that he was forced to participate in the raid on the Spanish galleon." He adds happily, "This gives us another reason to pursue our own inquiries—to find out the truth and get remuneration for the Africans Warwick stole from us."

Southampton sighs. "I wish you would consider dropping the matter altogether. It takes up valuable time better spent on more pressing issues."

"And miss out on the opportunity to set matters right with Warwick?" Sandys replies, his eyes shimmering maniacally. "Not on your life!"

29
CHRISTMAS AT ALDWARKE
December–January 1620–1621

A s a devout Puritan, Lady Isabel does not approve of Christmas festivities, believing them to be both pagan revelry and expressions of papist extravagance. But as the mistress of the primary estate in the area, she understands the obligations landlords and nobles have toward their subjects and indulges the customs beloved by many of her tenants and villagers. So she welcomes the wassailers, mummers, and Morris dancers who arrive at the manor during the twelve days of Christmas and holds a big feast for everyone in the district with a boar's head as the centerpiece of the lavish spread and plenty of cider and beer for refreshments.

She also allows decorations inside and outside of the mansion and turns a blind eye to Agnes observing superstitions and rituals, but she draws the line at bringing a Yule log into the drawing room and insists on holding the big banquet, along with the exchange of presents, on New Year's rather than Christmas Day.

For Margaret and John, it is an exciting time, full of fun activities. They didn't experience the joys of English holiday revels the previous year because Jope and Mary practiced Puritan austerity at Tavistock. Now they get to go with Agnes, Samuel, and other servants into the woods to help gather holly, ivy, and rosemary and festoon the windows, entrance gate, and interior common rooms with wreaths and garlands. Soon the manor is filled everywhere with holiday scents.

On Christmas Eve, Margaret and John come upon Samuel hanging a bunch of mistletoe from the ceiling of the main parlor. Looking up, puzzled, John asks, "Why are you doing that?"

"It's a tradition. If a young man catches a girl under it, she has to give him a kiss," Samuel says, grinning.

"Even Aunt Isabel?" asks Margaret.

"Yes." He adds in a conspiratorial whisper, "Don't tell Agnes, but I'm going to be on the lookout for her!"

In the afternoon, Agnes has the children help her carry a large bowl of cider and a bucket filled with pieces of toasted bread to the apple orchard. They place the bread on the branches and pour cider on the roots of all the trees. "It will give us a good crop next year," she explains.

As they head back inside, it starts to snow, small flakes drifting gently down in the late afternoon sky. Margaret and John stick out their tongues and run around the backyard trying to catch the tingling crystals.

That evening, they watch from a window in their wing of the mansion as the first group of mummers arrives in the front court, dressed in wild, colorful costumes. They perform their play for the servants, staff, and Lady Isabel. It involves St. George, a fair damsel, a doctor, and the devil. The knight gets killed and is brought back to life through a magic potion and the power of love to vanquish the villain. Although Margaret and John don't understand much of the goings-on—even with Samuel's explanations—they delight in the sword fights and the exaggerated death throes of the villain.

Lady Isabel thanks the players and gives them silver coins for their efforts. They bow to her and march off into the night, dancing and singing.

Later a group of wassailers comes by to sing carols and pass around a bowl of spiced ale. They, too, receive thanks and payment.

Margaret and John get to bed late and have a hard time falling asleep, wondering what new excitement Christmas Day will bring.

Over the next days, they get up early and work with Agnes and Samuel to finish their presents for Aunt Isabel. Margaret is knitting her a cap from the finest sheep's wool, and John is whittling away at a branch to make a small ship. They also help with preparations for the big feast. John participates in rounding up hogs, sheep, and cattle to be butchered. Margaret is in the kitchen and bakery. Surrounded all afternoon by the intoxicating odors of spices, baking breads, and puddings, and the warmth from the fire, she often returns to the manor in a pleasant trance.

So she doesn't pay attention late one afternoon when she comes into the parlor. Suddenly, John steps in her way. "What is it?" she asks, surprised.

Grinning, he points his finger toward the ceiling and says, "You owe me a kiss!"

Margaret glances up, sees the mistletoe, and can't help but break into a smile. She looks at John, who has tilted his head up toward her. She bends down and plants a kiss on his pursed lips and holds it until he draws back. Seeing the twinkle in her eyes, he laughs and dashes off before she can swat him.

In the evenings, more people from the village visit the manor house. The children especially like the Morris dancers, who perform in the great hall because the ground outside is covered with snow. Wielding sticks and swords they leap through the air. Their antics make the colorful ribbon streamers on their costumes and the small bells attached to their shins tinkle brightly. At some point, they lay a pair of long clay tobacco pipes on the floor, one across the other, and two men dance nimbly back and forth over them.

The season of revel, joy, and high spirits is in full swing.

* * *

But in the middle of the week, a messenger arrives after the midday meal. He has driven his horse hard. There is foam at the corner of its mouth, and when it comes to a standstill, it snorts heavily, sending vaporous exhalations into the cold air. The young man, bundled in a thick overcoat and hat and scarf, dismounts and doesn't even take the time to hand the reins to the groom who has come from the stables to meet him. He rushes to the entrance and knocks loudly at the gate.

Minutes later, Jake enters the study where Isabel and the children are reading the Christmas story in the New Testament.

"M'Lady, a courier with urgent news from Derbyshire."

Isabel rises in agitation—messengers in a hurry usually bring bad tidings. She waits until Agnes takes the children into the next room before letting Jake admit the messenger.

The young man enters with a pained expression, his cheeks still red from the cold outside. He bows and hands her a letter. She breaks the seal and starts to read. Suddenly she cries out. Her hand flutters to her chest like a wounded bird, and she starts to sway precariously. Jake rushes to her aid and helps her into a chair.

She waves him away and slowly gets control of herself. Then she reads the letter again and looks up at the courier. "What do you know of this?"

The young man's lips tremble with emotion. "Nothing but what is written there, m'Lady," he says haltingly. "Your son fell when his horse shied, and he hit his head on a stone wall. I was there when they carried his lifeless body into the hall. I'm very sorry for it and having to be the one bearing the news."

"What is your name, son?"

"Abner, your Ladyship."

"You must have ridden hard for several days, Abner, and I thank you for it." She turns to her butler. "Take Abner to the kitchen and have him seen after."

After they leave, sounds of scuffling come from behind the screen that conceals the door to the next room. Lady Isabel calls out, "No need to hide back there. You may come here."

The children emerge with glum faces. For the first time in many months, Margaret's cheek twitches, betraying her anguish.

Agnes follows behind them. "We couldn't help overhearing and I couldn't stop them. I'm so very sorry, m'Lady."

"It is all right." Lady Isabel takes a deep breath and continues, "It is the Lord's will. I am certain my Godfrey is with him now."

"Should I give word to cancel the festivities?"

"Under no circumstances," replies Lady Isabel firmly. For the benefit of Margaret and John, who stand there uncertainly, she adds, "We must carry on. So many others depend on us. It is our duty. Do you understand?"

The children nod with lips drawn tight.

* * *

Over the next days, Lady Isabel oversees with determination the festivities and preparations for the big New Year's Day banquet. The only sign of mourning is her raven black cap, which covers much of her white hair.

While John is sad, but not overwhelmed by emotion, for Margaret it ushers in a difficult time. She barely remembers the middle-aged man who visited Aldwarke earlier in the year. But the news of his death makes her worry about Jope and brings on dreams of her lost friends and family. They appear to her sailing on a ship, waving to her like fading ghosts. On several occasions, she wakes up in the middle of the night, frightened and with a piercing pain in her breast.

Observing Lady Isabel, Margaret notices her eyes drifting from time to time when she's not fully engaged in activities until someone asking a question reminds her of her duty and brings her back to the present. The tremors in her hand are more apparent. She also spends more time in the chapel next to the great hall, praying fervently.

When Margaret joins her now and again, sitting on the wooden bench next to her in silence, she doesn't object.

One time, she says, as if in a world of her own, "I was fifteen when I had my Godfrey. I never thought I would outlive him." Another time, she whispers in quiet anguish, "I don't know what I did for God to punish me so."

Margaret, sensing her deeper pain, impulsively puts her hand on Lady Isabel's trembling fingers and is gratified when her gesture finds acceptance.

She almost wishes they would not have to exchange presents on New Year's Day, but Lady Isabel insists on keeping up with all planned activities. She praises Margaret for the knitted cap, although she is not likely to ever wear it because it is dark blue, not the color of mourning. She accepts John's hand-carved sailboat with a smile. In return, she gives Margaret a pair of satin gloves and John a book of verses to encourage his reading.

Later, when tenants and villagers come to partake of the big feast, Lady Isabel has a kind word for everyone and receives their gifts and condolences with quiet grace. She hands out presents in return and distributes alms to the poor.

By the time Twelfth Night is over, bringing the holiday season to a close, Margaret has a better sense of what Lady Isabel meant by "duty" and "carrying on." She realizes that throwing herself into work allows her to keep going. It makes a big impression on her, and she vows to face any future hardships of her own with equal composure.

30

LORD RICH AND THE ANGOLANS

Aldwarke—Late Spring 1621

T he Earl of Warwick hates to travel by carriage. He feels cooped up, and no matter how many cushions and pillows line the interior, the rutted and potholed roads ensure that the ride leaves him sore and tender in more places than he cares to count. He has learned to tolerate the half-day journey from London to his estate at Leez Priory, but the three-day trip to Aldwarke puts him into a foul temper. With each shudder and jolt of his coach he gets more cross, and neither the beauty of the countryside nor the sunny springtime weather soothes his irritation.

Not that he needs any additional provocation to feel thoroughly vexed. Once again he seems to be beset on all sides. Things were looking up when the High Admiralty Court ruled that there was not enough evidence for him, Argall, or even Elfrith to be held responsible for the *Treasurer's* raid on the Spanish galleon. But Count Gondomar and Sir Edwin Sandys have pursued the question of ownership for the slaves from Angola with renewed vehemence, one in civil court and the other by initiating commissions in the Virginia and the Bermuda Companies to investigate the matter. Sandys keeps saying that Warwick stole the Africans from the shareholders of both companies!

Lord Rich and the Angolans

So far the levees Warwick has put up, with the help of his cousin Nathaniel, have held against all onslaughts. His contention that Elfrith purchased the Angolans from the Dutchman after being forced to accompany him on the raid has remained unchallenged. When some of the crew of the *Treasurer* who testified to his version became disgruntled about being stranded in Bermuda, Nathaniel Butler mollified them with suitable financial incentives.

But any unwarranted revelation that comes close to what really happened threatens to break through his carefully constructed barriers.

That is why the most recent effort to rally some of the Angolans on his behalf has been such a disappointment. If testimony from the men and women taken from the Spanish slave ship supported his case, he would have the weapon with which to silence the arrogant Gondomar and self-important Sandys.

Warwick was hopeful when he first met the three Africans—two men and a woman—identified by Butler and transported by ship by Elfrith to Southampton and from there to Leez Priory. Although they spoke English with heavy accents and were sometime at a loss for words, they were self-possessed and displayed none of the toadying qualities so many other menials affected in his presence.

They were able-bodied workers, too. The land steward put the men, Antonio and John Pedro, to work taking care of the cattle and goats on the estate, and Rich received only favorable reports about their knowledge and familiarity with his livestock. The young woman, Maria, made an excellent parlor maid and, according to the house steward, had as gentle a disposition as one could ask for. He also discovered that she and Antonio wanted to get married.

More annoying has been the Africans' insistence that they were devout Christians, brought up in the Catholic faith long before they were branded and baptized by the Spanish slavers. John Pedro, the oldest, even demonstrated his knowledge of catechism by starting to recite it in Spanish, and he has resisted every effort to convince him to renounce his faith. The other two, more amenable and eager to please, have participated in the Sunday services held in the estate's chapel, and agreed to convert and become good Puritans. They even took the English names of Anthony and Mary.

That act was enough to raise Warwick's hopes that that they would support his cause as well, but their account not only revealed the squalor aboard the Spanish galleon but also implicated Elfrith and the *Treasurer* as eager participants in the raid on the *San Juan Bautista*. They insisted that he himself selected them and the other Angolans for his ship, and that he traded several in Virginia for food before heading to Bermuda.

When Nathaniel Rich suggested that it might be in their interest to support a version more favorable to Warwick, Mary said in all innocence, "I couldn't tell a lie like that," and Anthony asked, with a more knowledgeable air, "You wouldn't want me to commit a sin?"

When the earl heard of it, he seethed with barely contained anger. Not only were these Africans stubbornly truthful, their testimony was so dangerous it could destroy his carefully erected bulwark and open the floodgates to disaster. After he calmed down, Nathaniel Rich convinced him that things would be all right if they were sent as far as possible away from England.

But having promised that they would testify before the Virginia Company's council, with one of the High Admiralty Court's judges in attendance, he had no choice but to produce at least one witness. After rejecting John Pedro as too dangerous and Mary as too naive, they decided on Anthony. They told him that he was not required to talk about everything—Nathaniel Rich would conduct the questioning and steer clear of dangerous waters—and he agreed.

Everything went according to plan. Anthony's account of the horrific conditions on the Spanish galleon shocked everyone in attendance.

But when Nathaniel Rich concentrated on Captain Jope and what Anthony could recall of him aboard the *San Juan Bautista*, one of his attorneys made the mistake of saying, "It looks like the Dutchman is entirely to blame for the attack."

When others started to chime in, Anthony, who remembered Jope's kindness, felt compelled to defend him and started to spill the truth about the *Treasurer*'s and Captain Elfrith's involvement. It was only Nathaniel Rich's quick thinking that prevented utter disaster. He claimed that, because Anthony was not a Christian, his testimony was not reliable or admissible, and the High Admiralty Court judge agreed.

Warwick decided to send Anthony to Virginia to the new plantation that his friend Edward Bennett was starting on the south side of the James River as a Puritan settlement. Out of spite, and in punishment for his insistence on being a good Christian, he would have to go alone. The earl would keep Mary a while longer at his estate so that Anthony would have plenty of time to worry about whether he would ever see her again.

Because John Pedro, older and more experienced, was politically even more dangerous, Warwick and his cousin determined that he needed to be separated from the others. Fortunately, the *Mayflower* returned in May with news that the Pilgrims had made land and founded a settlement. They named it Plymouth after the point of their departure in England. It was farther north than the place he and Argall had suggested. Although half of the passengers and crew died during the harsh winter, the survivors were determined to keep going and had made contact with the local Indian tribe, the Wampanoag, who seemed to be willing to help. Warwick has decided to send John Pedro to Plymouth with the next supply ship from the Council of New England.

It was his clever cousin who pointed out that the two African children harbored in Aldwarke could present a similar problem. At the very least, it would be prudent to find out if they remembered anything that could become troublesome.

But when Warwick wrote to his step-aunt Isabel, demanding that she bring the children to Leez Priory for a visit, she refused, claiming ill health after the death of her son, and pointed out the dangers of the journey for Margaret and John without her. Knowing how stubborn the family could be from his encounters with Lady Isabel's younger sister, Frances, Warwick decided not to press the point and cursed under his breath about the impossible Wray sisters. Nathaniel offered to go, but Warwick needed him to look after his affairs and put out fires at the trials and company inquests. He also wanted to see these two children for himself, who had charmed a hardened sea captain and now had Lady Isabel protecting them like a mother bear guarding her cubs.

And so he is suffering on the journey through Yorkshire and growing increasingly irritable.

* * *

Meanwhile, at Aldwarke the household staff and just about everyone is all aflutter in anticipation of his arrival. Although Lady Isabel has told her staff to treat the Earl of Warwick no differently than any other noble who has stayed at the manor, everyone is acting as if King James himself is coming for a visit. The maids, servants, and butlers have worked long hours to clean and polish every surface inside the house to make it shine. Margaret has been working in the kitchen, where the cook is preparing a feast to rival the Christmas banquet. John has helped clean the stables and make room for the earl's horses.

Lady Isabel has mentioned to the children that Lord Rich is coming to see them. Margaret knows he is the man Captain Jope talked to who is responsible for their being at Aldwarke, but she can't fathom why he would take an interest in her and John after ignoring them for a year and a half. Lady Isabel can't shed any light on that either, and the tension in the household rises with every day his Lordship's arrival draws nearer. Margaret and John are getting more anxious, too. The night before the earl is expected, neither of them sleep well.

Lord Rich and the Angolans

The morning of the day of Warwick's arrival, the children dress in their best outfits, but Lady Isabel conducts the lessons according to schedule to instill a sense of calm and normalcy.

"There is nothing to worry about," she says to allay their concerns.

Then the moment arrives. Margaret and John watch from a window as a large, handsome coach, drawn by six horses, pulls up to the front entrance. Footmen and servants gather, and a dark-haired man emerges from the carriage and steps uncertainly onto the cobblestones. He hunches his shoulders, then leans backward to work the stiffness from his body before straightening and heading inside.

In the parlor, Lady Isabel, with the children by her side, greets Warwick formally. "Welcome to my humble home, Sir Robert."

The earl is taken aback by how much she has changed since he last saw her. She looks as if she has aged a decade and seems smaller and frailer. The death of her son has clearly taken its toll. He gallantly takes her hand and, as custom dictates, kisses her on the lips. Then he says, "Lady Isabel, I can only express my deepest condolences at your loss."

"Thank you. That is very kind of you. We must go on as best we can, and I have my duties here." She turns to Margaret and John next to her. "Children, this is Lord Rich, the Earl of Warwick, under whose generous patronage you are here with me."

Warwick sees a thin young girl dressed in a rose-colored satin gown and a smaller boy wearing a green doublet and breeches, standing at attention. Radiating as much charm as he can muster, he smiles and says, "You must be Margaret and John. I am glad to meet you."

When they curtsey and bow in response, they look like miniature courtiers to him. What he finds unsettling is how they stare at him with large, unafraid eyes, just like the three Angolans at Leez Priory. He wonders if all Africans have this direct manner.

Margaret says. "I hope you had a pleasant journey, m'Lord. I know how rough a coach ride can be."

John adds, "It is more comfortable aboard a ship."

Warwick is amazed by their easy command of English and social grace.

Lady Isabel, noting his surprise, suppresses a smile and asks, "Will you be staying long, Sir Robert?"

"Just for the night. Unfortunately, my affairs in London don't permit me to stay away longer."

"You must be hungry. Why don't we have dinner and talk after?"

Warwick bows. "As you wish." It is just as well. The meal will allow him to get a better sense of the children before he asks his questions.

They repair to the large dining hall where a feast awaits them—veal, roasted capon, baked venison, tarts, and custards. Once again, he is astounded by the poise and manners that Margaret and John exhibit, from saying grace to washing their hands in the bowls provided by the servants to eating small bites and with refinement. They would be at home with any of his noble friends. Lady Isabel has taught them well.

Margaret feels his eyes on her and wonders what he wants from her and John. He seems pleasant enough, but it must be something very special if he traveled for three days just to see them.

She finds out after dinner when they all go to Lady Isabel's parlor. She and John sit on the sofa while Lord Rich settles in a large armchair like a monarch on his throne. Lady Isabel takes a chair opposite him and, in her usual manner, comes straight to the point. "Now, Sir Robert, what is it that you wish to know from the children?"

Warwick has always known her to be direct. He remembers the forthright honesty of Anthony and Maria and decides it is best to respond in kind. He turns to Margaret and John. "I want to know all about your journey after you were rescued," he says and smiles encouragingly.

When Margaret hesitates, Lady Isabel nods to her and John, saying, "You can tell the truth, children."

At first, Margaret speaks haltingly, but as she continues, she recalls memories and things she has not talked about before, and saying them out loud feels comforting. John nods from time to time but doesn't have much to contribute. Rich realizes that he was too young at the time. He will never be considered a reliable witness and represents no danger to him, but Margaret and her detailed reminiscences are something else altogether.

She can't recall much about the rescue and certainly not Elfrith's presence on the *San Bautista*, having been asleep in the cabin most of the time. But she does mention the *Treasurer* riding alongside the *White Lion* before the storm. When she gets to Virginia, however, she hesitates again, remembering her promise to Jope.

Warwick looks to Lady Isabel for help. She looks kindly to Margaret and says, "You can tell us everything. Remember, Lord Rich is our friend."

Margaret looks from one to the other and is met with kind smiles. Reluctantly, she tells what happened at Point Comfort. She provides a surprisingly thorough account of the arrival of the *Treasurer* and the meeting of Jope, Elfrith, Rolfe, and others in the cabin of the *White Lion*. Her imitation of Elfrith's rough manners and speech convinces Warwick that she's telling the truth.

When she relates that they all decided to "make up a story" in which her captain would take the blame for the raid on the Spanish ship, Warwick buries his face in his hands. Then he looks up with such an expression of hatred that Margaret draws back in fear.

Suddenly, like a snake uncoiling, he leaps from his chair and lunges toward her. His dark eyes glistening with rage, he hovers over her and shouts, "That is a damned lie and you know it!"

Cowering, Margaret can smell his dank breath. She says weakly, "No, m'Lord. I heard it. Every word."

Warwick hisses, "If you ever repeat it—to anyone—you will never utter another word, I promise you!"

Lady Isabel leaps from her chair. "Sir Robert, how dare you! Take hold of yourself!"

There is steel in her voice, and he draws back as she interposes herself between him and the children. Her eyes blaze with such fury that he raises his hands in appeasement and backs away. Lady Isabel gestures to Margaret and John to leave the room.

By the time they're gone, Warwick has himself under control. His voice is taut and thin. "If that story gets out, it's my head on the chopping block."

Lady Isabel shakes her head. "Is this what you came to find out? If they knew? I can promise you, it won't. Margaret has never talked about it before, and I'll make sure she won't say another word about it."

Warwick looks at her doubtfully.

Putting her hand lightly on his arm, Lady Isabel says, "You can trust me on this, Sir Robert. The girl has no reason to tell that story to anyone else. She can do you no harm, and you must not do her any either. Do I have your word? As a Christian?"

Rich notices her arm quivering. He tightens his lips and gives a slight nod. Then he pulls away from her. "I must be going."

Relaxing somewhat, she insists, "You will do no such thing. You will spend the night. I'll make sure the children stay in their quarters out of your way."

She rings a bell, and a servant enters.

"Joseph will take you to your room."

Warwick would like nothing better than to leave right away, but he knows it is getting dark and his horses need rest. He bows. "Thank you, m'Lady, for your kind hospitality."

After he is gone, Lady Isabel sinks into her chair, exhausted. She wonders how she can make Margaret and John understand what just happened, and in a way that doesn't frighten them. More worrisome is that she is not at all sure she can trust her powerful nephew to keep his word. When he has time to think it over, he will not want to put his safety and well-being in her hands.

31

EXILED

Tavistock–London—Late Summer 1621

When Jope returns to Tavistock from his most recent trading voyage overseas, he is happy to be back home, but also dissatisfied. Hauling cargo across the Atlantic Ocean and English Channel is not what he built the *White Lion* for. As a swift attacking vessel, she does not have a large enough hold, limiting what supplies and tobacco he can carry to and from Jamestown. As a result, his earnings are steady but meager, not as profitable as he had hoped. Being a merchant also goes against the grain of his adventurous spirit. He longs for the excitement of chasing after bounty and capturing a Spanish ship loaded with gold and silver.

As he alights from the coach and takes in the familiar exterior of his house bathed in the mid-morning sun, the front door flies open and his favorite hounds bound toward him and jump up at him yapping. By the time they have calmed down, Mary appears. She rushes into his arms, and her soft, passionate kiss makes him forget his discontent.

He breathes in her sweet scent, then pulls back to look at her. "I trust you are well, my wife."

"I am. And you, my husband?"

Jope forbears answering when he sees the driver and footman standing by. He gestures them to unload his trunks and take them into the house. Then he puts an arm around Mary's waist and walks leisurely with her toward the entrance.

"It has been a frustrating voyage, but I don't want to bother you with the details."

"My uncle tells me the Privy Council reprimanded the Virginia and Bermuda Companies for shipping tobacco to Holland to avoid taxes. Is that why you're home early, because you had to put into Plymouth directly?"

Jope laughs heartily. "I should have remembered that you spend much time at Sir Granville's house, where politics is part of the air people breathe."

Mary swats him affectionately, but her expression turns serious. "We didn't expect you so soon."

"Is something the matter?"

For a moment Mary seems lost in thought. Then she recovers. "You must be hungry, John. Let me have Sarah put together a cold collation for you."

Jope attributes her distraction to his long absence. It isn't easy to get fully accustomed to one another after so much time apart. He pulls her close to him and says, "There is time for that later. Right now I am filled with joy to see you."

Mary disengages herself before they head inside. She reaches a decision. "I don't mean to cloud your homecoming, John, but there are two letters for you that arrived within days of each other—one from Lady Isabel and another from Lord Rich. He visited the children at Aldwarke, and now he wants to see you."

Thunderstruck, Jope cries out, "Are Margaret and John all right?"

"Yes, yes. Lady Isabel says they're fine. But you should read for yourself."

Jope hurries into the house. While he pays the coachmen, Mary goes into the study and retrieves two letters with broken seals from the writing desk. She returns to the drawing room and hands them over with a somber expression.

Pacing by the window, Jope peruses them quickly. Relief and apprehension intermingle on his face. Suddenly he bursts out, "I gave Margaret and John explicit orders not to say anything about what happened to them!"

Mary puts her hand on his arm. "They're children, John, not used to sham and pretense. And they trust Isabel."

"You're right. It's not their fault."

"Of course not."

He resumes reading. At some point he exclaims, "Lord Rich wants to discuss 'our arrangement'! This does not bode well!" He rushes to the door and calls down the hallway for one of the servants. "Peter, go to the stables and have Martin saddle a horse. I must go to London right away."

Mary's face sags. "Is that really necessary? Won't you at least spend the night?"

Jope resumes his pacing. "This is a matter of great urgency!"

"You're here so rarely," she pleads.

"I'm sorry, Mary. This is something I must do."

A flash of anger crosses her face. "Sometimes I think the children are more important to you than anyone else in the world."

Stung, Jope responds harshly, "This is not the time, Mary."

"It never is!" she says and bursts into tears.

As Jope moves toward her, she runs from the room.

* * *

Once again, Jope makes the journey on horseback in record time, switching mounts at each postal station. It is a costly way to travel, but he doesn't care. It pains him to make Mary so unhappy, but he must make sure the children are safe.

As soon as he arrives in London at Sir Granville's house, he sends a message to the Earl of Warwick asking for an audience. He receives a swift reply, inviting him to call on him the next morning. The matter seems to be of urgency for all the parties involved.

Mary's uncle, who is in London while Parliament is in session, offers Jope a bit of advice. "Whatever happens, do not cross him. Warwick is unforgiving, and his memory lasts a long time."

When Jope knocks on the door of Warwick's townhouse estate early in the day, to his surprise, Alfred meets him and ushers him into the earl's study right away. The triumvirate of Lord Rich, his cousin Nathaniel, and Captain Argall await him.

Warwick is standing at a table with his cousin looking over papers, and Argall pores over charts on another table off to one side. The scene looks like it has been staged for Jope's benefit. When he advances, removes his hat, and bows, Rich gestures him absentmindedly to sit on a sofa while he finishes appending his signature to a document.

"Captain Jope, how good of you to come on such short notice," he says without looking up. "A missive from your home led us to expect you no earlier than a fortnight hence."

"The winds were favorable, m'Lord."

Warwick puts down his quill and looks at him askance. "Yes, one never knows from whence they'll blow when first setting out on a course."

Jope manages a smile. "One must learn to make the best of it, m'Lord, especially when at sea."

Relaxing visibly, Warwick turns to his compatriots and says expansively, "Didn't I tell you our good captain here is a man of reason?"

Nathaniel and Argall nod in turn. Their smiles seem forced to Jope, and it puts him on edge.

Warwick comes over and takes his seat on his favorite chair opposite the sofa. "Let me come straight to the point, Captain," he continues. "You have kept your side of our bargain admirably, and we appreciate it. But now our enemies are seeking to find all the Africans in my possession and take them away from me, here and in Bermuda. If they got wind of the children's presence on English soil, it would be dangerous and I could no longer guarantee their safety."

Jope is about to object that Margaret and John don't belong to Warwick when Argall blurts out, "Count Gondomar has his spies everywhere, and Sir Edwin Sandys—"

Warwick silences him with an irritated glance. Nathaniel Rich goes over to Argall and whispers something to him, while the earl turns his attention back to Jope with an indulgent smile. "Yes, our enemies are powerful and determined, and that is why I must alter our arrangement."

This is what Jope had feared, but he keeps himself well under control. "Margaret and John's safety is of utmost concern to me, too, m'Lord. What did you have in mind?"

Jope can tell that Warwick is surprised to have the matter tossed back in his court, but he hasn't reckoned with Rich's resources.

Warwick looks briefly toward his cousin and says, "I have given the matter some thought. We agree that the best course is to remove the children as far from England and the authority of the Spanish ambassador as possible." He rests his chin on his folded hands and fixes his eyes on Jope. "Do you know Edward Bennett, the merchant, Captain?"

Jope nods. "I do. I went to seminary in Holland with his cousin, William Bennett—he is a minister now—and I have encountered a number of his trading ships on my voyages. He is a pillar of the Puritan community."

"And a good friend." Warwick shifts in his chair. "He has just received a patent for a large plantation in Virginia on the south side of the James River. A ship with over a hundred settlers led by his brothers, Robert and Richard, will leave soon. In fact, the Reverend William will be on board as well."

Jope wrinkles his brow. "I'm afraid I don't understand, m'Lord."

Warwick leans forward and continues smoothly. "Have your charges join them, Captain. They'll be far away and safe from the clutches of Gondomar."

He nods to his cousin. Nathaniel Rich joins him next to his chair and says, "The colony is growing and thriving. They will have opportunities there they'd never be afforded in England. It really is the best course, Captain."

As Jope considers the offer, the others watch in silence, still as statues.

When he expels a deep breath and says, "I would want to take them there myself," the others come to life again.

Warwick settles back in his chair. "Of course, Captain. As you wish," he says indulgently. "Nathaniel will make arrangements with you and Edward Bennett." Gesturing to Argall, he continues, "Samuel here can show you on the map just where the plantation is located on the James River."

As Argall heads to the table covered with charts, he says, grinning, "Courtesy of the estimable Marmaduke Raynor, who is doing splendid surveying work for us."

Undeterred, Jope fixes his penetrating blue eyes on Warwick. "I need to be sure they will be safe, m'Lord. That is all I care about."

The earl's eyes flicker dangerously but meet the brazen demand head on. "I will make sure to the best of my ability, Captain. You have my word on that as a fellow Puritan. The rest is up to God."

"I'm glad we understand each other, m'Lord. I can't ask for anything more. Thank you."

Warwick offers a tight smile, and Jope bows. But he is seething inside as he follows Nathaniel and Argall out of the room into an antechamber where they go over the parchment chart of the Chesapeake Bay and the James River and discuss how to best secure Margaret and John's future. Jope has to force himself to pay attention because his mind is distracted. He hates being subject to a powerful yet cowardly man. Lord Rich may be an important Puritan leader, but he cannot be trusted to stay true to his word, and it worries him.

Nonetheless, he agrees with Warwick's assessment that Virginia is the best place to hide Margaret and John. He'll have to send letters to Mary and Lady Isabel informing them of the new developments, hire a coach to retrieve the children, and take them to Tavistock. In the meantime, he'll have his first mate, Gareth, ready the *White Lion*. Then, when he can safely smuggle them aboard, he'll embark on the voyage to Virginia and their new home.

32

LEAVETAKING
Aldwarke–Tavistock—Fall 1621

W hen Lady Isabel receives a letter from Captain Jope informing her of his arrival at Aldwarke within a fortnight to pick
up Margaret and John, "of necessity," and take them from England,
a sudden stab of pain in her heart makes her cry out loud. Her hand
flutters to her breast and she slumps in her chair. Fleeting images
of her son sweep through her mind before she can clasp her hands
in prayer and assert her will. Her attachment to the children runs
deeper than she has been admitting to herself.

She understands that Jope's hands are tied and that he is acting at
the behest of the Earl of Warwick, so she sends a letter to her nephew,
entreating him to change his mind and let the children stay. Her plea
falls on deaf ears. When she apprises her sister of what is happening,
Frances replies to explain what may have led to Warwick's decision
to "oust the Africans," but offers little sympathy. She has been set
against Margaret and John "hiding out" at Aldwarke all along and,
much as she hates to assent to anything her arrogant stepson says, on
this matter she agrees with him.

Lady Isabel's only option is to pray to God to help her face this
fateful development with the same strength and determination she
has harnessed for every difficult challenge in her life. But her resolve
is sorely tested when she summons the children to her study to tell

them that their time at Aldwarke is drawing to a close and that their captain will come soon to take them away.

John, as expected, tightens his lips, looks at his feet, and seems to shrink into himself before her eyes. But Margaret's reaction upsets her more. The girl bursts into tears and wails in anguish, "It is all my fault, isn't it?"

Lady Isabel is so shocked and alarmed, she is at a loss for words. Then she exclaims, "Oh no, child, you mustn't think that! You must never think that!"

"But I broke my promise and told, and now we have to go away."

Isabel has never seen someone look so lost and forlorn. She gestures for Margaret to come to her and enfolds her in her arms, rocking gently back and forth until her sobs subside.

Then she calls John to approach her as well. She looks steadily at both of them and says, "You mustn't ever think this was your fault. There are forces far beyond us at work here. The Earl of Warwick is but an agent executing God's will. Do you understand?"

The children look at her uncertainly. Margaret's cheek starts to twitch. Lady Isabel cups it with her palm, then rubs it with her thumb, quieting the quivering.

"Remember what I've told you about overcoming your fear?" she says intently. "There is no shame in being afraid, but the decisions you make in fear can bring you shame. Keep your mind clear and rely upon your faith, and the Lord will reveal your path. He will not betray you, because you have been chosen by him."

John nods seriously, and Margaret joins in reluctantly.

Isabel looks penetratingly at Margaret and says, "Promise me you'll do that."

Margaret's eyelids flutter briefly. Then she looks back with her large brown eyes and replies, "I promise."

* * *

For the next week, a melancholy atmosphere descends on the manor. Agnes and Samuel do their best to remain cheerful, but they, too, feel helpless, especially when John asks repeatedly, "Why do we have to go? I want to stay."

There is not much to pack. A small trunk suffices for each child to hold a change of clothes, an extra set of undergarments, and a few personal belongings. When Margaret hides her doll in the folds of a petticoat, Lady Isabel turns a blind eye. She decides that they should take their fancy outfits along as well, even though she knows that a satin gown and fancy doublet will be out of place where Margaret and John are going. But she doesn't want to make the parting any harder, and they will outgrow them soon enough. She also breaks with the daily routine and suspends lessons to give the children as much time as possible with the people and places they hold dear.

So John heads to the stables, talks to his pony, and feeds him special treats. Samuel overhears him say, "Don't worry about me, Berwick. When I come back, you and I will both be grown up."

Margaret spends hours in the garden, looking at the flowers and herbs, memorizing their names. At meals, she savors the smells of her favorite dishes. Every afternoon, she goes out to the pond and watches the ducks getting ready for their own migration. The fallen leaves crunch underfoot, their musty odor wafting pleasantly from the ground. At night, Margaret pays attention to the sounds of the manor quieting down and recalls her favorite times at Aldwarke. Many of her memories of Ndongo have begun to fade, and she wants to make sure to hold on to everything important about her sojourn here.

Lady Isabel spends much of her time in the chapel, praying. She knows she must preserve a strong, calm exterior for the sake of the children. It worries her that Margaret keeps looking at her doubtfully, as if she still believes she is to blame. She continues to talk to her and John to offer comfort and encouragement, as much for them as for herself.

Leavetaking

"Sometimes the true path can be hidden for a long time before it reveals itself. Don't let that weaken your resolve. The Lord has given you both strong minds. I am old and near the end of my days. You are young with your life ahead of you. I have prepared you as best I can. Now it is your turn to walk with courage unto your destiny."

* * *

It is late morning on a warm autumn day when Jope arrives. The leaves of the oaks and alders in front of the children's wing have turned bright colors and rustle in the balmy breeze.

He greets Margaret and John in the entrance hallway and notes their glum faces. But he is most shocked when he sees Lady Isabel. She seems to have aged years since he last saw her just a few months earlier, even more so since her son died. The tremors in her hand are more pronounced, and she walks stiffly with a cane. But her gray eyes are steady and clear and convey a sense of serenity.

They all go to her study, where the children kneel before Lady Isabel and ask her to give them her blessing. She does so, formally.

Then she draws Margaret to her feet. She reaches into a pocket in her gown and pulls out a necklace with a single pearl. Putting the chain around Margaret's neck, she looks deeply into her eyes and says, "You are on the verge of becoming a young woman. I want you to have this. Always remember that you are special and that I love you very much."

As Margaret's fingers clutch the hard kernel at her chest, memories of her mother flash through her mind, and for a moment she seems to be back in Pongo during the good times.

Lady Isabel puts a hand on Margaret's cheek and says, "Go with God."

Then she turns to John and hands him a small statue of a pony. "To remember us. You know you will become a fine young man."

John takes it and cradles it affectionately in his arms.

Lady Isabel nods to Agnes and Samuel to take the children out-side and ready them for the journey.

Alone in the study with Jope, she turns away and her body droops momentarily. When she has regained control, Jope takes her hand and says, "I am sorry this is happening all of a sudden, m'Lady."

She takes a deep breath. "Me, too, Captain. The children have been an unexpected blessing late in my life, and I thank God for the privilege."

Jope is surprised and moved. "I am glad for it and deeply grate-ful for what you have done for them."

Lady Isabel smiles. "I do have a request of you."

"Anything, m'Lady."

"Keep me informed of what happens to them as best you can."

Jope makes a small bow. "Of course."

"Thank you." She withdraws her hand and says, "Then let us not tarry."

He bows again, and they make their way to the manor entrance.

In the courtyard, servants, butler, cooks, kitchen maids, and stable hands—everyone in the household—have assembled. They are standing in line to one side of the entrance just as they would at the departure of any noble visiting the manor. Next to the coach, Agnes and Samuel are waiting with the children, dressed in coats and hats for the journey. Their small trunks have been stowed at the back of the carriage.

As Lady Isabel and Jope approach, without warning Margaret tears herself away. She runs to the older woman and throws her arms around her waist. John joins her. Lady Isabel puts her hands on their heads and, barely able to maintain her composure, looks to Jope for help.

He quickly steps forward and says, "Come, children, it is time."

Reluctantly they untangle themselves from Lady Isabel's skirt and climb into the coach. Jope joins them and signals to the coachman. The carriage rocks and moves forward, gradually picking up speed.

Leavetaking

Lady Isabel, Agnes, Samuel, and the others wave after it. Margaret and John stick their heads out of the window and wave back. The people at the entrance of the manor become ever smaller figures, and the children keep waving long after they can't see them anymore.

* * *

The rest of the journey over land passes like a blur for Margaret and John.

At some point, they tell Jope what happened during their encounter with the Earl of Warwick.

"He shouted at me and threatened to kill me," Margaret says, and her cheek twitches. "I am afraid of him."

"He's a bad man," says John.

"You don't have to worry about him," says Jope calmly. "You'll be safe from him where you're going."

But inside he's furious and would like nothing better than to wring Warwick's neck. He may be a powerful man, but to bully two innocent children because he is afraid is an action that deserves no respect. To take their mind off what happened, Jope tells Margaret and John stories of Jamestown and the plantations he has seen during his recent voyages, painting a rosy picture for them. When they nod off in exhaustion, he watches them carefully, pondering if taking them there is the best course of action.

At Tavistock, Mary welcomes the children with open arms, marveling how much they have grown. She seems genuinely glad to see them and does her best to make them feel at home during their brief stay. When she takes Margaret on a tour of her garden, she is amazed that the girl knows every plant by name.

Mary isn't one to bear a grudge, and physical endearments between her and Jope tell both of them that their previous argument has been laid to rest. At night in bed together, she and Jope talk about the children's future.

"Margaret will be fine," she reassures him. "But I worry about John. He's only eight and he seems very young for work in the fields with no one to look after him."

It gives Jope pause. Once again, he prays to God that this path is the right one.

Two days later, they head for Plymouth. It is a moonless night when he smuggles the children on board the *White Lion*, and the darkness hides their faces. Gareth, now first mate, greets them warmly. Seeing him, John immediately perks up.

The captain's cabin looks the same as before, and the familiar smells and sounds of the ship at anchor provide some comfort for the children. When they set sail early the next morning, John can hardly wait for the *White Lion* to clear the harbor entrance so he can go on deck and start exploring.

Margaret, feeling seasick, stays behind. She looks out the rear gallery window as the coastline becomes narrower and disappears. She has a premonition that she will never see England again. She closes her eyes and hears Lady Isabel's voice telling her to overcome her fear, trust in God, and look ahead with courage. She prays and whispers to herself, "I will keep my promise."

PART THREE

&

THE NEW WORLD

33

WARROSQUOAKE

Virginia—March 1622

T he creaking floorboards rouse Margaret from a restless sleep.
She sits bolt upright, disoriented in the dark. For a moment she
doesn't know where she is, and fear grips her heart. She gropes for
her doll and presses it to her chest. Then she makes out the familiar
shape of a woman kneeling by the fireplace, prodding the embers
and igniting tinder. It is Mrs. Breewood, the head of the household
at Edward Bennett's plantation, rekindling the fire in the hearth.
When the twigs and small branches catch with a crackling sound,
she lights a candle and puts it on the mantle. Its flame dimly illuminates other sleeping bodies on the floor.

Margaret relaxes and crawls out from under her blanket. Yawning,
she rolls up her blanket and stashes it under a side table next to her
trunk. She places her doll inside it on the soft silk of her rose-colored
dress. The room smells of fresh-cut timbers, the house having been
finished only a week before Margaret's arrival. In the corner, Lucy, a
housemaid, sits up and rubs her eyes. When she has put away her bed-
ding, she wakens the other servants. Then she and Margaret assemble
tables and move stools and benches to the center of the room to get it
ready for the day. Soon, the two masters of the plantation, Robert and
Richard Bennett, and their cousin, the Reverend William Bennett,
will be stirring in the adjoining bedrooms and gathering for breakfast.

When they are finished Margaret picks up two wooden pails by the front door and heads outside. The morning air is chilly, and she shivers. In the early hours before sunrise, she can make out the dark shapes of the smokehouse and storage shed. The cookhouse is busy already; flickering light from the fire inside shines through the windows.

Margaret makes her way toward the creek that meanders through the lands below the main residence. Without the moon lighting her way, she stumbles over the roots of a tree stump, left from clearing the forest. She manages to catch herself from falling and continues more cautiously.

Her thoughts drift to Captain Jope and John. By now the *White Lion* must be far away in the middle of the Atlantic Ocean, the wind lashing its sails.

* * *

A few days before they arrived in Virginia, Captain Jope had sat her and John down in his cabin and surprised them with the news that he was keeping John aboard ship as a cabin boy rather than having him join Margaret on the Bennett plantation at Warrosquoake. He had thought long and hard about it and decided that John was too young for the settler's life without a family or older sibling to watch out for him, and that Margaret would be too busy to play that role. John had been doing some chores on the ship already under the observant eyes of Gareth, the first mate, and would benefit from Jope taking personal interest in his education as well.

As John's face changed from surprise to delight, Margaret wanted to cry out that she was losing both her protector and her close companion, but she knew that the captain was right.

"What will become of me?" she asked plaintively.

Jope, hearing the anguish in her voice, looked at her seriously. "You will be safe with Robert and Richard Bennett, who are managing the plantation for their older brother. They're both good Puritans, as is their cousin, the Reverend William. He and I were at seminary together in Holland. They will look after you. I will arrange a contract of indenture for you. You will work at their plantation for seven years as a servant, and then you'll be free."

Seeing Margaret's bewildered expression, he explained that most newcomers to Virginia couldn't afford their passage from England and signed a contract of indenture. In return for paying their way, landowners and merchants had the right to use them as laborers and servants for seven years. During that time, they were clothed, fed, and housed by the owner of their contract, but received no pay. After that, they were free to go as they pleased. As part of the agreement, they would receive fifty acres of land to start their own farms, or they could stay on and earn wages for their work as free men and women.

"But why would you have me be an indentured servant to pay for my way when you are bringing me here on your ship?" Margaret asked, mystified.

"It is for your own safety. You must blend in with everyone else. Most of the newcomers to the plantation are indentured. If you came as a free woman, people would ask questions, and the news would soon be all over the colony. This way, no one will pay undue attention to you."

"We'll visit you whenever we can, won't we, Captain?" John piped up, trying to make her feel better.

Jope nodded. "Of course."

It was small comfort. For the remainder of the voyage, Margaret was miserable and forlorn. She had only her doll, Mary, to talk to about her worries. Seven years seemed like an unimaginable eternity to spend alone in a strange place.

Between bouts of nausea and sadness, she noticed the first terns and seagulls appear, gliding on the wind, diving into the waves for fish. The sailors saw them, too, and—knowing that land was near—performed their tasks with renewed energy and excitement. For Margaret they brought no joy, however. She treasured the times when John would join her late in the day after he had finished his chores and they sat in silence side-by-side on the gallery in back of the cabin, holding hands. At night, sharing the same bed, they wrapped their arms around each other as they went to sleep.

When they arrived at the Chesapeake Bay, Margaret recognized none of the landmarks from before. Point Comfort was just as foreign to her, although she had dim memories of it being a quieter, less bustling place. Captain Tucker greeted Jope like an old friend, acknowledged her and John, and let them proceed upriver immediately.

By the time they approached Warrosquoake on the south side of the James River, it was late morning. Another large ship, the *Sea Flower*, lay anchored near the wooden plantation dock, its sails rolled up and lashed tightly to the spars. While Jope went ashore, Gareth found out that it had arrived only a fortnight ago with 120 settlers from England aboard, most of them indentured workers. Some of the men who labored on land during the day were still sleeping in the ship's cabins at night while their living quarters were being built. The main house, belonging to the Bennett brothers, was already finished, sitting up high on the rocky bluff overlooking the river.

Margaret and John watched from the rear gallery of the *White Lion* as Captain Jope stepped onto the gangplank and strode down to the wooden dock and the group of men waiting for him there. Margaret's eyes settled on their leader, a slender, well-dressed man in Puritan garb. To Margaret, he looked honest and serious-minded, but with none of her captain's sparkle in his eyes.

Robert Bennett shook hands with Jope and introduced himself and the men with him—Ralph Hamor, captain of the ship at anchor, who had returned to the colony after an eight-year absence, and several broad-shouldered dockworkers, who stood by like protective guards. As business manager of Warrosquoake, Master Robert took a personal hand in welcoming any ship bringing goods and provisions. Since he had no tobacco to sell or trade yet, Robert was willing to spend money only on necessities.

He was about to say that they had no need for his cargo, when Jope said, "I bring greetings, letters, and provisions from your brother Edward."

Margaret could see that the announcement changed the whole mood of the encounter. A smile blossomed on Robert Bennett's face, and the dockworkers relaxed. Jope shouted orders to Gareth. While the sailors began to unload barrels, bales, and chests from the *White Lion*, Jope, Hamor, and Bennett climbed the cliff path up to the house to partake in the midday meal and conduct business.

As they waited for the captain's return, the children had their dinner in the cabin. Margaret picked at her meal; she had no appetite, and her stomach was in a knot. John kept watching her with sorrowful eyes. The fact that she would soon disappear from his life had sunk in.

At some point, Margaret reached a decision. "Let's say our good-byes now. It will be easier that way."

John nodded, close to tears. Margaret kissed him, and he drew her to him and held onto her for a long time. As she slowly disengaged herself, he hugged her again and said, "Remember what Aunt Isabel said."

Together they carried her small trunk outside to the quarterdeck, and she sat on it, fingering the pearl at her neck, awaiting her fate.

When Jope and Robert Bennett returned, their easy conversation made clear that they settled matters between them to their mutual satisfaction. The captain carried a rolled-up scroll with him.

Arriving on deck, he gestured for Margaret and John to join him in his cabin. He brought the inkwell and quill from his desk and unfurled the document on the table.

"This is the contract of indenture, Margaret. You must sign it."

Margaret saw Robert Bennett's name at the bottom and carefully wrote her name next to it.

When she was done, Jope waited for the ink to dry, then rolled up the contract and bound it with a leather strap. Then he invited her and John to join him in prayer. He closed his eyes and asked God to protect Margaret and guide her on her path of destiny. Then he prayed for a safe voyage home for himself and John and speedy returns for a visit. Margaret allowed his resonant voice to enter her and calm her fears.

Jope and the children sat in silence for what seemed like a long time. Finally Margaret took a deep breath, stood up, straightened her dress, and met him with a calm, detached expression.

"I am ready."

Jope handed her the scroll, kissed her on the forehead, and said, "You have my blessing, child."

He picked up her trunk as if it were light as a bird and allowed her to pass before him. John brought up the rear.

Outside, the sailors halted unloading the ship and watched as she walked to the railing. Gareth gave her an encouraging smile. Margaret nodded gratefully in return and proceeded down the gang-plank to the dock where her new master and Captain Hamor were waiting. They eyed her with undisguised curiosity.

Robert Bennett took a step toward her and said, "Welcome to Warrosquoake, Margaret."

Margaret curtsied and handed him the scroll. "Thank you for letting me come to live and work here, kind sir. I am pleased and grateful."

If Master Robert was surprised at her eloquent reply, he did not remark on it, but a look passed between him and Jope, as if he had not believed until this moment what the captain told him about the girl.

The rest was a blurry haze to Margaret—Jope handing her trunk to one of the dockhands and saying, "I'll be back before long"; look-ing back as she climbed the path and seeing John high up on the rat-lines waving good-bye; entering her new home and meeting a host of new people. The only one who made an immediate impression was Mrs. Breewood, the head of household, who scowled at Margaret, none too happy to have a young girl in her care. She had enough to occupy her already with her young son toddling about and left it to Lucy to show Margaret around the house and where she would sleep.

Toward the evening Richard Bennett, Captain Hamor, and Reverend William Bennett joined Master Robert for supper. In contrast to his brother, Richard was a muscular, burly man with a strong physical presence, although Margaret could see the facial resemblance between them. The captain had the leathery tan of someone who has spent considerable time at sea; he was plain-spoken and a bit rough around the edges. The Reverend William had a surprisingly soft voice and gentle demeanor. When Master Robert introduced Margaret as a new servant girl, they nodded to her but paid little attention as she and Lucy brought venison stew, bread pudding, and cider, and later collected empty pewter plates and mugs to be washed.

Although a radical change from her life at Aldwarke Manor, Margaret had no difficulty fitting in with the Puritan practices such as prayers in the morning and evening. Lady Isabel had prepared her well. At night, exhausted from the physical work of the day, she fell asleep quickly, but not before whispering to her doll and wondering how long she would have to endure this life. It couldn't be her destiny. Lady Isabel had told her she was special, and this was a most ordinary existence.

Mrs. Breewood remained a stern-faced woman, with none of the motherly kindness of Agnes at Aldwarke. She started Margaret out with simple tasks—serving food, fetching water, emptying chamber pots into the cesspit in back of the house, and helping out with carrying breakfast and dinner to the workers clearing the woods. Much as she disliked some of the chores, Margaret did without complaint everything asked of her.

Lucy, a plain, kindhearted girl, not yet twenty, tried to ease Margaret's entry into the new world, but was of little help.

When Margaret asked her why the plantation is called Warrosquoake, she shrugged helplessly. "I don't know."

Mrs. Breewood, overhearing the exchange, interjected, "It's what the Indians who used to live here called it."

"Indians?"

"The natives. Don't worry, you'll meet the heathens soon enough."

"'Heathens'? I have never heard that word. What does—?"

"Don't ask so many questions, girl. Just do what you're told," Mrs. Breewood cut her off curtly.

Margaret was certain that the woman didn't like her, so when she overheard Master Robert ask about her two days later and Mrs. Breewood grudgingly admitted that she was doing well, Margaret was pleased. She took it as a sign that she would be able to succeed in the New World.

* * *

By the time Margaret gets to the burbling creek, the day has grown light enough for her to make out the pebbles in the shallow water. She ties her skirt up and wades in to fill the pails close to the brim. On her way back she is careful of her footing. It is important to bring back as much water as possible. By the time she gets to the cookhouse, she has spilled only a little. Inside, the blazing heat of the fire is as welcoming as the smell of baking bread. Mrs. Breewood's husband, Thomas, the cook, and his helper, Hugh, a pockmarked young man in his early twenties, take one of the pails from her and pour it into a big iron pot to start the porridge. Margaret sits on the bench by the fire, draws up her skirt, and warms her feet by the flames. Then she returns to the main house to help set the table for breakfast.

By the time the sun has burned the morning mists from the surrounding fields, it is time to help Thomas and Hugh load up two separate wheel carts with pots of porridge, meat pies, boiled eggs, and several jugs of cider and ale. Lugging a basket heaped with bread, she accompanies them to where laborers are clearing the forest—felling tall pines, oaks, and beech and chestnut trees, and cutting down shrubs—to make room for more fields. Many of the workmen are bare to the waist. Sweat glistens on their pale bodies even this early in the day as they wield axes and saws, strip bark from the trunks, and hew them into planks for construction of more living quarters. Margaret likes the sweet, pungent smell of pine sap and fresh-cut timbers.

When the food caravan arrives, Richard Bennett wipes his forehead and calls to the workers to stop and come for breakfast. The bearded men line up by the carts, waiting for their portion of porridge and pies. Then they sit down, straddling hewn tree trunks and leaning against stumps, and dig in hungrily. As Margaret and Hugh walk among them serving hunks of bread, cider, and beer, there is no time to talk to anyone, just a moment for a brief smile and a hello. Richard Bennett is a strict taskmaster who wants the men to get back to work. Although they won't be able to clear enough fields in time to plant tobacco this year, he wants to sow a big crop of wheat and corn.

While Margaret and Hugh pack up the empty pots and baskets, the men rinse out their bowls, cups, and spoons by the stream, and pick up their tools to return to the arduous task of clearing the forest.

On the way back to the cookhouse, Hugh lets Margaret push his wheel cart. Oblong and heavy, with only one wheel, it is difficult to steer over the roots that crisscross the trail. Hugh laughs when she gets stuck and the cart tilts, spilling pots and baskets on the ground.

"Here, let me."

He jumps to her aid and rights the cart. Thomas grins as they load up again and continue, Margaret bringing up the rear.

The following day is Sunday. After breakfast, all the settlers—household servants, field hands, and owners alike—head for the makeshift woodland chapel at the edge of the forest. Although church attendance is mandatory, everyone is happy to go because it is a respite from the backbreaking work of clearing fields and putting up houses. They gather in the shadow of an old sail, which has been hung like an awning from four elms to provide shade from the sun. Instead of pews, there are the trunks of recently felled trees, and the altar is a few planks nailed to two neighboring beeches. The Reverend William Bennett stands before them, dressed in black, waiting for everyone to settle down. He seems deep in concentration, his expression stern and forbidding, unlike his kind demeanor at the dinner table.

Margaret sits with the other household servants behind Robert and Richard Bennett. She is curious what kind of sermon their cousin will preach. Perhaps she can catch a glimpse of her destiny in his words. What she doesn't expect is the roaring lion William Bennett turns into when he begins. Margaret is dismayed to hear his thundering diatribe about man as a weak, sinful creature, whose soul is a prisoner put on the earth by God and surrounded by temptation. The suffering in this world is only exceeded by the tortures that sinners and the nonelect will be condemned to on Judgment Day. Infants who die unbaptized are subject to eternal torment.

Margaret is appalled. Even in Lady Isabel's strictest teachings, she never painted God as such a wrathful, terrifying being. There is no room here for Jesus, who took the sins of humanity upon himself on the cross and who had a special love for children. Margaret shrinks into herself to hold on to a kinder vision in the face of William Bennett's angry, inexorable onslaught. She can't understand why he is so unlike her captain, whose beliefs have made him a kind and generous man.

Even when the reverend holds out a glimmer of hope, it is tarnished with contingencies. God is good; he has given man the free will and plenty of opportunity to overcome the evils luring him to sin. Still, even a life lived in purity is no guarantee of being called to sit in God's presence. That is only for those fortunate predestined few, chosen by God at the beginning of time.

Margaret can't help but recall the heated conversations between Lady Isabel and her sister, Frances, about her own fate. Would they still believe she will discover her destiny in this new land where people preach such gruesome sermons? What possible future could they believe would await her here? Did her fate really lie in the hands of such a mean-spirited God? She wishes that Captain Jope had not abandoned her here all alone.

When Reverend Bennett finishes, Margaret takes several moments to gather herself. As she heads back to the main house, she sees Master Robert talking with a tall, broad-shouldered African man she has not yet seen. He is pointing and gesturing animatedly as if to indicate the far boundaries of the plantation. She is intrigued. Who is he? Could he be from the *San Juan Bautista*?

"Margaret," Master Robert calls out and motions for her to approach.

"Yes, Master."

As she draws closer, the man's eyes settle on her with interest. She blushes but returns his look with equal curiosity.

"This is Anthony," says Bennett. "He came here several months before us, courtesy of the Earl of Warwick, and helped prepare the place for our arrival. He's been downriver near Nathaniel Basse's plantation, grazing our cattle."

Margaret, wide-eyed with surprise, gasps, "The Earl of Warwick?"

"Yes," answers Anthony. His face hardens. "He was supposed to return me to Bermuda, but I was brought here instead. Have you met him?"

Margaret likes the resonant sound of his voice and the lilt of his accent, but she is instantly on guard. She looks to Master Robert, wondering if he is aware that she, too, came to Virginia because of Lord Rich. But how much did Captain Jope reveal of her true circumstances? She doesn't want to betray his secrets again. She remembers all too well what happened when she told the truth to someone she shouldn't have trusted.

"Margaret?" Master Robert's voice stirs her from her reverie.

She looks up and says, "No, I have not."

For a moment he gives her a puzzled look. Then he instructs her, "Put some provisions together for Anthony. For the next few days he will be herding our livestock down by the Pagan River."

"Yes, sir. Right away."

As Margaret leaves, she hears Master Robert say to Anthony, "Just make sure to keep the herd this side of Basse's Choyse or it'll be lost to Nathaniel and his men."

She walks on briskly, her mind a whirl of thoughts.

By the time she reaches the cookhouse, Anthony catches up with her. "Just as well you didn't meet Warwick. He is not a pleasant man," he says with a somber look in his eyes.

Margaret doesn't know how to respond. She is dying to ask how Anthony knows Lord Rich. Were there other Angolans taken to England? And if so, where are they now?

"You weren't on the *White Lion*," she says tentatively.

"No. I came on the *Treasurer*, but I remember Captain Jope from the *San Juan Bautista*."

Margaret's heart leaps into her throat, but she decides to respond cautiously. "That seems so long ago!"

Anthony laughs. "Yes, it does. But where did you spend your time before coming here?"

Margaret avoids having to answer by escaping into the cookhouse and relaying Master Robert's orders to Thomas. The cook hands her eggs, bread, and cured meats. Anthony watches from the door as Margaret wraps them in a piece of linen.

As he takes the package from her and stows it in a leather pouch, he smiles and says, "Thank you. It's good to meet you, Margaret. We will speak more when I return."

On impulse, Margaret curtsies, ladylike, and replies, "I'd like that very much, Anthony."

For a moment he is taken aback. Then he grins, bows in return, and takes his leave. Margaret looks after him, her heart beating faster.

34

LEEZ PRIORY

England—March 1622

The Earl of Warwick declines the roast lamb that Mary, the lone remaining African servant at Leez Priory, offers to him on a platter. As she bows and withdraws, he pushes his chair away from the table, irritated. His dinner companions, Samuel Argall and Nathaniel Rich, exchange uneasy glances. Although the meal has been excellent, Warwick has hardly eaten, and for him to refuse his favorite dish does not bode well for the rest of the day.

He has been in a foul mood ever since Lady De La Warr; her champion, the Duke of Buckingham; and their buffoonish lout, Captain Brewster, brought yet another lawsuit against him. Since they received no satisfaction for their accusations of wrongful death regarding Lord De La Warr's demise in the *Neptune* affair, they now allege "misappropriation" of his property and demand damages on behalf of his widow. Warwick finally countersued Brewster almost out of spite for "losses incurred" when he interrupted the *Treasurer's* "fishing voyage." It is a frivolous legal case, but at least it will tie up the brawling windbag in court for another round of depositions and testimony, preventing him from taking another ship out to sea.

Once again, Warwick feels beset from all sides, like Hercules battling the Hydra, the ancient sea monster with many heads. Every time he cuts off one, two more sprout in its stead. He didn't even get a chance to celebrate the verdict of the High Court of Admiralty clearing him, Argall, and Elfrith of all charges in the raid on the *San Juan Bautista*. In no time, his two archenemies, Count Gondomar and Edwin Sandys, brought civil actions to remove the rescued Africans from his auspices. The reptilian Spanish ambassador claims ownership on behalf of his cousin Acuña, the ill-fated captain of the slave galley, and Sandys continues to insist that they belong to the Virginia Company and its shareholders.

Pacing ferociously, Warwick fulminates, "These miscreants will be the death of me!"

"You can't let your hatred for them cloud your judgment," Samuel Argall counsels cautiously. "The Admiralty Court's judgment removes all danger of us losing our heads. Now it is a civil matter, and we surely can outlast them."

"Of course, delay suits you," Rich rants on. "Nothing stands in the way of your precious knighthood now."

"Which will prick Edwin Sandys's spleen to no end," says Nathaniel Rich, hoping to pacify his hot-tempered cousin.

But Warwick is not that easily placated. He continues to pace like a baited bear. "I should never have agreed to let Anthony testify before the Virginia Company council! At least I got rid of that traitor along with the Dutchman's children."

"Why don't we take this conversation outside?" says Nathaniel, glancing meaningfully toward Mary, who is tarrying longer in the room than seems necessary to clear the table.

Warwick takes a hard look in her direction. "Very well."

As they exit through the double doors into the courtyard, his anger subsides in the brisk, invigorating spring air.

Walking toward the hedges ringing the gardens, Nathaniel resumes the matter at hand. "Why on earth have you kept her on?"

"She is a fine servant and good-looking, too. I have been loath to part with her," says Warwick, sulking. "Perhaps it is time to let her go."

"Yes, high time. Surely you can replace her with a comely flax-wench who'll let you fondle her under her skirts."

Warwick's eyes sparkle dangerously. "You know I only indulge my fancy in London, not here where my wife and children are."

Argall holds his breath, but Nathaniel Rich continues to look blandly at his cousin. "All right, Nathaniel! I'll ship her off to Virginia."

"Good. We have more pressing matters at hand."

Warwick knows he is right. At the last quarter court of the Somers Island Company, Sandys resorted to the same backstage maneuver he used when King James prevented him from heading the Virginia Company and managed to install the Earl of Southampton as treasurer, allowing him to maintain control behind the scenes. In many ways, this is more serious than his interfering with Warwick's privateering ventures at Jamestown. Unlike Warwick's plantation in Virginia, which has never borne fruit, the extensive lands he owns in Bermuda are turning a good profit. And they will continue to do so, if he can prevent Sandys and Gondomar from getting their hands on his African workers. Their superior skills at cultivating tobacco have been essential for his success.

"What can we do to curtail Sandys's influence and get him off my back?" he complains, picking up a stone and flinging it at an oak tree.

"We must find a way to put him on the defensive," says Argall, handing him another pebble to toss.

Nathaniel Rich strokes his graying beard. "Perhaps there is a way. The Virginia Company is in desperate need of money, and Sandys has started to negotiate with the King's ministers to take over the tobacco monopoly for England as a joint venture of the Virginia and Somers Island Companies. What if we succeed in preventing the deal?"

"How would that serve our cause?" Argall asks.

Warwick perks up. His cousin doesn't have to explain the details to him. He understands full well that if Sandys succeeds, it will entitle him to collect the custom levies for all tobacco imports. While he'll have to pay the Crown part of the revenue, there will be plenty left over—ample profits he can use to shore up the finances of the Virginia Company and consolidate his power. But if he fails, it will spell disaster for his reputation and standing as company treasurer.

"We must oppose him at all costs," Warwick says with renewed excitement.

"Even if it means financial disaster for the Virginia Company?"

"Yes, let it go to the dogs. It will serve them right for crossing me," Warwick replies, smiling ominously. "Our holdings in Bermuda will survive just fine."

"I will contact Thomas Smythe. I'm sure he and his faction are none too happy about it either."

"Good."

Nathaniel Rich has saved the best for last. "By the way, Count Gondomar—"

"Don't tell me anymore about that Catholic swine!" Warwick interrupts vehemently.

"Count Gondomar may have overreached," his cousin continues unruffled. "To be sure, he is a puppet master who dangles James from his strings at will, but the populace does not like the idea of a Spanish princess marrying the Crown prince."

"Perhaps we can encourage the rabble to hold further demonstrations against the union," Argall suggests brightly.

"There are rumors afoot that Spain soon will replace him with a new ambassador."

For the first time that afternoon, the earl is genuinely surprised. "How do you know that?"

A satisfied smile plays about Nathaniel Rich's lips. "Count Gondomar has his sources, and I have mine."

As they walk on among patches of snow and bare rosebushes, energy returns to the Earl of Warwick's step.

Perhaps things are looking up after all. He counts his blessings. Sandys's and Gondomar's meddling has not curtailed his privateering exploits. His fleet continues to scour the Atlantic Ocean and Caribbean for Spanish galleons. News from the Plymouth Company is guardedly encouraging. Although the pilgrims continue to face hardships in New England, they are determined to stay. And now they just might have found a means with which to frustrate Edwin Sandys's ambitions for good.

Listening to Nathaniel Rich lay out options, he marvels at his abilities and is pleased to have such a clever cousin, whose deviousness more than matches his own.

35

GOOD FRIDAY
Warrosquoake—March 1622

Over the ensuing weeks, Margaret becomes a regular part of the household. The Bennetts all treat her with courtesy, but Master Robert seems the most approachable. He makes a point to ask after her from time to time, and when she has a question for him, he listens and answers attentively. Even Mrs. Breewood warms up to her somewhat after Margaret plays with her young son, a button-nosed, pudgy boy, and makes him smile and gurgle in delight.

When Anthony returns midweek and again on Sunday to the main house for more provisions, Margaret is pleased. After Reverend Bennett's thundering sermon, they take a walk along the cliff overlooking the James River and talk. As they share their histories, she learns that Anthony grew up helping his father raise cattle on a farm on the high plains half a day's journey from Pongo.

When she mentions that her father was the *soba* of the region, he looks at her, his eyebrows raised in surprise. Then he nods and says, "I hear he was a good man."

Nothing changes in his attitude toward her. Their past social differences don't matter in the New World. When Anthony talks about his parents, his face hardens. He acknowledges that, like Margaret's, they were killed when the Imbangala overran Ndongo but says nothing more.

Margaret tells him about things she overhears at dinner as she serves the three Bennetts at the main house. The new governor, James Wyatt, is often the subject of conversation. He took over from Sir George Yeardley, who built the first windmill in Virginia on his plantation, Flowerdew. Apparently Wyatt is more religious and strict in enforcing laws, and the Bennetts hope that his Anglican faith won't interfere with their Puritan beliefs.

There are now enough houses on Warrosquoake, so the new settlers no longer need to use the *Sea Flower* at night, and Captain Hamor has returned to Hogg Island upriver, where he and his older brother are staking out a plantation of their own. Margaret misses his presence at dinner. She liked hearing his stories about his earlier adventures in the colony during "the starving time" when food was hard to come by, and trading for corn and venison with the Indians kept them alive. During one of his visits to a Powhatan village, he met an Indian princess named Pocahontas, who rescued one settler, John Smith, from certain death and married another, John Rolfe. At the mention of his name, Margaret's ears perk up. Could it be the same man who met with Captain Jope aboard the *White Lion* when they first came here?

Anthony doesn't know about any of that, but Margaret likes talking to him and listening to him. She feels safe and appreciated in his presence and comes to rely on his knowledge and good judgment. When English fails him, he uses Kimbundu words, which awaken good memories in her of their homeland. She experiences sudden smells and sounds, and a fleeting motley of images she hasn't had for some time. Anthony's presence soothes the inevitable pangs that come with them, the bitter knowledge that they belong to a time and place that can't be recovered.

Margaret also values Anthony's practical sense and optimism. Although firmly rooted in the here and now, he has big plans for the future. He wants to have his own farm and a large family after he attains his freedom. "We must make the best of what we have," he insists.

At some point, Margaret broaches the subject of the Earl of Warwick. Anthony's face clouds in anger as he recounts his time at Leez Priory with Mary and Don Pedro, and his falling out with Lord Rich over his testimony to the Virginia Company council regarding what happened on the *San Juan Bautista*.

Noticing Margaret's intent look, he asks, "Why are you interested in him?"

Before she can stop herself, she blurts out, "Because he is a monster!"

Now it is Anthony's turn to be bewildered. "So you have met him?"

Once the dam of secrecy is broken, Margaret doesn't hold back, and the whole story spills out—how she spent time in England and came to Warrosquoake. When she gets to her encounter with the earl, she shudders. "It was dreadful. He was so angry and vicious, like a savage beast. I'm sure he wanted to murder me. If it hadn't been for Lady Isabel . . . I'm still afraid he means to do me harm."

Anthony reassures her. "Not likely. He was a lot angrier with me and could easily have arranged to have someone kill me, but he sent me here instead. I don't think you have to worry about him."

His words provide partial comfort at best. "You mustn't tell anyone I told you!"

"Of course not. We traveled Kalungu together and survived—more than once. We're *malungu*, and we stick together."

Relieved, Margaret looks at him adoringly. When Anthony leaves that Sunday afternoon to tend the cattle, she admires his purposeful stride until he disappears over a hillock. For the next day she thinks about little else but his return.

Late in the afternoons when Margaret is finished with her chores, she sometimes explores the surrounding woods and meadows. It is early spring, and she notices plants that look similar to the ones that grew in the herbal and ornamental gardens at Aldwarke—snowdrops, monkshood, and hepatica. She wonders if there will be others as spring turns to summer, and she says the names out loud to remind herself—foxglove, yarrow, dandelion, orrisroot, comfrey, and mugwort. She would like to plant a garden near the smokehouse and plans to ask Master Robert for permission.

One morning, after feeding the workers clearing the woods, she looks out the window of the cookhouse and sees two strange-looking men walking up the slope from the creek toward the main house. They are wearing skirts of animal hides, which cover their lower bodies above the knees but leave their muscular torsos exposed. The older has a dead deer slung over his shoulders, and the younger carries three pheasants, their lifeless heads dangling toward the ground.

Margaret marvels at the dark-reddish tan of their skin and the three feathers stuck in their dark hair, tightly woven and close to their heads. These must be the Indian natives she has heard Captain Hamor mention.

As the men reach the front porch, Robert Bennett emerges from the house and welcomes them like good neighbors. They shake hands and start to converse, communicating more in gestures than words.

Thomas Breewood comes up behind Margaret, wondering what has attracted her attention.

"Are those Indians?" she asks.

"Yup, them are the heathens," he says with the same dismissive tone of voice as his wife. Then he calls to his helper, "Come, Hugh, let's go and bring their gifts in here. We'll have a fine feast at supper tonight."

Margaret watches from the window as they go to greet the Indians and take the dead game off their hands. Meanwhile, Robert Bennett returns from inside the house with beads and a small dagger. He offers them to the older man, who holds them up to the sunlight. Smiling happily, he and his companion exchange several bows with Master Robert and take their leave.

As they pass the cookhouse, Margaret hears them talking to each other in a language she doesn't understand. She looks after them, fascinated, until Thomas tells her to get back to work.

The next time she sees Anthony she asks him what he knows about the Indians.

"They're probably from the Warrosquoyacke or the Nansemond, two of the local tribes here allied with the Powhatan," he says.

Margaret has heard of the Powhatan before, but knows little more than their name.

"They're the most powerful tribe in the area," Anthony volunteers. "Their chief, Opechancanough, is like a king, like *ngola* Mbandi in Ndongo."

Margaret is amazed that the Indian names roll off his tongue so easily. "Is he the Kalungu Ngome, the god of the underworld my father told me about?" she asks, wide-eyed.

Anthony shrugs. "I don't know about that, but they lived here long before we came and pushed them off their land into the forests."

"Doesn't that make them angry?"

"Actually they've been very friendly and kind. When I first arrived here, I was in Jamestown for a few days, and they came and went freely, trading food and hides for beads and weapons. I'm told that they taught the early settlers how to grow corn and other crops, and where the best oyster beds and fishing grounds are. Without them, I doubt that any of the settlers would have survived, and we wouldn't be here."

It is a lot for Margaret to take in. The Indians aren't like anyone she has ever met. "Have you talked to one of them?"

Anthony shakes his head. "Sometimes they watch us from the edge of the woods, but they have never come close. Maybe they're afraid of our cattle."

* * *

Over the next week, the two Indians and others Margaret hasn't seen before return, bearing gifts of food, furs, and deerskins, and bartering for small broaches, bead necklaces, and hunting weapons. Their presence soon becomes a natural, familiar part of her days. So she doesn't pay any special attention when a small contingent appears on the Friday morning before Easter. She briefly looks up as they pass the cookhouse window on their way to the main house and returns to kneading dough.

Suddenly, there are shrill yells she has never heard before, followed by a desperate, piercing shriek. She hurries to the window. One of the Indians is standing over the prone figure of Mrs. Breewood, screaming and holding up her defenseless arms against his raised hatchet. There is a terrible thud and a moment of silence. Then Thomas rushes from the cookhouse and plunges a butcher's knife into the back of his wife's assailant. As the Indian yelps in pain, blood gushes from the wound. In no time, other Indians surge from the main house and storage shed with hammers and axes. They surround Thomas, bludgeon him to the ground and hack away at him. Their high-pitched victory cries mingle with war whoops and sounds of gunshots coming from the woods where the settlers are clearing trees. The Indians are attacking everywhere!

Inside the cookhouse, Margaret sinks to the floor, covers her ears with her hands, and clamps her eyes shut. Imbangala! Here in Warrosquoake! She doesn't understand why the natives, so peaceful just a few moments ago, are suddenly slaughtering everyone. She only knows she is in mortal danger.

Cowering and shaking with fear, she is about to accept her fate when she hears Lady Isabel's voice echoing inside her head. "Control your fear, Margaret. You must control your fear."

She takes a deep breath, calming herself, and rises to peek over the window sill. Two Indian warriors are heading her way. Their savage faces, painted in bright red and black markings, are terrifying masks.

Margaret dashes to the door and closes the latch. Looking desperately for a place to hide, she remembers that the storage cellar has a back door. She hurries to the rear of the kitchen, goes down the stairs, and feels her way among the barrels of corn and flour. As her eyes adjust to the darkness, she makes out Hugh sitting in a corner and hugging his knees.

She kneels by him and whispers urgently, "We have to leave. They'll find us down here."

He nods, terrified. For a moment, he remains frozen but then follows her to where a narrow beam of light shines through the barrels. As Margaret squeezes past them and pushes the door open, they hear a crash above them. The Indians are breaking into the cookhouse.

There is no one in sight out back. Margaret takes a deep breath and runs to the rear of the storehouse. Crouching low, she peers around the corner. The Indians at the main house are occupied with looting—bringing clothes, jugs, and dinnerware from inside to the front porch. One of them holds up Margaret's doll, baffled, and her heart clenches in pain. But there is no time. Farther down by the new workers' houses, more Indians are struggling with settlers. The only way to safety is through the cleared fields. If they can make it to the edge of the woods, they can hide and survive. But they'll have to cross the creek, swollen from the recent rains.

Margaret hitches up her skirt and calls to Hugh, "Now!" and starts to run.

As she leaps over roots and tree stumps, she hears a shout, followed by the shrill war whoop. They've been seen! Her feet fly over the dark earth, and there is a hideous scream behind her. Hugh! They've caught up to him. Redoubling her efforts, she races on blindly. Before she knows it she tumbles through the air and ends up sprawling on the ground. She tries to scramble to her feet, but trips again and falls down. She hears the sound of running feet halting close to her. Terrified she fumbles on her back to face whatever fate has in store for her.

A large Indian warrior stands above her, his face covered in bright red coloring, his fierce eyes boring into her. His battle-ax is raised, ready to strike. Margaret clenches her eyes shut in anticipation of the blow. But the blow doesn't come. When she opens her eyes cautiously, the native is looming above her. His painted face comes so close she can smell his fetid breath. His ferocious expression turns to bewilderment. Suddenly he straightens, turns, and jogs back up the hill.

Margaret doesn't think twice. In no time, she is on her feet and racing to the creek. She wades into the dark, chilling water, unaware that it comes almost up to her neck. Flailing, she makes her way across, scrambles up the bank to the tree line, and plunges into the dense shrubs.

From the safety of the bushes, she looks back. Flames engulf the workers' homes, main house, and outbuildings. As she watches the dark, angry smoke billowing into the sky, she thinks of her trunk and fancy dress burning up, and it breaks her resolve. All the screams and horror of the day come pouring in on her, and she bursts into tears. Sobbing, she pushes deeper into the woods, oblivious to the brambles scratching her face and hands. When she reaches a section of swamp impossible to pass, she sinks to the ground in exhaustion. Looking up, she finds herself under a canopy of wispy, floating foliage. Gray strands of moss sway from the branches of budding trees covered with delicate green leaves. The screams in her head diminish to a ringing silence, broken by the rustle of squirrels chasing each other over the branches.

Feeling her hands burn and sting, she looks and discovers them bleeding from where the briars and thorns scratched her. She starts to cry again.

Once again, she hears Lady Isabel's voice. "Margaret, control your fear. Trust in the Lord."

Closing her eyes, she begins to pray, "Dear God, give me your strength. I am lost. Please show me the way."

The tranquility of her surroundings engender in her a welcome sense of serenity that, much to her surprise, turns to defiance. She opens her eyes, gets up, and takes a deep breath. She doesn't know how long she's been here—minutes or hours—but she hopes the Indians have withdrawn by now.

As she retraces her steps, the musty smell of the swamp yields to smoke and a sweet, noxious odor that she recognizes as burned flesh. When she reaches the tree line that overlooks the fields, Margaret is stunned to see the houses all in smoldering ruins, black smoke still wafting in columns into the early afternoon sky. There is no sign of the Indians.

She fords the stream in a shallow spot and cautiously walks up the hill. The nauseating smell gets stronger, and she pulls her wet and muddy apron over her mouth and nose trying to mask the stench. Halfway up, she comes upon Hugh's body. His legs and arms have been hacked off, and his head is a bloody pulp where the Indians scalped him.

Margaret averts her eyes and moves on. As she reaches what's left of the workers' houses—remnants of walls and skeletal chimneys— she sees clothing ripped to shreds and other personal items scattered all over the ground. Impaled on spears, as if left for display, are the remains of those slaughtered—hands, feet, limbs—burned, swollen, and dripping with the pungent juices of death.

Startled, Margaret backs away and, unable to hold on to her innards, vomits.

At the ruins of the main house, she comes upon the disfigured remains of Mrs. Breewood and her husband. Behind them lies the mutilated corpse of their young son. Nearby, the grotesquely twisted shapes of Lucy and the other housemaid rest in puddles of blood.

The grisly vision of slaughter takes her back to Pongo. Surrounded by devastation and the memories she has tried so hard to forget, she mumbles, "Why? Why has this happened again?"

Suddenly, she hears voices coming from the direction of the James River. Then Robert Bennett, the Reverend William, and a few other men appear. They look battered from fighting.

"Margaret, are you hurt?" asks Master Robert.

She shakes her head. Behind them Anthony arrives, carrying an assortment of weapons. Her heart leaps with joy that he is alive and well.

"We must search for survivors, anyone who is still alive," says Master Robert. He points to the workers' quarters. "There are no survivors there. Let's go and check by the woods."

Together they march in silence beyond the fields. They soon come upon more slaughtered bodies. This is where the gunshots came from. Margaret is surprised that there are no Indians among the dead, just as the one Thomas Breewood killed at the main house has disappeared. The Indians must have taken their fallen warriors with them as they retreated.

Fanning out, the survivors comb through the area. Searching near the stream, Margaret finds a large man slumped against an oak tree. He is holding onto his left arm, which seems attached to his shoulder by only a piece of pulpy skin. At first she doesn't know who it is because his head hangs low, and his face is covered with blood seeping from a gash on the crown of his head.

As Margaret kneels beside him, she hears him mumble, "They've gone mad," and recognizes his voice.

She jumps to her feet and hollers, "Master Bennett! It's your brother Richard!"

She pulls off her apron, rips the binding, and ties it tightly above the remains of his arm. Reverend Bennett is the first to arrive, with Master Robert hard on his heels.

"He is barely alive," she says, looking to the men for guidance.

They kneel by his side, but it is too late. She recognizes the cold stare of death and turns away. Before she can go looking for others, a cry comes from the direction of the main house.

A sable-haired youngster comes running toward them, yelling, "Help! Help! They're killing everyone! Help me!"

He arrives out of breath, hair disheveled and cheeks flushed. His eyes are wild and dart everywhere, taking in the slaughtered remnants in the clearing, the lifeless body of Richard Bennett propped against the tree.

"We are all going to die," he wails, shaking his head in distress.

Robert Bennett, struggling with his own emotions, stands up and addresses him in a firm voice. "Get a hold of yourself, son. Where have you come from?"

The boy swallows and says, "Basse's Choyse. The Indians attacked us!"

"What is your name, child?" Reverend Bennett asks.

"Samuel. Samuel Basse."

"Nathaniel Basse's son?

"Yes, but my father is yet in England. Everyone is dead!"

Robert Bennett grabs him by the shoulders to steady him. "No survivors?" he asks.

"I don't believe so, sir."

With a heavy heart, Master Robert turns to Anthony. "Take him and go over to the plantation. Stay off the creek bed, so you can go unnoticed. There could still be Indians about. Collect any weapons you find. Bring back anyone alive and leave the dead. You must return before the sun sets. Should the Indians attack again, we must be able to mount a defense."

Anthony nods and disappears with the boy into the woods.

"We must continue our search," Master Robert proclaims, his voice cracking with emotion. "There may be someone alive."

It is a thankless task and bears no fruit. Throughout the plantation, they find only bodies, many of them unrecognizable pieces of severed flesh and bones.

The good news is that as the afternoon wears on, survivors trickle in from the surrounding woods where they've been hiding. By mid-afternoon, a little more than half of the settlers are making camp in the field behind what's left of the workers' quarters. Under Reverend Bennett's direction, they gather as many of the bodies and remains as they can find and put them in a large, hastily dug pit in the most recently cleared field by the forest.

Robert Bennett keeps a tally and writes down the names of those killed they can identify. By the time they have finished, comparing his list with the survivors present, he counts fifty-three settlers lost.

Meanwhile, Margaret and Lewis, a young man assigned to help her, sift through the charred remains of the kitchen and smokehouse for food and anything else salvageable. Under a mound of ash she discovers the iron cooking kettles. When she ventures into the cellar, much of it exposed now since the floor collapsed, she sees that most of the barrels have been burned. But then she finds two by the rear door that haven't been damaged. Prying them open reveals partially ground corn, enough to feed everyone for several meals.

By the time Anthony and Samuel Basse return just before sunset, carrying only a few weapons, a fire is going, and Margaret and Lewis are preparing a porridge.

Anthony reports to Robert Bennett, "Basse's Choyse suffered a total loss, and all our cattle have been slaughtered."

Master Bennett, sensing the dismal mood of the survivors, tries to reassure everyone. "The Indians are not likely to come back tonight. They attacked another plantation in a coordinated plan. If anything, we will need to be watchful tomorrow."

His words bring some relief, but huddled together for warmth, there are few who catch more than a wink or two that night. Surrounded by the lingering smell of death, they lie awake listening, startled by the snap of a twig or rustle of a wild animal.

Margaret, huddled with Anthony and comforted by his presence, finally gets a chance to rest, but she can't fall asleep either. Although she is exhausted, images of the day continue to whirl through her mind. Above all, she returns again and again to the Indian warrior looming over her who came within an inch of killing her. She has no idea why he spared her life.

36

TO JAMESTOWN

Virginia—March 1622

As the sky lightens in the east, the survivors rise slowly from the dew-covered ground. At first they stand around like dark statues, numb from the events of the previous day and cold night. Then they start to move about and slap their limbs and chests to loosen stiff joints and banish the chill from their bodies. Slowly, low murmurs fill the crisp morning air. When Margaret stokes the fire, coaxing the embers to life, the settlers congregate around the licking flames. With the first rays of sun peeking over the treetops of the forest, she and Anthony haul water from the creek to prepare more porridge for breakfast. In the pale mists, they can make out the skeletal remnants of the ruined buildings, thin lines of smoke still rising into the cloudless sky.

When everyone has eaten their meager gruel, Robert Bennett stands up and addresses the assembled settlers. "I will send messengers to Jamestown for help. In the meantime, we must bury the dead."

He calls on two burly young men and hands them a letter. "Take the rowboat down by the dock and deliver this missive to Governor Wyatt."

Then he assigns a few men, Anthony among them, as lookouts to guard against further attacks by the Indians. The rest go about the grim task of digging graves for their lost friends. They work in silence. About half of the bodies, mangled but more or less in one piece, have been identified, and they get their own, individual burial places. Mrs. Breewood; her husband, Thomas; and their son share a family grave. The remaining body parts are put in the ground in a large pit. A few settlers make simple crosses, lashing small branches together with leather thongs.

It takes most of the day to get ready for the funeral. When Reverend Bennett steps forward to say a few words, it is late in the afternoon already. For once, he doesn't rant on about man's sinful nature but simply recognizes the courage of the poor immigrants who hoped to make a new life for themselves and met with a gruesome end that none of them deserved. Then he exhorts the survivors to honor their memory by becoming better human beings themselves and asks the Lord for mercy on their souls.

By the time the settlers cover the bodies with soil and place the crosses on the mounds, it is getting dark. There is just enough time to have supper at the makeshift campsite and huddle around the fire for a while before spending another cold, fearful night under the stars.

Margaret and Anthony once again nestle close together to keep warm. She would like to ask him about the Indian who spared her, but they are both too tired to talk and drift off into a fitful sleep.

The next day, Robert Bennett divides the survivors into small groups to start clearing the rubble from the burned buildings. He assigns Margaret and Lewis to see what they can salvage from the cookhouse and smokehouse before they get the midday meal ready.

The smell of scorched flesh still lingers as they pull charred logs out of the way and dig through the ashes. Margaret wishes she had her gloves, but they burned along with everything else. She is excited to find more cooking implements—kettles, stirring spoons, ladles, knives without their wooden handles, earthenware bowls and baking dishes, and a wrought-iron trammel from which to hang pots over the fireplace—and another undamaged barrel, which contains flour. Unfortunately, nothing edible is left in the smokehouse; all the dried fish and meats were burned to a crisp.

Outside, Margaret notices the wheel cart resting on its side. Her defiant old workmate has survived the Indian onslaught intact. With Lewis's help she wrestles it upright, loads it up with their meager treasures, and pushes it to the camp.

That afternoon a messenger arrives from Hogg Island upriver. He is one of Captain Hamor's men and carries a dispatch for Robert Bennett.

"From the governor in Jamestown," he explains.

While Master Robert reads it, the messenger talks to the settlers who have gathered around him. "We were attacked by the Indians, too, at the captain's new house," he explains. "We drove them back with brickbats, axes, and spades. His older brother suffered an arrow in his back, and his cousin Nathaniel Powell was killed."

When Master Robert is finished, he announces, "The governor has ordered us to evacuate everyone from the south bank. We will go by ship with Captain Hamor's man to Hogg Island tomorrow to meet up with the other survivors. From there we'll get ferried across to Jamestown."

There is guarded relief on some of the survivors' faces. Others remain fearful of yet another night out in the open, but it passes without mishap.

The next day, everyone is up at dawn. For the first time in days, there is a sense of eager restlessness among the settlers as they prepare to evacuate Warrosquoake.

"Take only what you can carry," Robert Bennett tells the settlers after they have had their last breakfast at the plantation.

The Reverend William commandeers the wheel cart, stacking it with guns and other salvaged weapons, and boots removed from the dead, to take to the cliff edge above the river dock. Margaret manages to find a place on it for the remaining barrels of corn and flour, but she, Lewis, and another man end up lugging the iron pots and kitchen implements to the waiting *Sea Flower*. Margaret is happy to see Captain Hamor on deck, even though he doesn't pay any attention to her, not even a quick greeting in passing. Instead he engages the Bennetts in conversation and, when everyone is safely on board, gives the order to push off.

With the wind in their sails, the trip to Hogg Island takes little time. Upon their arrival, they find that the plantation there fared no better than Warrosquoake. The houses are charred ruins, and the weary survivors there are eagerly waiting to leave the uninviting marshland. Once they've come aboard, the *Sea Flower* heads across the river to Jamestown.

It is the first time Margaret has laid eyes on the place she has heard so much about. She is initially impressed by the row of well-kept houses overlooking the river. But when they dock at the Jamestown fort, she is disappointed. As she walks off the ship toward the gate, she realizes that the north side of the river is no safer than where they came from. If the Imbangala could penetrate the great rocks of Pongo and its protective fortifications, how can these stripped saplings lashed together into feeble palisades keep them safe from the Indian savages? The worried faces of the residents greeting them confirm her fears. Nor do the barns and warehouses lining the pathway inspire her with confidence. When soldiers guide the arrivals into one of the large sheds, Margaret finds her new home to be no more than a hovel with straw on the ground, and iron tools and hides hanging on the timbered walls.

But it is comfortable and warm after spending three days and nights out of doors. The Jamestown inhabitants are generous with blankets and extra clothes. Margaret also appreciates the meal they serve that night as a welcoming gesture. It is the first supper that she hasn't had to cook herself or help to prepare, and she and her fellow survivors relish the vegetable stew and meat pie as a welcome relief from corn gruel.

Over the next days as they settle in, they hear different accounts of what happened and gradually piece together the extent of damage to the colony. The Powhatans staged a coordinated attack on all plantations up and down the river from Jamestown, hoping to wipe out the entire population. As at Warrosquoake, they brought fish, turkey, and deer to trade and sell to the unsuspecting colonists. Once inside their homes, they grabbed any tool and weapon they could find and killed as many men, women, and children as they could.

Jamestown and its immediate surroundings were fortunate that they received early warning when an Indian youth named Chanco, living at the home of Richard Pace across the river, warned him of the impending assault. His older brother had visited him the night before and told him about a meeting of chiefs and elders of many tribes and the decision to wage war on the settlers. He told him that it was Chanco's duty to kill his white godfather, but the boy had grown close to Richard Pace and couldn't bring himself to do it and told Pace about the planned surprise attack. Pace rowed to the fort across the river and sounded the alarm, allowing the settlers there to bolster their defenses.

A number of plantations were also able to repel the Indian attacks, suffering only a few casualties. Others were not so lucky, including Captain Berckley's plantation at Falling Creek and Henricus, the fledgling college plantation for children of natives and settlers. The worst affected were Warrosquoake and Wolstenholme Towne at Martin's Hundred, seven miles to the south of Jamestown. Together, they had more than 100 fatalities, nearly a third of all the men and women killed. There were rumors that the Powhatans also kidnapped twenty white women from Martin's Hundred. Altogether, more than 350 settlers perished, more than a quarter of the population.

As a precaution, the House of Burgesses under the leadership of Governor Wyatt decided to abandon nearly all of the eighty plantations and small settlements along both sides of the James River. The surviving colonists were brought to the remaining seven that had the best defenses, including Flowerdew, Southampton Hundred, Newport Newes, and Point Comfort, where Captain Tucker and his men valiantly repelled the Indian attackers. The rest took refuge at Jamestown.

Surprisingly, no Africans were killed. At first Margaret thinks it was just an idle rumor, but when she hears it from a number of different people, she wonders again what happened with the Indian who was ready to strike her dead and then changed his mind. She finally decides to tell Anthony about it.

When she asks if he knows what it might mean, his eyes narrow and he ruminates for some time. "I have heard that the Indians think we're ghosts because of our dark skin," he says. "Perhaps they believe we're already dead walking the earth, and to kill us again will bring bad luck."

The thought frightens Margaret. That night, missing her doll, she yearns for Captain Jope and John. Feeling abandoned and homeless, she wonders if she will ever find a place again where she belongs.

37
RIPPLES IN ENGLAND

London—Summer 1622

In June the *Sea Venture* arrives in London, carrying as passengers a group of frightened survivors of the Powhatan attack on the colony. It is the first news of the massacre, and it unleashes a firestorm of shock and horror. For most Englishmen, aristocrats and commoners alike—whose only knowledge of Indians is based on the visit of the cultured and well-spoken princess Pocahontas—the accounts of savagery and destruction are almost unbelievable. A few remember the prophetic words of John Smith, whose warnings of the Indians' threat and bloodthirstiness just a few months earlier fell on deaf ears.

At the hastily called emergency meeting of the Virginia Company, Nathaniel Rich does his best to fan the flames of anger and discontent against the company officials. He rails against their incompetent leadership, taking care to exempt the Earl of Southampton of any blame, and puts the onus squarely on the shoulders of Edwin Sandys and Nicholas Ferrar.

"Not only have they displayed an astonishing degree of ineptitude in managing the affairs of the company, but they have repeatedly thrown the wool over our eyes regarding the precarious state of affairs in the colony," he proclaims.

He continues his condemnation with such vicious oratorical guile that the attack hound of the Sandys faction, the irascible Lord Cavendish, begins to snarl and threaten him with bodily harm.

When the Earl of Southampton, ever the peacemaker, intercedes and reminds the hotheads of the crisis at hand—the settlers are in desperate need of food, weapons, and other provisions—Cavendish delivers a diatribe of his own. Blaming the natives, he calls them "ye cursed race of Ham, unworthy of evangelization," and calls for their extermination. What gets lost in all fault-finding is any attempt to provide relief for the endangered colony.

Instead, one of the merchants in Sir Thomas Smythe's faction speaks up. "We must quickly determine who has died, so that their lawful heirs may take speedy order for the inheriting of their lands and estates."

The assembly authorizes Edward Waterhouse, a company secretary, to publish a list of the dead at once. He warms to his task with speedy efficiency. Not only does he offer a comprehensive list of settlers killed at each plantation, his *Declaration of the State of the Colony and Affairs in Virginia* provides a detailed account of the massacre, based on letters from Jamestown officials and eyewitness reports. Mincing no words, he calls the attackers a "viperous brood of hell-hounds and wicked infidels" who "despise God's great mercies," and concludes that the assault justifies a change in policy toward the Indians. The English colonists should "destroy them who sought to destroy us."

The declaration sparks renewed outrage and recriminations, causing Sandys and the Virginia Company no end of grief.

* * *

When Nathaniel Rich arrives with the list at Leez Priory, he is met by Samuel Argall as he emerges from his carriage. Recently knighted and resplendent in his brand-new leather doublet, the captain makes a splendid figure, but he seems subdued.

As they walk toward the large entrance doors, he warns, "The earl is suffering from an attack of gout."

The lawyer sighs, anticipating a difficult meeting.

Inside they encounter a flustered physician in panicked flight, a victim of Warwick's wrath. They find the earl sitting in his study by an open window in his most comfortable chair. Wearing a silk nightshirt and propped up by a multitude of pillows, he is resting his bare foot on a cushioned hassock. He winces at the slightest movement, but when he hears what Nathaniel Rich has brought, he is eager to have a look. Not knowing that the Dutchman has kept John on board the *White Lion*, he searches for the names of Margaret, Anthony, and the boy on the list and is disappointed not to see them among the forty-seven casualties at Warrosquoake.

"It would have taken care of that problem in one fell swoop," he mutters.

Argall reassures him, "Give it time, m'Lord. The Virginia climate is most unforgiving."

"We can only hope."

"We did ship Mary and John Pedro a fortnight ago to Jamestown and New England," Nathaniel Rich comments judiciously.

Warwick glares at him. "May the waters of the Atlantic Ocean swallow them," he grouses. "Give me some good news."

Nathaniel Rich smiles indulgently. "I can report that King James is still in mourning over the loss of his favorite, the Spanish ambassador. I'm told that he has taken to his bed, and grasps and hugs his pillows and sheets like a swain mooning for his departed lover."

The image brings a grim smile of satisfaction to Warwick's lips. "May Gondomar rot in hell," he hisses.

"And take Edwin Sandys with him," Argall adds fervently.

Walking to the window, Nathaniel Rich takes a moment to enjoy the balmy summer breeze and listen to the wrens and larks warbling in the apple orchard outside.

"Speaking of Sandys," he resumes, his back to the room, "I may have stumbled upon something that will serve our purpose." He turns to his cousin. "You know how hard at work he has been to obtain the tobacco monopoly for the Virginia and Somers Island Companies. My sources tell me that, should he succeed, he plans to pay himself a pretty penny as its administrator."

"Hah!" Warwick shouts, slapping the armrest with glee, and instantly pays the price. His face contorts in agony from the searing pain in his big toe.

Argall grimaces in sympathy, and Nathaniel Rich looks on dispassionately. He waits until Warwick recovers and ventures, "When the time is ripe, we will use it to drive a wedge between Sandys and the other investors in the company. I'll make sure of it."

Warwick nods carefully, his lips pressed together in pain.

"In the meantime, we must remain on guard. Sandys is a formidable adversary. Even with this crisis on his hands, he continues to agitate about our Africans in the Somers Islands."

The earl grasps the armrests with such force that his knuckles turn white. He wants to erupt in anger but knows any sudden movement of his leg will bring infernal torments. Between clenched teeth, he sibilates, "What do you suggest?"

"We must make preparations in case a royal commission or committee of the Virginia Company ships out for Bermuda to investigate," his cousin offers. "Nathaniel Butler has served us loyally as governor, but we can't expect him to hold his own against an organized inquisition."

Warwick's eyebrows contract as he thinks furiously.

"Why don't we send a ship ahead of them and evacuate him?" Argall pipes up. "It worked well when Sandys dispatched George Yeardley to Virginia to investigate me."

Brightening, Warwick compliments him. "That is a most excellent suggestion."

"But if we bring him home to England, they'll just depose him here," Nathaniel objects.

Warwick's eyes sparkle mischievously for the first time that afternoon. "Why don't we send him out of harm's way to Virginia when the time comes?"

Nathaniel Rich can almost read his cousin's conniving mind. "On a very special mission," he adds, and is rewarded with a nod and satisfied smile from the earl.

In the brief silence that ensues, the songbirds outside chirp and trill merrily.

38

STARVING TIME
Virginia—Summer 1622

If Opechancanough's warriors and their allies counted on the attack frightening the survivors into packing up and leaving Virginia, they failed to reckon with the settlers' fierce spirit. Except for the few immigrants who fled on the first ships back to England, the colonists are more determined than ever to make the lands around the James River their home. For many, the attack engenders an aggressive desire for revenge. Others use the Indian assault to justify their plans to expel them from their native territory for good, asserting divine right of conquest of the "heathen" lands.

Governor Francis Wyatt appoints a number of plantation owners with military experience to his council, among them the veterans of earlier wars with the Indians. Former governor George Yeardley, Captain Ralph Hamor, and Raleigh Crosham all fought with John Smith and Samuel Argall against the Powhatans in the years when Jamestown was first established. Some held negotiations with Opechancanough's father, the great chief Wahunsenacawh, and participated in the abduction of Pocahontas. Lieutenant William Pierce and Captain William Tucker are experienced Indian fighters, too. Captain Henry Spelman even spent a year and half among the Powhatans and learned their customs and battle tactics. Over months following the massacre, they conduct a series of devastating raids against the Nansemond, Appamatuck, Wayaock, and Chickahominy tribes, and other Indian communities along the banks of the James River, looting their villages for food and burning their homes.

The Indians set ambushes in return, and the seven remaining occupied plantations and Jamestown are on constant alert. For many months, the colonists feel under siege and live in perpetual fear, struggling to survive. As food supplies become scarce, they contemplate their meager existence with a sense of impending doom.

Yet for Margaret it is a surprisingly pleasant time. Soon after the Warrosquoake survivors arrive in Jamestown, Robert Bennett honors his promise to Captain Jope to take special care of Margaret and invites her to become a servant in the house of Governor Francis Wyatt, where he and the Reverend William Bennett are quartered. All the gentlemen planters have found refuge with Jamestown's wealthier citizens and merchants—George Yeardley, Abraham Piercey, and John Chew—whose larger homes line the river east of the stockade. The governor's mansion is by far the biggest, with an addition to the original building that can accommodate a number of guests.

Margaret joins the other domestics, helping in the kitchen where her cooking experience is appreciated, sharing household chores, and becoming one of the servers at dinner and supper. Because there are extra servants now, she has more time to herself than on the plantation. She often seeks out Anthony, and they take walks together along the river and explore the immediate area surrounding the town. They visit the ironworks and tannery, lying fallow now because they are too far from the fort and the workers fear further Indian attacks. With the coming of summer, Margaret recognizes more familiar plants in the surrounding woods.

Governor Wyatt keeps a large table. Regular invitees include his brother, the Reverend Haut Wyatt; his wife's uncle, George Sandys, a poet and the secretary of the colony; and Doctor Pott and his wife. The rest vary from important military and merchant members of the community to visiting burgesses who bring news from the remaining plantations. Captain Hamor attends from time to time. Margaret recognizes Abraham Piercey, the colony merchant, from her first visit, when he negotiated the sale of her fellow Angolans aboard Captain Jope's ship. She is pleased that he seems to have no memory of her at all. That is not the case for John Rolfe, who arrives one afternoon and eyes her with unabashed curiosity until it dawns on him where he has seen her before. Then he nods to Margaret with a conspiratorial smile. Throughout supper, she worries that he will give her away. Fortunately, he pays her no mind for the remainder of the meal and ignores her later on, too, while the men smoke tobacco and talk among themselves.

On the way out, however, he slows as he walks past her and murmurs, "Your secret is safe with me."

Margaret curtsies gratefully.

Conversations at dinner and supper are usually lively and filled with laughter. At first, it surprises Margaret. She expected a more subdued atmosphere, considering the danger to the colony.

When she mentions it to Anthony, he says, "Sometimes people want to escape the difficulties they face. Some do it with prayer, others drink spirits that make them happy. In Ndongo, we used to dance until we were delirious."

Margaret understands how it works with prayer, but she has no familiarity with the other ways. Yet she nods seriously as if she does.

While Jamestown has laws requiring mandatory religious observances, it is an Anglican community with less stringent practices than the Puritans at Warrosquoake. Every morning and evening the household assembles in the main room for recital of the Common Prayer. Margaret watches Reverend William Bennett bow his head and participate in silence. On Sundays, they all go to the church inside the fort to attend the service of Reverend Richard Buck. He reads from the scriptures and prays for the souls of the assembled settlers. His sermons are considerably shorter than Reverend Bennett's, and while he, too, has plenty to say about man's sinfulness, his is a more forgiving God; Reverend Buck preaches more about mercy and charity than the eternal torments of hell. Having ministered to the settlers there since 1610 and seen difficult times before, he knows how important it is to keep up the spirits of his congregation. Margaret's ears perk up at the frequent mention of Jesus and his divinely inspired words, and she leaves many a service feeling bathed in God's grace.

The feeling doesn't last long, however. Immediately afterward, the congregation assembles in the square to watch the punishment meted out to those settlers who failed to attend church the previous week. Standing amid the crowd of gossiping onlookers, Margaret can't cover her ears to the screams and whimpers of the men and women being lashed at the whipping post, or avert her eyes. But she refuses to participate in the cruel mockery of the offenders on display in the stocks. To her, it all seems a brutal, unseemly spectacle—an unbecoming diversion on the Sabbath, the Lord's Day—and she walks away as swiftly as possible when the sentences have been carried out.

As the weeks go by, there are plenty of difficulties to face. A ship arrives from London bearing more settlers but no food supplies. The accompanying letter from the officers of the Virginia Company reprimands the colonists for leaving themselves vulnerable to the attack. It responds to Wyatt's pleas for provisions by reminding them that they had been forewarned a year earlier that the company's funds were "utterly exhausted" and that they would have to rely on their own resources. The news making the rounds in Jamestown upsets everyone because it feels like rubbing salt into open wounds.

As ships continue to arrive with holds empty of provisions, but bulging with settlers who left England before word of the massacre reached its shores, the scant food supplies become even more strained. Margaret hears from Anthony that the refugees are often going hungry, and she recognizes how dire the situation is by the reduced offerings at the governor's table—fewer courses, reduced portions, and no desserts. If food is that limited at the Wyatt house, it must be even scarcer among the rest of Jamestown's inhabitants.

She is not alone in her concern. One evening she heads to the storage shed in back of the house to get some tallow. The door is ajar, and as she slips inside she hears voices. In the dim, mildewed interior, she cannot see who it is, but she recognizes the voices as belonging to Francis Wyatt and his brother, Haut.

The governor laments, "What have we done that God has cast evil down upon this land? We have lost almost a third of Virginia's inhabitants. The Lord has abandoned us!"

"You must not say so," the reverend replies with urgency.

"Our people suffer terribly."

"You must not waiver, or you'll only add to their dread."

"I don't know what to do!"

The anguish in the governor's voice touches Margaret, and without meaning to, she speaks up. "You must be strong. We're counting on you. It is your fate. You must not question the Lord."

There is a sudden silence, broken by the Reverend Haut's commanding voice. "Who is there? Show yourself!"

Margaret is suddenly afraid, but she steps forward. In the failing light from a window, she sees the governor get to his feet. The knees of his britches are covered with dust.

"Margaret, what are you doing here?" he asks incredulously.

"I . . . I came to get some tallow."

Reverend Wyatt advances on her. "You will not speak of this. Not a word to anyone!" He fixes her with an iron-hard stare.

Margaret shrinks from him. She has not seen such angry eyes since the Earl of Warwick glowered at her at Aldwarke. "No, no, of course not, never," she promises.

"Now go!"

As Margaret turns and runs from the shed, she hears him say to his brother, "She will not tell. And who would believe her over our word?"

For the next days, Margaret lives in desperate fear of what they may do to her. When she encounters Sir Francis or the Reverend Haut, she lowers her eyes and feels relief when they ignore her. In time, when nothing happens, the constant knot in her stomach loosens and she feels reasonably safe again.

Whether her words or something else influenced the governor, she never finds out, but in the days and weeks following their encounter he wears with renewed vigor the mantle of colony leadership. He sends Captain Hamor on a voyage up the Chesapeake to form alliances with tribes there not favorable to the Powhatans and to trade for food. His orders: If all else fails, use force. When the *Tiger* returns a month later with 4,000 pounds of corn and enough dried fish to feed the settlement until the fall harvest, there are celebrations throughout Jamestown. The jubilation is marred by news that Captain Hamor also received a secret message from Mistress Boyse of Martin's Hundred. The desperate plea to the governor to help her and her fellow sufferers obtain release from Indian captivity confirms that she and the nineteen other missing women were kidnapped during the attack. Although much discussion takes place in the Governor's Council and informally among Jamestown's denizens on the streets, nothing is to be done, and the feeling of helplessness dampens everyone's spirit.

The extra bounty of corn and fish helps feed the stream of new arrivals from England, undeterred by the news of the massacre. Most of the newcomers who swell the ranks of Jamestown inhabitants are men, and there is little to do for them. With too much time on their hands, they become ever more difficult to control. The sight of drunken men stumbling along the river in broad daylight becomes a common sight. By late June they are such a nuisance that Governor Wyatt issues proclamations against drunkenness, swearing, and taking boats without permission. Depending on their social station, gentlemen offenders earn fines, free men spend time in the stocks, and servants and apprentices earn an appointment with the whipping post.

Virginia—Summer 1622

In late July the *Margaret and John* docks at Jamestown. Margaret finds it odd that a ship would bear her and John's names and dismisses it as a coincidence, although its arrival brings significant change to her life because one of the passengers aboard is Mary, the last African at Leez Priory. When Anthony hears of it, he is beside himself with joy. Margaret witnesses their reconciliation with mixed feelings. She is amazed at the open affection the two have for one another, hugging and kissing with no concern of what bystanders may think. Although Margaret is glad for Anthony, she also feels hurt. Until Mary's arrival, she thought he cared for her as more than a sister, but now she observes a passion she has witnessed only one other time in her life between two people—with Captain Jope and his Mary. She realizes that she was foolish to think that a grown man would care that way about her, a twelve-year-old girl, and she wonders if she will ever experience such feelings herself.

Although Anthony and Mary sometimes include her in their company, they spend most of their free time together on their own, leaving Margaret feeling all alone, deprived of Anthony's companionship.

A week later, the *Abigail* brings Catherine Bennett to Jamestown. The greeting between her and the Reverend William is more formal than the reunion of the two Africans. Margaret observes that they are glad to see each other, but after the customary welcoming buss, there is little physical contact between them. There is also a world of difference in how the two women travel. Mary, on her own, brings with her only the clothes on her back. Catherine Bennett has her own maid and two large trunks, one filled with fancy dresses, the other with silver utensils, books, and linens. When Margaret helps unpack them, she sadly remembers her small trunk and her own beautiful, rose-colored dress and scarf all burned during the Indian attack.

After a summer of intermittent skirmishes with the Powhatans, the English settlers put a price on Opechancanough's head and let all their allies know about it. With the coming of fall, they continue to raid Indian villages. Unfortunately, the harvest is smaller than usual, leading to more food shortages. The colonists can only hope that they have inflicted enough hurt on the Indians that they will have to struggle to survive the winter as well.

By October, when the leaves start to turn, the militias encounter no more Indians on the south side of the James River.

One evening after supper, Robert Bennett takes Francis Wyatt aside. "I would like to go back to my plantation," he informs the governor. "My brother Edward has sent ships with enough supplies for us to make it through the winter."

Wyatt considers the proposal. It is timely, and there are considerable benefits—not the least that it will remove the servant girl whose presence continues to irritate him. There will be fewer mouths to feed in Jamestown, and retaking the southern banks, even if only by establishing a beachhead for now, will send another powerful message to the Indians that the settlers are here to stay.

"Propose it to the council, and I will offer my support," he says. "But we must make sure you are safe."

By the time Master Robert makes his application official, the governor has met with some of the military veterans and come up with a suitable plan. He orders a fort to be built on the cliffs overlooking the river next to the plantation. It will have the dual purpose of serving as a fortification against any Spanish attacks from the Chesapeake to the east and provide a place for housing soldiers who can protect the settlers against the Indians.

Margaret, with a heavy heart, helps Catherine Bennett pack. Despite her awkward encounter with Francis Wyatt, she likes living in his house; it reminds her of Aldwarke and Lady Isabel. She is not looking forward to the rough life on the plantation, but she accepts her fate and imagines she will have an easier time of it than the wife of the reverend.

39

BENNETT'S WELCOME

Virginia—October–December 1622

As the boats travel past Hogg Island on the way to the plantation they left six months earlier, Margaret and the other returnees are apprehensive. They all wonder what new adventures lie ahead and whether to trust the promises the Bennett brothers made prior to their departure from Jamestown.

When Master Robert and the Reverend William addressed the assembled survivors of the massacre at Warrosquoake and spoke of their plans, they didn't make it sound like a return to paradise, but offered many reassurances nonetheless. Master Robert told them that a fort would be built for their protection at the highest point on the cliff overlooking the James River, and that they would get help from other plantations to rebuild their destroyed homes. After being idle for so long and living on starvation rations, most of the workers were ready for a change, but what convinced even the most reluctant among them was the announcement that three ships had arrived from England with more than plenty provisions to make it through the winter. That news trumped any thought of eking out a living within the Jamestown palisades.

Including new hires, more than seventy workers are going to the plantation, which Master Robert has decided to rename "Bennett's Welcome" in order to erase the memories of the bloody past and mark a new beginning.

Bennett's Welcome

Margaret glances at the eager faces of her fellow returnees. Only Anthony, seated next to her on the wooden bench, looks serious and unhappy, because Mary is not with them. When Catherine Bennett heard that she had been a house servant of the Earl of Warwick, she arranged for Mary to become her personal maid. She also insisted on staying behind at Governor Wyatt's in Jamestown until the new home at Bennett's Welcome is built for her and the reverend.

Up ahead, anchored in the wide bend of the James River, three large galleons are rocking gently on the lapping waves. Margaret's heart leaps into her throat. Could one of them be Captain Jope's? Has he come to take her away from this dismal place? As their pinnace comes closer, she looks eagerly for familiar signs, but by the time they pass the second schooner, she is deeply disappointed. The *White Lion* is not one of them. She turns to the dock where men are scurrying back and forth, unloading barrels and wooden planks from smaller boats and carrying them up the cliff. Looking up, she sees the front wall of a new, large house at the top, greeting them like an emblem of hope. The ships' crews have been busy preparing for their arrival.

The pinnace comes to an abrupt stop at the dock, rocking Margaret forward. She disembarks with the others, climbing onto the wooden timbers and from there onto solid ground. The wet sand and stone pebbles feel oddly familiar under her feet, as does the winding path up the cliff. When she reaches the top, she is surprised by how much of the plantation has been rebuilt already. Smoke rises from the brick chimney of the partially completed cookhouse. Workmen are filling the skeletal walls with wattle and daub, while carpenters and joiners are putting up timbers for a new smokehouse and shed next to it. Farther down the path to the meadow, where the workers' homes were, a row of makeshift tents awaits them. There are even a handful of cattle grazing nearby. The only remnants of the attack are charred timbers and planks, which have been cut up and stacked here and there for use as firewood.

Margaret closes her eyes. A few fleeting images flash past, memories of the horror she experienced, but the banging of hammers and shouts of the workmen echoing in the woods across the creek drown out any ghostly whispers of the victims whose blood drenched the soil.

Toward evening, as the workmen return to the ships, Margaret notes some apprehensive glances toward the dark forest among the settlers. The returnees are not convinced that the area is safely cleared of all Indians. Huddling around the large campfire by the tents, they speak louder than normal to cover their anxiety. No one sleeps well that first night, listening for any unusual sounds coming from the woodlands.

Over the next days, however, as other workers arrive—people whom Robert Bennett hired from other plantations to help out—everyone relaxes. The returning settlers fall back into their former roles. Anthony takes the cattle farther afield to better grazing grounds. He has a few more young helpers with him than before, carrying muskets for protection. Margaret returns to kitchen duties, assisting a ferret-faced man named Humphrey, who has replaced Thomas Breewood as the main cook. He seems pleasant enough, but Margaret can't tell how experienced he is. Until the new cookhouse is ready, everyone survives mostly on sailors' fare: rock-hard biscuits and porridge that is easily prepared in large pots over the campfire.

One morning a detail of four soldiers, led by a young, bearded lieutenant, appears at the main house. After conferring with Master Robert, they head east along the cliff to determine the best spot to build the fort.

The following day after dinner, as Margaret returns from the creek, hauling water, she meets Master Roberts coming from the cliff path. He is normally serious, but today a small smile plays about his lips.

"I'm glad I found you, Margaret," he says. "I need your help down at the dock. Why don't you go ahead while I talk to Humphrey for a moment?"

Puzzled, Margaret leaves the heavy water buckets by the cooking house and heads for the edge of the cliff. What she sees takes her breath away. Another ship is anchored near the three schooners. It is flying a Dutch flag. It can't be . . . the *White Lion*! She blinks to make sure she isn't dreaming. It is!

In no time, Margaret is flying down the steep path, stumbling, tripping, barely able to stay on her feet. Halfway down, she stops and sees a familiar figure looking up toward her. The man breaks into a run, and Margaret flies into his arms for a long embrace. Her heart feels like it is about to explode with joy.

Finally Captain Jope puts her back on the ground. He holds her at arm's length and asks, "Are you well, Margaret? We have been terribly worried about you."

Overwhelmed with emotion, she is unable to speak and nods rapidly. Then she looks around for John.

"He is aboard the ship." Jope says. "We didn't want to draw any more attention to you here. Come." When she hesitates, he assures her, "It's all right. Master Bennett doesn't expect you back until the morning."

He takes her to a small rowboat waiting at the dock next to a pinnace from which all kinds of barrels, chests, and trunks are being unloaded. On their way to the *White Lion*, Jope points to the rigging high above the quarterdeck. A small figure is hanging onto the ratlines, waving madly. As they get closer, he scampers down the ropes. By the time Margaret climbs aboard, John is waiting for her, dancing in anticipation from one foot to the other. They look at one another for a moment, then come together kissing and embracing. The other seamen look, pretending to be indifferent, but even the most hardened hearts are melting a bit at their affectionate reunion.

Gareth, the first mate, steps forward and bows. "Welcome back on board, Margaret. It's good to see you."

"It is good to see you, too," Margaret says and curtsies.

As the crew applauds, Jope ushers Margaret and John into his cabin, where a small feast is laid out on the table, the likes of which Margaret hasn't seen for some time—cheese, bread, meat, and fish.

After saying blessings, they dig in. Between bites they chatter about everything that has been happening to them.

Jope heard of the massacre from his wife when he returned from a long trading voyage to Bermuda and the Caribbean. He hardly took the time to register that Mary was six month's pregnant with their first child before he was out the door again and on his way to Plymouth. There he tarried anxiously waiting until the *White Lion* was loaded with food, supplies, weapons, and other provisions before setting sail for Virginia.

Margaret claps her hands in joy. "Mary is going to have a baby, that's wonderful! What are you going to name her?"

Jope blushes, embarrassed. "We haven't had time to discuss it. Probably Joane, after Mary's grandmother."

When Margaret tells them what happened during the massacre, omitting only the moment when the Indian almost killed her, John's eyes grow wide as saucers.

"We haven't had any adventures like that," he says, sounding disappointed. "We've just been carrying merchandise back and forth."

After the meal, Jope gives Margaret and John time alone together to get reacquainted. To Margaret, John hasn't changed all that much. He is a bit more sinewy, but still boyish. He shows her proudly around the ship, overwhelms Margaret with his newly acquired nautical terms—all the names for different kind of knots, sails, and rigging. He shows her the astrolabe with which the new navigator determines the latitude of the ship. Then he brings her to the cabin where he sleeps, a dark nook he shares with two other cabin boys. Jope affords him no special treatment, having placed him under the second mate's supervision. Only one thing sets him apart from his shipmates. After the day's chores are done—swabbing the deck, darning sails, repairing ropes, serving food to the crew—John gets to spend some time in the captain's cabin being tutored by Jope and reading the Bible and books about law and maritime trade. John especially likes *Hakluyt's Voyages*, which are all about travels of discovery in the New World.

"It reminds me of you and where you are," he says seriously.

Margaret muses that his life is not so different from hers, except for having the time to read and the joy of being with their captain every day. She is glad for him and feels just a little bit jealous. She wishes she could share their lives, but she knows that is an unattainable dream.

She spends the night in Jope's cabin, breathing in the smells, before she goes to sleep. In the morning, they all have breakfast together. Before it is time to go, the captain blesses Margaret and presses some coins into her hands.

"Keep them safe for when you may need them!"

Their good-byes in front of the men are more measured—a simple embrace and kiss for John, a longer clasping of Jope. Then Margaret steps on deck, says good-bye to Gareth and the crew, and climbs down into the rowboat. Captain Jope joins her, and two seamen row them back to shore. After they step on the dock, Margaret impulsively hugs Jope once more, feeling the rough surface of his leather jerkin through her dress.

Then she says, "Good-bye," and her lip starts to quiver.

Jope looks deeply into her eyes. "Be well, Margaret. We'll be back before long."

She turns quickly to where Master Robert is tallying goods and talking with other seamen. He nods to her once and returns to his tasks. Margaret hurries toward the cliff path. She doesn't look back, not wanting Jope to see the tears that blind her vision.

By the time she reaches the top, she has herself under control. When she arrives at the cookhouse, she is grateful that Humphrey doesn't ask where she's been. Master Robert must have given him a suitable explanation. She is glad that there is plenty to keep her occupied. But in the evening, she stares forlornly into the curling flames of the campfire.

Her melancholy mood lasts until more soldiers arrive, along with additional laborers, to start building the fort. In their wake, Margaret notices a plump young African woman who breaks away from them to come down the path from the cliff toward the cookhouse. She is wearing a simple brown dress with a white collar, carries a small child on one hip, and looks vaguely familiar. Her lively face lights up when she sees Margaret, and she hurries toward her.

"Master Robert told me to find you, Margaret," she says. "My name is Frances, and this is my son, Peter. I'm here to help out with the cooking for the soldiers and the other workers."

Margaret's confused expression is easy to read. Frances smiles and continues, "I remember you. You were aboard the ship that brought us here, you and the boy. We all wondered where you were taken. Is he here, too?"

Margaret shakes her head no. She doesn't remember a woman with a baby on the *White Lion*. She points at Peter. "How old is he?"

Frances face turns radiant. "He is almost two. He was the last gift bestowed on me by my husband." Her expression becomes somber. "When I was taken from Pongo, I didn't know I was pregnant and—"

"You are from Pongo?" Margaret interrupts her excitedly. "Did you know my mother and father?"

Frances looks at her questioningly.

"He . . . he was the *soba*."

Surprised, Frances says, "Why, everybody knew him. Your father came to my house after my husband was killed in the second battle with the Imbangala. He had kind words for me and my parents. He said we would be looked after."

Tears well up in Margaret's eyes.

Frances reaches out and touches her cheek. "We've all had a terribly difficult time, but we're survivors. We're *malungu*. We must stick together and look out for one another."

Margaret nods gratefully.

Over the ensuing weeks, she gets to know Frances and Peter well. It is wonderful to have someone to talk to during working hours, and afterward at night. They share memories of Pongo, stories of the brutal trek to Luanda, their memories of the unspeakable journey across Kalungu, and their miraculous rescue. For Margaret it is the first time that she can fully unburden herself to a stranger. Although she was happy to share some of her past with Anthony, talking with Frances is a deeper, more healing experience. Soon Margaret trusts her enough to tell her all about the time in England. In turn, Frances relates her experiences at Floridew plantation.

When she and the other Angolans from the *White Lion* arrived there, it was a rundown place owned by then governor Yeardley. But in the past two years, the presence of the Africans has turned it into a thriving plantation. Most of the white indentured workers come from big cities in England and have no farming skills whatsoever. She and the other African farmers from Ndongo showed them how to cultivate the tobacco plants and guided them through the complicated process of pruning, harvesting, drying, and curing the leaves. Now hogsheads filled to the brim are being loaded on ships bound for England.

"Without us they'd still be scraping the soil like hogs rooting for truffles," she says, laughing proudly. "But they don't appreciate what we're doing for them, or at least they don't show it."

Margaret, who has experienced the kindness of Captain Jope, Lady Isabel, and even Robert Bennett, isn't sure she agrees, but she keeps her own counsel.

Frances is happy to be at Bennett's Welcome. Unlike Warrosquoake, Floridew survived the massacre with only a few casualties, but with the arrival of refugees from the surrounding plantations, supplies grew scarce there as well. Here provisions are plentiful, and she doesn't have to skimp and scrounge to find food for her son.

Margaret enjoys watching her dote on Peter, a happy, energetic boy. When she has fun playing with him, she often wonders if someday she will have children of her own. In the meantime, she relishes spending time with her new friend and almost believes that life in Virginia has more possibilities for her than she can imagine.

40

UPROAR!

London—December 1622

The winter session of the Somers Island Company takes place at the residence of the Earl of Southampton. Henry Wriothesley, who has been reelected as treasurer of both the Bermuda and Virginia Companies over the objections of King James, knows that he is presiding over a powder keg that could explode at any time. The most important item on the agenda is the discussion of the tobacco monopoly, a potentially contentious issue, and the monarch, angry that the shareholders have ignored his royal advice, is waiting for any opening to disgrace the leadership of the companies. Another riotous meeting would give him that opportunity.

When Southampton brokered the uneasy compromise that embarrassed Warwick into forswearing Jamestown as a pirate base, the earl never forgave him and has treated him as a member of Sandys's faction ever since. Their relationship remains polite and cordial, but frostily distant. Southampton doesn't care about that, but it has become increasingly difficult for him to act as a mediator because he no longer has access to Warwick's thinking and never knows when he and his conniving cousin will stir up trouble.

While Warwick no longer attends the meetings of the Virginia Company, he still is very much a presence at the governing sessions of the Somers Island Company. He and his family own large estates in Bermuda, and he overcomes his deep loathing for Edwin Sandys long enough to conduct business and look after his financial interests.

Not that he has an easy time of it. It is clear to Southampton that everything about Sandys rubs Warwick the wrong way, from stroking the ends of his silver mustache to screwing up his face when he is about to embark on one of his long-winded orations. It doesn't help that Sandys continues to use his influence in Parliament to thwart Warwick at every opportunity. He recently passed legislation to deny the New England Company exclusive fishing rights for the whole east coast of America. Of course, Warwick knew that obtaining the rights was unreasonable in the first place; he pursued them in part to irritate his rival and has decided not to challenge their termination. The Plymouth Colony in Massachusetts will survive without them. Despite the harsh northern winter climate, it is doing better than Jamestown, where hostile Indians have made the life of the settlers a precarious existence.

The exclusive tobacco contract for Virginia and Bermuda is another matter, though. For months Edwin Sandys has pursued obtaining the monopoly with representatives of the Crown, and his labors are about to bear fruit. Although the negotiations have been conducted in secret, some of the provisions have leaked out and are raising questions and concerns. The plans for how to distribute the fees paid into the royal coffers are especially worrisome, as the terms are unfavorable to Warwick and his family. Sandys means for the Virginia and Somers Island Companies to bear the costs equally, which would cut heavily into Warwick's profits.

So when the meeting turns to a discussion of that part of the tobacco contract, Southampton prepares for the worst. He watches Warwick purse his lips, barely hiding his contempt, while Sandys outlines the plan for equal division of the royal charges.

Expecting an outburst, Southampton is surprised when Warwick rises and addresses him directly, acting as if Sandys were not in the room. "This arrangement is patently unfair, my Lord. Virginia tobacco has a greater value and should therefore carry a proportionately larger share of the fees."

Nicholas Ferrar, speaking for Sandys and his minions, interjects, "Bermuda is on sounder financial footing and, being closer to Europe, has an easier time transporting tobacco to English ports."

Again, Warwick shows remarkable restraint as Thomas Smythe and members of his faction, who share his financial interests, chime in.

Before the wrangling becomes contentious, Southampton suggests a compromise. Why not leave the final decision to a Bermuda court, which will meet two months' hence? Its consent is required to ratify the contract, and the decision made at that time will be binding. It is an elegant solution, offering a concession to Warwick and Smythe by suggesting a venue more favorable to their cause without eliminating the chances for Sandys and his plan to carry the day.

After conferring briefly with Nathaniel Rich, Warwick catches Smythe's eye and receives a small nod in return. He rises once again and says, "We accept this arrangement."

Southampton is relieved and feels almost jubilant when he gavels the meeting to a close without a single eruption.

He doesn't realize that Warwick gathering his fur coat, beckoning to Samuel Argall and his cousin to join him, and abruptly leaving the great hall is a sign of trouble. On their way out, the three men chuckle as if they have scored a victory, but Warwick is churning inside.

* * *

He gets his revenge by proxy at the December meeting of the Virginia Company. The initial agenda items raise no hackles, although the report on the state of the colony is hardly encouraging. A recent letter by Governor Wyatt to Southampton in his capacity as treasurer describes ongoing hostile encounters with the Indians and asks for more military reinforcements and food supplies.

"We have sent the frigate *Abigail* with armor, gunpowder, and new settlers to offer relief," Henry Wriothesley assures the shareholders. "It is due to arrive in Jamestown this week."

But when the time comes to discuss the tobacco contract, which needs ratification by the company members, Nathaniel Rich rises and, pointing an accusing finger at Edwin Sandys, utters these fateful words: "Five hundred pounds!"

Taken aback, Southampton makes the mistake of replying with a question that had been better left unasked, "What do you mean, sir?"

In a voice dripping with sarcasm, Warwick's cunning cousin says, "Perhaps we should ask our worthy auditor why he negotiated a salary of £500 for himself to administer the tobacco contract."

He pauses and lets the stunned silence sink in among the assembly before continuing. "Not to mention £300 for his second in command, Nicholas Ferrar, and so on for the rest of the managers of the contract." Before any of his adversaries can jump in, he drives the point home. "The total exceeds £2500, and at a time when our company is in dire financial straits!"

Immediately, a chorus of well-coordinated cries of indignation bursts forth from the Warwick and Smythe factions.

"For shame!"

"Fraud, deceit, corruption!"

"Sandys is taking food out of our mouths!"

"This is a contemptible conspiracy at the top!"

"Down with the Machiavellian mountebank!"

As the shouts of displeasure get increasingly personal, Sandys jumps to his feet, but all he can do is glare daggers in Nathaniel Rich's direction. His supporters weigh in with insults and hollering of their own. Lord Cavendish is nearly apoplectic, his handsome face crimson with fury and twisted into an ugly grimace. If there wasn't a phalanx of shareholders between him and Nathaniel Rich, he would do the lawyer bodily harm.

The meeting descends into such chaos that the staid and usually effective Southampton is unable to restore even a semblance of order. He hammers his gavel on the table repeatedly but is drowned out in the din and bedlam of the different factions heaping insults at each another. He looks for help to Nicholas Ferrar, whose temperament is closest to his own among the leaders of the company, but receives an exasperated, helpless shrug. Sandys, his lips white with suppressed rage and eyes darting across the tumultuous crowd, suddenly turns away in disgust.

When the raucous shareholders on all sides have shouted themselves hoarse, there is a momentary letup in invective. Southampton bangs his gavel again, and this time the lull lasts long enough for him to shout, "This is offensive and undignified behavior!"

When his exhortation is greeted with derisive peals of laughter, he bellows with all his might, "This meeting is adjourned!"

Nathaniel Rich nods to Smythe, a self-satisfied grin on his lips. He is looking forward to reporting the outcome to his cousin. He knows the Earl of Warwick will be pleased.

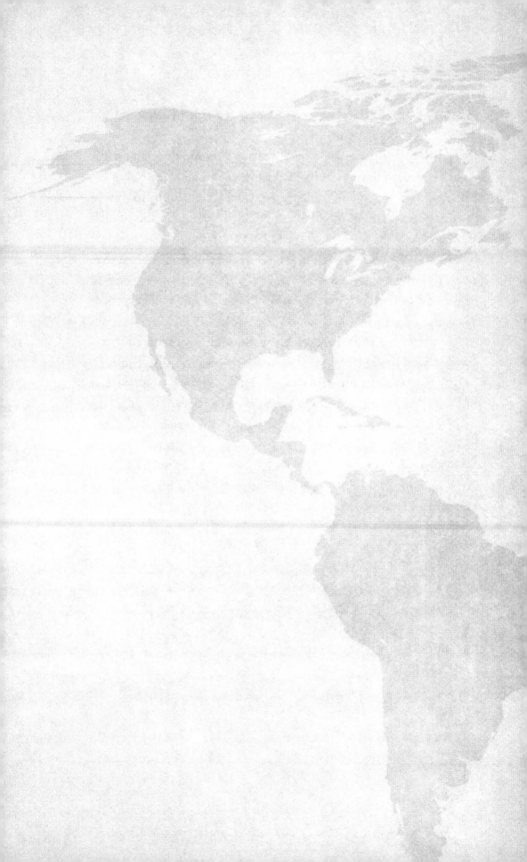

41

PESTILENCE

Bennett's Welcome—Winter 1623

By the time the first snow flurries arrive, enough homes have been built to accommodate all of the returning settlers. The climate is quite chilly, but not worse than anything Margaret experienced at Aldwarke, and plenty of wood is available to keep the hearths and kitchen fires going. When snows blanket the grazing fields, Anthony and his helpers bring the cattle closer to home and herd them into a pen where a shed provides shelter from the freezing cold at night.

With the ground hard and frozen, work at the fort comes to a halt, and most of the soldiers return to Jamestown. A small detachment remains behind to protect Bennett's Welcome against Indian attacks—not that any are expected. Veterans of previous winters know that everyone, natives and colonists alike, hunkers down until spring. The soldiers stay in a log house inside the unfinished fortifications, but the settlers often invite them for meals into their homes. Lieutenant Sheppard is a frequent guest at the main house. He always wears his uniform and is unfailingly polite to everyone, including Margaret.

From time to time he and Master Robert travel by boat to Jamestown for meetings with the governor's council. They come back with news of what is happening throughout the colony and occasionally bring along provisions purchased from the rare English ship that shows up at the harbor.

One time, they return accompanied by an English gentleman who is dressed in a fancy doublet, britches, and fur-lined overcoat. While serving dinner, Margaret learns that his name is Nathaniel Butler. The former governor of Bermuda is paying a visit to the colony to report on its current state. When he mentions the Earl of Warwick in conversation, Margaret becomes especially alert and tries to catch as much of the conversation as she can. It upsets her that their guest knows Lord Rich well. What if he mentions her to the spiteful earl? She has not thought for some time how easily his long arm could reach her.

When she shares her fears with Anthony, he laughs dismissively. "Not to worry," he reassures her. "We are tiny minnows in his lordship's pond. He has many bigger fish to catch."

When Margaret looks doubtful, he continues, "Besides, the man probably hasn't noticed you. When he came by the paddock, he went right past me without a hint of recognition, even though he met me several times in Bermuda and even talked to me before I shipped out to England."

Margaret wants to trust Anthony's judgment, but does her best to avoid Butler as he walks around the plantation and inspects the progress on the fort. She breathes a sigh of relief when he departs the following day.

Christmas passes without any special celebration, in keeping with the austere practices of the Puritans. Margaret notes that Reverend Bennett's sermon barely mentions the birth of Jesus and says nothing about his redeeming the world from sin. But what she misses most are the fragrant holly and rosemary decorations at Aldwarke.

On their next trip to Jamestown, Master Bennett and Lieutenant Sheppard bring back several guns, a keg of gunpowder, and a young soldier, fresh from England. His name is Phillip, and he is eager and excited like so many youngsters in uniform. He came to Virginia shortly before Christmas on the frigate *Abigail* with other recruits and immigrants. Unlike many of the settlers aboard, he did not become sick during the voyage.

A week later, Master Robert appears in the doorway of the warm cookhouse with Phillip at his side. They both look somber and serious. It is rare for the master to visit the work areas, and Margaret looks questioningly toward Frances.

"Several of the soldiers have fallen ill," Master Robert says. "They are unable to travel to Jamestown and are in need of attention. Lieutenant Sheppard has asked for our help."

"Is the lieutenant all right?" Margaret asks.

"Yes, yes," says Master Robert impatiently. "Take what you can and see what relief you can bring to them."

Margaret and Frances pack in two baskets several jugs of cider, some bread, and the remains of the morning porridge. Phillip picks up the heavier of the two. Together, they take the cliff path to the fort.

Margaret is eager to see the unfinished stronghold for the first time. It turns out to be about a quarter the size of the Jamestown fort. The partially constructed palisades remind her of the walls of Pongo. Inside is much open space. In one of the corners overlooking the cliff she sees a raised mount with a cannon aimed downriver. There is also a log house and, off to one side, a hastily constructed lean-to no bigger than a hovel.

As they approach the log house, Lieutenant Sheppard and several soldiers come out and help carry the baskets. They set them down a short distance from the lean-to. The lieutenant points toward four men lying on makeshift cots, shivering and moaning. Their faces are pale as ashes. As Margaret draws near, one of them stirs and his eyelids flutter open. He stares vacantly at her, the white of his eyes a sickly yellow.

Putting her hand on his forehead, Margaret exclaims, "He is burning up with fever."

341

She walks back to Lieutenant Sheppard and says, "If they can manage a sip of cider, they may find some relief. I don't know what else I can do."

He runs his fingers through his dark brown hair. "They need to be confined, or all of us will be on our backs in no time."

"Has a doctor been sent for?"

"Yes, we sent a dispatch to Jamestown this morning."

For the remaining daylight hours and into the night, Margaret ministers to the sick as best she can, cooling their burning heads with a wet cloth and getting them to sip cider from a small ladle. She bundles them up against the cold and prays for them, but when dawn finally comes two of the soldiers are lifeless corpses and the other two are close to death.

Later that day, a messenger returns from Jamestown. The remaining soldiers stop digging the graves to bury their comrades and gather around as Lieutenant Sheppard reads the dispatch. "Illness is rampant here and at the other plantations. Keep the sick isolated. May the Lord be with you."

He turns to his men, looking stricken, and says, "It is signed by Governor Wyatt. There will be no doctor."

There is an uncomfortable silence until Margaret speaks up. "Shouldn't we send for the Reverend Bennett to administer last rites?"

"Yes. It's the least we can do," says Lieutenant Sheppard.

* * *

Over the next weeks, the pestilence overwhelms Bennett's Welcome. All work comes to a halt while the healthy settlers care for the sick. The few remaining soldiers move into the plantation's empty houses. Every day someone else comes down with the debilitating fever and is soon too weak to move about or eat without aid. Not everyone gets the disease, and some who do survive. Still, many die. Surprisingly, none of the four Africans—Margaret, Anthony, Frances, or

Peter—contract the sickness. It also seems to prey more on the weak and ill-fed, sparing the halest, including Lieutenant Sheppard and Humphrey, who as cook eats better than anyone on the plantation.

Still, neither Robert Bennett nor his cousin the Reverend William are spared. They both contract the disease in short order, and Margaret cares for them to the point of her own exhaustion. After languishing for a week, they slowly recover, but they remain weak for several more days.

Those not afflicted divide up the tasks. Frances and Humphrey prepare food. Anthony heads the burial detail. Digging into the ice-hard ground is hard work. Margaret and the rest nurse the sick.

One day, emerging from one of the worker's homes, she finds Anthony resting briefly, warming himself by a small fire.

"Another has died," she calls to him.

He sighs and joins her inside the house's lone room. They pull the emaciated body of a middle-aged man, one of the field hands, outside, lifting him onto the wheel cart and transporting him to the burial grounds. When they arrive, Anthony starts to attack the ground with a pickax to break through the rocklike surface.

"You don't have to stay, I can manage," he says between blows.

"I don't wish to go back inside," Margaret responds.

Looking at the fresh mounds topped by wooden crosses, Margaret suddenly feels overcome by the magnitude of the devastation and begins to cry uncontrollably. "I can't help enough of them," she sobs. "I keep praying, but they just slip away."

"You shouldn't care so much," Anthony says gruffly as he starts to dig into the softer ground below the icy crust. "They wouldn't care if you were bitten by the fever."

By now, Margaret is familiar with Anthony's low opinion of the white settlers. But she can't help but ask, "How do you know that?"

"They are English," Anthony retorts with a scowl. "Their hunger for power is boundless. If you aren't of use to them, they simply discard you."

Disagreeing with his harsh view allows her to get hold of herself. "I don't believe that," she insists. "They're not all like that!"

"Believe what you will. You'll see," he says, jabbing at the ground with renewed force. "It will be much worse for you. They treat their women without regard and their servants even worse."

Margaret decides to leave him. She doesn't understand why he is suddenly so negative. She knows there is more to do, even if it is a losing battle, and Anthony's angry mood makes it harder, sapping her energy.

She and the few healthy survivors continue daily to look regularly after the sick. The worst time is early in the mornings when they find the bodies of the settlers who didn't make it through the night. Margaret prays that their journey ends with them in the arms of the Lord and then calls on Anthony and his men to bury them. Death becomes their constant companion as the pestilence decides who lives and who perishes. For her own preservation, Margaret begins to shut out any feelings for the deceased or herself. She performs her tasks like a ghost, walking through life disconnected from her body and feelings.

So when she wakes one morning and finds blood on her dress, she looks at it with detachment and wonder. Upon further examination, she realizes it is coming from between her legs. It baffles her. None of the sick women she has tended to have ever bled like that.

By the time she finds Frances and tells her about it, she is frightened. To her surprise, her friend breaks out into a bright smile. "This is wonderful news, Margaret!" she exclaims. "It means you are a becoming a woman."

Margaret is dubious. "Is my life in danger?"

Frances laughs. "Of course not. You have the flowers. Soon you'll be able to have babies." She adds mischievously, "Where there are no flowers, there can be no fruit!"

Uncertain, Margaret asks, "What is going on with me?"

"Don't worry. This happens to every woman. It lasts about three days every month. I'll make you up a small bag of cinnamon to carry with you and mask the smell of blood."

That triggers a distant memory for Margaret. Once in a while her mother stayed inside the house and refused to go out. There was an aura around her, a scent, for several days. Then it was gone and she ventured outside again.

When Francis notices Margaret relax, she hugs her and says, "When this terrible time of pestilence passes, we will celebrate!"

The reminder of the scourging sickness jolts Margaret back to the present. There is work to be done aiding the afflicted, and she hurries to start her morning rounds.

* * *

Several months pass before the disease runs its course. By then, more than half of the settlers who returned to Bennett's Welcome have perished. A census taken in February shows only thirty-three settlers alive on the plantation.

The figures are just as dismal for the rest of the colony. The sickness has killed more people than the Indian massacre a year earlier. Along with losses due to starvation, the colony has shrunk from 1,400 settlers to barely 500 in just one year.

With the first signs of spring, there are hopeful developments. The survivors at Bennett's Welcome sow corn and other crops. Robert Bennett writes to his brother Edward in England that he expects to plant the first tobacco crop the following year on the way to finally making the plantation financially profitable.

In March, Catherine Bennett joins her husband at the plantation. With her comes Mary, who nursed her back to health when she contracted the pestilence and everyone else, including Dr. Pott, had given up on her. Her English maid succumbed to the disease. She and the reverend move into their new home next to the main house. It is not as large, but quite comfortable.

At the sight of Mary, Anthony all but melts. His mood improves overnight. He smiles again and casts tender glances toward her whenever he is in her presence. He no longer talks with unrelenting hostility about the English, and Margaret muses about how love can brighten someone's outlook.

With work on the fort about to commence again—more soldiers, carpenters, and joiners arrive from Jamestown—Lieutenant Sheppard surprises Margaret. After he packs his trunk to move back to the log house, he seeks her out at the cookhouse, removes his cap, and says, "Thank you, Margaret. We could not have survived without you. We are all in your debt."

42
SPRINGTIME
Bennett's Welcome—March–April 1623

S oon after the pestilence has subsided, Master Robert and Lieutenant Sheppard resume their regular trips to Jamestown to confer with Governor Wyatt and the other burgesses and militia leaders. Settlers at Bennett's Welcome eagerly await their return for the latest news of the other plantations and what is happening to protect the colonists from further Indian attacks.

As Anthony and his helpers take the cattle to grazing areas farther inland, they sight Indian patrols on several occasions, but none of the encounters are hostile. So it comes as a shock when the settlers get the news that Henry Spelman and nineteen men on a trade expedition for corn and food on the Potomac River were all killed by Anacostan Indians. The report is a grim reminder that everyone needs to remain vigilant, and the soldiers renew their perimeter patrols around the houses at Bennett's Welcome.

Early April brings confirmation that the raids on Indian villages and destruction of crops the previous summer were more effective than hoped for. Two Powhatan emissaries arrive in Jamestown bearing a message from Opechancanough. The Powhatan chief wants to declare a cease-fire because "enough blood has been shed on both sides," and he acknowledges that his people are starving. He wants to negotiate a truce so that his people can sow corn and tend to their crops for the coming year. In exchange, he promises to return the English women who were kidnapped during the massacre.

To demonstrate his good faith, Opechancanough releases Mrs. Boyse a week later. She arrives in Jamestown, emaciated, wild-eyed, and attired like an Indian queen with pearl and glass bead necklaces and copper medallions. Her deerskin dress is dyed red and covered with furs and feathers. Her appearance shocks the colonists, and her harrowing account of her captivity brings renewed calls for rescuing the other women prisoners.

Governor Wyatt and his council debate the merits of Opechancanough's proposal. Most of the members are dubious about trusting the Powhatans. The veterans of previous Indian wars—Hamor, Yeardley, Pierce, and Tucker—want nothing to do with it. They think it's better to kill their enemies than to save a few female English captives. At the same time, they know that their plantations need a respite from warfare, too, especially if they want a sizeable tobacco harvest this year.

Master Roberts and Lieutenant Sheppard continue the discussions at the dinner table at the main house. Margaret, listening in as she serves the meals, has mixed feelings. She understands why the Reverend William calls for the extermination of "the heathen brutes"—he is still livid and upset about the death of his cousin Richard—but Lieutenant Sheppard also takes a hard line. Margaret is surprised to hear Master Roberts argue for peaceful coexistence.

Despite the danger of encountering natives, she takes to walking in the forest on her own. She proceeds with caution, knowing that the Indians are starving and likely to be foraging for food, but the woods beckon. Alone, surrounded by the smells of springtime soil and delicate dogwoods in bloom, she feels at peace for the first time in months. She watches the squirrels chasing each other across the bare branches, listens to the twittering mating calls of birds, and surprises families of deer. Startled, the adult does raise their heads, then dart away with their young offspring.

Margaret looks for medicinal plants similar to the ones in the garden at Aldwarke and Tavistock. She is delighted to find moss and early signs of yarrow and foxglove, but so many of the plants peeking through the earth are unfamiliar to her. Some flowers have blossoms that look like Indian moccasins and mushrooms with corrugated hoods.

As the weather warms, delicate green leaves appear on the branches of oaks, elms, chestnuts, beech trees, and ash trees. One day she ventures farther into the woods until she comes to the edge of the swamp, where cedars and cypress trees rise from the wetland. The day is balmy, and a mild breeze rustles the fledgling leaves. Sunlight pouring through the green canopy creates golden, diaphanous curtains. Margaret's heart tingles with pleasure. She extends her arms and whirls around in circles, caressing the warm air and feeling at one with her surroundings.

When she stops, she sees an Indian gazing in her direction from across the clearing. She freezes, hoping he hasn't seen her. But he comes toward her, moving lightly on his feet. Margaret is terrified. As he nears she wills herself not to tremble. The young brave has strange drawings on his arms, and his face and shoulders are painted crimson red. He is wearing a woven loincloth with a leather pouch and sheathed knife at his side, and he carries a large bow. There are feathers in his braided hair, but no war paint on his cheeks.

The young Powhatan brave circles all the way around her, examines her dress and face closely, circles her again, and stops in front of her. Margaret holds still, remembering Anthony telling her that Indians think Africans are ghosts. When he looks into her eyes, she holds his glance without blinking. He extends his hand tentatively toward her face and slowly touches her cheek and hair, like a blind man exploring an unfamiliar creature.

Without thinking, Margaret smiles. The Indian draws back, startled. Margaret holds her breath, expecting him to strike. But he reaches into his pouch and withdraws a handful of mushrooms with pitted caps, like the ones she noticed before. He lifts up her hand, turns it over, and places them in her palm.

A hesitant smile plays about his lips. Then he turns and vanishes into the forest.

Margaret lets out her breath and sinks to the ground in relief. She looks at the mushrooms in her hand. The young Indian has made her an offering, a gift. He could just as easily have cut her throat. Anthony must be right. The Indians see Africans as different creatures from the white Englishmen and women.

She takes a tentative bite from one of the mushrooms. It has a nutty taste. On her way back home she gathers more in her apron and brings them to the cookhouse. Humphrey looks at her questioningly, but Frances recognizes them.

"They are good to eat," she says.

The next afternoon at dinner, when Margaret serves the cooked mushrooms, Catherine Bennett wrinkles her nose in disapproval. "What are these?" she asks haughtily.

"They're mushrooms," Margaret replies simply.

Master Robert smells the dish and asks, "Where did you get them?"

"I picked them in the forest. They are tasty and leave no ill effects."

He gives her an odd look, but takes a spoonful on his plate and ventures a taste. "Not bad," he decides.

Margaret wisely doesn't say anything more about how she got them.

The next day, she returns to the spot where she and the Indian brave first met. She doesn't quite know what to expect, or whether he'll even be there, and is pleasantly surprised when he emerges from the underbrush as if he has been waiting for her.

This time Margaret is more assertive. When the young brave approaches, she takes a step toward him. When he halts, uncertainly, she holds out one of the coins Captain Jope gave her. It glints in the sunlight, throwing a bright spot on a nearby chestnut tree. The Indian draws closer and cautiously puts out his hand. Margaret places the coin into his palm. He examines it carefully, then drops it into his pouch.

When he looks up, she purposely puts her hand on her chest and says, "Margaret."

He nods in understanding and replies in kind, "Askuwheteau."

The next time she sees him, he is wearing the coin as a necklace and seems pleased when she notices it and smiles.

In the following weeks Margaret explores the forest with him whenever she can. Askuwheteau shows her roots, trees whose bark can be peeled and used to make ointments, and bushes with unripe, green berries. He points out poison ivy and which mushrooms to pick and which to avoid. He shows her vanilla leaf, skunk cabbage, sassafras, jasmine, sweet gum, mustard, and saw palmetto, and he mimes what to do with them.

The information is more than Margaret can absorb, and she doesn't know all of the uses yet. But she always returns home with a new plant or two, which she dries in the shed behind the smoke-house. In return, knowing that the Indians have had a hard winter, she always brings him something to eat—leftovers from the meals at the main house.

Her encounters with Askuwheteau give her a very different sense of Indians than what she hears from the men around the dinner table, who have never met a native face-to-face.

43

INVESTIGATION

London—February–May 1623

After hearing the dispute over the tobacco contract charges, the Bermuda court holds for Edwin Sandys and his associates. The fees for operating the monopoly are to be carried equally by the Virginia and Somers Island Companies, and the salaries for the administrative officers are considered appropriate. Sandys is not the kind of man who openly celebrates such a decisive victory, but for several days after the verdict a smile of satisfaction remains on his lips. He derives great pleasure to have bested the Earl of Warwick and won a significant battle in their ongoing war.

When Lord Rich hears of the ruling, he hurls yet another wineglass against the wall of the study in his London home, adding another layer to the growing, unsightly stain on the woodwork next to the fireplace.

"It is not fair. How does this imbecile get away with it?" he rants on in impotent rage.

For the next week he is morose, nursing his defeat. Servants and close allies tiptoe around him, afraid to set off another explosion. Even the normally imperturbable Nathaniel Rich admits behind his back to being at a loss as to how to rouse his cousin from his ill humor.

Then Nathaniel Butler arrives from Virginia. His accounts of the colony's trials are like sunshine breaking through the dark clouds of Warwick's despondency. The more Lord Rich hears about the troubles at Jamestown and the surrounding plantations, the more his mood brightens.

"We will use this to our advantage," he says when Butler has finished.

Over the next weeks, he and his triumvirate—the two Nathaniels and Samuel Argall—meet frequently to map out a strategy.

The Virginia Company council plays into their hands when it publishes a report it has delivered to King James. *A Declaration of the Present State of Virginia Humbly Presented to the King's Most Excellent Majesty*, while acknowledging some of the difficulties resulting from the Indian attack, paints a rosy picture. Hearing about silkworms thriving on mulberry bushes, vineyards producing sweet wine, and a developing shipbuilding industry, not to mention the abundant tobacco crops, one would think that the colony is a virtual Eden poised on success. The report concludes by condemning "diverse troublesome opposition at home by persons little favoring Virginia's prosperity," which "must be borne with patience and with constancy overcome."

After reading a copy, Warwick is nearly ecstatic. He knows well who is meant by "troublesome opposition" and understands who is behind the report, although his signature does not appear at the bottom of the document.

"Give a man enough rope and he'll hang himself," he asserts and rubs his hands together with glee. "Sir Edwin has just given us everything we need to destroy him."

Two weeks later, the conspirators present their answer to the King's Privy Council. *The Unmasked Face of Our Colony in Virginia, as It Was in the Winter of the Year 1622*, written by Nathaniel Butler, is a devastating assessment of the colony's situation. Mincing no words, Butler disparages Wyatt's government in Jamestown. He describes the settlers' houses as worse than "the meanest cottages in England." He notes that the plantations are built on "infectious bogs and muddy creeks and lakes." Having seen no fortifications against Indian attacks, he is not surprised that the colony was vulnerable to obliteration by the infidels.

But the most damaging claim is that, of the 10,000 settlers transported from England to Virginia over the past five years, fewer than 2,000 are still alive. While the figures are somewhat exaggerated, they support an earlier estimate brought to the company's attention: during Edwin Sandys's tenure, more than 3,500 men, women, and children were shipped to the colony, and after the Indian attack and pestilence only about 500 remain—a shocking rate of mortality. It seems that sending people to Virginia was sending them to their death.

When Warwick makes the report public, it causes a sensation. But that is only the first broadside against the Sandys administration. For round two, the earl releases a collection of supporting documents that Nathaniel Rich has quietly gathered. Much of it is direct evidence from Jamestown that John Pory has been only too happy to supply, as all letters coming from and going to England pass through his hands.

One accusatory epistle from the company board of directors to Francis Wyatt after the massacre refuses to offer help to a starving colony. A desperate letter by a young settler named Richard Frethorn, written to his parents, describes in agonizing detail the times of famine and pestilence in Jamestown. Its plaintive tone tugs at heartstrings of its English readers.

But the crowning blow is the private letters from Sir Edwin's brother, George Sandys himself, which not only support the figures of the terrible death toll among the settlers in Virginia but condemns the company leadership. Many readers focus on his statement that "the living have been hardly able to bury the dead through the London Company's imbecility."

It causes inescapable embarrassment to Sandys, Southampton, Ferrar, and the other council members of the Virginia Company.

Sandys seethes with rage when he hears of it. "How could Nathaniel Rich, that snake in the grass, have gotten hold of these letters?" he rails at Nicholas Ferrar, the bearer of the bad news.

Ferrar has no good answer. "There must be a traitor to our cause within the government in Jamestown," he ventures.

Stating the obvious doesn't bring Sandys any relief. He spends the next few days huddled with Southampton, avoiding any public attention, trying to figure out how to weather the storm.

But that is not the end of his troubles. Encouraged by the revelations, Alderman Johnson, a member of the Smythe faction, delivers a petition to the Privy Council. It claims gross mismanagement on the part of the governance board of the Virginia Company over the past four years, further impugning Sandys's leadership, and calls for an investigation.

As a result, representatives of King James resolve that the officers can't be relied upon and cancels the tobacco contract. The decision keeps the company in financial straits and deprives Sandys of a lucrative salary. The accusations also give the monarch the opportunity he has been waiting for. With Sandys and Cavendish in the House of Commons acting as thorns in his side, he has long believed that the London Company for Virginia and the Somers Islands is "just a seminary to a sedition parliament," and that they have turned Jamestown into hotbed of antiroyalist sentiment.

He has the Privy Council summon the company leaders—Southampton, Sandys, and Ferrar—to answer the various charges. They respond with unexpected courage and cogency and present a paper, written by Lord Cavendish, which addresses many other allegations as well. It includes a forceful rejoinder to the claim that the government of the companies is "democratic and tumultuous, and ought therefore to be altered, and reduced into the hands of a few." While acknowledging some truth to the charge, it argues that the administration is the "most just and profitable," and most conducive to achieve the ends everyone desires: a stable colony in the New

World. In addition, it reproaches Thomas Smythe's faction, which militates most loudly against democracy and calls for installing an oligarchy instead.

None of the fine words of rebuttal ultimately carry the day. In early May the Privy Council establishes a commission to investigate the London Company, both its Virginia and Bermuda branches. The commission demands that all of its records be turned over, including the court book, which contains all financial records—not to mention all letters, petitions, lists of names, invoices of goods, and more. Nicholas Ferrar, as deputy treasurer, has no choice but to comply.

Sandys may have prevailed in many battles, but the Earl of Warwick, bent on destruction of the Virginia Company, is about to win the war.

The result is a relentless unleashing of bitterness and bile between members of the Sandys and Rich factions. They start to quarrel openly in public when they encounter one another. The exchanges grow so violent that the Privy Council, in charge of keeping peace in London, commands both sides to avoid all quarreling.

So when Sandys and Cavendish publish a lengthy denunciation of Warwick, accusing him of conspiring against them, they miscalculate badly. The earl, prompted by Nathaniel Rich, complains directly to the Privy Council, which holds the authors in contempt for libel and places them under house arrest. Making their apology and promising better behavior, Sandys and Cavendish attain their release a short while later, but the wrangling and bickering continue unabated.

44

REVENGE

Virginia—May–June 1623

The settlers at Bennett's Welcome keep busy sowing spring corn, wheat, and beans, and planting a small field with tobacco seedlings as an experiment. They want to learn how to grow the crop in order to cultivate larger tracts of land the following year and to start reaping big financial rewards. When Margaret expresses curiosity about the process, Frances, who has spent more than three years at Floridew, one of the most successful plantations in Virginia, becomes her teacher. She explains all about seeding and transplanting the seedlings to another bed; growing, priming, topping, and harvesting the plants; curing, striking, sweating, and sorting the leaves; and finally packing them in hogsheads for transportation.

"Don't rub the leaves on your skin. They can make you sick," she warns. "At the height of the season after a day in the fields, some of the workers feel nauseated."

Margaret continues to make trips into the forest to spend time with Askuwheteau. Every week new plants emerge from the rich soil, and more bushes and flowers break out in colorful blossoms. The Indian brave continues to point them out and mimes what to do with them, adding to Margaret's store of medicinal knowledge. With the late spring, humidity returns in full force, but the woods remain cool and pleasant.

Revenge

Work on the fort continues to move forward, but toward the end of May there is a stirring among the troops. Lieutenant Sheppard, attending a dinner at the main house, announces plans for a great powwow with the Powhatans and their allies. He and several soldiers from Bennett's Welcome will accompany a delegation led by Captain William Tucker to meet with Opechancanough and his chiefs at a neutral site on the Potomac River. The purpose is to hold peace talks and to discuss the release of the women still held prisoner.

Margaret is glad to hear it. She remembers Captain Tucker from both times she arrived at Point Comfort on the *White Lion* and is surprised that he is in command rather than Captain Hamor or George Yeardley.

Phillip, who is now Lieutenant Sheppard's adjutant, explains the reason on one of his stops at the cookhouse.

"Captain Tucker is a hero after his defense against the Indian attacks at Point Comfort during the massacre last year," he says with pride.

Phillip has become a frequent visitor, always looking for an extra morsel of food. He and Humphrey get along well, and Margaret likes him well enough after working by his side during the pestilence. He has a mischievous side and entertains them by wrinkling his nostrils like a rabbit, sniffing the air, and trying to guess the ingredients in what they are cooking.

It is the first time Phillip will encounter the Powhatans up close, and the morning of his departure he is nervous when he comes to say good-bye. Margaret wishes him luck, and Humphrey slips him an extra hardboiled egg and biscuit for the journey.

While he and the lieutenant are gone, construction on the fort continues apace. Margaret marks its progress when she and Frances bring food to the workers for the midday meal and notices that the fort will be finished soon. She doesn't want that day to come because she knows Frances and Peter will have to return to Floridew.

Margaret will be sad to see them go and miss them. Frances has become a friend like no other.

Returning from the fort one day, they talk about the future, and Frances mentions her contract of indenture. "I have four more years before I get my freedom," she says. "What about you?"

Margaret only knows what Captain Jope told her. She'll be a servant for seven years.

Frances chides, "I hope you're sure about that. It's one thing to be an unpaid servant for a while, but I don't want to do this forever. I want to have a place of my own, where I can raise Peter and have more children."

"But you're not married!"

Frances laughs. "That won't be a problem. There are many more men here than women. By the time I get my freedom, I'll be twenty-five and quite a catch." She adds, "Someday you'll find a man and start a family of your own."

Margaret hasn't given it much thought. She has been too busy, but she remembers Anthony talking about his freedom and owning his own land. Did all her fellow survivors from the slave ship have that dream? On her solitary walks in the forest, Margaret tries to imagine what it would be like to have a place as big as the main house for herself.

A few days later, Robert Bennett brings astonishing news from Jamestown. The soldiers have returned from their mission unharmed. The parlay was a tremendous success, but not the way anyone imagined. Captain Tucker and his men have killed many Powhatan warriors, including a number of important tribal leaders.

When the Reverend William hears of it, he is jubilant and exclaims, "It's the just and mighty revenge of the Lord on the infidels."

Everyone at the plantation eagerly awaits Lieutenant Sheppard's return to learn all about what happened. Delivering food for the victory dinner, Margaret overhears him boast, "We surprised them. They had no idea what we had planned."

Revenge

But she doesn't get the full story until Phillip visits the cook-house later that day. He accepts a crust of bread and hunk of cheese from Humphrey in celebration.

"When we stepped ashore, there were more than 300 Indians from all different tribes," he says.

Between bites and chewing, the story emerges. By the time they made it to the meeting place, Opechancanough and other promi-nent Powhatans were already waiting. They looked fierce and impos-ing, arrayed in leather tunics and feather headdresses, and carrying bows and battle-axes.

Captain Tucker, knowing that he had to impress the Indians, had Lieutenant Sheppard and his soldiers line up behind him like an honor guard.

"We stood at attention, carrying our muskets on our shoulders," Phillip recounts.

"Did you feel scared?" Humphrey asks wide-eyed.

"Scared? Me? Not at all!"

Margaret and Frances, hearing under the bluster how anxious he must have been, hide their smiles and exchange knowing glances.

Then Captain Tucker and the Powhatan chief exchanged many fine speeches, negotiating. It took a long time because interpreters had to translate every word. When they finally came to mutually agreeable terms, the Indians brought out tobacco and pipes, and Tucker had the sailors carry several kegs of wine from the ship to offer a toast to the accords and to celebrate a lasting peace.

"You should have seen the eyes of the heathens light up," says Phillip. "We couldn't fill all their cups fast enough."

What the Indians didn't know was that the two kegs marked for them had been laced by Dr. Pott in Jamestown with a potent poison. After the toast, the braves who downed their wine went into convulsions.

Phillip looks up and his eyes flit back and forth rapidly as he relives the event. "They fell to the ground, writhing in pain and foaming at the mouth. The others went for their weapons, but we fired our muskets and killed many more. One of them came at me with an axe, and the lieutenant shot him through the throat with his pistol. We fought them off as they were dying around us. The rest ran away."

Margaret is horrified. Images of the Imbangala and the Indian hovering over her flash through her mind. A change in Phillip's voice brings her back to the present.

"Then we made sure the ones on the ground were dead and took a bunch of their scalps," he says, more subdued.

The memory of cutting and ripping the hair and skin from the heads of the dead Indians seems to trouble him and he shudders. Dismissing the thought, he continues, "We got about 250 of the heathens. Too bad that Opechancanough escaped."

"What about the women captives?" Frances asks.

"I don't know. They're still with the Indians. I guess we won't be able to rescue them." He swallows. "But this was more important. We showed the heathens that we mean business. Made them pay for the massacre."

He sees Lieutenant Sheppard passing by the window in the company of his men. They're laughing loudly as they head back to the fort. Phillip quickly says his good-byes and runs after them.

That afternoon, Margaret goes into the forest. She cautiously approaches the spot where she first met Askuwheteau, but there is no sign of him. For the next week, she returns every day. She hopes that he didn't go to the parlay—perhaps he was too young—and prays, if he did, that he wasn't among the braves killed. He doesn't show himself again, and Margaret never finds out what happened to him.

* * *

Over the next months, they see less of Lieutenant Sheppard and his soldiers at the plantation. The "fraudulent peace" has worked, and

Revenge

Governor Wyatt and his council decide to take a more aggressive stance toward the Indian tribes in the area. Under the leadership of William Pierce, Captain William Tucker, and George Yeardley, the militias launch ruthless offensives against the Chickahominies and Weyanocks. Even George Sandys, the company treasurer, leaves his poetry behind for a season and leads an expedition against the Tappatomaks. The soldiers kill many Indians, burn their villages, destroy the crops they have sown in abundance, and carry what food they find back with them to Jamestown.

Knowing that Frances and Peter will be leaving soon, Anthony and Mary advance their wedding plans. He tells Robert Bennett that they want to get married even though they are both still indentured to him, and he gives his blessing. The ceremony takes place one Sunday afternoon following the Reverend William's sermon. All of the plantation workers and a handful of the soldiers attend, standing in a clearing near the makeshift chapel.

Having spent most of her time at Anglican Floridew, Frances is surprised how simple the wedding ritual is. Because Puritans view marriage as a civil contract, not a religious sacrament, Robert Bennett presides in his role as magistrate of the plantation. Margaret is just as happy not to have to listen to the Reverend William rant on about sin and damnation again that day.

Anthony and Mary appear before Master Bennett, dressed in their regular clothes, and he asks of them in turn, "Do you want to marry?"

They look at one another with glowing eyes as they both say, "Yes."

Margaret, seeing how much they are in love, is happy for them.

Master Bennett pronounces them man and wife and has them sign the new plantation record book. After they make their X's, there is a small, celebratory dinner where Margaret and Frances serve sweet pies and puddings in addition to the usual fare.

That evening, Anthony and Mary move into one of the small workers' cottages—a home of their own. Still, he is away with the cattle a great deal, while she serves as housemaid to the Reverend William and his wife.

The day of Frances's departure arrives much too soon for Margaret. With a heavy heart, she, Anthony, and Mary accompany Frances and Peter to the dock. A pinnace is waiting for all the workers who have helped the settlers at Bennett's Welcome get back on their feet to take them back to their plantations upriver. Master Robert and the Reverend William thank them and wish them Godspeed.

After Frances kisses Anthony and Mary good-bye, Margaret gives Peter a toy boat she had Phillip carve for him. She hugs him and then buries her face in Frances's arms. The young woman gently strokes her hair, then holds her firmly by the shoulders and looks into her eyes.

"We will see each other again, Margaret," she says resolutely. "We are *malungu*. We stick together and look out for one another."

Then she picks up Peter and steps onto the ship.

Margaret, Anthony, and Mary head back up the cliff trail. When they reach the top, Margaret heads for the forest. She wants to be alone in the only place where she can feel at peace.

Later, as she walks among the soft underbrush and the lush canopy of the oak and chestnut trees, the seeds of freedom Frances has planted in her mind begin to take hold. She wonders what happened to her contract when everything burned during the massacre. She thinks about what a home of her own would look like. She can't imagine owning a house as big as Master Bennett's place. Anthony and Mary's cottage seems more manageable, but too small to house a large family, and she knows Anthony has bigger plans when their day of freedom comes. She wishes she could have such dreams.

45

DUEL

London—July 1623

Edwin Sandys and his cohorts do everything in their power to stave off the dissolution of the Virginia Company. They send a copy of Nathaniel Butler's *The Unmasked Face of Our Colony in Virginia* to Jamestown, asking Francis Wyatt to draft a point-by-point rebuttal. In London they continue to petition the Privy Council and work back channels to appeal to the King's advisers. Meanwhile, any encounter in public between members of the different factions unleashes a flurry of insults and threats of fisticuffs.

The truce between Warwick, Sandys, and Cavendish lasts just until the next boardroom meeting of the Somers Island Company. With a new court case brought against Lord Rich by Lady De La Warr and the Duke of Buckingham, Sir Edwin once again lambasts the earl for keeping the Africans taken from the Spanish slave ship for himself.

"They rightfully belong to the Bermuda Company and its shareholders," he insists.

Warwick is incensed. He is fed up with the lingering troubles stirred by Lady De La Warr and the duke. He has put out feelers trough Nathaniel Rich about the possibility of reaching a financial settlement with her.

"Anything to get that pernicious woman and her vexing spaniel out of my life!" he gushed, wishing he could take a hatchet and cut her head off.

So when Sandys confronts him once again with the accusations he has thrown for the past three years, all his frustrations with her, not to mention his vexation over losing the *Treasurer*, being ousted from the Virginia Company, and having his enemies hound him in what he perceived as a determined effort to send him to the scaffold, burst forth, and he retaliates with venom.

Puffing himself up to his full height, Warwick declares, "Why should a man bankrupt of ideas, moral compass, and human decency dare accuse me of anything? Let him cleanse his own barn and pigsty first."

That brings Sandys to his feet, a vein throbbing dangerously in his flushed forehead. "You may hide behind your title and access to the King, m'Lord, but your actions are no better than a common cheat's!"

"And you and your lackeys are libeling, conniving carbuncles whose words curdle milk and sour beer."

Stung, Lord Cavendish joins the fray. "That is a cheap, traitorous accusation," he fumes.

Warwick laughs harshly. "Cheap? How droll, coming from a notorious rampallion who never pays his debts."

Southampton, Ferrar, Nathaniel Rich, and the other board members jump up, trying to intervene, but they are too late. All semblance of civilization has surrendered to an onslaught of verbal thrusts worthy of a brawling street fight.

"A pox on you, you villainous coxcomb!"

"Clapper-clawed maggot!"

"Lying whoreson of a mongrel bitch!"

There is a sudden silence as everyone realizes Cavendish has gone too far.

Warwick, trembling with barely contained fury, his eyes ablaze, advances on the offender and spits out, "I challenge you, m'Lord!"

Cavendish, his face having lost all color, stares back. He raises his eyebrows, and a smile begin to play about his lips. He nods his head ever so slightly and replies, "I am at your service."

By now, the others have gathered around them, the pressing issues of the meeting forgotten. Everyone watches the two adversaries with rapt attention. The fateful decision having been made, Warwick and Cavendish relax to work out the details.

"We will have to find a neutral venue," Sandys's attack dog says.

Everyone understands what he is talking about. King James not only doesn't condone dueling, he abhors it. Ever since two of his favorite retainers killed each other in an "affair of honor" more than a decade earlier, he considers dueling butchery. He even passed a proclamation against it, which curtailed the practice but did not eliminate it. But while the opponents can't wait to skewer one another, neither wants to run afoul of the law.

"We must go to the continent," Rich suggests. "Ghent in Holland will do. A week from now?"

Cavendish nods. "Agreed."

Within hours, all London is abuzz about the impending duel between the two nobles. When the news reaches the royal chambers, the King immediately condemns it and instructs his law officers to order Cavendish and Warwick to remain in England under house arrest until their tempers have cooled. The two agree to comply, officially, but they have no intention of obeying the royal command and exchange secret messages to move ahead with their plans.

Nothing Nathaniel Rich says to his cousin can dissuade Warwick from pursuing his revenge. An accomplished swordsman, he has no doubt that he can fence circles around his opponent, who is considerably older than him, and he is looking forward to running him through and through. As a military man, Samuel Argall, who acts as Warwick's second, agrees with the earl: it is time to put a stop to the loudmouthed spokesman for Sandys's faction and teach him and his cohorts a lesson.

Duel

So on July 17, an overcast day, the Earl of Warwick sneaks from his London home disguised as a merchant. He takes a carriage to Margate, a small port near Dover, to go to Holland as a trader of woolen goods. He and Argall board a small sailing ship. It is the first time Warwick rides in a seagoing vessel larger than a rowboat. The channel is choppy, and a cool breeze blows across the bow. Warwick thinks about his fleet of ships and what it means to cross the Atlantic Ocean where, he imagines, the waves are even bigger. He feels a greater appreciation for what his captains and sailors have to endure. That thought takes him to Captain Jope, the Dutchman, and his young African charges. He remembers the defiant girl with the big eyes—Margaret was her name—and hopes an Indian will cut her throat. Images of Anthony, Mary, and John Pedro, the Africans he had at his home, crowd in on him in rapid succession.

He shakes his head to banish them from his mind and focuses on his upcoming duel. The nerve of Cavendish to impugn his mother's reputation! Warwick will make him pay dearly for his insults.

Arriving in Ostend, he and Argall lose no time hiring a coach to take them to Ghent, a bustling mercantile town, thirty miles inland. They arrive toward the evening and spend the night in an inn near the Saint Bavo Cathedral. The next morning, they head past the madhouse of the Castle of Gerald the Devil to the outskirts and town common, where they await Lord Cavendish.

But they wait in vain because Warwick's nemesis never makes it across the channel. King James's constables intercept him on his way to the Sussex coast at a roadside and detain him. Not that Cavendish goes through a great deal of trouble to elude them. In fact, he lingers most of the morning at the hostel, and when the officers find him, he is dressed in one of his fancier outfits and claims that he fell ill during the night.

By the end of the day, other officials catch up with Warwick and Argall in Ghent and escort them back to England. The earl is in a funk the whole way back to London, although as they cross the channel with not a cloud in the sky, he can't help but note the irony of having smooth sailing after his utter failure to gain any satisfaction.

Upon arriving at home, and being placed under more stringent house arrest, Warwick doesn't know which is worse: Having his distraught wife fling herself at him and cover him with kisses for his safe return, or learning that his adversary found a way to avoid the duel, sending him on a fool's errand.

In an unguarded moment, he confesses to Nathaniel Rich, "I feel I played a buffoon worthy of Shakespeare's *Comedy of Errors.*"

His cousin wisely refrains from making any comment in reply.

Eventually, Warwick swears an oath before a magistrate that he will not pursue his quarrel with Lord Cavendish any further and earns his release. Leaving the courthouse he stoically endures the smirks and amused glances of his acquaintances. As he marches across the stained cobblestones to his waiting carriage, he vows that he will let nothing stand in the way of his taking revenge and making sure of the destruction of the Virginia Company.

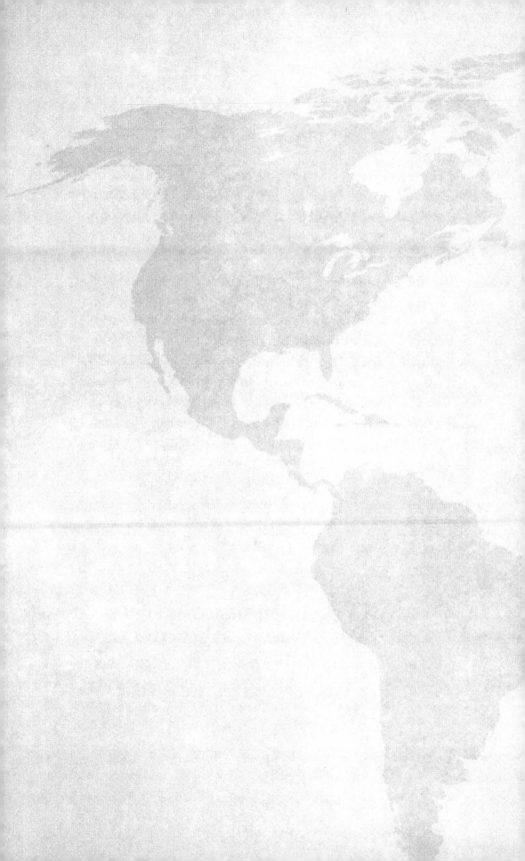

46

REUNION

Bennett's Welcome—July–August 1623

Once again Captain Jope and John return to Virginia in haste. This time, news of the havoc the pestilence wreaked among the settlers has brought them rushing back to check on Margaret. Upon arrival, Jope orders his men to unload the provisions he's brought for the plantation—barrels of olive oil, rock-hard cheese, flour, and dried fish. Then he and John climb the cliff path as fast as they can.

When they reach the top, they hurry toward the main house, where they meet Robert Bennett, who is surprised to see him.

"Is Margaret all right?" Jope bursts out without greeting.

Master Robert eyes him thoughtfully and looks at the young African boy a few feet away, who can hardly stand still, an anxious expression on his face.

"We have had another difficult time, but she is fine," he says. "In fact, she helped us all get through it. Nursed me back to health when I got sick."

As Jope and John look at each other, the tension seeps from their shoulders.

"Is that her brother?" Master Robert asks.

Jope hesitates for a moment. Figuring it will forestall further questions, he answers, "Yes." Then he looks around. "Where is she?"

Reunion

Master Robert points past the tobacco field to the creek and the woods beyond. "This time of day, she usually goes into the forest, looking for mushrooms, berries, and plants." He looks at the position of the sun in the sky and continues, "She's on her way back by now. You can probably meet her halfway."

"Much obliged, Sir Robert," says Jope. "My men are unloading supplies I've brought for you."

"Thank you. I will go and check on them." As he turns to go, he stops and adds, "It is all right for her to spend the night aboard ship with you. I'll make her excuses."

Jope bows gratefully. Then he and John head down the path toward the creek. They hurry past tobacco plants as tall as a small house. Field hands, inspecting the greenish-yellow leaves for worms and other pests, look up with curiosity at the tall man dressed in a fancy leather jerkin and the small boy in breeches and a linen shirt hastening along.

When they reach the creek, there seems no easy way to get across, so Jope picks John up, throws him over his shoulder, and wades in. The water reaches past his thighs. On the other side, he sets him down, and they walk through tall grass dotted with yellow flowers to the edge of the forest where dense underbrush blocks their way.

Unsure of where to go next, they stop and look around. Suddenly, John pokes Jope and points excitedly to where Margaret emerges between two bushes a stone's throw away. She wears a dark purple dress, has a cloth tied around her head, and is carrying a small woven basket.

When she sees them, she stands still as a deer sensing danger. Then a smile of recognition blossoms on her face. She puts her basket down, hikes up her skirt, and starts running. Jope and John rush toward her, and they meet halfway and throw their arms around one another.

After they untangle themselves and greet each other more formally with kisses, Margaret says happily, "I didn't expect to see you so soon."

"We were so worried about you when we heard that everyone here got sick," says John.

"You look good, Margaret," Jope comments, inspecting her from head to toe. "You are becoming quite a young lady."

The compliment takes her by surprise and makes her blush. She has not thought of herself that way.

On their way back, Margaret offers them a taste of the mushrooms in her basket. John wrinkles his nose and declines, but when he notices the dark purple elderberries and wants to try them, she warns him, "They have to be cooked first, or you'll get a stomachache."

By the time they make their way to the *White Lion*, Margaret has told John and Jope all about Frances and Peter, Anthony and Mary getting married, and the fort getting built. Jope is pleased to hear that there are now soldiers stationed nearby to protect the plantation.

In Jope's cabin, a fine meal is waiting as before, and Margaret digs in with enthusiasm. After the meal she continues her account of the pestilence, Lieutenant Sheppard, and the poisoning of the Indians. Jope shakes his head in disbelief at what she has endured and looks at her with renewed admiration. John is amazed, too, and a bit jealous. Except for sailing through a frightening three-day storm, his life is filled with routine; loading and unloading cargo in various ports doesn't make for much of a story. Once again, he wonders if he will ever have exciting adventures like Margaret!

At some point Margaret asks the captain, "Did Mary have her baby?"

A smile lights up his face. "Yes, a daughter, and she's pregnant again," he says. "But I haven't seen them much. Haven't even had time to christen my firstborn yet. We'll do that when we get home next month. We'll invite all of my Cornish relatives and have a real celebration."

"What does 'Cornish' mean? Are they like Cornish hens?" Margaret asks, mystified.

A hearty laugh escapes Jope. "No. Well, yes. It refers to people and things from Cornwall, my home."

Reunion

He is quiet for a moment and his face sags. Margaret thinks he is missing his family, but Jope is trying to figure out how to share sad news in the midst of their joyful reunion.

The last time he visited Tavistock, Mary told him that Lady Isabel died in February. Her uncle heard about it in London and, knowing it mattered to Jope's family, paid Lady Frances a visit of condolence. Apparently, in her final year Lady Isabel got weaker and her tremors worsened. At some point, she fell and broke her hip, and never left her sickbed again. What surprised Jope most, having met Lady Frances and taken a strong dislike to her, was how perceptive she was about her sister. She mentioned that Isabel had brought herself, late in her life, to love once more with all her heart, and she gave all of that love to Margaret and John. When they left, with her son gone as well, she had little else to live for.

Jope does not tell Margaret all that. He only says, "She died peacefully and is with God."

"Everybody is leaving me," says Margaret and bursts into tears.

Jope doesn't know how to comfort her. John tries to help, putting his arms around her. Having heard about Lady Isabel's death a month earlier, his feelings are no longer as raw, but seeing Margaret so upset makes him sad all over again. They sit quietly together on the gallery for a while and go to bed with heavy hearts.

By the next morning, Margaret feels better. She feels the warm sunshine on her face as she steps out onto the main deck, where Jope is conferring with his new navigator, a sunburned man with large, protruding teeth and pockmarks on his cheeks. When the captain notices her, he smiles and joins her by the railing.

Margaret takes a deep breath and asks him about her contract and when she will be free.

"Five more winters," Jope says, surprised. "Why do you ask?"

"I have never seen the paper," Margaret explains. "But when the Indians attacked, everything here burned. I don't know if Master Robert will remember."

Jope becomes serious. "I am glad you told me, Margaret. This is very important. I will speak to him before I leave."

He accompanies her up the cliff to the main house. While she returns to the cookhouse, he asks to speak to Master Robert. Half an hour later, Jope pokes his head in and gestures to her. Margaret leaves the mushrooms she is chopping, wipes her hands on her apron, and follows him outside.

"You were right. The contract was destroyed, but it's taken care of now," Jope says.

Margaret feels relieved. She walks with him to the edge of the cliff, where their good-byes are heartfelt as ever. This time she feels calmer, certain that she will see her captain again. She watches him stride all the way down to the dock and onto his ship before she returns to her work.

Later that afternoon, Master Robert searches her out. He looks at her with guarded respect. "You have good friends, Margaret," he says. "No one else I know has people go out of their way for them like your captain."

Margaret keeps quiet.

"I'm sorry it slipped my mind that your contract burned along with everything else, but I will draw up another, as soon as I come back from Jamestown. I promise."

"Thank you, sir. I am grateful."

"You will get what you have rightfully coming to you. We owe you a great deal for what you have done for Bennett's Welcome."

Margaret goes back to finish her work in the cookhouse, feeling less forlorn. It helps to know that she is appreciated. Having enjoyed her time on the *White Lion* with John and her captain, she decides it is important to savor all the good moments that come her way. She decides to spend a long time in the forest the next day.

But a big summer storm keeps her and everyone else inside, as raging winds whip torrential rains across the plantation for the next two days. Margaret prays that John and Jope don't get caught in it and remain safe aboard their ship.

Reunion

* * *

Two days later after the weather clears, Robert Bennett returns from Jamestown in a pinnace. He is exhausted. The meetings he has attended with the governor and other council members have gone late into the night. They have worked to draft an answer to *The Unmasked Face of Our Colony in Virginia*, Nathaniel Butler's diatribe, which has caused a stir in London. Francis Wyatt impressed on them how important it is to refute the unfair criticisms point by point to counter the negative impression it made on the Privy Council. Nothing less than their freedom and independence are at stake.

As he climbs the cliff path wearily, Master Robert recalls that he had liked Butler when he came to visit Bennett's Welcome. He was mild-mannered and curious, even complimentary of what they were accomplishing in restoring the plantation after the Indian massacre. As a fellow Puritan, he seemed to understand the value of having a safe haven for their religious beliefs. It never occurred to him that he came with the purpose of destroying the Virginia Company.

Letters from his brother Edward in London have made him aware of the vicious battles being fought in London over control of the company and the governance of the colony. Although loyal to the King and England, Master Robert is a good Puritan who firmly believes in the separation of church and state. He worries what will happen if King James, a devout Catholic, revokes Virginia's charter. Will there be renewed prosecutions of the sort that drove him and his family to Holland?

Reaching the top he walks along the cliff to get a better look at the whole plantation. He notes with satisfaction the smoke issuing from the newly built houses, and the lush green fields dense with cornstalks and tobacco plants ready to be harvested. He looks for signs of damage from the storm and sees a damaged roof on one of the worker's homes.

Distracted, he does not notice the depression where the heavy rains have loosened the soil, and when he steps forward, it slides out from under him. Flailing his arms wildly, he tumbles down the steep cliff. He hears the desperate outcry of the servants who followed him from the ship, unable to help. Then he smacks against the rocks below and his neck snaps. His inert body comes to rest in the sand.

In the cookhouse, Margaret hears the panicked cries for help from afar. She drops the carrots she's been dicing for the evening's soup and rushes outside with Humphrey. Running toward the cliff with the servants from the main house, she does not realize that fate has once again struck a blow that will change her life irrevocably.

EPILOGUE
Virginia and England—August 1623

Although everyone on the plantation is in attendance, the funeral for Robert Bennett is a simple affair. In reaction against the ostentatious rituals of the Catholic and Anglican Churches, Puritans have no sermon, no reading of the scriptures—just a hand bell ringing that brings everyone to the freshly dug grave. Six men, including Anthony, solemnly carry Master Robert's body and lower it into the ground near where Richard Bennett lies buried.

Lieutenant Sheppard, Phillip, and his soldiers have come to pay their last respects, as have several important men from Jamestown. Margaret, standing next to Mary, recognizes John Chew, the wealthy merchant, who is representing Governor Wyatt and his council. The Reverend William and his wife, Catherine, who are expecting their first child, stand by the graveside, looking somber and stricken. He mumbles a few words and turns away, wiping tears from his eyes.

As the men start to shovel dirt on top of the pale body, Margaret starts to cry, too. She liked Master Robert. He always treated her with kindness and respect, and he deserved better.

After Master Robert is laid to rest, the Reverend William addresses the assembled plantation workers. He does his best to instill a sense of hope, but it is difficult for him, being more used to focus on the negative and rail against man's sinful nature.

"Letters have gone to London to Master Robert's brother, Edward Bennett. He will surely send a new overseer," he says. "Our job is to keep the plantation going until then to the best of our abilities. I count on all of you doing your best."

If there are dissenters, they hold their tongue. In the wake of mourning for the loss of their popular master, they don't want to appear ungrateful. But they are all worried about the uncertainty of their future. Margaret has the same doubts. She wonders what will happen to her, since Master Robert died before fulfilling his promise to write another contract for her.

She receives an answer to her question a few days later. John Chew, who has been named executor of Master Robert's estate, spends considerable time at the main house with the Reverend William, going through what papers are there. Master Robert has left no children behind, but there are holdings on both sides of the Atlantic Ocean, and it will take some time to sort out his affairs.

Margaret sees him seek out various workers and converse with them in private. Word soon gets out that he is discussing their terms of indenture. Apparently, Margaret's contract wasn't the only one that burned up in the Indian attack.

One afternoon Chew intercepts her on her way to the forest. "A moment of your time, Margaret."

He gestures her toward a bench by the side of the shed, away from the sunlight, and indicates for her to sit.

Leaning toward her, he says, "The Reverend Bennett and I have been talking, and we cannot locate any papers for you. Many documents were destroyed during the massacre."

Margaret nods. "Master Robert was going to write another contract for me, but then, he . . . he . . ."

"I know," Chew says gently. "Don't worry. We will take care of you."

Margaret isn't sure what he has in mind. "The captain who brought me here can vouch for my contract next time he comes," she says.

Chew rubs his chin thoughtfully. "That will be fine, but until he confirms the terms of your indenture, I have a proposition for you.

My wife, Sarah, came to Jamestown this summer, and I am building a house for her. When it is finished, I want you to come work for us as her servant. I will have to go to England from time to time and need someone trustworthy to be with her and our two children. Would you be willing to do that?"

Margaret knows she is dealing with a powerful man, no matter how soft-spoken he appears, so she doesn't hesitate. She nods eagerly. "I would like that very much. Thank you, sir."

"Splendid. It's settled then." Chew rises quickly. "When the time comes, I will call for you and draw up another contract. What name shall I put on the document?"

Margaret looks up at him in surprise. "Why, Margaret, of course."

Chew smiles indulgently. "I mean your full name."

Margaret doesn't remember what name Captain Jope chose for her before. She thinks for a moment, then states with resolve, "Margaret Cornish."

Chew looks at her, surprised. "Margaret Cornish?"

"Yes. Margaret Cornish!"

"Very well."

As Chew returns to the main house, Margaret picks up her basket and heads into the forest to her favorite spot. New flowers have sprung up, and the first cranberries, dark red drops hanging from low bushes, are ready for picking. A few ripe chestnuts lie on the ground already, the hard maroon fruit peeking out from cracked, spiny outer shells. Margaret remembers when they were bright green high up in the branches among the leaves, and Askuwheteau pointed to them and mimed them falling to the ground. She gathers them in her basket and then sits with her back against the firm trunk of the tree.

"Margaret Cornish, Margaret Cornish." She has been trying out the name and likes it—likes the way it sounds and that it connects her to where her captain is from.

Then her thoughts turn to what is ahead of her. Having survived two disasters in rapid succession unscathed—the Indian attack and the pestilence—she feels confident for the first time in many years that she is ready to face whatever fate has in store for her next. She is actually looking forward to it.

* * *

Three thousand miles away, Captain Jope has safely returned home to Tavistock. It is Sunday, and he is standing in church in front of a large congregation with John by his side. Next to them, Mary, visibly pregnant, holds a baby girl, not yet a year old—her and Jope's firstborn. There are a good number of Cornish men and women witnessing the christening, as well as many members of Mary's family.

In good Puritan tradition, the minister does not make the sign of the cross, but holds his hand over the infant and says, "I baptize thee in the name of the Father, of the Son, and the Holy Ghost: Margaret."

CPSIA information can be obtained at www.ICGtesting.com
Printed in the USA
LVOW07*0821150115

422878LV00002B/4/P

9 780990 836506